REVELATIONS
OF THE
RUBY CRYSTAL

"Played out in the story of uncovering the abusive power of male sexuality at the heart of the Vatican, this romance offers an introduction to what is a significant religious movement by providing insight into the character and attraction of the Gnosticism of New Age belief and practices. A page-turning novel of love and desire, abuse and corruption, and the cosmic quest for redemption, this is the best of introductions to the appeal of astrology and New Age spirituality over and against common perceptions of Christian faith and the Church."

TIMOTHY F. SEDGWICK, PH.D.,
CLINTON S. QUIN PROFESSOR OF CHRISTIAN ETHICS AT
VIRGINIA THEOLOGICAL SEMINARY, ALEXANDRIA, VA

"Barbara Hand Clow's *Revelations of the Ruby Crystal* is a unique revelation about deep cosmic processes and actors in the dimensional ecology of our planet as well as a page-turner story about loss, redemption, and transformation of beings who are deeply in love. As a legal advisor, I can vouch for the authenticity of the darker aspects at work in the action set in Rome and in the Vatican itself. It is truly a novel for our times."

ALFRED LAMBREMONT WEBRE, AUTHOR OF
*THE OMNIVERSE: TRANSDIMENSIONAL INTELLIGENCE,
TIME TRAVEL, THE AFTERLIFE, AND THE SECRET COLONY ON MARS*

"Barbara Hand Clow's book *Revelations of the Ruby Crystal* opened my eyes even further to the world-creating artistry—the 'fictive power'—of the imagination to shape our world and influence our souls. The story that she weaves is a perfect example of how storytelling is the shamanic art par excellence that helps us to de-literalize our own reading of the world and remember who we are."

PAUL LEVY, AUTHOR OF
DISPELLING WETIKO: BREAKING THE CURSE OF EVIL

"A well-researched narrative with intriguing insights seamlessly blended into beautiful evocations of the Italy of our dreams."

CAROL M. CRAM, AUTHOR OF *THE TOWERS OF TUSCANY*

"Esoteric Christianity, buried secrets, psychic powers, karma, and kundalini entwine in this lush, vivid erotic romance set fittingly in eternally romantic Rome."

PEGGY PAYNE, AUTHOR OF *COBALT BLUE* AND
OTHER NOVELS OF SEX AND SPIRITUALITY

"As a software trainer and developer and a published author of two books on word processing, I often encounter many technology users who are longing for a vision of what might be possible as a 'next step' in our evolution. *Revelations of the Ruby Crystal* is a divinely inspired web of transcendent energy that has a magnetic appeal. This book is a visually rich, sensual, non-social-media-driven trans-Atlantic adventure using revelatory information about the historical past that moves us through a complex romance quite unlike any that has ever been written. A must read!"

MARIANNE CARROLL,
BUSINESS PRODUCTIVITY CONSULTANT

"*Revelations of the Ruby Crystal* is a gift for anyone interested in unmasking a time line of deep secrets and hushed discoveries about the life of Jesus; the ossuary of Peter found in Jerusalem; the earliest years of Christianity; Marcion, a so-called heretic; and Christianity's critical 'wrong turn' and its eventual takeover, distortion, and corruption by the Roman patriarchy. The intense dramas are played out against the backdrop of a powerful paradigm shift jolting world events into chaos, the Vatican into a meltdown, and a time of transformation into the ethers, finally welcomed in Rome by the surprising and sudden election of Pope Francis, the 'revolutionary.' It is an intense, exciting read."

JEAN RICHARD,
POLARITY THERAPIST FOR RITUAL ABUSE

"I find this [*Awakening the Planetary Mind*] book mind expanding, provocative, and offering an important contribution to our self-understanding as a species, especially as we face important decisions in these critical times."

MATTHEW FOX, AUTHOR OF *ORIGINAL BLESSING*

The Pleiadian Agenda

"An uplifting message from a multidimensional mind . . . a document that will be talked about for hundreds of years."

JOHN MAJOR JENKINS, AUTHOR OF
TZOLKIN: VISIONARY PERSPECTIVES AND CALENDAR STUDIES

"An intriguing kaleidoscope of galactic interdimensional cosmology that offers an intimate overview of the star histories as they play themselves out in our current planetary judgment day."

JOSÉ AND LLOYDINE ARGÜELLES, INITIATORS OF
HARMONIC CONVERGENCE AND CO-CREATORS OF
DREAMSPELL: THE JOURNEY OF TIMESHIP EARTH 2013

Astrology and the Rising of Kundalini

"Barbara Hand Clow has identified the hidden key to evolution: the rise of suprasexual energy experienced as the passion to express our full potential self through joining in love with others to create. She gives us practical guidelines to go through our personal midlife crisis to become co-creative humans, a global species at the next stage of our evolution."

BARBARA MARX HUBBARD, AUTHOR OF
THE EVOLUTIONARY JOURNEY

The Mayan Code

"A very wise human being has poured her heart, her soul, and her mind into these words. *The Mayan Code* is a great gift to us all."

WHITLEY STRIEBER, HOST OF
DREAMLAND RADIO AND AUTHOR OF *COMMUNION*

REVELATIONS

OF THE

RUBY
CRYSTAL

BARBARA HAND CLOW

Bear & Company
Rochester, Vermont • Toronto, Canada

Bear & Company
One Park Street
Rochester, Vermont 05767
www.BearandCompanyBooks.com

Text stock is SFI certified

Bear & Company is a division of Inner Traditions International

Library of Congress Cataloging-in-Publication Data
Clow, Barbara Hand, 1943–
  Revelations of the ruby crystal / Barbara Hand Clow.
    pages ; cm
  ISBN 978-1-59143-197-8 (hardcover) — ISBN 978-1-59143-778-9 (e-book)
  1. Mysticism—Fiction. 2. Psychic ability—Fiction. 3. Conspiracies—Vatican
City—Fiction. I. Title.
  PS3603.L689R49 2015
  813'.6—dc23

                                                                    2014046514

Printed and bound in the United States by Lake Book Manufacturing, Inc.
The text stock is SFI certified. The Sustainable Forestry Initiative® program
promotes sustainable forest management.

10 9 8 7 6 5 4 3 2 1

Text design by Debbie Glogover and layout by Virginia Scott Bowman
This book was typeset in Garamond Premier Pro and Legacy Sans with Goudy
Oldstyle used as the display typeface
Artwork by Liz Clow
Edited by Meghan MacLean and Julia Waterman

To send correspondence to the author of this book, mail a first-class letter to the
author at PO Box 30905, Bellingham, WA 98228 or to c/o Inner Traditions •
Bear & Company, One Park Street, Rochester, VT 05767, and we will forward the
communication.

For Gerry Clow and Liz Clow

—◂▸—

In May 2011 all the characters in this book except for one—the Jungian analyst Lorenzo Gianinni—appeared in my office, gave me their names, ages, and professions, and described what fascinates them. I was very intrigued by these appearances and described them to my partner Gerry, who was excited and enthusiastic and wanted to hear about their lives. I wrote this novel to tell their stories. Because of his enthusiasm and support, you have this book in your hands.

When I told my daughter, Liz, about this novel vigorously springing to life, she wanted to illustrate it. Because she poured her heart, soul, and artistic talent into this book, you have this beautiful artwork in your hands.

Hearing is the sense of Faith and seeing is the sense of Glory, because Glory is the vision of God. Seeing is the sense of light, of space, of plasticity; vision is the immensity of space; it sees what there is and what there is not.

ANTONI GAUDÍ

Contents

PART ONE

The Sibyl of Cumae

PART TWO
Armando's Redemption

PART THREE
The End of the Mayan Calendar

PART ONE

The Sybil of Cumae

1

Rome

On a soft and aromatic April morning in the city of layered secrets, Sarah strolled down a small street south of the Piazza del Popolo. Strange movements to her left caught her eye; in a deep square pit below the street level something odd was going on. She stopped and looked down into the pit, where white marble columns rose mysteriously amid scattered stone blocks.

Surely it wasn't a new building site in the midst of ancient ruins? She noticed a bronze historical plaque to her right and scanned it eagerly. It read: "Ancient foundations of an important early Roman villa with significant mosaic floors circa 150 to 50 BCE. Protected by the Roman Antiquarian Society. See the Antiquities Director, Dr. Allesandro Cinelli, for tours available on Tuesdays." She was relieved to see it was a protected site. But what was that movement she had noticed when first walking by? Peering more closely into the layers of fallen stones, she discerned moving colors—gold, black, gray, and stripes. Cats, a dozen sleek flashing cats! How odd.

An ancient bell rang to call people to Mass in the church down the street, but Sarah barely registered the sound. She was mesmerized by the strange acrobatic cats and their flow of moving color. They jumped up on the rocks to fly from ledge to ledge, and then froze, ready to pounce. In the center of all this movement, a sleek, muscular black cat gripped a brown rat in his jaws, biting deeper and deeper into its neck. Without ever looking directly at this central cat, the other cats were fixated on the prey clenched in his jaws. Switching their long snakelike tails, they shared the murder.

I suppose they want him to play with the rat, to kill it slowly, Sarah thought. She was right. The black cat bit into the back of the rat's neck just long enough to stun it, and then he slowly passed it back and forth between his long-clawed front paws. He was grinning. The other cats—a golden tabby, a gray-striped Abyssinian, a steely gray Persian, a dirty and mean-looking white cat, and a scrubby orange cat—circled in closer to watch the show. Sarah recoiled. *They're like leering Romans watching the lions torture Christians in the Colosseum.*

Completely engrossed in the sacrificial ritual on the ancient hearth, Sarah suddenly felt a man's presence on her right. She tightened her grip on her leather shoulder bag, preparing to move quickly down the street.

Simon Appel had been about to cross the narrow street to revisit the historical villa site for some last-minute details for his latest article when his gaze had been caught by the young woman. Her lithe body was outlined invitingly in a black wool miniskirt. Knee-high light brown suede boots over black tights showcased her athletic legs. Her upper body was shrouded in an ivory tunic, but still he could see she had broad shoulders. Long, wavy dark brown hair with red highlights—his favorite—streamed down her back. *She must be Celtic.* He crossed the street silently and came to stand next to her, scanning the plaque he had come to read. He sensed her tension at his sudden appearance, and before she could move away, addressed her, "Excuse me, madam, do you speak English? May I tell you some things about this site?"

His words, spoken in smooth and well-educated English, stopped Sarah. It had been a long time since anyone had addressed her in English. He sounded American, like her. And since it was daytime and there were a few people walking quickly by on the way to Mass, she let her body relax. She didn't look at him, although his presence felt commanding.

"You're guarded, as you always should be in Rome," he said. "But I couldn't help but notice you seem to share my interest in this site. It goes right back to one of the most fascinating periods in early Roman history when there was a lively Greek pagan culture in this region. Archaeologists believe this may be the House of Cumae." Sensing by the tilt of her head that he'd captured her attention, he continued. "The mosaics are especially interesting. They have many unusual esoteric symbols that have not been officially identified."

She turned to look at him and saw a vibrant young face. He looked intelligent with sunken cheeks, a strong jaw, and a slightly hooked well-formed nose. Large, clear deep brown eyes flashing with sapphire lights dominated his face as he smiled.

As she took all this in, her intense green eyes captivated him. They were watery as if she were in another world, maybe in the bizarre cat drama going on down below? Caught slightly off guard, she flushed a delicate light rose tint. All this passed in seconds, but it was recorded in the consciousness of both. They knew this fated meeting on an ancient street on a crisp April morning in Rome was full of meaning.

"I'm Sarah," she said. "Sarah Adamson."

"Sarah," he repeated. "Sarah, what brings you to Rome?"

"I'm a student, from the University of Birmingham. The one in England, not the one in Alabama. Are you a student, too?"

"I'm a freelance journalist," he said. "My name is Simon Appel. I'm working on a story about this villa for a local paper and also some stories about the Vatican for the *New York Times*."

He paused, holding her gaze. "You know, I've been up since 5 a.m., and I'm starving. Will you join me at my favorite trattoria? I'd love to chat with someone in English."

That was something Sarah normally would never do. But she'd

been in Rome for more than three months doing research in the libraries and touring ancient sites, and she was lonely. She was also very tired of struggling to communicate in her limited Italian. "I'd love to join you. It would be nice to talk in English for once." They walked away after she took one last glance at the battle going on down below. The cats were taking turns pummeling the hapless rat, a scene that reminded her of the Christian mobs stoning Stephen while Saul stood by and watched.

At the trattoria Simon hung up his green corduroy jacket on a hook as Sarah pulled her sweater over her head and shook out her hair. She felt him look her over, his gaze seeming to linger on her breasts, which she knew were large for her tall, slender frame, and she reflexively hunched her shoulders. She was relieved she was wearing a high-necked, long-sleeved white cotton blouse, her typical attire for the Vatican Library. They sat down at a small wooden table covered with a red-checked vinyl tablecloth. *How did I get myself into this?* she wondered as she slid onto a wooden bench. *I usually know better.* Red table wine arrived immediately, and she realized he must be a regular at the trattoria.

"Are you a grad student or undergrad?" he asked. "And why are you studying here in Rome?"

Relieved to think about something other than his eyes on her body, she replied, "I'm getting my Ph.D. in patristics, which is the study of the early Church Fathers of 150–400 CE. Many of my sources are here in Roman libraries, especially in the Vatican Library. I finished one year in England, and I have to go back periodically while I write my thesis. I hope to write about Marcion of Pontus, the first heretic refuted by the Church Fathers." She smiled ruefully. "Sounds dull, doesn't it?"

"Not at all," he replied. "I've long been fascinated by Marcion."

Sarah's eyes widened in surprise. "You've heard of Marcion? Forgive me, but even here in Rome, most people have never heard of him. Have you researched him for your work?"

"In a way. As you may have guessed from the name Appel, I'm Jewish. When I was an undergrad at Williams College, I discovered Marcion because I was trying to understand the source of anti-Semitism. The blue-blood New England judgment at Williams was excruciating; so different from where I grew up, in Brooklyn Heights in New York. I just wasn't prepared for it. My parents thought I might be unhappy at Williams, but I had a full scholarship and was thrilled to have my college education paid for." He shook his head. "Soon I realized I'd gotten the scholarship as a token Jew on campus. Anyway, while seeking the source of anti-Semitism, I ran right into Marcion, since theologians say he was the first anti-Semite. What really grabbed my attention was that as one of the first bishops he didn't want the early Church to attach the Old Testament to the newly forming Christian literature. But as you know they did it anyway, and then he was mostly lost to history."

Sarah couldn't keep the smile from her face. Simon was the first person she'd ever met outside of moldy academics that knew anything about Marcion. *But he is a Jew and I'm a Catholic,* she reminded herself as her body heated up with the thrill of finding somebody to talk with about her most passionate interest. She had been raised to be deeply suspicious of Jews. If her father, a strict Boston Catholic, knew what she was doing right now, he'd be furious. She had better just enjoy lunch and get out of there fast.

"Well, I'm amazed that you've heard about Marcion," she said. "I came across him because I was interested in the formation of the New Testament canon. It wasn't until I read about Marcion that I thought about how demeaning it was for the early Christians to call Hebrew scripture 'Old' just because their scripture was newer."

"I couldn't agree more," Simon replied heatedly. "I've always thought Marcion had it right, that the Jews should have retained their own wisdom literature and practices and that the new Christians should have written whatever they wanted about their Christ, or Jesus, that Christianity should be a totally new religion.

So my ancestors probably agreed with Marcion on some level. Their scriptures were their sacred culture, their heritage. Maybe they felt the Christians were *stealing* their scripture to legitimize their new religion. If Jesus was the Christians' teacher, a divine visitation from God, then why would they need anything more?"

Simon spoke from a burning inner pain that had ignited when his sneering, cold, rich college classmates treated him like a pariah. Even now, more than fifteen years later, the disdain and rejection burned inside him as a core wound. His education at Williams and later Harvard had, however, given him the ability to write and speak incisively about Judeo-Christian issues in a way that never insulted non-Jews. He was still deeply intrigued by the anti-Semitism lurking under the surface of Christian culture.

Sarah sympathized greatly with Simon's experience of anti-Semitism. Her studies had brought her face-to-face with the pains Jews suffered over the centuries from Christian judgment. Listening to Simon talk while watching his passionate facial expressions, she also felt his body. Somehow she actually felt the sensation of his thigh muscles tightening as he recalled those days in college. I wonder if he's married? Feeling heat in her pelvis, a new sensation, her mind wandered. Her cheeks and chest warmed as she watched deep blue lights flashing in his dark eyes. I like watching his fine hands and taut arms while he talks. I wonder if it's the red wine? Thankfully, a marvelous plate of antipasto served with crisp garlic crackers arrived, and they dove into the vegetables soaked in rich Italian olive oil.

Admiring her piece of toast slathered with capers, mushrooms, garlic, and shaved Romano cheese, she replied, "Well, I'm Catholic, from an old Irish family in Boston. Until I encountered Marcion's point of view, it never would have occurred to me that the early Christians *stole* the Hebrew Bible from the Jews. But after studying the sources, I can see Marcion was really afraid the newly emerging religion would lose sight of the authentic Jesus if it was too attached to Judaism. I often wonder how our Christian beliefs would have evolved if they hadn't attached the Hebrew Bible to the Christian canon.

"When I was twelve years old, I was given a Bible. Being a typical Catholic girl, I'd never before read the Bible, but I dove into it right away thinking it was strange that the Old Testament was a thousand pages long, yet the New Testament tacked on at the end had only around two hundred pages! I wondered if a mistake had been made and they'd given me a Jewish Bible! I forgot this until just now."

Hearing Sarah describe her strong religious background, Simon found himself wondering if she'd ever had sex. He could tell she was trying to control strong energetic responses to him. *She's eating a lot to calm her body, and she seems to get cerebral when she's having erotic feelings. She must be very inexperienced.* Tasting his wine thoughtfully, he put it all together in his mind. *Maybe she's younger than I thought, maybe only twenty-one or twenty-two?* He blurted out, "Sarah, how old are you?" He was embarrassed at the way the question had just slipped out, but Sarah responded without skipping a beat.

"Oh, I'm twenty-five, but with the studies I've chosen, sometimes I feel like I'm ninety. I just can't get rid of my obsession with the possibility that early Christianity took a wrong turn. I am so delighted to find somebody else who is interested in what people actually believed during this crucial turning point in religion. In my studies, 99 percent of what I have to focus on is scholarly arguments by writers who don't think about what they actually believe. Well, I think Marcion may have been on the right track in 150 CE! Yet when you get into early Church dogma, the first thing you notice is the big Marcion cover-up directed by the early Church Fathers. There were and are a lot of powerful people—Jews and Christians—who don't want anybody to hear anything about Marcion of Pontus. I don't know what they were afraid of. By the way, Simon, did you know in Marcion's era there was a significant teacher named Appelles who agreed with Marcion?"

He smiled at her obvious excitement. "Really? I imagine you and I could stay here all afternoon, but unfortunately I have to get back to the office. Can we have dinner sometime soon and get more deeply into Marcion?" As soon as the words popped out, he realized how much he was hoping she'd agree.

Sarah hesitated only a moment. "Okay, but on the condition that we share the expense. 'Go Dutch,' as they say in the States."

"Of course," he responded, and they exchanged e-mails and phone numbers.

2

Reviving the Sibyl

Simon's article about the early Roman villa appeared in the weekend edition of *Corriere della Sera,* and Sarah read it with great interest. In spite of her difficulty reading in Italian, his painterly skill with words brought the beauty of the site right back. He hadn't called her yet and she wondered if he would; it had been four days. *Was he as interested in our conversation as I was, or was he just being polite?* But Sunday afternoon he called and asked if she'd like to join him the following Tuesday for a private tour of the site and lunch at the little trattoria. She agreed, finding, to her surprise, that she could hardly wait.

Simon used a key to open the gate by the sidewalk and then led Sarah down the steep, narrow steps. The sun had already warmed the street above, yet the stairwell was moist and cool. Noticing the way she grabbed the handholds on the sidewall as she made her way down, he offered her his hand.

"You look great," he said. She wore tight and faded jeans, a gray cotton top, and a blue jean jacket. Her reddish-brown hair waved back and forth across her back. It was full and wild as if she'd just washed it. When she took his hand for support on the rocky stones, he felt an intense hot rush that took him by surprise. *What the hell is this, Cupid's arrow?*

Sarah was about to take her hand back once she had her footing. But she fell sideways right into Simon when a flash of dirty gray fur scraped against a stone near her ankle. The cat flew past her knees and bolted. Simon held her up, reaching under her arms to stop her fall as she muttered, "Damned things, they are all over the place! Thanks." She caught his scent, sweet like good essential oil, maybe frankincense.

Simon felt like using the hand that had moved up to her left shoulder to turn her and kiss her. But he could sense by the rigidity of her body that this would be a disaster. Meanwhile, at the base of her spine, Sarah felt the same heat she had felt while talking to him last week. To regain her bearings, she looked away and scanned the site.

They were more than twenty feet below street level. Although the ceiling was gone, allowing the late-day sun to dapple the stones, the air was musty and acrid from cat spray, black moss, and dry plants growing wild in patches of dirt. An inscription or a scratching on a stone caught Sarah's interest. Relieved to be back in her mind, she moved closer, asking, "Is this one of the unusual symbols you mentioned last week?"

Simon followed her over to the stone. "Yes, this is a very interesting one. It's on the back wall of what was once an inner courtyard where the archaeologists say there may have been a fire altar because they found charred stone bowls and a few figurines."

Together they examined the symbol, which was the upper half of a woman's body on top of a small triangle. It was as if the triangle was her skirt. The woman's arms were raised and holding sticks, possibly snakes. Simon and Sarah stared at the symbol, transfixed. Nearby, large bumblebees hummed lazily, dipping into blue cornflowers.

He continued, "I think this is a version of the Middle Eastern snake goddess, Tanit. But the archaeologists did not identify it. The main work on this site was done more than a hundred years ago, when such an idea would have been anathema since Tanit was pagan. So as usual, they say it's an unknown religious symbol."

"Can I touch it?" Encouraged by his favorable nod, she lightly ran her fingers over the defining lines to see if she could feel grooves.

Simon watched her long delicate fingers, and he felt that strange disorientation again—a few minutes zipping by in a second. Her amethyst bracelet slipped down over her wrist and caught a flash of light. He felt a strange swirling feeling in his mind, as if watching something he had already seen somewhere else.

He snapped himself back into place. "Come over here to see something that I think is related to it."

He led her a few feet away along a partially ruined inner wall of the ancient courtyard and pointed out a deep niche in a part of the wall that hadn't collapsed. The niche, which was eight inches deep and about a foot square, was cut into a stone block, a perfect little outdoor altar.

"This is where they found a standing figurine with a triangular skirt and a few grains of wheat, so they concluded it was a place to make offerings. Of course the rats ate all but a few fragments of the wheat long ago. I will take you to the Museo Romano to see it someday if you want."

"I'd love to do that, but luckily I read your article in last weekend's paper, so I've already seen your photo of the figurine and read your comments about it. I have the same impression that it's Tanit. You're an excellent writer in Italian, as far as I can tell by my limited reading ability."

Simon was genuinely touched and thanked her for the compliment. "So now that you already know some things about this house, what would you like to see next?"

"To tell you the truth, and I don't know why, I just want to feel this place." Sarah didn't know how Simon would feel about such a thing—perhaps he'd think she was a weirdo—so she struggled to explain. "Normally I'd want to examine every significant thing there is, but since we have the place to ourselves, I'd just really like to, well, sit and feel it first."

Simon knew what she meant about how special this place felt. After reading the archaeological reconstructions he'd collected for the article, he had come back to the site two weeks ago for what he thought would be his last visit. He had sat on the hearthstone where the cats carried out the sacrificial ritual, closed his eyes, and entered into a meditative state, trying to visualize the house as it was in the beginning. A fuzzy white screen appeared in his mind that seemed to be suspended in front of his face. Then on the screen, the original house precipitated into form like a watercolor emerging on paper or a photo in the developing fluid. During this brief moment, he saw pastel blues, pinks, and beiges and a green garden. He heard metal clinking, dogs barking, children's laughter, and saw a beautiful woman's face. It was enchanting, quite unlike anything he had experienced before, a mystic dream. He'd erased it from his mind until this moment. Was she experiencing something similar?

"Maybe you should take a moment to be alone here while I wait for you?" he offered. He walked quietly over to a partially standing column and leaned against it.

Grateful that Simon didn't seem to think her request at all out of the ordinary, Sarah sat down on the edge of the same hearth where Simon had sat two weeks before. She closed her eyes as soft breezes carried the sounds from above down into the pit. The sounds faded to be replaced by the low hum of bees sucking on nectar. She shivered when she heard a soft, lilting voice say, *Follow it; follow it where it will go. You know how to use the thread leading back to your heart.*

When the voice was gone, she felt a chill in the back of her neck as she opened her eyes to see Simon still leaning against the crude stone pillar. She told him she was ready to go. After they emerged from the steps, he unlocked the gate as she said quietly, "Thank you for giving me that moment. It sounds silly, but I think I heard a woman's voice that encouraged me to keep on going with my work.

I can't imagine whose voice it was; I've never had a message like that before. It was very real and it means something, so thank you for bringing me here."

Simon nodded. "A few younger archaeologists think an ancient oracle lived in that house. They believe the family was called Cumae, but they can't prove it. The famous oracular school of the Cumaean Sibyl was near Naples, so it's possible that family had a house here since Romans often sought her wisdom. She was more famous in early Rome than the priestesses of the Delphic Oracle in Greece, but we don't know very much about her everyday existence. So maybe you heard the Sibyl's voice? To me, this place feels magical." He smiled. "Let's have lunch."

They were back at Simon's favorite table sipping red table wine. They ordered and nibbled on fresh bread dipped in olive oil and balsamic vinegar while they waited for their meals. They looked so comfortable together the diners around them thought they'd known each other for years. Normally Simon—a great seducer and lover of many women—would be putting his hand lightly and insistently on her outer thigh by now. Or he might have drawn his body up close to the table's edge, taking her hands by the wrists, softly pressing her inner palms with his thumbs. But something was causing him to act very differently. *I wonder if I'm restrained because she's frigid, afraid of men in some way. But, no, that isn't it. It's something else . . .*

He searched her face, capturing her eyes for a fleeting moment. He saw Sarah take a deep breath as her gaze flickered uncertainly. As he struggled to hold her tentative gaze, he experienced another time distortion, the third one, as if a whole hour of the distant past was swept away in the wind. *Where is my mind going when this happens to me? The flashes of light from her eyes are hypnotic.* She seemed to be waiting for him to say something, anything.

"Strange things seem to be happening to me, Sarah, since I've met you. I wonder if my edges are thinning?"

She still didn't say anything, so he continued. "After I met you last week, I looked up that Appelles guy, conceivably my ancestor, who lived in Marcion's time. Did you know Appelles believed in a psychic or channeler named Philumena?"

Simon was curious as to how Sarah would respond. He suspected her inquiries into Marcion were forcing her to get honest with herself about her religion. To his surprise, however, she didn't take him up on his invitation to discuss her favorite subject, Marcion.

Instead, Sarah set down her bread and blurted, "Simon, you are having an effect on me, a huge effect, and I'm not used to that. For the moment, please listen to me and do not interrupt. If my father had any idea we were having lunch together, he'd put out a Mafia hit on you! My father is a bigwig in Opus Dei. I don't know if you've heard of it, but it's a Catholic power group kind of like the Freemasons. I don't really know what they are or what they do. To be honest with you, I think they're kind of weird. But because of his involvement with them, I'm expected to be a power Catholic like him. That's why he supports my expensive religious education, the reason I'm here with you this afternoon. Lucky for me, he's never heard of Marcion. He thinks I'm just a studious Catholic girl who's interested in the early Church Fathers, which I am. It never occurred to him or to me that my studies could change my beliefs." She took a deep breath. "Now I've run into you, a Jewish guy who knows all about Marcion, and you have the perspective from the other side of the question. You are a person I can talk to, somebody who can help me get the wider view on issues that could change the course of my life. But how can I forget that my father would shoot you on the spot just because you're Jewish and having lunch with me? Never mind the other stuff!"

"Whoa!" Simon tried to interject, but Sarah held up her hand.

"Please let me finish. I haven't had much experience with men. I've been so busy with my studies, plus my father has drilled into me that I need to avoid men until I'm ready to marry."

Simon thought Sarah was building a wall between the two

of them, but he resisted interrupting her. Painful memories of Williams and Harvard welled up in his mind, including the day Martha Mills's father ran him out the back door and across the lawn, screaming he'd kill Simon if he didn't stop sleeping with his daughter. It had been a favorite anecdote of his Jewish friends at Harvard, but they had never realized he was still suffering inside through every retelling even as they screamed with laughter. *Are Catholic girls all like this?*

Meanwhile, Sarah was still speaking earnestly. "So even a friendship with you goes against the way I've been brought up. Regardless, when you looked into my eyes the way you did a moment ago . . ." She hesitated and then raised her eyes to his. "You are special, Simon, but it can't happen. The only way we can spend more time together is if this relationship never becomes more than it is right now. Otherwise, we could lose our chance at friendship. It seems like we have so many things to share, a bond that would be valuable to us both. I have to ask you to, to control yourself, to block your natural feelings." She stopped, seemingly at a loss for any more words.

He watched her intently. Her facial muscles seemed to be in the grip of something, something that was making her puppet-like. Could she be bipolar? That didn't seem to fit with what he had learned of her so far. He was taken aback by the earnestness of her little speech. What kind of father had laid down such strict rules? Could he have beaten her up or abused her? He felt a powerful urge to get up from the table and leave his lunch, but he was rooted to his chair. *It's time to vow to never pursue a non-Jewish girl again, especially a Catholic from Boston.*

Instead what came out of his mouth in a kind, brotherly voice was, "Sarah, you are only twenty-five, and if you haven't had any experience by now, your time *will* come. It might not be with me, since your father would kill me, but it has to be somebody unless you become a nun or a celibate scholar. You are beautiful and desirable. You can't let your father rule you to the point of never being able to have a lover!"

Sarah's eyes grew wet and she blinked rapidly, but she maintained firm control.

Simon went on gently. "If I may ask, did your father tell you that you have to be a virgin when you marry?"

To Simon, such a thing was unbelievable. This whole conversation was making him feel like he'd been thrown a century back in time. *Maybe I've landed on another planet and found a lost species?*

"Simon, he not only expects that, on Sundays he made me *promise* it to him many times when I was a little girl. But look, my father is a good and well-intentioned man—strong, successful, and self-made, the lord in his own house. I think you'd like him, actually. However, he totally believes what the Church teaches and nobody ever crosses him, not even my mother."

Again his peripheral glance was drawn to the tight muscle group that pulled in her mouth and reshaped her whole face for a moment. He'd seen expressions like this before with people who were mind-controlled—Christian fundamentalists or people who had been brought up in cults. He shivered. *It's time to run; run, Simon, now!*

Her face soon returned to normal, however, and for the first time she intentionally touched him by reaching for his left hand and gently holding his wrist. Her touch sent a strong electrical shock through his arm up to his shoulder and up in his neck.

She said, "Can we share more of these ideas and explore Rome together? Can we just be friends for now? I don't know if it could become something else; who knows that? Can we be friends?" She captured his gaze. "Maybe I was wrong to assume you are attracted to me. Perhaps that is my issue, not yours? I hope you can offer me some more time because I'm having feelings for you that I've never felt before. That's why I'm asking you to help me. For now can we stick with the sheer joy of exploring ideas together? Can we be enlightened Stoic philosophers, friends in moderation in all ways?" She giggled.

Simon wondered if she knew she was flirting with her eyes. He was thinking along very different lines. *I'm going to get someplace with this strange and evocative girl, regardless of her damned father. She just propositioned me with the wackiest set of rules I've ever heard, and we're going to break every one of them in due time.*

As she went on and on, a realization struck him as if an unseen god or an angel had just knocked him on his head: He was in love with this woman. He was already more in love with her than any woman he'd ever met. It had begun when he first laid eyes on her last week, and he felt it would never end. Instinctually his eyes slowly travelled along her right thigh, which she didn't seem to notice because she was so excited about her grand proposal. *I can wait until she's ready, but I don't give a shit about her damned father, Opus Dei, or the pope. She doesn't even know what kind of challenge she has just proposed to me. Eventually she will change her mind. No daddy is going to have his way because I have the patience of Job. It's time for Daddy to get real about how things work when you have an enchanting and beautiful daughter.*

"Okay," he agreed. "You shall be the virgin Sibyl of Cumae, and I shall be Cicero or Appelles listening to Philumena. You shall attain wisdom while I learn how to attain a peaceful old age. If you succeed in repressing your sexuality around me too long, then perhaps you will have ecstatic visions of god and the angels like Hildegard of Bingen and Teresa of Avila. If I repress mine, perhaps I will attain peace of mind. You may go crazy, but I will be sane. This will be fun. And if I recall, weren't the members of Marcion's community vegan celibates? Perhaps we both can empathize better with the Marcionites if we live by their rules?" He laughed. "One more thing. Don't expect me not to have sex with other women anytime I want to."

Sarah nodded, smiled sweetly, and returned to her lasagna and salad, leaving Simon staring at her fork as it cut into the oozing pasta.

What a crazy flirt she is! Does she realize how seductive she is in her innocence? We will be like the characters in a nineteenth-century Anthony Trollope novel where the marriage always occurs in the last chapter.

Luigi the cook was watching them from afar. Firing up another pan, he muttered with a smile on his lips, "Che bella!"

3

Borghese Gardens

Walking briskly along the Via del Babuino approaching the Piazza del Popolo, Simon couldn't keep a broad smile from his face. The sun shone as radiantly as his mood, brightening the pink magnolia blossoms that lined the street. Sarah had agreed to spend the whole day walking with him in the Borghese Gardens and discussing Marcion and patristics. He spotted Sarah standing below the obelisk, craning her neck to look up a hundred feet to the deeply incised hieroglyphs that were very readable in the angular light of the clear morning sunlight. Her strong body, arching in response to the tall obelisk, turned him on.

Lost in another time for a moment, Sarah shivered back into reality when she heard Simon's soft voice behind her. "Odd that anybody would go to so much trouble to bring this huge obelisk all the way from Egypt a few thousand years ago, isn't it?"

"Hello again," she said. "Yes, when I visited Egypt I had no idea so many obelisks had been removed and taken to Rome. Of course, this occurred when the Romans conquered Egypt, so they probably believed the obelisks would enhance their power. Yet it does seem odd. Let's see if the marker says anything about it."

Moving over to the historical marker they read: "This obelisk was removed from Egypt to Rome during the first century BCE.

The Emperor Augustus erected the obelisk in the Circus Maximus to commemorate the conquest of Egypt. After Rome fell, it was lost in the ruins of the circus for more than a millennium. It was re-erected here in the Piazza del Popolo in 1589 CE. Seti I incised three sides of the obelisk, and the fourth side (west facing) was cut by his son Ramesses I. Originally it was located at Heliopolis, the Sun Temple in Cairo."

"Well, of course," Simon said. "Rome became the Temple of the Sun once the Republic ended. When the emperors stripped the temples in Egypt, they brought the power objects to Rome."

His black curly hair shining in the morning sun, he charmed her with his laughing dark eyes as he took off his soft tan leather jacket. Taking her arm like an English gentleman, he steered her over to a bench on the side of the fountain. "This piazza is just plain beautiful whether you like obelisks or not."

Carved lions in the Egyptian style spouted water into cool basins below the obelisk, which was raised high on a marble platform with benches on all four sides. Mothers and small children played in the fine spray made luminous by the rays of sunlight warming the stones.

Sarah took a seat on the bench. "It's ironic that this is here while there is almost nothing ancient left at Heliopolis near the Cairo airport. Only one obelisk remains there, in the middle of a wealthy suburb. It's one of the oldest temple sites in Egypt, but now people go there to walk their dogs. Little attention is ever given to its archaeological importance. It was significant when Egyptian religion was pure and devoted to the reception of light."

Simon pulled an apple out of his backpack and crunched into it while listening to her. A mangy butterscotch dog stared hungrily at the apple. Air wheezed in and out between his sharp teeth and pronounced ribs, which protruded so far they seemed close to puncturing his skinny sides. Simon dug deeper into his pack, pulled out a dog biscuit, and held it out to the starving animal, who quickly snatched it with his teeth. Multicolored pigeons perched on the edges of the fountain basins dropped down to the pavement and moved quickly in their direction.

Sarah said, "It's funny. When I visited the temples in Egypt, there were always dogs like this one faithfully guarding the sites from bad energy. I always took food with me for them."

"Well, dogs really are our best friends. So I always carry treats when I go out. Do you suppose this obelisk is related to the things we're trying to figure out?"

Despite his casual tone, Simon's words, and their implication, were very much intentional. *Women love synchronicity, even Ph.D. candidates.* It felt to Simon there was a fated quality to the way they were getting to know each other. The only cover Sarah had was the subjects they had agreed to discuss, but it didn't matter to him what they talked about. He could happily gaze at her all day.

She took the bait and replied, "Well, many people think Jesus got his knowledge in Egypt. He could have studied with Egyptian masters in the temples, and he also must have studied with the Jewish Gnostics in Alexandria who lived close to the great library, the repository of thousands of years of wisdom. Considering the influence Jesus has had on religion, he *must* have mastered ancient knowledge. But trying to nail down anything historically accurate about him is like chasing a phantom, since all we can do is guess where he got his knowledge based on what we *think* he said."

He smiled at her encouragingly. "If Jesus had studied at the Sun Temple, what would he have learned there?"

"He would have learned all about the Heliopolitan mysteries—the most multidimensional teachings in ancient Egyptian wisdom. Until recently, they were thought of as incomprehensible riddles with hidden messages. In the light of modern science it seems that when these mysteries describe how things become solid in our world—the language of light—they are actually describing the basic principles of quantum mechanics and string theory. According to one linguistic scholar, Laird Scranton, hieroglyphs are a quantum mechanical language! I think this obelisk is engraved with these dimensional principles."

Watching her face as she examined the tall red granite form, he wondered if her information came from inner knowledge as well as academic study.

"Back to Marcion, if I may," Simon said. "Like Jesus, maybe he knew something that threatened the status quo? What else explains the concerted cover-up of everything he said? Do you suppose Marcion knew anything about what Jesus studied, even *where* he studied?" Simon paused, looking off into space he searched for an answer to his own question and then continued, "Let's go walk in the gardens. It's one of the most magical places on Earth. Maybe the setting will help our insights flow."

They stood up and gathered their belongings as the hungry hound followed closely behind, hoping for another treat.

As they walked along, Simon admired Sarah's off-white loose linen dress. Her elegance thrilled him. Her long and muscular legs and dark leather sandals reminded him of an early Roman patrician woman. Simon wanted to touch her; however, he was totally committed to the strategy that he was sure would eventually get him everything he wanted. Maybe, when she knew him better, she'd be willing to move beyond discussing ideas.

Strolling along they marveled at the five-hundred-year-old umbrella pines. The thick canopies way up high were sculpted by salty wind and afforded delicious coolness below. The ancient pathways under the proud trees seemed to be in another dimension, the world of ancient gods and Roman aristocrats. As they neared the Villa Medici, Simon remarked that Galileo had been imprisoned there by order of the Inquisition from 1630 to 1633 CE, a powerful example of thought suppression in those days. While he spoke, sun warmed the moist cool air rising out of the gardens; everything shimmered.

Lake in the Borghese Gardens

Sarah forgot all about heretics as they selected the perfect spot to spread out the blanket on a small rise sloping down to a sparkling blue lake. The lovely Roman temple across the lake looked like a temple for Venus. She laid out fruit and sandwiches while Simon uncorked red wine. Everywhere around them were delightful glimpses of the villas and gardens of the Renaissance elite. Sarah wondered if they could focus on anything as serious as Marcion in this enchanting setting.

But as Simon poured the ruby liquid into her glass, he said, "Sarah, I've been wanting to ask you, why was Marcion so determined to start a new religion based on cutting out the Hebrew Bible and any references to it?"

Sarah wished he'd just let her relax for a moment and enjoy lunch, but this discussion was the reason they were together today, so she sat up and replied in her lecture voice, "He believed the god of the Hebrew scripture—Yahweh—was not the same god as the one Jesus described. He believed the new religion could not develop if it retained the old Jewish god. This attitude was common during the early second century, so Marcion wasn't really that extreme. For example, although Marcion wasn't a Gnostic, many of the Gnostics of his day had a more negative attitude toward the Hebrew god than Marcion did. For many Gnostics, Yahweh was a jealous, murderous, and avenging monster! Many firmly believed that Jesus came to *abolish* the worship of this ancient tribal god. They said he came to Earth to teach people god is compassionate.

Sarah's voice grew more animated. She had forgotten all about her desire to relax and enjoy lunch. "Marcion said that Yahweh was the god of law and Jesus was the teacher of love. Regardless of who the Hebrew god actually was, Marcion wanted Christians to start out fresh with a New Covenant based only on what Jesus said. So he founded his own churches and wrote his own scripture based on these principles. Back then, a lot of people agreed with him. By 150 CE his church was the largest Christian church in the world! Marcion brought more converts to Christianity than any other preacher during the second century, and they used his bible, now lost. His church was a threat to the supremacy of the emerging church in Rome based on Peter as the vicar of Christ. In reaction to Marcion, the Petrine Christians attached their own writings to Hebrew scripture. The truth is, Marcion inspired the creation of the New Testament!"

Simon had been lying on his side watching Sarah as she spoke. Now he propped himself up on one elbow. "Okay," he broke in, "So if Marcion had his way back then, Jews today would have our own scripture; Christians would have theirs. If it had gone that way, maybe there'd be less fighting in the world now? Regardless, the early Christians who followed Saint Peter erased Marcion from history, and they must have had their reasons. What were they?"

Sarah nodded vigorously. "That's what I ask myself every single day. It's the core topic of my dissertation," Sarah responded. "Around 150 CE, early Roman Christians began suppressing the Gnostics and the Marcionites. When Constantine adopted Peter's Church in the early fourth century, this religious-political fusion produced a violent and insanely bloody culture. At the end of this period, dark ages ensued that weakened militaristic Roman Christianity, barbarians took Rome, and the lights went out. The more I look into this period—when time wound down to zero and then moved forward through 500 CE—I see it as a great big wrong turn. Next came a thousand years of schism, brutality, and holy wars."

He watched her animated face and her hands, which pulled compulsively at blades of grass as she spoke. *I'm sitting here with a beautiful girl I can't touch. Maybe it goes all the way back to that wrong turn? I'm the guy who is supposed to find a Jewish girl so that my children will be Jewish. She has a father who'd shoot me if he saw me with her today. Maybe this weird separation is coming from some kind of strange shadow, some kind of divisive force from way back in time that separates us now?*

"Can you be more specific?" he interjected. "You say Marcion was not a Gnostic. Most of what we hear about the Gnostics is that they saw everything as black and white, dualistic, and that they hated their bodies. Was Marcion like that? Maybe he was since his communities were ascetic and taught people to avoid sex. What was that all about anyway?"

Sarah turned to look at him, her eyes wide with excitement. "It fascinates me to see you take the same path I've taken. Right now I'm deeply immersed in Gnostic sources looking for answers to those questions. *Gnostic* simply means "to know." Many Middle Eastern, Druidic, and Greek philosophical schools were Gnostic. When the Essene and the Nag Hammadi scrolls were discovered and translated, finally we could read what these forgotten people thought about, *not* just what their enemies—the Christians—said about them.

"Now we know that the period just before Jesus and just after was tumultuous. For example, as you said, what we always hear about the Gnostics is how they hated their bodies. But in those days marriage and childbearing were the kiss of death for women who married in their teens and who usually died very young after having many children. How could a woman like that be spiritual and have time to think as I do? No wonder people seeking spirituality often avoided sex! Many thinkers hoped that religions would adopt entirely new beliefs that could bring peace; Jesus was that hope. Marcion is pivotal because he built a religious establishment based on his belief that Jesus came to our world to abolish the old law and establish a new religion. But even though the calendar dates wound down to zero and then started up again, *Christianity did not start fresh!* Like a stinky old garbage dump, more layers were piled on the moldy old ideas, the old angry god growled in the trash, and Marcion and the Gnostics were crushed."

Simon nodded. "From a Jewish point of view, the winners—the Roman Catholic Church—set themselves up as legal murderers. They carried out genocide against the heretics and conspired to control the world from Rome. This lethal combination of religion and imperialism gave wings to the angry jealous god of the Hebrew Bible. This is exactly what Marcion said would happen! When Christians retained the old god, they allowed Yahweh to possess Christianity. Religious fanaticism intensified during the Dark Ages, became perverted during the Inquisitions, and now the Church is collapsing morally and financially in a wasteland of priests abusing sex and their vows. When I look at it as a Jew, Christians are more atavistic than we are. Just when the Jews were evolving and outgrowing the ancient characteristics of the old tribal god, the Christians put frosting on him and spread him globally! During the Inquisitions, the Jews became more compassionate and cried out for mercy when Christians persecuted them."

Sarah threw her hand up in excitement, releasing a fistful of the grass she had been pulling. "Simon, you've said some things I wouldn't dare utter! Now that we can read the original Gnostics, we have perspective on what they said during this crucial turning point. The Gnostics were embroiled in awesome spiritual ferment reconsidering ancient beliefs. The second century was transformative, very much like our times with old ways ending and new things coming in."

She exhaled slowly and let her posture relax. "Phew, I think we need a nap."

They both lay back lazily in the warm sun. She was grateful for trust, companionship, and intellectual stimulation.

Simon dozed off thinking of ways to seduce her as well as just be with her in the world of ideas.

They woke up when coolness came in the late afternoon and enjoyed a leisurely walk back through the Borghese Gardens into the city just before rush hour jammed the streets of Rome.

4

The Vatican Museum

I bet Simon thinks the Vatican is a secret den of evil world controllers, Sarah thought as she poured hot water over coffee grounds while staring absentmindedly out the window at the cool, moist garden below. She loved the view from her apartment into the high-walled garden with a rococo marble fountain in the center. A smiling lion spouted water that flowed into a waterfall cascading into the large fountain bowl.

Sarah lived at 9 Via Ovidio near the Vatican in a small apartment owned by a friend of her father. As a visiting scholar, she spent many hours in the Vatican Library, a comfortable and stimulating place to read, with the sources she required, the prodigious background material on the early Church, close at hand. Yet what she loved the most were her thoughtful mornings at home.

Her kitchen was a little shoebox. To save counter space, her French press was on a wide stone ledge in front of a deep window casement where she contemplated her garden in the morning. The fine Renaissance house, now divided up into twelve small and very elegant apartments, was her first apartment since leaving her childhood home. The parlor had a single bed set in an alcove, leaving just enough space for a desk and a cozy chair. Deep window ledges built of thick-cut stone greatly expanded the room. The window seat at the end of her parlor had thick leaded-glass windows with circles pocked by blurry bubbles of trapped air. The original and elegant floors of checkered six-inch black-and-white marble squares were bordered by lacy gold filigree. According to the small cloisonné plaque on the door, her room was the bedroom of a very special daughter, Luciana Amelia—1583–1606 AD.

Coffee cup in hand, Sarah pulled in the tall window casements and leaned out to the flower garden below. Her hair fell around her neck and over the soft stone ledge. *I am like Rapunzel leaning out of my tower window, imprisoned by my father to keep my lover away.* She smiled at the strange thought.

Pulling back inside, she closed one of the leaded windows and snuggled down in the plush, emerald green velvet cushion of the window seat. Taking a deep draw on the warm liquid, she pushed Simon's number on her cell phone. It was Saturday, and after a week of heavy reading she thought it would be fun to meet in the nearby Piazza San Pietro. Tapping idly on her cup, she listened to the phone ringing and ringing. Funny. He always answered right away. Where could he be?

Just as she finally hung up, the morning sun broke over the corner of a garden wall in a flash of clear light that illuminated the thick window glass. Sarah sat up in anticipation of her favorite time of the day. Sunlight struck the outside surfaces of the ancient bubbles as each one transformed into a convex lens that reflected miniature images of the garden below. With intensified light, color spectrums illuminated the bubbles, clarifying the reversed images of the garden. Like holograms of floating worlds, for a moment her window was a kaleidoscope of tiny flower gardens.

Today, however, Sarah couldn't quite enjoy the beauty before her. Where was Simon? Did he really sleep with other women the way he said he would? *He's so attractive and charming, he must. I wonder what it would be like if I . . .*

Hugging her knees and sipping more coffee, she opened the

Sarah's window seat

other window to let in more of the aromas wafting up from the flower garden. *Am I crazy to insist he just be a friend?* Sarah sighed. Maybe it was time to move past the rules of her father. Sometimes she wondered just what century she was living in.

The ringing cell phone woke Simon, who was wrapped in the embroidered covers of a giant four-poster bed. Slowly and carefully, he reached for the phone and turned it off, hoping not to wake the woman beside him. He slid back down into the cool ivory silk sheets and listened. She was breathing softly, still asleep, her black hair cascading over her pillow. He exhaled slowly, glad for the time to think.

Last night's long dinner with Claudia had ended perfectly—exciting perfume, the aftereffects of expensive Chianti, and wild sex with no resistance. Claudia was one of several women he dated when he had time, a woman who always had fun and kept it light. She ran a successful boutique specializing in expensive shoes and bags. She was as beautiful as any Roman woman, gorgeous, in fact, and she liked to talk about the things that interested him. Last night, they had had a salacious conversation about scandals in the Church, the hot topic these days all over Rome.

He'd dated her on and off for a few years, but last night something had been different. When they came back to her apartment to make love, it had been great at first. Yet in the middle of their lovemaking Simon had realized he felt like an efficient machine. Claudia had seemed to be excited and satisfied, but he felt like he wasn't really with her. Her constant laughter irritated him. Even now, he felt as though somehow a part of him wasn't there.

He slipped quietly out of Claudia's enveloping bower, tiptoed noiselessly across the thick carpet, and crept into the kitchen to brew coffee. He wanted to leave, yet that was not how he usually behaved. Still, Claudia knew where to reach him, so after he finished his coffee and she still showed no signs of waking, he decided to go.

God, at least I'm not horny for a change, he was thinking when he closed the door. Spending lots of time with Sarah when the rules were "No Touch" had really screwed up his energy balance and his ability to think straight. Not a good thing, in light of the article he was writing about Vatican connections to the sexual abuse scandals in the Boston Archdiocese. *I wonder what old daddy Adamson will think when my story appears in the* Times *next week. I wonder what he'll think about celibacy when he reads what I have to say about what went on in the Boston rectories?*

Simon returned Sarah's call as soon as he got home, and he and Sarah arranged to meet later that morning outside the Vatican. As he approached, he saw Sarah standing in front of the obelisk in the middle of St. Peter's Square. Oddly, he felt like he was seeing her in a dream. It was early May, just getting hot, and she wore a blue paisley skirt and a thin white camisole, her wavy hair flowing over her shoulders.

She's like the goddess Athena visiting from another world.

Simon was suddenly so grateful for his night with Claudia. Otherwise he'd break all the rules today. After all, it had been two months. How much could a guy take?

Feeling very much in control of his feelings and his body, Simon came up behind her and put his right hand lightly on her bare shoulder. Sarah felt a jolt of electricity and shivered as her nipples hardened. She turned to face him, searching his dark eyes. Desire and curiosity lurked in her own green eyes. *Can she guess where I was last night? Does she know?*

She swallowed and turned toward the obelisk they'd come to see. He could see from the rise and fall of her chest that her breathing had accelerated.

"Another Egyptian obelisk," she said. "This one is not incised, which is unusual." As always, returning to the world of the mind had calmed her, and she was now more in control of her body's responses. "It's as if the pope who set it up chose to avoid having the beliefs of the Church compared to Egyptian symbols."

They decided to go the Vatican Museum to see if they could find more information about the obelisks. As they wandered through the Egyptian rooms, Sarah reached for Simon's bare arm below the sleeve of his seersucker shirt; his skin warmed to her tentative touch. They stood in front of a large seated statue of Sekhmet, the famous lion goddess who towered imperiously above them and the surrounding crowd. Simon glanced sideways and noticed Sarah's slender body becoming rigid as she faced the great royal lioness. Her eyebrows furrowed as if she disapproved of something.

"Look around this big room," she said. "There must be a dozen or more of these huge seated and standing statues of Sekhmet! Like the obelisks, there are more here in Rome than in Egypt! When I was on a tour of Karnak a few years ago, I paid a guide to spend some time in the temple with the only Sekhmet left in her original temple. She is the principle of chaos, the goddess who rages and causes destruction when people sin against the gods, the goddess of cataclysm and disorder. She watches when evil enters the world. Her seated statues protected the dynasties, the power of royalty. Now the Vatican uses them as devices to ground and protect their global power base; but, Sekhmet is pagan!"

Simon had been working on his article about priestly sexual abuse in America for weeks now, and he was on edge and low on sleep. He blurted, "As I stand in front of the great lion goddess, she's being used to cover up misogyny, the virulent hatred of women in the male hierarchy. I've spent the last few weeks reading the reports on what really went on in the Boston Diocese since the 1980s. The ugly reports of abuse inflicted on young children, mostly boys, turn my stomach. It's an unstoppable nightmare that got bigger and bigger and went out of control. Sekhmet rages right here in the Vatican!" Before Sarah could respond, a sea of tourists flowed around them.

The subject didn't come up again until dinner. As they sat in a very private cubicle at Giovanni's Wine Cave near Sarah's apartment, she realized Simon was really upset.

As soon as the waiter poured their wine and left the table, Simon began ranting. "It's just so abnormal for anybody to abuse bodies that way, to entrap and torture little boys like squashing bugs on the floor. I'm sorry; my brain is still flashing with all the graphic reports I've had to read. As horrible as they are, I think everybody should read them. When you really look at it, such systematic and continual abuse has to go right to the top."

"Do you think the pope knew what was going on and didn't do anything? Is that really possible?" Sarah pictured her father's pudgy, trusting Irish face in her mind as she spoke.

Simon set his wine glass down on the table with a firm clink. "Sarah, he had to know. Look at how the Church is structured. It's a pyramid with all the power in the capstone—the cardinals and the curia with the pope at the tip. Nothing happens in the lower levels of the hierarchy without the knowledge of the top." Simon could tell his words were upsetting to Sarah by the way she sipped her wine more quickly than usual. As she reached for the bread, he placed his hand over hers. "Look, Sarah, I watched Benedict's career when he was Cardinal Ratzinger in charge of the office that used to be called the Inquisition. He knew exactly what was going on. They elected him as the pope just because he knew! He was supposed to orchestrate the cover-up, but he botched it. He could be counted on to protect the guilty ones in the hierarchy, since he had so much to lose if he got caught. This agenda possesses the whole Church. Apostolic succession from Christ is baloney; it was invented to funnel the power falsely claimed by Peter through all subsequent popes."

As a lifelong Catholic, Sarah was more than familiar with the hierarchy he described, but hearing Simon put it all together to point out the pope's complicity in the abuse scandals was profoundly upsetting. She took a deep breath. "In Boston our whole family watched in horror as the truth came out piece by piece. I knew a few priests who were exposed, and I knew several families that had children who were abused. Looking back, I can now guess why some of the kids I was in parochial school with acted like zombies. My father and probably everybody else in Opus Dei has been giving the Church gobs of money to help pay for the lawsuits. It is just so painful, so sad. Sometimes even I can't believe these stories are true even though I know they are. A lot of Catholics I've known for years refuse to admit it or even think about it. It is the ultimate taboo, a terrible time to be a Catholic and hold our faith. Maybe I've been drawn to study the early Church to retain my faith.

Suddenly, she looked up. "You know, Marcion warned that the angry, avenging god Yahweh would pollute Christianity if the Hebrew Bible was retained and the new religion of love and compassion couldn't take root. The sexual corruption in the Church could be exactly the kind of thing Marcion warned about. The early Jews struggled to end child sacrifice, and now children are sacrificed *sexually*!"

Sarah's green eyes were filled with pain as she sought his, but Simon was someplace else, his inner mind flashing with last night's smooth white thighs, rippling breasts, soft fingers, and luscious lips. He realized the night had been tainted by his long days poring over the disgusting reports and he wondered if evil was an eruptive force.

He looked down at his plate and said in a strained voice, "I'm going to say something to you I never thought I'd say. Considering the work I'm doing right now, I'm grateful you want our relationship to be platonic, to be pure."

Inside his strong cynical side noted, *Boy, this is the best one-line come on I've come up with yet! Here I am with the most gorgeous and sweet woman I've ever known; Claudia is nothing compared to her. How could I have fallen down into a sex pit last night just when I'm reaching so high, just when I want to be more?*

She reached across the table to touch his arm. "It is really special that you say that. Sometimes I feel like I'm a weirdo. Your respect for me makes me feel what's happening between us really matters. I have to face what's going on in the Church and stop being Daddy's daughter. I've really only been out of my home for half a year. All the rest of my life I was in dorms or at home. I can't just toss everything I've believed while growing up. I still don't feel free. I feel like Ariadne trying to find her path out of the Cretan labyrinth, except my labyrinth is the Roman Catholic Church. I'm following a thread through the dark that I hope leads to light. The Marcionites believed sex was created by the demiurge, a limited god who was so potent and dangerous that they believed they needed to be celibate to avoid being controlled by him! Considering what's been going on in the Church, maybe the Marcionites were right? What else explains a world where dragons consume infants? Abusers pollute the Church's altars like the Canaanite rituals stained the early religion of the Jews."

Simon was impressed by Sarah's ability to face the truth about her religion so quickly. "Forgive me, Sarah, if I go too far, since I am not quite myself today. Some anti-Catholics say Christ created the Communion to supplant the blood sacrifices being practiced in his time. Maybe the Mass was invented to lift people out of blood lust. With time, however, I think the constant repetition of Mass in churches all over the world has built up a tremendous sacrificial force, an evil power that perverts good men into torturing children. This must seem like blasphemy to you, but the abuse reports stir up these kinds of thoughts because it's impossible to comprehend what people do. What goes on is even worse than you know. Often boys were seduced by priests approaching them with words of pious Christian love that the boys couldn't protest against. Handicapped and deaf children were used; orphans were fair game."

"As for blasphemy," she interjected, "the more I study the Gnostics and Marcion, the more I have similar thoughts, ideas that would have angered and offended me a few years ago. The Gnostics believed sex was the easiest way for good people to be invaded by evil, something that certainly seems to have happened to the priests who have done these terrible things. I've also wondered whether the Mass serves evil as well as good forces, since the Mass is the central ritual of a power-based global religion. When I've taken Communion, I've felt many levels going on. For example, what goes on if I take Communion from a priest who just raped the boy who is serving the altar?

"I still go to Mass when I'm home in Boston, but not here in Rome where the man at the top is so close; he looks and feels evil to me, almost reptilian." Her eyes widened. "But if you ever meet my father, be sure you don't mention any of this to him!"

"Don't worry about it, Sarah," Simon said with a teasing grin. "I'm afraid you have something bigger to worry about. What is your father going to think about Simon Isaac Appel's article about the Boston Diocese in the *New York Times* next week? And, by the way, I won't be able to see you for a week because I have a nasty deadline to meet."

And I won't be seeing Claudia either, he noted as he walked Sarah home with his arm resting happily on her shoulder. *It is over.*

5

A Visitor in Rome

Simon's priestly sexual abuse article stirred up great interest in the United States during May 2012. He was the first major reporter to focus on a reason for the abuse, namely, the hierarchy that funneled all decisions directly to the top. He contended that the archbishops, bishops, cardinals, and pope had to have known what was going on in the parishes. What else explained all the documented sexual predators being moved by bishops and archbishops from parish to parish and all around the world?

Predatory priests had been callously unleashed on the innocent and trusting laity. The reports from Boston parishes were sad stories from people suffering in a climate of abandonment and terror. They had bravely struggled to be obedient and keep the faith because they didn't want to lose the way of life they'd practiced for generations, but the hierarchy's cruel lack of concern about their pain was eroding their trust in the Church.

Simon's story came out just as the hierarchy was realizing there was no way to hide the ugly truth. Initially, when the reports of rampant abuse during the 1960s and 70s began leaking out during the 1980s, priests, bishops, and archbishops closed their circles and conspired to maintain absolute control. They played a twenty-year global shell game moving known abusers from parish to parish and to other countries. They got away with it because the laity simply could not believe the rumors and reports; they couldn't conceive of such things. In 2002, however, when the Boston media courageously reported on the extent of the abuse, a rising tide of the faithful began leaving the Church, taking their financial support and their children with them. The hierarchy in America responded by selling Church property to pay for the victim lawsuits. By 2004 parishioners realized they had no ownership rights over properties their own grandparents and great-grandparents had originally donated and developed for the Church. Padlocks snapped shut on old doors of beloved churches and schools, while many bishops and archbishops continued to live like royalty in the mansions gifted to them by the founder Catholics. Hard-working Catholics were losing their culture and their access to sacred space while old neighborhoods decayed around them. Simon's vivid description of the Catholic sexual and financial crisis was a compelling story of voracious greed and rotting lust. It hit hard.

Sarah read the article on her laptop while snuggling in her velvet window seat. She felt as though Simon was writing from his heart, and she was hearing him deep in her mind. They were both obsessed with the same things. Sarah wondered if she would ever get her Ph.D. She was struggling to approach Marcion academically. She was so interested in what the early Christians thought that she found she had little interest in objectivity. Instead the more she studied, the angrier she became about the way the Marcionites and Gnostics had been silenced when Constantine created his alliance with the Church in the fourth century. The great cover-up in the early Church had advanced during the struggles over Christology in the early councils; she believed they had cut the subtle thread leading back to the real Christ. The battles over dogma then raged for centuries while the Church attacked and murdered anybody who went against orthodoxy. The hierarchy prevailed for more than a thousand years, and now they were blind to the evil they claimed to fight because they were not in touch with divinity. Sarah saw Simon's article as the story of a metastasizing cancer spreading through the Church.

Her cell phone rang, and she reached for it eagerly, thinking it was Simon. Instead, a loud and exasperated male voice growled, "Sarah! Is that you?" It was her father.

Sarah moved the phone a short distance from her ear. "Yes, Daddy, are you all right?"

"You're damned right I'm all right, but the New York Jewish rag sure as hell isn't. Did you see the article about priests in yesterday's paper? Part of it focuses on unsubstantiated reports of abuses in Boston parishes over the past forty years. Just when the sit-ins finally went away and we're getting back in the black, now this! It's going to get everyone stirred up all over again about the church and school closures. Dragging up these sick accusations after the fact just makes things worse."

Sarah sighed. She couldn't pretend to agree with her father about this. "Well, Daddy, it's not like the people in Boston hadn't already noticed the connection between the closures and payments for the lawsuits. They resent losing their family churches and schools just because the priests were out of control."

"Oh bullshit, Sarah. The archdiocese has been cleaning up its financial act, so it's time for forgiveness and reconciliation, you know, healing the pain. This damn article is a stink bomb on Boston just when everyone was getting over it and moving on.

"But that's not why I'm calling. We'll be able to talk about all this in person, sweetheart, since I've been called to Rome to attend some meetings as a representative of the Boston Archdiocese. I can't wait to see you. I'm going to hop on a plane as soon as possible. We can talk about how your studies can help the Church—like father, like daughter! I'll call you later about when I'm arriving. Your mother says hello."

"Okay, I'll see you soon then. Bye, Daddy." She wondered how this would turn out. *What on earth will Simon think of my father?*

Two days later, Sarah's father picked her up and took her to dinner at the home of his old friends, the house where he always stayed when in Rome. She'd already visited their house when she first arrived a few months ago and was blinded by the sheer joy of being in the ancient city. Now that her reality was clouding with complexity, she couldn't wait to return. Life felt simple and unchanging at the ancient house by the back side of the Borghese Gardens on the Via Lombardia.

Sarah and her father knocked on the imposing door of the Pierleoni home. It creaked slowly open, and a wizened servant showed them the way in and through a cavernous room where seventeenth-century scarlet and sapphire tapestries softened the cold stone walls. The echoes of William's and Sarah's footfalls emphasized the profound silence.

They entered the library, where a lively discussion was going on around a huge fireplace covered by a large metalwork screen. Count Pietro Pierleoni, an elfin and elegant man, and his lovely, birdlike wife Matilda warmly greeted Sarah and her father with cheek kisses.

A third man, a Catholic dignitary wearing a white cassock cinched with a kelly green embroidered surplice, embraced William, who introduced him to Sarah as Father Sean McBride, head of the Vatican office for American parish affairs. Sarah greeted him and then withdrew to a nearby leather window seat to observe the scene. Her father joined the others by the fireplace.

Pietro was saying, "Yes, this scandal is of such proportions that now we even hear about it in Rome. At first we thought the Americans were fussing about things we tend to ignore here in Italy. After all, little peccadilloes do happen. We all know the Vatican is not lily white and that life must go on."

The Pierleonis, descendants of an old Roman family that originated in Tuscany, fascinated Sarah. Family crests and elaborate genealogies tracing their ancient bloodlines adorned the walls around her. The Pierleonis had come into prominence when their family produced a few popes more than a thousand years ago, and to this day they were still involved in Vatican intrigues. Sarah settled into the window seat, surrounded by leather-bound, gold-embossed books arranged in shelves so high ladders were required for the top rows. Near her a golden tabby curled up under a heavy gabled desk glared at her with hot amber eyes, switching his fluffy tail to express annoyance over the invasion of his space.

Matilda Pierleoni smiled at Sarah from the fireplace, over her crystal glass of amber scotch. She sensed that Sarah, whom she'd first met in Boston when Sarah was only a little girl, needed a few moments for reflection. A few months ago during a dinner, Matilda had shared some wonderful stories about her family history with her and had been utterly charmed by Sarah's keen interest and her dark-haired beauty, which was particularly enhanced when she was thoughtful. Matilda thought of her eldest son, Armando, who had been born in Tuscany years before Sarah was born. *I wish I could get the two of them together in the same room.* She discreetly looked the young woman over, enjoying the sensation of the warm liquid sliding down her throat, and decided she was going to make it happen.

Sarah crossed one leg over the other, cognizant of the older woman's scrutiny. She wondered if the Pierleonis would have welcomed her so warmly if they knew about her new ideas about her religion. A maid dressed in a black dress covered by a starched white pinafore offered Sarah a glass of wine on a silver tray. Sarah felt like she was in another place in time. Accepting it gratefully, she strained to catch the conversation in front of the fireplace. Apparently, Father McBride had asked for a meeting with the Pierleonis and her father. Father McBride, a corpulent man with fierce gray eyes, seemed to be attempting to use his size to over-whelm them all. Sarah didn't find him very convincing, mostly because of the way his right wrist went limp when he made a point. In a low whisper barely audible to Sarah's sharp ears, Father McBride said, "Our concern is connections are being drawn between the Holy Father and the scandals in Europe, especially Belgium. Of course, the Holy Father is an innocent man of God who must be involved in Church affairs and political issues. It is unavoidable that he would have made some difficult decisions in the past. His decisions will be scrutinized if his private documents ever became public. Maybe you can describe to me how Church records are arranged and stored in America, William? And Pietro, you know how records are kept in Italy. I wanted all of us here to share ideas on how to handle these administrative processes more efficiently. I need direction for how we can, ah, protect documents for the Holy Father's privacy. How can we keep things for our eyes only, if you know what I mean?" Sarah touched her lips to the etched wine glass and stared at the annoyed cat still gazing at her.

The conversation was interrupted by the appearance of the maid announcing that dinner was ready. They retired to the din-ing room, where they enjoyed pasta primavera with linguini steam-ing in colorful pottery bowls and rich red wine from the Pierleoni cellars in crystal goblets. The room was a cavernous crypt with heavy dark beams looming over a heavy oval table. Wall sconces with candles emitted soft light as the servers' footsteps shuffled on the worn alabaster floors. A heavy door led into a cavelike kitchen, and whenever it opened or shut, audible suction pulled through the ancient dining room. Sarah was seated next to Pietro, who wanted to know everything about her studies and whether she was still enjoying Rome.

"I love being able to do reference work in the Vatican Library," she told him. "When I've had enough, I walk all over the city where the visible layers of time lead me deeper and deeper into the fabric of history. It's so much easier to understand the past by actually being here instead of just reading about Rome at home. Now I see why Europeans have such a firm grasp of history, deeper knowledge, beyond what's possible for most Americans."

"Yes, of course, my dear," Pietro replied in cultured English with a smooth Italian accent that made every word sound sensual.

Pietro was a charming older man who enjoyed life, and tonight he was exceedingly taken with Sarah. Matilda always seated him next to the prettiest woman in the room. Sarah wore a richly embroidered, tawny empire-waist dress with a dark blue bodice, and he was enjoying the deliciously low neckline. Pietro considered beautiful breasts to be man's gift from God. "Yes, and I wonder exactly what you are studying? I believe it is very early Church affairs?"

She murmured yes, aware that Father McBride was listening to their conversation while he chatted with Matilda. Her soft response thrilled Pietro, making him feel like she was sharing a secret.

"I'm investigating the three centuries just after the time of Christ when Peter's church in Rome formulated the Gospel canon."

"Ah, yes," Pietro nodded. "But what are you *seeking*, my dear?"

At this point everybody stopped talking as Father McBride aimed a pointed glance at Sarah over his small silver eyeglasses.

She took a deep breath and boldly spoke to the table while the fat prelate leered at her chest. "I'm investigating Marcion of Pontus, an early theologian and bishop who was excommunicated in 144 CE, even though he was the founder of bishoprics all over the known world."

Father McBride dropped his knife on his gilded Spode plate and almost cracked the gold rim. Sarah's father stared at him, wondering why he was so upset.

Pietro persisted, "Well, what a fascinating subject! I know

very little about Marcion except that he is said to be the first and greatest heretic refuted by Tertullian. I suppose you're poring over the Gnostic sources and recent biblical redaction, discoveries, and research that have been offering many new insights about the early Church?"

Pietro was enjoying himself mightily. Wine warmed his throat, and he observed appreciatively the rosy flushing on Sarah's chest and cheeks.

Sarah rallied. Her earnest green eyes sparkled in the candle-light. "Well, yes," she replied, peeking under her thick black lashes to see if her father was listening. He wasn't, which was not surprising since he wouldn't know a Gnostic from an early Church Father, so she went on. "All the recent discoveries, like the Nag Hammadi and Essene scrolls, make it possible to reconsider the early days of the Church. I'm interested in this new perspective and what it may mean to us in the modern world."

"It's easy to see why you'd be so interested in this period," Pietro responded. "However, my dear, the early Church must have had good reasons for suppressing the Gnostics, good reasons for laboring to refute them. That's why there were so many early councils to define Christ's nature. What if you inadvertently raise the lid on Pandora's box? What do *you* think, Father McBride, since you've been listening to our conversation?"

Father McBride's salacious snooping amused Pietro, since the priest was supposed to be paying attention to Matilda. Matilda had also been listening to Sarah while she talked with Pietro, since she kept her eye on Pietro when he was drinking wine. He loved to stir people up and flush out what they were thinking about, especially pompous clerics. Her task during dinner was maintaining harmony.

Matilda was afraid Pietro was igniting an explosion, since Father McBride looked like he was on the verge of apoplexy as he responded, "Well, of course, I could not avoid hearing the discussion, since this young lady is talking about things that are rarely spoken of in polite company. We believe it is dangerous for Catholics to look into the Marcionite heresy and dangerous for them to read the Gnostics. The Church buried these ideas years ago for the protection of the faithful, so they are best left forgotten. As I understand it, Sarah, you are a devout Catholic. At least your father certainly is. So how do you justify this research in the light of your faith?"

Sarah felt her neck get hot; however, she'd already thought plenty about what to say to people like Father McBride. Noticing her father put his utensils down to slug more wine she retorted in a sweet, calm voice, "If my faith is strong, things I discover will strengthen it. How can seeking the truth be wrong in any way? Divine providence guides us when we explore new insights about Christ's life, things that have been hidden for so long. After all, every century brings forth a new Christology, a new interpretation of His meaning to help us keep our faith. I think it's time for a twenty-first century Christology."

Matilda saw William's perplexed look and arched her eyebrow pointedly at Pietro to cue him that he must be concerned with all the guests, especially his old friend. Even when they were students together at Yale, William had never shown the least interest in theology.

But Pietro ordered a double bourbon for Father McBride and boomed, "I started this discussion, so I will say what I think! We are here tonight because of a crisis in the American Catholic Church that is spreading into Europe and around the world. We could be having a Second Reformation. We all know something is very wrong. Perhaps this is a crisis over celibacy, even some kind of chal- lenge to the hierarchy itself. The Church does evolve although it is slow like an aging turtle. We must trust God's providence, just as Sarah says. As a devout Catholic girl from a good Boston family, she is an ideal person to look into the new information coming to light. Sarah, you love history and want to know what happened in the past. I commend you for this, since our greatest danger would be to ignore what we've already learned. So, I look forward to reading your reflections on early Christianity!" He proposed a toast to his pretty dinner guest as she demurely smiled at Father McBride, who suppressed a cough with a slug of bourbon.

After dinner they returned to the library for cognac and chocolates. Matilda scooped up the sleeping golden cat from the window seat and beckoned Sarah to sit with her. "My dear, I am impressed by your courage and determination. I've been curious about some of these recent discoveries in early Christianity, and I've read a few sources. Gnostic theology seems like New Age gibberish about conspiracies and spacemen. I've never heard of Marcion. Why are you so interested in him?"

Her clear blue eyes sparkled with genuine curiosity, lighting up her delicate face. Her skin glowed like fine marble in the light from the fire. Sarah thought it was a face Botticelli would have painted. Sarah also noticed her hostess was wearing the family jewels, an exquisite necklace of two- to three-carat emeralds separated by brushed gold beads. It sat heavily on her delicate neck, leaving indentations in her fine skin.

Sarah replied, "The most compelling thing about Marcion is that around 150 CE his early church was much more extensive and developed than Peter's. Also it continued for many years around the world. Marcion's main belief was that Christianity should let go of the Old Testament and start fresh by using only new Christian sources. He believed the emerging religion would be distorted if it added its new scripture to the old Jewish scripture. After all, Christ spoke of a New Covenant."

Matilda frowned. "But Jesus himself was Jewish, so I've always thought it made sense to study the scriptures he himself knew so well. I can't imagine what our faith would be like without the Old Testament scriptures."

Sarah leaned forward eagerly. "I've been thinking about the same thing. I think our faith would be more about Jesus. It's Jesus who I think was lost when his teachings were grafted right on top of the Jewish scriptures. Even though I have my faith and feel close to Christ, the Church is in the way of what I feel in my heart. The Church has erected a great wall of dry scholasticism around Christ's true nature, a castle that imprisons his warmth and passion. When I consider early sources, Jesus comes alive for me as a real person. I want to *know* this man and hear what he came to say to us."

Matilda considered this idea for a moment. "I do wonder if things could have been less contentious throughout history between Christians and Jews if the Christians had just created their own religion. Looking back through our family's history over a thousand years, we have had many dealings with Jewish bankers and merchants. Their stories are sad ones of good people having their property taken and being moved into ghettoes. I wonder whether we Christians just took what *we* wanted of Jewish wisdom. We've even been taught Isaiah anticipated Jesus, but to be honest, that has always felt fishy to me. After all, we know translators were always rewriting things. Worse, we used *our* Bible to persecute the Jews whenever they got any power and money." She sighed. "I see why you're looking into this."

Sarah felt a strong sense of relief that this valued friend of her family was open to her emerging ideas, and she continued eagerly, "I feel that we are living in an exciting time of great reflection. We have access to all of these lost sources even at the same time people are still fighting and killing each other over their gods. It is said Jesus came to redeem us, yet everything is collapsing! I wonder what Jesus would really think of what's happening today."

Father McBride was listening to the discussion between the ladies while he stood by the fireplace with Sarah's father. He said, "William, I think you'd better ask your daughter some questions about her research. She may be investigating things that should be left to the theologians who protect the Church against error. That's why the early Fathers defined these questions in the first place. I have to wonder, why would a woman, even if she is your daughter, be investigating things that are meant for theologians?" Swigging his double cognac, he actually was thinking: *She is too beautiful to have much of a brain. She won't last long around here, but she bears watching. I'll phone Father Ignatio about Sarah Adamson tomorrow morning.*

William Adamson met Father McBride's intense red-rimmed eyes. He vowed to spend some time alone with Sarah before returning to Boston.

6

Dinner at Alfredo's

Bliss overwhelmed Sarah on the morning after the Pierleoni dinner party while she gazed out to the garden as her coffee brewed. Her garden, the only green space amid multistoried apartments, was the street's nature preserve. Stimulated by rising heat drying the morning dew, dragonflies unfurled their wings and flew around in circles above the fountain's surface. Iridescent rainbows shimmered in the mist generated by water pouring from the lion's mouth into the white marble basin. Sunrays flashed through the tall cypress trees that edged the circular drive, reflecting on crystalline specks in the marble. Pungent eucalyptus, yew, and cypress aromas perfumed the mist.

The phone ringing in the parlor startled her out of her garden contemplation so she grabbed her coffee mug and walked into the other room. Anticipating her father's voice, she was instead pleasantly surprised to hear Simon eagerly wishing her a lovely morning and apologizing for not being in touch for more than a week.

"I didn't anticipate such a big reaction to the priestly abuse article. I had to spend hours on my blog answering people's questions and dealing with a tidal wave of objections. I'm not everybody's favorite right now. So, how've you been? Did you like the article?"

"It was excellent. And I'm so glad it's gotten so much attention. I wasn't at all surprised not to hear from you."

"I miss you," he continued. "I still have a lot of work today, but can we have dinner tonight?"

"Well, sadly I can't, and for reasons that involve you," Sarah said. "You're not going to believe this, but my father is in Rome. He came three days ago, and I've been spending all my time with him. Actually, it has been very challenging. We had dinner at my father's friends, and he introduced me to the Vatican official in charge of American parishes. This priest got wind of my research and told my father he should watch out for what I'm looking into. So my dad gave me a hard time all the way home in the cab. Except he doesn't know the difference between Marcion and Tertullian. "Sarah grinned. "Actually, I was pleasantly surprised by my own confidence about my research in the face of a pompous Church official. So although I would love to, I can't have dinner with you tonight."

"Hey, wait, I want to meet your father," Simon replied. "I assume he doesn't come to Rome that often? I must meet him; I insist. Can I take you both out to Alfredo's tonight? It's really hard to get in there, but the owner is a friend of mine. Americans love the place. It would be a real treat for your father and a great way for me to meet him."

Sarah moved her laptop aside and dropped heavily down onto her window seat, making an effort not to spill her coffee. "Oh, Simon, I don't think it's a good idea at all! He just read your article and it really got him going. That's actually why he rushed to Rome. He's dealing with terrific pressure in our parish, and he thinks you just made it all worse! The minute he hears your name, he'll launch into a tirade." She paused, considering. "Well, he might. He is usually respectful and polite when he's socializing regardless of what he actually thinks."

"I'll take my chances. Look, I'll make you a deal. Just tell him a good friend of yours insists on hosting him while he's in Rome. It's better if he starts out in debt to me. Just introduce us. I'll bet he won't even realize it's me at first. When he does, I can handle whatever comes up. Who knows? We might end up having a great conversation. After all, we have mutual interests." Simon kept talking, deliberately not allowing Sarah the chance to break in or protest. "I'll reserve for 8 p.m., so bring him a few minutes early and get seated and then I will join you. Since he's an Irishman, order him a stiff drink. That way he'll already be relaxing at his table before he hears my name. I want to meet him. I insist!"

Sarah had her doubts about Simon's plan but, charmed by his determination to meet her father, she assented.

Evening was settling in as William and Sarah were led to their table at Alfredo's, and the restaurant was already jammed with glittery gossiping Romans. The beefy older man following a stunning young woman got their attention. *Mistress or daughter? Must be a daughter, since she's so understated.* Her upswept hair revealed diamond and pearl earrings, and the deep V neckline of her elegant light blue sheath showed off another large pearl on a small gold chain. *What a beauty! Could they be Americans? He looks like it.*

While they were being seated, diners near William and Sarah's table continued to indulge in periodic quick glances at the mysterious pair. Next a tall, elegant young man in a black Armani suit slowly and deliberately approached the table. Resting his hand on the back of the remaining seat, Simon smiled sweetly at Sarah and conversation hushed at the nearby tables as Sarah and her father rose for introductions. Simon turned to gaze directly into the eager and friendly Irish blue eyes of William Adamson, who extended his hand while taking the full measure of the confident young man—Sarah's "friend."

Reaching for the hand perfectly encircled by starched white cuffs cinched in gold bars, William liked the look of this friend's fresh smiling face and direct dark eyes. *Whoever he is, his manners are impeccable.* When Sarah announced a name he thought he'd heard before, William was surprised to realize Simon was an American. He responded, "Nice to meet yuh," but couldn't quite register the name—*Apelle, Apple, Amen?*

Simon, amused by all the nosy Romans sneaking peeks while gossiping heatedly at their tables, seated himself. He'd spotted a few people who knew him, but he didn't acknowledge them because he wanted to focus on Sarah's father. Simon took in William's typically Irish florid face, balding reddish blond hair, bright blue eyes, and happy, solid round body and noticed, from his protective glances at Sarah, that he also seemed like a loving father.

Drinks arrived right away, and William raised his glass, followed by Simon and Sarah. "To you, Simon, for hosting us this evening in this beautiful city and for being a friend here to my gorgeous and intelligent daughter."

In response to Simon's polite questions, William explained that he was a developer in Boston and then got right down to business by asking where Simon was from, what he did for a living, and why he was in Rome. Simon explained about his upbringing in Brooklyn Heights and his work for the *New York Times* and other papers. Then William asked Simon to repeat his name again.

"Simon *Appel*, sir." Simon said clearly and enthusiastically as Sarah touched her lips to her Manhattan, demurely sniffing the sweet cherry. Simon watched William's eyes narrow as the sound landed in his brain.

"Well, young man, I believe I know who you are! Are you the author of the recent article in the *Times* about the priestly scandal in America?"

"Yes, sir, I am. I wanted to host you in Rome because your daughter has become a good friend, and she says you had quite a reaction to my article. Sarah tells me you are very active in your parish in Boston, in one of the parishes that thankfully was not closed a few years ago. So I think we have some common concerns, although I could see why you might not welcome my article. Oh well, as a journalist, I'm used to that," Simon said, smiling broadly with a twinkle flashing in his dark eyes.

For the first time, Sarah noticed the well-bred and sensual curve of Simon's upper lip, as he looked expectantly at her father. Simon exuded self-confidence and was so incredibly good-looking in the Armani suit that she knew her father was impressed.

Simon's comfortable boldness and directness had also disarmed William, who had just been about to get testy, especially at Sarah for setting him up without so much as a warning. *This guy sounds like a damned Jew, like a nosy, know-it-all kike! But he's got balls. It took a lot of nerve to set up this dinner with me as a guest. And what the hell, it's a balmy night in a great Roman restaurant.* With a Rob Roy sliding down his throat and warming his belly, William felt magnanimous. Being a man with a big heart, he put fun and good cheer first. He also felt expansive like he always did when he travelled in Europe. It wouldn't be good manners to badger his host. But what was that name, Appel, exactly? Italian? Greek? French?

"Well, I can't say your article thrilled me. But you've got the right to write about it; anybody does. Your paper, the *New York Times*, of course has a heavy Jewish influence, so we Catholics don't like it much. We prefer the Boston Globe, don't we, Sarah?"

"Yes, Daddy, but I like the *Times* too, and I think Simon is a very good writer. I liked the depth of his sources and comprehensive coverage, didn't you?"

"Well, it creates a lot of trouble for me, since you suggest that the Vatican knew some things, which is ridiculous, just plain ridiculous. No way that's possible," he said, still trying to figure out whether Simon was French Jewish (which would have been not so bad) or what. But mainly he was just enjoying himself. *Damned good-looking buck, that's for sure. Smart dresser, warm smile with engaging eyes.*

All three agreed that the butter lettuce salad with goat cheese croquette and candied pecans drizzled with balsamic vinegar was outstanding. William ordered an expensive bottle of wine, insisting it was his contribution to the dinner. As the waiter poured the rich, ruby red liquid just before the arrival of pasta carbonara, he felt warm and fuzzy. He wondered if she was dating this guy. At least he was no peon. Williams and Harvard, hmmmm . . . He still couldn't believe Sarah hadn't given him any background about Simon prior to this dinner.

"So how'd you two meet?" he wondered. "Did you know each other at Harvard? Probably not, since I think you are a little older than Sarah?"

"Yes, I am, I'm thirty-five. I'm aware Sarah also went to Harvard, so we have that in common, but I graduated a few years ahead of her. After I graduated, I went out to become a journalist because I like to write. Luckily, I got a lot of breaks, I'm making a living, and I get to travel a lot. The *Times* sent me here as a stringer covering Vatican news, and they don't care if I write for other papers. Needless to say, my understanding of how the Vatican works is valuable for the *Times,* and so they asked me to write this recent article."

"But how did you two meet?" William persisted.

Sarah quickly popped in. "We were both interested in an early Roman archaeological site, and we met there during a tour."

Simon sent an amused glance Sarah's way. Obviously she didn't want to say she'd just met him on the street. "Mr. Adamson, don't worry, we are just friends," Simon said, which made all three of them laugh.

Funny thing is, her father likes me. He can't help it. Of course he likes me, since his daughter likes me. Simon was using his journalistic eye to discreetly study William whenever Sarah was chatting with him. *He's a hard-working man, callused hands and a healthy outdoor face. He must be second- or third-generation American since he's easy with money for her education, for her travel. The diamond ring on his right hand is a dead giveaway: he must have made a pile at some point and treated himself. This is a man I can respect. He's not a Mr. Mills, the father of my old girlfriend, who was snide, took pride in his patrician blood, never worked a day in his life, and scorned anybody who was not a certified blueblood. I think I can trust Sarah's father.*

"Now I'm ready! And call me William, Simon!" William announced once the main course was served. He rolled Alfredo's famous homemade spaghetti in freshly pureéd tomato sauce on his fork and said, "Let's not mince words about your article. How long do you think everybody has to feel guilty about what happened, Simon? Do you understand what these financial settlements are doing to our parishes? Do you realize the Catholic Church in America is reeling financially like a drunken circus elephant? Is it worth it to hype up the public by bringing out all the dirty laundry just when the people in charge are dealing with it as best they can?"

Sarah flushed. *What's Simon going to do with that?*

Simon, however, wasn't the least bit nervous. Instead he was eyeing Sarah, thinking she looked sexy as hell. *Sitting here with big Daddy tonight, I feel like I'm going to know her for the rest of my life!*

Sarah felt his gaze warming the side of her long neck, so she glanced over at him with green eyes flashing excitedly. Her moist shell-pink lips narrowed slightly as she wondered how he'd respond to the challenge.

She likes it! She's enjoying seeing her father go at it with me. Great!

Simon set down his fork and met William's eyes. "With all due respect, William, there's no sign the hierarchy has or ever intends to create systems that will protect children from these abusers. To be candid, I've been here in Rome for almost three years, and I see no signs that anybody here gives a damn. They just want the problem to go away. They want Catholics in America to obey again and go back to Church, pray, and send the money. But how can you do that when your parish church closes? How do you educate your kids as Catholics when the school is closed? I don't write about these things just to get paid. I care a great deal about these problems. The pain in New York over shrinking parishes is terrible, just as it is in Boston. Catholic communities have been a fundamental American social system in cities and towns for generations. I write about this because I believe the Vatican will clean up its act only if people keep the pressure on them. Italian society is ancient and decadent and not aware how destructive these losses are for a young culture like America."

Two bulls were about to charge and lock horns, so Sarah interjected. "Hey, I'm the third part in this trinity, and I'd like to say my piece. What if this disaster—a crisis that really is on par with the Reformation—what if it's really about celibacy?" She lowered her voice very delicately as she cut into a firm slice of sweet lemon and basil chicken on arugula, wondering what her father would think about what she had to say. Neither man replied, seemingly preferring to focus on their entrees, so she went on. "I assume you both know that the Church adopted celibacy only about one thousand years ago for financial reasons? The Church needed to hold assets in perpetuity, yet property was leaking out into the families of married priests through inheritance. The Church wasn't accumulating enough money, and now the financial basis of the Church is shrinking anyway. Maybe marriage for priests needs to be allowed again, since it would appear that lifelong celibacy is impossible for most men."

Simon noticed that her cheeks had flushed slightly since they had gotten into their second bottle of wine. *Her pouty lips are just asking for kisses as she sits here talking about celibacy when she won't have sex with me. Oops, better control my thoughts or Daddy will know something is going on.* Simon looked over to William. "This wine is fabulous with my steak. How is it with your food?"

"Great! And if the problem is celibacy, then maybe it's because there are too many gay priests because, you know, gays screw around a lot. I don't know if it has always been that way, but it sure is now. Did you run into the gay issue during your research, Simon?"

"Of course I did, but I'm not sure if it's anything new. I tend to think the priesthood has been a refuge for gay men for a long time before the 1960s sexual liberation movement. Before that, homo-sexuals had to deal with a lot of judgment and suffered with heavy guilt. So for a gay person who was inclined to be spiritual and also moral, it was easier to become a priest and try to be celibate than it was to live in society as a homosexual. Then with the sexual libera-tion during the 1960s in America, suddenly many gay priests came out. I don't really think the Vatican knew this was happening at first, especially since many older priests had managed to be celibate, at least most of the time."

"Well, I agree with you, Simon, so I'm wondering if our visiting scholar sees any connection to her studies and the current crisis in the Church?" He turned to his daughter and waited for her reply.

Sarah paused, not yet ready to formulate her thoughts but feel-ing safe enough to float a few ideas.

Simon wondered what on earth would come out of her mouth, noting he liked her comfort with her father. *That's a very good sign. They probably don't agree on a lot of things, yet they share their thoughts easily.* He was happy he'd pushed for this dinner.

"Daddy, that is a very tough question, especially since I'm still determining what I want to focus on. It's challenging because I wouldn't be interested in the moldy old past if it weren't relevant now. Considering what people actually thought about two thousand years ago, invariably they were obsessed with the question of how evil got into our world. Jesus said God was good, so they couldn't reconcile why a good god would allow evil into the world. Well, considering the feelings of a mother whose child has been abused and scarred for life by a trusted priest, I feel her angst. Just read-ing the abuse reports has traumatized Simon. I'm investigating what people thought about evil during the time of Christ and when the Church formed. This question is compelling now, when evil lurks in the highest levels of the Church."

"How is getting into that stuff going to get you or any Catholic anywhere? Can't say these ideas would do me any good!" But

William felt strange and wondered if he'd had too much red wine. He didn't want Sarah to have any part of these ideas. Hell, people had been murdered and burned at the stake just for thinking about these ideas. But he had to admit that the hideous evil oozing out of the rectories in Boston made him wonder how so many priests could've ever acted the way they did.

Sarah gazed earnestly at her father. "Daddy, it is so good to talk to you about this. I'm the next generation that is supposed to carry on the faith, but will there be schools for my children? The historic churches I loved as a child are turning into wastelands. So if God is good, how can this happen? The Gnostics said the highest god is pure and good, but during the creation, an evil god was unleashed in the world. Well, there is an evil force in the Church, and I think we must find out how this could happen. Some answers may be found in the period when Christianity first defined itself. What if decisions made a long time ago are causing the current crisis?"

Eventually, after tiramisu and ice cream for William, the lively conversation ended. After Sarah and William said goodbye to Simon, William finally had his chance. "So Sarah, what is Appel? Is he a Greek or a Frenchman?"

Sarah suppressed a tiny smile. "He's Jewish, Daddy. He comes from an old New York family of successful industrialists going back more than a hundred years, a very well-educated and good family. But before you get worried about that, since I know you are, he's just my friend, not a potential boyfriend since he's Jewish. That's how you brought me up, so I honor your expectations."

William sensed something more, but there was no point saying anything about it since he felt like Simon had bagged him in the first round. *Maybe those are Sarah's intentions, but what about Simon's? Oh well, dinner was a thoughtful gesture on the part of a very nice young man, even if he is a Jew.*

7

A Dinner in Tuscany

On the morning after Alfredo's, another special invitation came to William and Sarah from Pietro and Matilda Pierleoni. The Pierleonis had begun their Tuscan summer residence at Castel Vetulonia near Siena, so knowing William had a few more days in Italy, they invited him to visit. William hadn't been to the castle in forty years, so he couldn't wait to return and bring Sarah with him. He hired a driver and soon they were past Orvieto on a rural road, passing rustic little villages clustered around churches. Vineyards and fertile fields bordered by ancient stone walls surrounded stone villas on hills under tall trees, a landscape where the works of humans fused with nature.

Sarah had the sense this visit was somehow going to change her life, and in the meantime she enjoyed her father's mounting excitement. As she listened to him describe his previous visit to Tuscany, a trip that had become legend in their family, he was young again.

"I'm just so happy you can share this special visit with me, Sarah. What luck! You may recall that I first got to know Pietro in college when he was a dapper and popular Italian *cognoscente* who had been sent to school in America. After we graduated, he went to work in finance in New York and I didn't see him for a while. Then he asked me to come to his family estate in Italy for his wedding. Although the estate had been in Pietro's family for more than a thousand years, it had only recently been returned by the government after Mussolini seized it during World War II. "I know you've heard all this before, Sarah, but when I knew him at Yale, Pietro had decided to make money in business in America to restore his patrimony. He retained control over his American business interests and went back to claim his land as a count. Imagine that! Like a fairy tale come true, he met Matilda of Lucca, fell madly in love, and they married. She was very rich, which meant he could restore his estates without limitation, but when I was here for the wedding it was still nothing more than a wreck. Still, they strung the walls with flowers and served fabulous food in tents. It was like something out of a dream. I can't wait to see it again now that it's been restored," he said as the driver went through the gate into the castle grounds.

The sun cast lines across the cypress-lined drive up to the top of a tall round hill. They glimpsed the castle briefly each time they drove around curves edged by stonewalls. Eventually they reached a long, straight drive flanked dramatically by ten-foot high stone walls and then continued through a high, arched tunnel connected to a tall square tower. Finally, they came to a spacious parking area in the back area of a large three-story stone building. When they got out of the car, Sarah looked back to examine the tall square stone tower they had passed. It appeared to be a very old defensive structure.

William took her hand. "That's the oldest part of the castle, built in the tenth century to harbor soldiers that protected the family during the dangerous time when Italy was coming out of the Dark Ages. The rest of the castle was built during the fourteenth through sixteenth centuries, but come, you'll see," he said as he lifted her bag out of the car and gave it to the driver.

Pietro and Matilda appeared near a back coach gate set in a round arch to greet them warmly. Their hosts led them through a cobblestone courtyard to a back entry and then through a narrow hallway with creaking floorboards. After climbing narrow stone stairways, they emerged through an arched entry into the great hall, the castle's front entrance. The ceiling rose twenty feet, braced at the top by huge dark beams.

"This is the Renaissance section of the castle," Matilda said, taking Sarah's arm. A wide stone staircase rose out of the great hall. Arched and cavernous hallways on the sides of the staircase led out into the two first-floor wings of the castle. The stone floors in the great hall were worn smooth and partially covered by a large oriental rug. The last vestiges of late afternoon Tuscan sunlight flooded in through windows set high in the thick walls.

"It's lovely," Sarah breathed.

Matilda smiled. "This is my favorite time of the day in the great hall. Come with me to your room." She escorted her up the grand stone stairs to a large upper hallway and through a set of rounded double doors into a bedroom. "This was a very special one for the daughters in the family way back in the sixteenth century."

Sarah was speechless with excitement over the castle and her room. The canopied bed was draped with fabric covered in jewel-toned embroidered small wildflowers. Old iron lamps with amber shades rested on small ancient side tables. A tall narrow dresser painted with country scenes bordered by leaves and grapes rested on a soft, thick, beige wool rug. Faded wallpaper portrayed early Roman mythic scenes of gods and heroes dancing by fountains in the forest.

"There, dear, now you have a few hours to just relax, or you are welcome to come down and join us in the library in about an hour for sherry. But do feel free to do whatever you want, and that includes exploring the castle. We love it when people come to just enjoy this marvelous ancient home. Really, it's a museum." Matilda smiled, slipped out the door, and closed it.

Sarah felt like she'd landed in heaven. Golden light still streamed into the west side of the room, which looked out over the front entrance into the great hall. Leaded recessed windows were set in two small round corner towers, so the first thing she did was go into one of the narrow towers to survey the rolling Tuscan countryside surrounding the tall castle. The last dimming view of late spring greening fields divided by winding stonewalls and edged by small patches of forest was otherworldly.

The driver brought in her luggage. She thanked him and after he closed the door, she put her things away in a small armoire after selecting a sapphire-blue dress and silver shoes for dinner. She placed a book on the side table, then peeked out of the wide double doors to look left down a long hallway. No one was about, so she slipped out, taking note of her father's satchel at the door of a nearby room. Matilda had said it was okay to explore and Sarah was not about to miss that opportunity. About twenty feet beyond that, she noticed a mysterious-looking ancient pine planked door. *I wonder if that odd door leads to the square tower?*

Creeping quietly down the hall, she stood by the door to listen. No sounds. She grasped the heavy iron key in the ancient iron faceplate, and it turned easily. It engaged and clicked as she turned the doorknob and pushed. The heavy well-fitted door opened noiselessly into a dark room, yet some light from the hallway penetrated the gloom as her eyes adjusted. *Oh my god, the family chapel! It is ancient and right down the hall from my room!* Slipping into the room, she nearly bumped into a thick metal stand holding a large white candle. Matches were placed conveniently on the thick rim, so she struck a match. As the candlewick flared, instantly the space was illuminated. She moved back to shut the door, and then continued to explore the room.

Twenty feet into the gloom there was a simple but substantial wooden altar set with a white cloth bordered by light blue flowers. The side walls were dark and hung with gloomy Stations of the Cross paintings. The rickety chairs under the Stations seemed long forgotten. Behind the altar, a dark and brooding painting of Christ on the cross was dimly visible when she lit two more candles on the altar. She almost bumped into an old wooden kneeler for four or five people. The room was musty with traces of incense, old wood, and dank spider webs. *It looks hardly used. Once I've had dinner, I will be back in here to pray. Oh, how will I ever get through a long formal dinner?* She knelt on the kneeler and opened her heart. *Later I will be back to ask for guidance; here I will ask for a sign.* She crossed herself reverently and rose up to extinguish the altar candles. She blew out the thick beeswax candle and returned to the door. After she pulled the heavy door shut, she walked silently down the long hall to her room to dress for dinner.

I hope my father was right about such formality, she mused, unzipping her dress. Luckily she had all the right clothes. Her mother, murmuring something about how Romans would never accept the terrible way college students in America dressed, had given her a liberal clothing allowance for the famous Roman shops. Her light gray silk patterned stockings felt delicious as she slipped into them and then stepped into a classic wrap dress before adding elegant silver heels. Turning around in front of a gilded triptych mirror, she thought the length of her dress just above her knees looked demure yet sexy. She finished by fastening the clasp of a gold chain holding a large and very old diamond pendant. *I wonder if there will be any other guests? It is nice to have dinner in a home where I can wear these heirlooms.*

A maid led her to the library, a large room lined on all sides with bookcases. The group was already seated in front of the fireplace on comfortable chairs arranged around a dark oak coffee table. Her attention was drawn to the grand carved stone fireplace with one great log resting on iron rails. It was truly baronial. By the side of the fireplace stood a tall, dark, and elegant man wearing a dark green velvet dinner jacket. As she walked into the room, he made no attempt to hide his frank appraisal of her; his eyes burned into her body. Cradling a deep-cut crystal tumbler with two inches of dark amber scotch in his left hand, he stepped forward and reached for her proffered hand as Pietro performed introductions.

"Sarah, this is my son Armando, who just happens to be with us this weekend. We are so lucky to have him, and I hope you will enjoy spending some time with him."

Armando took her hand and grasped it a bit longer than might be expected, brazenly enjoying the charming pink flush on her exquisite face. Her eyes sparkled in the subtle light of the great crystal chandelier hanging down from the high ceiling. Light also flashed inside the deep-cut diamond pendant resting between her breasts. She met his eyes only momentarily as she politely acknowledged him, but Armando was already captivated. *I'll have to hand it to my dear old father. He isn't missing a beat on this one. She may be the most beautiful woman I've laid eyes on. And she looks contented, enthusiastic, and even sincere. I'm sick of the boring, bratty European women I always date.* As the oldest son of a wealthy count, Armando, who was forty, had had his share of women. His parents had persuaded him to come up to Tuscany for the weekend just to meet this young lady, and now he congratulated himself for agreeing. She could be a model, yet supposedly she is a scholar, a serious one, so this could be interesting. *She's exactly the right age too—old enough to be experienced yet still fresh . . .*

Sarah reclaimed her hand and sat down on a nearby golden velvet chair with a high puffy seat. When she crossed her legs and pointed one toe down to the floor, her dress hiked slightly up her thighs. Feeling exposed, she fluttered her hands into her lap.

Pietro and Matilda shared some of their favorite stories about the restoration of the castle. It had proceeded well because the local men were grateful for the jobs and were honored to revive an esteemed old estate. All the work had been mostly finished before Armando was even born, and then Armando and his older and younger sisters grew up at the castle until they were sent away for school in Rome when they were ten or eleven. Since Matilda was from nearby Lucca, it had been natural for her to raise her children in Tuscany.

"As children we used to hide here in the library in hidden

passages in the backs of some of the bookcases," Armando inter-jected in precise English with a heavy Italian accent. "One of them leads down to a lower floor where there is a small secret room where they hid precious books from the Jesuits."

They bantered on for a while and then went to the dining room, where Armando seated Sarah next to his place. Conversation resumed once everyone was seated around the large and very heavy round table and wine was poured. Pietro sat next to his schoolmate with Matilda on the other side. Armando was between his mother and Sarah. When he turned his body toward her to address her, Sarah was assaulted by a great divide between her inner thoughts and her outer manners. While she responded to him calmly and politely, her mind was racing as hot nervous energy coursed through her whole body. *It's the castle, not Armando, that is causing all this energy,* she told herself.

Armando noted her rising nervous excitement while she chatted with him. *This will be a very easy one. Oh god, I hope she doesn't fall all over me.*

Sarah gestured to the lovely room in which they were dining. "Armando, I can't imagine what it must be like to be the son of an ancient and titled family, a family that goes back a thousand years."

Armando's attention was caught by her long, graceful arm, set off by a simple gold bracelet set with small but perfect rubies.

"Well," he responded in a slightly nasal voice. "My mother taught us we are lucky to have position in Italy, a real place in society. But, she also believed we must work and find something that matters to us. So I became a painter, and since I have an eye for beauty, she encouraged me. I paint Tuscan landscapes. My work sells, which actually is very important to me. I wouldn't be happy just living on an income, which of course does allow me to paint. I have a studio here in the medieval tower, and I'd love to show you some of my work tomorrow morning as well as the old tower. Would you like that?"

Sarah found it difficult to concentrate on his words as she scanned the stunning dining room. The dark cherry paneled walls were delicately painted with tiny cornflowers climbing wild geometrical trellises, giving an effect like that of Renaissance embroidery. Candles gleamed subtly from enameled art nouveau fixtures with lily tendrils. The timeless floor was laid with herringboned terra cotta tile. The ruby stained glass windows above the panels glowed with light from the kitchen, giving the room a medieval touch.

Matilda saw her looking around. "Oh, Sarah, I see you are interested in the dining room's décor? This was the original dining room, but it was a ruin, so I used William Morris designs and other art nouveau favorites that were inspired by medieval themes. Do you approve?"

"Oh yes," Sarah responded, trying to process both Armando's invitation to his studio and Matilda's comments about the décor. "I am so captivated by the beauty in this room that I'm barely hearing what your son is saying to me. Please forgive me, Armando."

She was breathing heavily, feeling more out of control than she liked to be. She was so elated by the beauty of the room that Pietro's strong vintage wine immediately went to her head. She didn't even notice Armando's upper thigh pressing gently against her leg.

I want to stroke her thigh, Armando thought. *She is so gorgeous that I am aching. Women like her are God's gift to men.* He glanced at his mother, knowing she could see that he was extremely attracted to this American beauty. Frankly, feeling attracted to a woman picked out by his mother was the last thing he had thought would happen tonight. When he was younger, Matilda had tried to get him interested in various women she approved of, but he'd never had more than a passing interest in any of them. Finally she had just given up, realizing her son was a lazy connoisseur of easy women in the art world, women who liked his money and his style. Used to getting any woman he wanted, Armando found himself surprised to be so taken by this American woman's beauty.

William was keeping an eye on his daughter. Before Matilda or Sarah had come into the library, Armando, Pietro, and William had shared a drink. William had decided Armando was a smooth Italian roué, and a lazy one to boot. After all, all he did was paint. For his part, Armando dismissed William as a boring American Irishman, an unsophisticated, fat, and pushy man. Even though William was a friend of his father's, Armando treated him like a boor. William had always felt intimidated by Europeans, so Armando's rudeness made William extremely uncomfortable. When Matilda had joined the men, proper manners had prevailed and rough edges softened as she expertly steered the conversation between restoring the castle and the older men's days at Yale. Regardless, the first impression between William and Armando had been a strong mutual dislike. William was less than pleased to see the sophisticated older man lean into his innocent daughter at the dinner table. *Matilda might harbor some hopes for her only son with Sarah, but he's thoroughly distasteful.* He wasn't happy to hear her agree to visit Armando's studio the next day, but he trusted her.

As charming as he had been, Armando was the last thing on Sarah's mind as she changed into casual pants after dinner and crept down the hall to the chapel. She lit the candles and knelt down to pray, crossing herself when the painting of the crucifixion emerged in flickering candlelight. *Generations have been married, received Communion, and been baptized here. This is where they came to solve their problems. This is the perfect place to ask: am I losing my faith?*

Closing her eyes to shut out the sickly greenish-white alabaster Jesus hanging on the cross with a bloodied dripping crown of thorns, she wondered, *Do I believe he died this way, or was scripture rewritten to support the Church's agenda too? The fairy tales are dissolving, and I can't lie to myself anymore. Regardless of who the historical Jesus was, I still feel Christ deep in my heart.*

The brightly burning candles flickered in the fresh air moving through the old walls, having a hypnotic effect on Sarah even through her closed eyes. Her logical mind lost its grip in the blinking light, and her inner skull expanded. She almost jumped when a deep, authoritative, yet incredibly loving voice sounded in the center of her head: *Sarah Adamson, follow your heart. I live deep in your soul, within your mind, and I will always be there with you. Tell my story! I came two thousand years ago to open the light in the heart of each person on Earth and many still know me. Now brother turns against brother, sister against sister, all in the name of powerful and cruel men who use my name. Evil lurking in their corroded hearts poisons them. Tell my story! You've chosen the right course and nothing will stop you.*

Inner fire rising in her body illuminated the small chapel when the glow from another dimension penetrated her cells. Hot energy rising in her spine warmed her skin and thickened her inner sacrum. She had never felt anything like this before. Tiny pulsations ached in her base of her spine as waves moved slowly up through her sacrum and into her spine. Fire feathered up her back and golden light encircled her head. *Is that you, Lord? Are you taking me?* Her spine was a rod of fire. She felt energy moving exquisitely from the back of her head down into her lower body and then back up again. The energy popped into her skull as otherworldly bliss flooded her mind. Enjoying the waving warmth, she struggled to open her eyelids, sensing she must orient herself. The inner fire calmed when she opened her eyes. Looking up at Christ on the cross, the most sacrilegious thought of her whole life came into her mind: *I will get Him off of it. I will tell His story so that He can be freed from that obscene rack of hatred and abuse.*

8

The Golden World

The Pierleonis and their houseguests enjoyed Sunday morning breakfast in the castle kitchen. The harvest table was piled with fresh fruit, homemade biscuits, and raspberry jam from last summer's pick. The cook served made-to-order skillet omelets. Rich, freshly ground coffee satiated Armando and Sarah before they walked out of the kitchen to head for the ancient tower. Golden rays of light illuminated the Tuscan landscape; everything sparkled. Exuberant farmers came up the back road singing while bringing loads of fruits and vegetables to the pantry. Four strong young men laughed after singing a particularly robust chorus as they balanced a taut burlap square piled high with a perfect pyramid of bright red tomatoes. They nodded discreetly to Armando while slyly assessing Sarah. A girl followed behind them with a large bundle of dark green spinach on her back. It must really be something to run this place, Sarah thought as Armando heaved open the old planked door into the south side of the square tower. She wondered if his studio was on the first floor or if, as she was hoping, they would go up to the tower.

"This will be quite a climb; however, you have the right shoes," he said, noting her ankle-high leather boots, tight jeans, and loosely woven white cotton sweater, which fell over her shoulders like a shawl. As they entered the cavernous space, rays of light filtering down from the top flashed on the reflective surfaces of dust particles and penetrated the deep gloom. Armando indicated the way to the stairs by stepping up onto a stone platform, a secure foundation for the open wooden stairs firmly attached to the ancient walls. They rose reversing back and forth, platform by platform, up to the top. Climbing the narrow steps with Armando behind her, above Sarah could see a flat wood ceiling, the floor of his studio. When they'd climbed around eighty steps, thirty feet in the tower, they came to a landing with a slit open to the outside. She stopped to peer out over the red-tiled roofs and gables of the castle to the rolling Tuscan landscape around the tower. Armando stood close behind her on the narrow landing.

"Is this staircase original?" she asked.

"The stone platform is original, and we rebuilt the wooden stairs. There once was a rotting wood floor between this landing and the lower area. You can see where the beams were in the square indentations in the walls by the landing below."

"And what was the tower used for in the beginning?" Sarah asked, turning to look out the slit once more.

"A thousand years ago, the family lived on the two upper floors, one of which is now my studio but with a new floor. The lower level was very tall and garrisoned soldiers during the tenth century." He pointed toward the castle. "When life became safer in the fourteenth century, the early stages of the castle were built, such as the area of our kitchens and servants quarters. The section you are staying in as well as the dining room were built during the Renaissance, a vital period in this region. Even then this tower was occasionally used to garrison soldiers and store supplies. Excepting San Gimignano, this is one of the few remaining early medieval towers in Tuscany, so we restored it. As for me, I like to work in a space infused with the layers of time because it helps me imagine many realities. Come, we're almost to my studio."

They climbed up a dozen more steps to the last landing where he pushed open an old creaking door. They stepped into a bright 30-by-30-foot-square room filled with racks for canvases. Subtle north light from a wide panel of windows in a high dormer streamed down onto a large easel. A few dozen canvases were strewn about, leaning against posts, against a garish red divan, or suspended on hooks. Sarah walked straight to the canvases and began studying them. She had taken several art theory classes, since art was used to express religious devotion for hundreds of years, and had, in the medieval period, been used to convey esoteric ideas through hidden symbols.

Armando watched her move excitedly from one painting to the next, pleased at how captivated she seemed to be by his work. Sarah's sense of time and place faded while she soaked everything in. Finally she told him, "I am so struck by your realism, your perfect depiction of your subject matter as color and form, yet what intrigues me is there is something else going on in them, and . . ." She felt him standing very closely behind her right shoulder and detected his aroma, pungent, moist oak leaves warmed by strong fall sunlight. As he moved tantalizingly closer to her body, she smelled lavender in his cologne. Until this moment, she hadn't really noticed him very much. *I felt him watching me last night as I walked into the library, so I shut him out.* Like most truly beautiful women, she was used to people watching her, and she generally ignored the attention because it took away her sense of self. *Armando is different from anyone I've ever encountered; he's like an exotic cat.*

"Yes, you were saying—and . . .?" he said in a soft and very silky voice as he moved his body closer to hers. His chest was inches behind her back. She spun gracefully to face him while simultaneously taking a few steps back. Startled by the vibrant intensity in his dark eyes, she tensed her lips, hoping words would distract him.

"Yes, I meant to say I see another world in these paintings. I wonder what it is and how this could be, since on the surface they are totally realistic. Take this one," she said, adroitly moving farther away and gesturing to a canvas depicting a rustic Tuscan villa surrounded by sturdy, crude walls with fields receding deep into the background. "The view is of this lovely villa, yet I also see odd touches of color, like over here on this windowsill, a dash of deep red. Or, there on the side of the doorway, a touch of sienna plus these touches of deep blue dotting the stonewalls in front of the house. Something else is happening that is not an element of the realism. These touches suggest there is another world in this painting."

Armando was charmed by her earnestness and intelligence as she struggled to express what she saw. He sashayed closer to her. "What do you think this other world might be?"

Sarah searched his face. "I want you to tell me what you see when you're painting." *I think what he's doing is related to a whole lot of things I want to know.*

As her desire to know took over her mind, he was even more drawn to her and then something shifted deep within him: a potent and lusty shining dragon merged into his lithe body while she stood there breathlessly waiting for his reply. Instead of answering, he grabbed her shoulders and kissed her fully and passionately on her lovely mouth while pressing her gorgeous large breasts to his chest. He moved his arms around her back and forcefully pulled her pelvis close.

Instinctually she rammed the palms of her hands into his shoulders and shoved him backward. "Armando! Stop!"

He almost fell over, but recovering his footing and expelling air from his lungs, he slurred, "I'm sorry, I am truly sorry. I have never done anything like this in my studio. I apologize; I am terribly embarrassed. I just lost control of myself because you are so beautiful and see so much in my work. Most people think those extra touches are like the extra colors in a Cézanne. In fact, my work has been compared to his. I really don't know what Cézanne intended, but I know what I intend with my work. I will try to tell you what I'm really doing here if you will just say you forgive me. Please forgive me so I can forgive myself. You carried me away with your delightful enthusiasm! I am excited because you see what I create. This means you think what I do is meaningful!"

Sarah was shaking. She hadn't been kissed like that since just after college when she dumped her last serious boyfriend who had annoyed her with knee-jerk seductions. Since then she had buried herself in the world of ideas, deliberately forsaking the physical. *This is a new level. That kiss nearly overwhelmed me, and I almost didn't stop him. I pushed him away only because he startled me.* She retreated to the place where she was always safe—words—and said, "Yes, I forgive you if you will tell me what you see, tell me what you really intend with your art."

Armando was relieved. He rushed around the studio grabbing canvases and placing them in a row. He put a photograph on a stand and muttered that he always worked from one. As he explained the steps he went through, it became apparent the other world she detected was actually a *first* painting. Then he layered over it with the realistic landscape in the photo by tying the first painting to the landscape with geometrical color nodes. Sarah questioned him until she really understood his technique. His approach was utterly fascinating. *But what is this other world?*

While they were carrying on this serious discussion, a fast and furious train of thoughts assaulted Armando. He struggled to control himself as his breathing intensified, and he realized that her excited mind was incredibly arousing. Here he was, forty years old, and trying to stop an erection! *What is it about her? Yeah, she's beautiful, but when she talks about ideas, she's amazingly sensual. Does she have any idea how seductive she is?* Breathing hard, he searched for words to answer her.

Sarah thought the struggle to describe his work was what was causing his chest to heave and his eyes to bulge slightly. As he went on more about his technique, she began to feel hot energy in her solar plexus. The fine, sensual, and aristocratic curve of his lips captivated her.

Responding to her shy eyes on his mouth, he desperately extended his right arm with the elbow facing out down over the front of his loose slacks. *I never thought I'd be grateful to talk about ideas to calm myself down!*

Armando continued, the words rushing out, "Even though I work from a photo in my studio, I begin by going back to that same view again when the light is right. I sit and contemplate it for hours and maybe take more photos. As the light comes and goes, I become it as I integrate the various elements—the curve of a wall, a space that suggests emptiness, colors that draw me deep into the Earth. Then finally the moment comes that I've never tried to describe to anyone before now. Warmth comes in as energy suffuses me, and I feel crackles in my brain. They produce flashes of light in my inner eye that thicken my body. Viewing the landscape while perceiving this way, I find the elements in the landscape that bridge our world to the other world, the place the Jungians call the golden world. Once I see it, I can paint it.

"The first painting is sometimes just a cluster of stars, such as the Pleiades or Orion, with connecting lines. Sometimes it is a series of nodal points that require strong colors to express their emergence and intersections, like a 3D hologram on a flat canvas. Then back in my studio, I anchor in the realistic landscape of the photo. That second painting goes very fast, maybe just a few hours, and it is easy and enjoyable, even relaxing. I'm not satisfied until the landscape comes through, so I get it done as soon as possible after I've gotten the first image. This has made me very prolific. People always buy my paintings because they take people to another place in the landscapes they've already learned to love."

While he was speaking, Sarah was discreetly studying his strong, masculine jaw accentuated by prominent, well-formed cheekbones. His intelligent and slightly arched brows drew attention to his dark eyes; his expressive mouth made her feel warm. *This good-looking man just kissed me!* She returned to examining his paintings, and as he explained she realized she could see even more of the golden world by detecting a magical imprint of the primary light pattern in her own retina.

Sarah said tentatively, "I've always wondered about the golden world. I understand what the Jungians mean when they talk about it, but I never thought someone could depict it in realistic art. Your work makes me wonder if some medieval painters, such as Sandro Botticelli, Allesandro Lippi, or Fra Angelico, also captured that world. I am truly impressed!"

"Lucky for me, so are my parents as well as a few collectors. It is strange you mention Fra Angelico. Our family has retained a story about him. The rumor always was he fathered a child with one of our ancestral daughters. She was sent to a convent, and our family raised the boy. His name was Armando, my namesake! My full name is Armando Angelico Pierleoni. I've often wondered if I'm actually related to Fra Angelico even though the story is from six hundred years ago. I suppose I will always be happy painting as he was."

He stopped, his face growing somber. "But what happened today makes me very unhappy. I lost control simply because I am a man. I feel terrible. Will you promise me you forgive me? Can you show your forgiveness by accepting a dinner date with me when we are both back in Rome soon?"

Sarah was intensely stirred up. Today felt like a turning point in her life, a doorway was opening, an unknown portal. She felt a strong attraction to Armando, the most sensual and potent man she'd ever met, so she agreed to see him in Rome.

Before dinner Sarah crept back into the Pierleoni chapel. This time when she knelt at the altar, she fell into deep thought but not about Jesus. She was thinking about the two intriguing men who'd suddenly appeared as if out of nowhere. *What on earth is going on? After avoiding men for a few years, suddenly I'm spending time with two older, very sensual men. And that kiss . . . even though I shoved him quickly and hard, his mouth locked onto mine. I can still feel him and taste him; he could have taken me. He reached into me and grabbed me. I am going to have to be very careful because nothing will stop him.*

While Sarah was in the chapel, Matilda entered the library on her way to the dining room to check the table and chairs before dinner. She was startled to see Armando reading in a chair. "Armando! How nice to see you here. I know this is your favorite room, but lately you always seem to be in your studio. How are you, dear? How are you *really*?" She knew that he often came to the library when he wanted to talk to her.

"Well, Mother, I suppose I do feel like saying something. I am so taken by Sarah! I don't think I have ever had such a strong response to a woman. You've surprised me with this one. She is beautiful, intelligent, and cultured, yet not in an artsy and superficial way like most of the women I know. She is spiritual like me, something I didn't think I would ever find in a woman. We've agreed to see each other in Rome, which I hope will make you happy?"

Matilda smiled. This was just what she had hoped would happen. "Of course it makes me happy, Armando," she responded. "She is a lovely woman from a very good family, and Pietro and I hope you will find someone to love. Your father and I have always been so happy together, so it is hard to imagine you not finding your love. Have you been paying any attention to what your father is doing tonight? We are serving the boar he hunted on the day before everybody came. He's been roasting it all afternoon, ever since he got back from Siena. He is offering us a Tuscan feast! He called in vegetables, fruits, and desserts from nearby farmers to create a true celebration of spring. Perhaps it will be a celebration of the day you found your lady love!"

At 7 p.m. the sun moved down in the western sky, warming the front of the castle. Sarah enjoyed the view from the large courtyard by the front entrance.

Pietro also stepped out to see the sunset and immediately walked over to her.

"Oh, Sarah, I wonder if you have any idea what's going on tonight? Your father was with me today in Siena touring the square where the Palio goes on in the summer as well as seeing the Gregory VII murals in the Cathedral library. Thus he may not have told you? We invited some of our neighbors to come for a feast tonight to meet you and your father, just a few."

"How delightful, Pietro! And who are your neighbors?"

"Ah, it is lucky I walked out right now or you'd never understand where they come from. Look out to the distance on the right and then scan to the left, but don't look too much at the sun. Do you see the little rolling hills out there with stone buildings and towers on the top? Do you see the rows of cedar and old walls winding up the hills to the castles and villas, just as our driveway rises here?

"Yes, I have been looking out at this view as much as possible since I arrived. I've wondered if they are small villages and if I could go see them."

"Those buildings are the castles and villas of my neighbors, and some of them will come tonight. These are the real old Tuscan families like mine, and you will love meeting them. Dress as you did last night, and you will be perfect. They can't wait to meet you and your father. Of course, they never miss my roast boar served with our private reserve wine."

At 8 p.m. the guests started arriving. Each minute or so another car came up the hill, and the drivers unloaded the guests in front of the castle where Pietro and Sarah had been standing. Then the drivers parked behind and went into the kitchen for supper. As the guests came in, Sarah and William stood with Pietro, Matilda, and Armando inside the great hall to greet them. Sarah found the ladies, in their long dresses and heirloom jewels, to be like relics emerging from the past. *I never imagined I would witness a scene like this— ancient nobility arriving.*

The guests were very curious about Sarah, addressing her in slow lilting Italian that she barely understood. They were charmed by her attempts to speak their language and her natural beauty. Once all the guests had arrived and were formally introduced, off they went to the library for cocktails wondering whether Armando was involved with her. They'd guarded their daughters against him years ago because of his reputation as a notorious rake. Maybe, they mused, he was past that now that he was forty. Their daughters were all safely married now, and they wondered if he was finally going to settle down.

Eventually the dinner bell rang and they flowed into the dining room in a pack, the guests moving through the house with the familiarity bred of long acquaintance. The large room was filled with a long table covered in a white tablecloth. One end was partially covered with the feast and the other was set for guests. On guard was the cook, slicing into a twenty-pound roasted boar. As Armando slyly observed, Sarah winced when she saw the grinning face of the boar with a crimson apple crammed in its mouth and a red bow tie around its neck. The space in front of the wild pig was piled with platters of vegetables, potatoes, salads, and sauces. Everyone lined up with their plates to enjoy the feast, and then some sat down at the other end of the long table and others went to round tables in the entry hall.

William was enjoying the celebration immensely. When Armando took an empty seat next to him, he decided to give him another chance. They toasted each other with red wine.

Armando said, "I must say, William, your daughter certainly knows art. She came up to my studio this morning, and we talked about my work for hours. There are few people who have been able to analyze the deeper levels of my paintings; most just see the surface realism. It was a joy to share with her. Her intelligence is impressive, just delightful."

Despite his reconciliatory feelings, William found the sound of Armando's voice grating. *There is something slimy about this guy, something disturbing about him. He covers it up with his perfect manners and elegant clothes. This guy is a snake.*

"Her intelligence and her seriousness have been a challenge and a source of great enjoyment to her mother and me," William replied. "Things have worked out quite well because she pursues her studies diligently. We miss her, being so far away in Rome, but she'll be right back as soon as she finishes this phase of her research."

"Ah, well, she and I never got around to talking about her work, come to think of it."

William tuned in more deeply to Armando's voice. As Armando continued, "She has agreed to have dinner with me in Rome, and I hope you won't mind if I see her. I'm so happy I came out this weekend. Otherwise, I might never have met her," William heard instead a disembodied voice whining in a barely audible high pitch, *"I want your daughter, and when I want something, I get it."*

William looked over his left shoulder at Armando, pulling his lips tight and showing his teeth. "She's studying patristics, the early Church Fathers, and the sources in Rome are excellent. She is working on her Ph.D., and she will have to write a very challenging thesis. I do not think she is in Rome to date." He grinned at Armando like a mean Cheshire cat while sticking his left elbow on the table by Armando's arm and shoving it, seemingly inadvertently. Then he raised his glass with his other hand to indicate he wanted more wine.

Armando turned away from the fat flushed elbow and sank his sharp knife into the pink, buttery boar flesh. He cut a piece and skewered it on his fork, raising it slowly to his lips. William's elbow came off the table again when he cut into the tender boar flesh.

When the time to exchange places for dessert came, both were relieved to part.

Armando made the chatting rounds with each of the guests. Then he stole Sarah away from a few of the ladies and led her to a small table with two chairs back in the library. They shared a few more thoughts while sitting together in the low, flickering firelight amid books and family genealogies. He didn't ask her about her studies, since he'd never heard of patristics.

For Sarah, the evening was perfect. The profound quiet in the library calmed her soul, and the glowing fire soothed her mind. *I can still feel his kiss. I feel like a princess in this ancient home with Armando.*

9

Ossuaries and Etruscan Tombs

As they drove out through the stone archway by the tower and descended the winding road the next morning, William and Sarah left the magical world behind. Sarah nestled down in her seat, hoping to tune back into the golden world. No such luck: William was ready to speak.

He fixed his gaze on his lovely daughter. "Well, Sarah, tell me exactly what you think about Armando, who seems to be very taken with you. Pietro and Matilda certainly set him up for his big chance, don't you think?" *Sometimes I wonder just how sophisticated she is. Does she know what goes on? Is she attracted to glamour? To aristocrats?*

"He's a fine painter," she said, ignoring his implications. "He paints these landscapes that at first look realistic until you look closer and see that there's another world hidden in them. First you sense it, next it grabs you emotionally, and then the landscapes take on an otherworldly cast. I found myself getting lost in his work, and apparently he is very successful." *I wonder if Daddy noticed that I'm attracted to Armando?*

"Yes, well, Pietro and Matilda are very proud of him and they should be. But, isn't it odd that he's not married yet at age forty? To tell you the truth, I think he's a playboy, an Italian aristocrat who chases beautiful women like you!" *There, I said it. If she does like him, will this get her to wake up? Or will I alienate her and push her toward him?*

"Hmmm, interesting. I can't say I was really checking him out in that way. He is very handsome, beautifully mannered, and his landscapes are in his blood. Whether he is a playboy or not isn't my concern. I'm too busy with my studies. He asked me to join him for dinner in Rome and I accepted. It might be fun! After all, he is the son of your dear old friend." *Did her father sense her misgivings?*

"Sweetheart, since I won't be seeing you for quite a while, may I offer you some fatherly advice? Don't say yes unless you are sure. You may be quite surprised by what I have to say." *I hope she goes for it; this guy is dangerous.*

Sarah paused. The way it worked in the Adamson family was if you agreed to listen to advice, then you were honor-bound to consider following it. That had been just fine until she was seven years old. After that, she had avoided his control by not asking for his opinions. Now at twenty-five she still was reluctant to ask his advice, but she felt she needed it now.

They were passing through a lovely small village. Its location right by the road meant it was ancient. They were returning to Rome via the narrow old Roman high road that went through Etruscan cemeteries and ancient villages. *I've always wanted to see an Etruscan necropolis . . .*

"Daddy, we will be passing by Cerveteri. Can we stop there for a little while?"

William tapped on the glass and the driver opened the window for new instructions. This was a fair trade, so Sarah replied, "Sure, Daddy, why not offer me your advice. It has always helped me so far."

William sank his solid body down into the plush leather seat, squared his shoulders, and went for it. "In my grandmother's day, when ladies were ladies and men were real men, you'd have a chaperone. When I was growing up, all that ended, and let me tell you, we guys thought that was great. Now that I'm older and have two beautiful daughters, I wish both you and your sister Susan had chaperones. Before you giggle and ignore me, Sarah, I have something very important to say about the loose times we live in." He paused.

"You've admitted to me lately that you wonder whether some kind of evil force has been unleashed in the world. Well, I have my own ideas about that. Evil has always been in the world, but it affects less those who guard against it. That was the purpose of chaperones for hundreds, maybe thousands of years. Lusty men always prey on beautiful and innocent young women. It's in the Bible, for God's sake, like the story of the gods who came down, took the women, and created the giants! I hope you will not go out with Armando or Simon alone. Since I know you probably will, I have one little request: as your father, I ask you to never go to their home or apartment alone, never! Hey, I'm a guy and I know what I'm talking about. That's asking the demons to come out."

Automatically Sarah responded, "But, Daddy, you already know I would never do that. I wouldn't consider going to a man's place, ever." As soon as she said the words, the old rule recorded by her cells sank down into her brain, yet at the same time she realized she felt ambivalent about obeying him. *My father's rules have always protected me, but now I'm older. Following his dictums narrows me too much. It's time to widen my experiences, time to explore myself. This doesn't feel exactly right to me.* Despite her reluctance, she couldn't resist him. He had accessed her reptilian brain, the mind-controlled robotic part of her—*It is Easter and I have to wear white gloves and a hat to Mass, to Mass!* She felt diminished, riding along for a few more hours while William snoozed. As much as she loved him, she realized she was happy he was going back to Boston.

He woke as the driver pulled into the parking lot at Cerveteri.

Sarah was looking eagerly out the window. *Nobody is around. How lucky!*

They found a local guide and stepped down into a round underground tomb, a perfect miniature house for the dead. It was cool and shaded, and the walls were decorated with graceful paintings of nymphs, satyrs, sphinxes, and mythological chimeras. The ancient and pristine tomb made her forget all about her father's remarks about men preying on women. Then she spotted a strange relief on the wall that made her feel dizzy. *What was that flash, that image?* Her eyes fixed on a drawing above the stairs—a young dancing boy bent over the back end of a large red bull. A muscular older man with a huge black phallus was penetrating the boy from behind. The whites of the man's eyes leered through the centuries while he broke the dancer in two. *Synchronicity, synchronicity, the only way I ever figure anything out. Why do I see this here now?* The other reliefs waved and stretched into a blur while the guide droned on. That night, she dreamed of an old priest rushing down a hallway after slamming a door to silence the moans of a boy in pain.

Finally William was gone, and Sarah had a delightful day. That evening, as cool air penetrated the garden, the trickling water from the fountain soothed her senses. Being alone was such a relief that it almost worried her. *Do I spend too much time by myself?* As she finished a bowl of pasta and a salad, the phone rang and she hoped it was Simon.

"I miss you!" he said sweetly into the phone, and she told him she missed him too. *Funny, whenever I hear from him or see him, I feel very special.* She happily agreed to meet him at La Fontana for wine and dessert. "I can't wait to hear what you've been doing while I was away!" she told him. "It's still light, so I can walk there. See you in twenty minutes."

She rushed out the door; within a few blocks she was disgusted when an older Italian man pinched her ass. She waited at a small table for Simon because she wanted to observe him walking into the room. As he came toward her, she felt balanced and peaceful. *He is so damned good-looking. He's different from Armando, who is a determined man always seeking a target. Simon is contained within; he's not always aiming at some object.*

Simon quickened his pace as he spotted her. "It is so great to see you! It seems like weeks since we had dinner with your father at Alfredo's, even though it was only last Wednesday. I really liked him, and I think he liked me despite his concerns about my article."

Simon continued, the words pouring out in his excitement, "A million things are going on in Rome! At the Vatican this weekend there was a flap over Jerusalem ossuaries, the bone boxes. An ossuary with an inscription that reads 'James, son of Joseph, brother of Jesus' came on the antiquities market in 2002. Israeli officials declared it a forgery and went after the man who found it. The case against the finder was finally thrown out of the Israeli courts a few days ago, and a great theological controversy has erupted, which favors opinions expressed in *Biblical Archaeology Review* that this ossuary is the earliest link to Jesus."

"Do you mean the magazine published by the Biblical Archaeology Society?" Sarah asked.

"Yes," Simon replied. "You and I could talk about this ossuary all night—it directly challenges the Catholic fairy tale of Mary's perpetual virginity. If it is authenticated, it exposes more of the lies about the family of Jesus. Piece by piece, the whole story fabricated by the Church sixteen hundred years ago is falling to pieces. I will have to go to Jerusalem for some fact finding."

Hearing Simon talk about these topics that so interested her reminded Sarah why she loved being with him. She hadn't thought about it until now, but she and Armando hadn't discussed her work at all. "I can't wait to read all about this! We had no news at the castle near Siena where I was with my father. I wish you could have been with me to see the villa, a truly authentic Tuscan castle that was built and added on to over a thousand years. It has such a special feeling because it has remained in the same family. My father really had a good time with his old friend. I was free to explore, so I spent some time meditating in an ancient chapel." She was so excited by seeing him that her hand slipped onto his arm. Simon reached for her hand to press it, and Sarah flashed back to the painter's studio and to the guy who'd just pinched her. She ripped her hand away.

Simon looked at her oddly, and she realized she had put her hand on his arm in the first place. She heard his voice. "Sarah, are you all right? You look like you've seen a ghost!"

She recovered herself, but she was flushed and hot. "Oh, I'm sorry. Suddenly I felt funny." She put her hand gently back on his arm and said, "I forgot where I was for a moment because I was so excited to tell you about the castle. Then I found myself holding your arm." *Like a princess in a tower, like a maid with cascading locks down to the ground, I touched a man, but Daddy said not to touch a man . . .*

Simon watched her, his reporter's eye scrutinizing the deeper set of tense muscles altering her face. She was a different person—still beautiful, still Sarah, yet a phantasm had passed through her mind. He blurted out, "Don't you think you're going a little bit too far with this sex-avoidance thing? I mean, I'm not going to do anything to you that you don't want, never would with any woman. So why are you so jumpy?"

Now what can I say? I'm cornered. She muttered in a low voice, "You have a weirdo on your hands. When my father and I were driving back to Rome, he actually told me he wishes I had a chaperone! I was introduced to the Pierleonis' oldest son, Armando, a painter who has a studio in the castle tower. My dad thinks he is a playboy who will go after me. Isn't that just too much?"

Simon had heard of the old and powerful Pierleoni family. He didn't like the image forming in his mind. *A Pierleoni playboy painter in the perfect castle tower and the beautiful woman . . .* As usual, Simon blurted out his thoughts without thinking, "Well, from what I saw of your father, he may be right. Your father is a very smart man, Sarah. Also, you know what? I'm not sure you realize how captivating and alluring you are, and sometimes you are a flirt! A lot of men would lose control just by getting close to you; I easily could myself. But we agreed to be just friends, which I will honor. Would this painter guy agree to just be your friend? I doubt it."

He grinned at her, trying to lighten the mood. "Do you think your father would like us to have a chaperone when we see each other?"

They both laughed at that idea.

Simon brought the conversation back to safer waters. "The collector who was just acquitted, Oded Golan, has been fighting this battle in the courts since 2003. Because of the ongoing legal battles, there's been very little attention paid to what has actually been discovered about Jesus and his family. There have been two major discoveries of Jesus family burials since 1980, and Golan's acquittal calls attention to these findings in spite of the extreme resistance of Israeli archaeologists. Now the lid is finally flying open, excuse the pun."

Sarah nodded. She remembered reading about the ossuary in the news after it was first discovered, since the inscription in Aramaic clearly read *James, son of Joseph, brother of Jesus.* It had been linked to an earlier discovery of ten ossuaries inscribed with the names of various members of the Jesus family in Jerusalem in 1980. One of the boxes, that of James, the brother of Jesus who led the early Church in Jerusalem after the crucifixion, was not found among the nine remaining bone boxes when the inscriptions were tallied. James was very prominent in the early Church, so it had seemed strange that his name was not among those on the ossuaries. Then in 2002 the ossuary turned up mysteriously on the antiquities market.

"Some think Golan's ossuary was the one that was stolen in 1980, right?" asked Sarah.

"Exactly," said Simon. "Scholars who believe in the authenticity of both finds are screaming for worldwide attention, since these finds need protection against Vatican cover-ups and the Israeli authorities. Outrageously, the Church ignores archaeological discoveries that contradict the Christian fairy tale!"

Sarah frowned. She still felt a little twinge of discomfort with Simon's term "fairy tale," yet her own research had challenged the Catholic doctrine stating that Jesus had no brothers or sisters because Mary's conception was immaculate and she had perpetual virginity. The ossuary discoveries were powerful evidence that Jesus had in fact had siblings. "I remember when the James ossuary was sent to Ontario in 2003," she said slowly. "It was damaged during shipment, which was so sad. It was repaired and the inscription was protected, but people just forgot about it. Maybe they didn't want to think about what the discovery might mean for their faith. These findings call direct attention to the fourth century Church cover-ups."

Simon brought his hand down on the table with a thump. "That's just why I'm so excited about this! You and I have met just as these big secrets about Jesus are being uncovered; we are in the middle of a revelation. Sexual degeneration in the Church is calling attention to their ultra-secrecy, which includes the cover-up of the real story of Jesus. I think demonic clerical behavior comes out of a weird Jesus complex. Victims have reported some priests say they are Jesus while seducing them! Maybe sexually repressed priests go over an edge when they seek divine connection. The truth is, celibacy makes them lonely and dries them up. It warps their character and then demons take them over when they seek spiritual contact."

I wonder if enforced celibacy is warping me, Sarah reflected. *The other side of the coin is that if I were sexually active, demons could be unleashed in me. That is what I'm afraid of.*

"So, Simon, isn't there *anybody* in the hierarchy who is curious about these finds? Don't they feel the desire to see and touch an ossuary that might have contained the bones of saints they supposedly adore? After all, you and I saw all the bejeweled reliquaries in the Medici Chapels in Florence that contain the bones of saints and wondered why the Medicis were so obsessed with them."

"This is where it gets weird. I'm obsessed with the cover-up because I think if the news gets out, the Church will collapse," Simon responded. "Have you ever heard of the Tomb of Mary, mother of Jesus?"

Sarah shook her head.

"Almost no Catholics have, yet it's a major sacred site on the Mount of Olives for Eastern Christians, who call her Theotokos, the mother of God. Muslims also revere the site as the tomb of the mother of Issa, their name for Jesus who they believe came to their land to teach. Yet the Vatican takes no interest and Catholics know nothing about it! What's at stake here? Merely the truth! So *why* do Western Christians deny the existence of things that should be of such great interest to them?"

"This is why I'm investigating the Gnostics," Sarah responded passionately. "Until the recent finds, we only knew what the Church Fathers who distorted Gnostic beliefs said about them. Maybe orthodoxy was afraid Jesus was a Gnostic?"

"Okay, Sarah, give me a good synopsis of Gnostic beliefs; I'm all ears."

Sarah's eyes glistened. "Okay, here goes: The Gnostics say that an error occurred that brought in evil when the world was created. When the world was not yet manifest, they say it was filled with hierarchies of spirits and angels. Eventually, the goddess of wisdom—Sophia—wanted to use her power to create a world for new creatures to adore the divine, creatures that would be half animal and half angel. But instead of doing so with a partner, out of impatience she made the mistake of creating the world by herself. When the creation unfolded, her potential partner, Lucifer, fell into matter and became overly physical. His fall created all kinds of imbalances, such as male energy dominating and abusing women, and children being used by adults instead of simply nurtured by them. The new beings—humans—were cut off from divine access, so they got trapped in their egos."

While she spoke, Simon was entranced by the way her nose flared while she was figuring something out, and her right hand rapped the table lightly as if she was winding up her left brain. *This girl knows more than I even realized.*

"As this fundamental imbalance evolved through time, humans and angels forgot the cause of their confusion. They struggled to find their way back to the divine world, and Lucifer struggled to find his way back to divinity. Amid these titanic struggles, they say Fallen Angels were created who wanted to control the world, such as the Jewish god, Yahweh. Modern Gnostics believe the Vatican is Yahweh's throne perpetuating evil in the world. The original Gnostics said Jesus came to correct the error that occurred during the creation by teaching about love, which is why Mary Magdalene would have been his disciple, maybe his wife." She paused.

"That fits right in with some of the things I've been thinking about," Simon responded eagerly. "Organizations need power, so getting people to do what the priest says is the obvious way to run a church. So the Church uses the people, who are pushed and pulled by the struggle between good and evil. Also the Church ended pagan rituals by building churches on their sacred sites, and then they conducted their own rituals to hypnotize the people. Being half human and half divine, people experiment with sex to find the fire in their bodies. Believe me, sex is direct access to the divine. What if priests possessed by the Fallen Angels have been *culling* sexual energy, most particularly the potent and pure energy of little children? Based on evidence in the Hebrew Bible, child sacrifice was rampant in the land that spawned Judaism. Yahweh commanded Abraham to sacrifice his son Isaac to prove his faith. That is insane!

As you said, systemic sexual abuse in the Roman Church is the newest form of child sacrifice."

Sarah was nodding vigorously, her wine and tiramisu completely forgotten. "You're right, Simon. What will it take to get people to see this? *What?* Perversion rots the heart of the Church, and this cover-up of the family of Jesus is part of their game. Who would tolerate the hierarchy once they realize Jesus was a normal man endowed with advanced divine consciousness? People would begin to see the dangers of the hierarchy. Funneling all the power to the top leaves the clerics at the bottom so powerless that it actually encourages them to become abusers so they can have a sense of power. "

"Yeah," said Simon. "And if people did wake up, we could bypass the story of a celibate weirdo with no brothers and sisters who had a mother who didn't conceive him during sex." Simon looked at his watch and said apologetically, "It's getting late, and I have to catch a flight to Jerusalem tomorrow. The *Times* knows this is a hot story, and I have the right background for it and I know more because of you, Sarah, a lot more, so thank you. I may be gone as long as a month. Tune in and picture me as I'm visiting the Tomb of Mary."

The two of them left the café and walked in silence, both feeling somewhat spent from the frenetic nature of their conversation. The night air was soft and warm, and Sarah wished he wasn't going away, especially for so long. They turned into the curved driveway in front of her apartment and then stopped in front of the massive carved door.

"Will you hold me for a moment?" she asked. "Hold me so that I can remember your touch. We may be two different people when you return to Rome."

Happily he pulled her to his body and held her tenderly. *She feels sacred.* Her hair exuded a delicious light scent, juniper. Her soft cheek nestled into his neck, and time stopped for both of them while they stood there together like one body. Finally, reluctantly, he pulled away. "I will not be different when I get back, but maybe you will be," he said. He held her away from himself searching her eyes for a moment, and then walked away trembling. *I belong to her now that I've held her. Someday I will have her, but it is going to be a long journey. I remember my mother telling me how long it was before she gave herself to my father.*

Sarah turned the key thoughtfully and slipped quietly into the silent hallway. Every cell in her body vibrated with his strength and integrity. She thought about how much she would like her mother to meet him as she ascended the curving grand staircase up to her apartment. She knew her mother would respond to Simon's warmth and integrity. *I know he will always be a part of my life. But I feel like I am poised on the edge of an abyss.*

She was.

That night she slept so soundly that she had no memory of her dreams. Her psyche moved right into universal consciousness, an unexplored region of her mind. She found herself in a garden filled with marble carvings of ancient Greek gods and goddesses. They cracked open and oozed dark liquid that swirled around their white forms and transformed into ravens. Raven eyes switched back and forth like signals in her mind of gossamer shrouds made of angel feathers that sometimes come to turn the world white.

10

The Limestone Grotto

The night Simon flew to Jerusalem, a big storm descended on Rome and flooded the ancient streets. Sarah spent the next day in the library and came home to dinner alone. She found herself really missing Simon. *Maybe our converging ideas flowed out with the rain and went down the Tiber.* She felt a strange twinge in her belly, the palpable feeling she always had when a new idea was emerging. *Seems like we go so deep when we talk. Maybe that is why I miss him?*

She'd spent some time reviewing articles about the St. James ossuary, so she turned them over in her mind while she ate chicken salad. The ossuaries were used for burial for a hundred years, from 30 BCE, a period of messianic fever, through 70 CE, when the Temple of Jerusalem was destroyed by the Romans. Upon burial all of the ossuaries had been aligned to the Temple Mount.

The destruction of the Temple not only ended these burial practices, it had shredded the social fabric of the Jews. Significantly the timing exactly paralleled the period when Jewish Christians awaited the Messiah's return. Sarah wondered if the ossuaries had been aligned to the Temple so the dead would have front-row seats to the fervently awaited apocalypse. *What an odd thought, yet I feel as if it's true.* Again she wondered why she was able to sense so much about this period.

Sarah thought the ossuaries could reveal the real story of Jesus and his family, including whether or not Jesus survived the crucifixion in 33 CE and then taught in the East for around thirty years, as many people in the Middle East believed. The date of 70 CE also corresponded to the Eastern date for the death of Jesus (Issa) in the Middle East when he was seventy years old. Those ossuaries held secrets about what the Jews and early Christians believed, yet the current Jewish authorities and the Vatican hid them as much as possible. It was outrageous! Why weren't all Catholics, especially the hierarchy, seeking to protect the authentic relics of the Holy Family?

There had been a monumental shift in human beliefs during this short period when time ran down to zero and then started up all over again in the West. What did this restart have to do with ossuaries? If studied, would the ossuaries reveal the life of Jesus in the East after his supposed crucifixion? That would get him off the cross!

While Sarah mulled over these wild ideas, the late spring storms ended and were followed by a few days of perfect weather. On a particularly beautiful morning, she picked up the phone hoping it was a call from Jerusalem. Instead, it was the call she had been beginning to dread.

Armando Pierleoni's smooth, entitled voice said, "Oh, I'm so happy to reach you, Sarah. I'm back in Rome and I managed to reserve for two at La Fraschetta, which you will love. It is intimate with delicious food, so I do so hope we can share an evening? Will you join me tomorrow night? Is that possible?" Armando's sophisticated Italian accent caused him to slightly roll his consonants when he elongated his vowels in a high pitch. She visualized him gesticulating in alignment with his body while he spoke into the phone.

She didn't see how she could get out of it, since she'd already agreed to dinner with him. And he was the son of a family her father adored that she too was growing to love. *If I don't go, Matilda will be disappointed. Hell, I'm a big girl, I can handle Armando.* Sarah was also tired of being alone. Until this year, her life had been filled with constant activity. With some hesitation, she agreed to his proposal for Friday night.

Her bell rang at exactly eight o'clock just after she'd nervously finished dressing. Despite the care she'd taken, she felt like her clothes wouldn't protect her as she buzzed open the front door.

Armando strode into the entry hall and stood there watching while she descended the tall curving staircase. Her long, muscular legs were eye-catching below an ivory shift that accentuated the beauty of her pretty feet in light tan flats. *This was a good idea, a very good idea; she's in for a very big surprise.* When she came to the bottom of the marble stairs, he exclaimed, "You look lovely, just like the dream I've always waited for. It is so good of you to join me!"

She was completely taken by his easy manner. It was so very male. Ushering her smoothly out the door, he said, "I hope you won't mind. I changed our dinner reservation to my private club under the Hotel Circus Maximus where I stay sometimes when I'm in Rome. When you gave me your address yesterday, I realized your apartment is only blocks from the Vatican and therefore close to my club. So we can walk together," he said as they passed by an antique Karmann Ghia. He patted the small forest green sports car. "Father's car. If you can believe it, he didn't want it anymore!"

Gallantly being steered by her bare arm at the elbow, Sarah felt amazed she was going out with him. *I don't have any idea where we are going! What am I doing?*

As they walked down the Via Ovidio approaching the back of the Castel Sant' Angelo, Sarah said breathlessly, "It's so kind of you to keep your promise after meeting me in Tuscany. But what do you mean by private club?"

"Oh, my darling, you make it sound like a seduction!" he joked as he looped his arm tightly into hers and bent over her in a catlike way, a very smooth and intimate gesture that made the hairs on the back of her neck tingle. "Roman restaurants are so noisy you can't hear your companion's voice. Everybody shouts and it is so boring. When they built the Hotel Circus Maximus, the antiquities department allowed them to build a private area inside the early Roman grottos below the hotel so that people can see an ancient part of the old aqueduct system. It's now a private club, the Doria Pamphili, and luckily I got a membership fifteen years ago. You will love it, just as all Romans love it. It is like dining in the tufa cave restaurants of Santorini in the Aegean where the club owner got his idea!" Armando was fluttering inside as he envisioned walking into his club with Sarah on his arm. *The old guys will be really jealous.*

As they veered off onto the Via Aurelia, the lights of the Vatican façade above St. Peter's square switched on and illuminated the saints and angels on the top rim. *I wonder what the saints think about what I'm doing tonight?* Sarah mused. Soon they walked into the lobby of the Hotel Circus Maximus and down a long flight of stairs to a large, dark, carved double door. The tuxedo-clad doorman greeted them both in Italian and opened the doors. After they stepped inside, the heavy doors closed soundlessly, and damp air called them to a lower world. As they descended limestone stairs, the bizarre two-story anteroom rose up through natural limestone layers topped by a painted dome.

"Fascinating, isn't it?" Armando said, eyeing Sarah's reaction.

As they walked through the anteroom, Sarah's attention was caught by an ornate mosaic floor in bright but subtle color depicting Cupid riding a lion. "Is this original? Is it early Roman, even late Etruscan?"

Armando watched her keen eyes scan the mosaic. "It is very ancient. They discovered it in a buried villa when they excavated for the hotel, so they moved it here to save it. Originally this was a water tunnel, so of course there was never anything like it here before. It is lovely and very pagan. Our Pierleoni lineage fades back into the late Etruscan times, so my ancestors might have once seen

Club Doria Pamphili

it in the villa. Maybe they brought someone beautiful just like you in to see it!" He was fascinated by how viscerally she responded to art, as she did to his paintings. *She really has an eye for beauty, even, in this case, pagan beauty. Maybe she can feel the free love of art and sensuality that characterized the ancient days. She will love the delight we Romans seek. I picked the right place for our first evening together.*

His Etruscan roots fascinated her. The Roman conquerors had totally absorbed and then forgotten about the Etruscan culture, but Armando carried the heritage of this lost civilization. She replied, "When I toured Pompeii I saw a mosaic as lovely as this one. This one is in such charming contrast to the natural limestone grotto." Her eyes swept a path over the pocked and irregular walls up into the ceiling. Sarah felt the deep and flowing sense of joy that always took her over when she encountered true beauty. The soft, damp limestone cooled her skin. *I could drop all my studies and just live like this.* The insight surprised her.

Her vibratory field flowed out beyond her body while Armando visualized her nipples, and she registered the frequency shift of his root in her body. Narrowing his eyes slightly at her, he responded in a low voice, "Yes, the limestone is beautiful with the mosaic, an exquisite man-made work of art. It is always the combination of these two elements—nature and art—that creates the most exquisite feelings, the same as your emerald and diamond necklace resting on your beautiful swanlike neck."

This remark jolted her awareness back into the grotto as potent fire energy in her sacrum moved up her spine and coursed up into her skull where she felt a ping. Looking sideways, sloe-eyed, at his perfectly cut slacks and dark shirt open at the neck, her emerald and diamond filigree pendant burned her chest as she cast her eyes down to the mosaic border of waves and masks. She felt like bolting out of the cave. *He just unzipped me!*

This hot energetic interchange was merely a few seconds. Satisfied, Armando deftly took her arm to lead her through a large rounded portal into a cavernous limestone grotto. When they entered the room, all eyes turned in their direction. The elegant Tuscan aristocrat accompanied by a young woman of great natural beauty and grace stopped the conversations for a moment. *Who is she? Where did he turn her up? She is unknown, yet I think I've seen her. She literally glows; she shines. She must be a celebrity.* Sarah felt a strange heady energy from all the people in the room. It was as though she were a vision conjured by them for their own purposes. She was relieved when they passed out of the main area.

Several other grottoes opened up on the edges of the main cave, and Armando led her across a travertine floor to their own private grotto, with a table set with linen, silver, and flickering candles. The candlelight caused the crystals in the limestone to sparkle and her dangling diamond earrings to glow.

The elegant and very private setting made Sarah feel off balance. She said nervously, "This is lovely, Armando. Thank you for bringing me here tonight. I've never eaten dinner in a cave before! Do you mind ordering for us, since this is your club?" Before she had time to take her words back, he'd already ordered two double martinis from the waiter who had suddenly appeared at the table's side. With a smile, he said, "I noticed you liked having a martini with my mother in Tuscany, and that you like them up, dry, and with a twist."

In mellifluous Italian he ordered an appetizer, salad, and a rack of spring lamb for two, and then turned back to Sarah. "You may be interested in the source of this club's name, Doria Pamphili. It comes from a nearby villa and gardens, the seventeenth-century playground for the Pamphili and Doria families. The Pamphili family produced Pope Innocent X, a very scandalous and controversial pope. He is of interest to me because he was the model for the face of Satan trampled by St. Michael the Archangel in a painting by Guido Reni. We can go see it at the Church of the Conception, Santa Maria della Concezione, if you like. Reni's painting inspired the Portrait of Innocent X by Diego Velazquez that subsequently inspired Francis Bacon to paint 'The Screaming Pope.'"

As Armando spewed out this crazy story known to most Romans, he was enjoying her décolletage perfectly displayed in her low-cut dress. *Her eyes are smoky green pools, and her perfect facial bones record centuries of good Celtic breeding. Her face is as perfect as any marble by Michelangelo.*

Sarah's head spun with all the detail, as well as from the effects of her smooth double martini. She felt him studying her though he covered up his scrutiny with a wry smile, laughing eyes, and constant gesticulating. Armando was the most elegant man she'd ever dined with, and so she did not mind his attention. At the same time, she knew he was toying with her, testing her with unusual ideas to see where she'd take them. She responded, "Really! 'The Screaming Pope' is modeled on Pope Innocent? Hmmm." His knees insistently rubbed the outsides of hers, making her feel edgy.

"Well, yes. Actually, I've thought a lot about it," he said as he poured her a glass of unfiltered red wine with a high percentage of alcohol. She wanted to take a piece of bread and dip it in olive oil, but since he didn't, she resisted. "Bacon must have been obsessed with the true insanity of being a pope, a supposedly infallible human who is usually very sinful because he had to play nasty power games to get elected. I think Bacon's screaming pope is a disturbing depiction of the total evil that invades almost any pope during his tenure, an infallibility neurosis that fascinated Bacon.

"The other interesting story about this family is that Olimpia Maidalchini, the wife of the pope's deceased brother, was the *mistress* of Innocent X!"

Sarah took a serious sip of wine. The air around them seemed to crackle when he spoke, and then she caught a flash of another entity, a gray wraith, entering his body. Although the odd sight startled her, she didn't consciously register what she saw because of the wine, the ideas being discussed, and Armando's touch stimulating delicious sensations inside her thighs. It all happened in a moment, causing a palpable shift in the grotto.

Slightly disoriented because she needed to eat, Sarah made the mistake of looking too deeply into his ancient eyes and apprehended pure evil, but again not consciously. Sensing evil too close to Sarah, her alarmed soul jumped into her body exactly when Armando hooked her. Armando hid a satisfied smile. He knew precisely when his carnal desire anchored in a woman because after many seductions he'd learned to recognize the signal—an intense almost painful electric snap in his right testicle. After that, just like any sadist, having his pleasure was a matter of time.

Surrounded by sparkling crystal light and across the table from a gorgeous, elegant man whose focused dark eyes held her gaze, Sarah nonetheless felt her heart constrict into a tight knot. Her throat closed and she coughed. From what seemed like a distance she heard his voice saying, "The story of Olimpia Maidalchini is really intriguing, because nobody really knows what was actually going on behind closed doors. We know for sure that she controlled the papal court, which makes it likely she was his mistress. She locked the Pope in his chamber sometimes! This was a fascinating period in history—the time of the Thirty Years' War in Europe, Cromwell's rebellion in England, and the Reformation. While Europe was in turmoil, Innocent X took advantage by greatly increasing the power of the papacy with Olimpia manipulating the agenda. Religion is more about power than it is about faith. The villa near this club was Olimpia's summer residence, and now Rome owns it and its wonderful gardens are public. So Olimpia lives on with us here in this club."

The waiter placed a large steaming rack of lamb in a rich brown sauce on the table. It melted under the waiter's knife as he sliced off a few chops for each of them. Another waiter brought vegetables and potatoes on platters, and they helped themselves while the waiters poured more wine into their glasses. She felt a strange alienation, a great resistance to something. *I'm the one who should've been named Innocent! I wish I weren't here right now. But also I love being here, in an ancient grotto as a guest in a mysterious private club. Everything is so elegant, so perfect, so compelling.*

The lamb was tender and aromatic, the mint sauce sharp and fresh, and the wine tasted even better with dinner. Sarah began to relax again, so Armando said, "Please tell me what you're looking into. I have been talking way too much about history and my club." As he spoke, she glanced out into the room and noticed a sleek, curvaceous woman stuffed into a gleaming green satin dress. A much older man was feeling up the woman's rear end with a hairy, long-fingered hand. The woman's head was thrown back, her dark shadowed eyes closed and her red-lipsticked mouth open in laughter. Armando followed her gaze and took note of Sarah's shocked eyes.

"Ahem," he broke in, clearing his throat. "They do get going down here, since it's kind of a sexy place with grottoes. That's Italians."

Something about this didn't quite square up with Sarah as she watched the man shove a fleur-de-lis cocktail stirrer between the woman's breasts and then pull it out and lick it. The woman laughed again, and then they both got up and strolled over the black-and-white floor and out a back door. Something was disconcerting about that door so she asked, "Where are they going?"

He hoped she wouldn't also notice the painting of an erect Priapus on the lintel above their table as he said, "Oh, there is another part of the club, a small casino, and they go there to gamble. We can do it too, if you want to?" Noting the suspicion in her face he quickly added, "I'd love to hear more about your work, please?"

"Oh, you know, sometimes I just get sick of my studies. Meanwhile, I'm fascinated by what you have to say about Innocent X, especially since your family produced a few popes." Sarah wasn't ready to talk about her discoveries with Armando, so she evaded him, and they bantered on while enjoying their dinners. He ordered two cognacs and a delicious chocolate torte slathered with cherries in brandy sauce, and then it was time to walk her back. His arm rested lightly around her waist as they walked along, enjoying the warm spring air. Soon they stood by her front door. With practiced ease he used his other hand to spin her to face him. Smoothly, like a potter molding a vase, he drew her closer; their lower bodies touched. He swept her cheek with his lips very delicately, saying softly, "I hope you will allow me to take you out again, soon?"

Sarah felt his soft breath near her ear. The sugar had taken her slightly out of her body and the alcohol had melted her guard, leaving Sarah in a wild mood. The cedars swayed, her lower body felt warm against his, and she felt energy rising in her chest and neck as she felt his lips on her cheek by her ear. Like a silly teenage girl, she felt a desire to have him kiss her on the mouth, but she knew if he did, she would push him away. Armando had learned his lesson from the way things had gone in his studio, so he drew his head slowly back as she still felt his soft breath. Then she put both her hands on his chest, softly separating their bodies, and replied, "Yes, I'd love to see you again."

Lying in bed finally feeling safe and herself again, she wondered as she fell asleep, *What on earth am I doing? Am I under his spell? How can I be responding so strongly to two men at the same time? How can I enjoy Simon yet also feel so excited by Armando? Of course my parents would love to see me marry a man like Armando, and they would never accept a Jewish guy. Daddy may want me to be a good girl, but he'd love it if I married the son of his old friend.* "How wrong you are, Sarah, how wrong you are," a voice whispered in the deepest recesses of her mind when she was sound asleep.

As for Armando, as soon as he closed the door to Sarah's foyer, he leaned on his Karmann Ghia and called Giaconda on his cell phone to ask her to meet him in the lobby of the Circus Maximus. They gambled in the casino for a few hours, surrounded by other couples openly making out and feeling each other up to get excited before going upstairs. Giaconda and Armando went up to his room in the hotel where he stripped her and braced her against the back of a settee while he sucked on her small, hard-nippled breasts. He pulled four leather strips out of his night bag and slid them all over the front of her body likes snakes as she arched her back and moaned. Then he tied her firmly to the bedposts, enjoying her willingness and enthusiasm. He got between her outstretched legs, ripped off her flimsy thong, and pushed in his huge penis. He held her ass high, watching her heaving breasts as he plunged in harder and harder while her breathing quickened and her body got hot. As he pushed and she moved with him, he felt the hot rising energy flooding his brain with light when she screamed, "Yes, oh yes, oh-oh-oh yes!"

As Armando lay there while Giaconda fell asleep, he felt himself slipping into the twilight zone where he saw a distant temple. Walking up to the temple on a curving path lined with multicolored flowers, he entered the round open building with ten white columns, the Temple of Venus. Moving deeper into his dream state, he saw a thin and beautiful woman dressed in a gauzy white robe sitting on a bench in the center. He approached her with reverence, as if he were Cicero seeking Livia. She said, "Ah, fine. You have finally come to me, the goddess of love and of the hearth. You have found me in a woman, a lovely woman, but she is my Vestal Virgin! If you choose her for your wife, remember you will ruin her if you take her before she is willing. Do not forget, Armando." And then he fell into a deep sleep. He didn't recall the dream, but he got the message.

11

What about Marriage?

As spring passed into summer in 2012, many commented on what a peculiar year it was. People talked of the world coming to an end based on the Mayan Calendar. In Europe people took to the streets to express their frustrations when economic austerity caused high unemployment, and the viability of the euro was threatened by tension in Greece. People in the Middle East had fought for their rights during the 2011 Arab Spring, and in 2012 Egypt, Syria, Iraq, and Iran became very unstable. Globally a great malaise was building due to stress over constant wars and climate change, but for Sarah a romantic future was beckoning.

Early one June morning her apartment was warm and humid even before the sun rose. She sat in her window seat wondering if she was in Rome to find her partner. And if so, who would it be? Simon or Armando? Armando sent her lovely flowers every other day; he was such a romantic. And their long daytime walks and sensual, languorous dinners made her happy. But just as the idea of Simon started to fade in her mind, he called her with the latest news on the ossuaries, saying, "Many people are beginning to revise their beliefs about the origins of Christianity. Orthodoxy is challenged."

Enjoying fresh coffee while delighting in the aroma of the

morning dew, she thought about how she lived in two different worlds. *Who created this script—a dashing and intense Italian aristocratic artist in hot pursuit while at the same time I share ideas with a heart-warming, sweet, intellectual man?* Watching a young couple linger by the garden wall to stop and kiss near the fountain, she felt like she'd never had so much fun. *What's changed in me? Why now? I feel myself opening like a rose.*

At this point the media was calling the pope "God's Rottweiler" because he ranted and raved against movements in Austria that collected the signatures of priests who demanded an end to celibacy, permission for woman's ordination, and Communion for divorced Catholics. The desperate pope called the faithful to "radical obedience," which enraged them because they were horrified by the priestly abuse and financial erosion of their parishes.

In May an Italian journalist, Gianluigi Nuzzi, had published *Your Holiness: The Secret Papers of Benedict XVI,* a collection of leaked private Vatican correspondence—"Vatileaks"—concerning struggles over the control of the Vatican Bank and hidden details about widespread corruption. For example, large sums of money from powerful business leaders and politicians for private audiences were doled out to the pope's secretary, Georg Gaenswein. Nuzzi's book described systemic disorder in the ancient institution. Romans chortled gleefully over these revelations. The Vatican was in total chaos! Clearly the so-called infallible pope was not in control.

A few days after Nuzzi's book was published, the president of the Vatican Bank, Ettore Tedeschi, was fired. And the day after that something truly bizarre happened: the pope's butler, Paolo Gabriele, was put under house arrest. Romans assumed the butler was a scapegoat, since the volume of leaks was far greater than files he could have gathered himself. In fact, Nuzzi said in an interview that one of his sources told him there were at least *twenty* whistleblowers in the Vatican. Change was in the air, according to Nuzzi, who said his book would never even have been published twenty years earlier.

Sarah was still obsessed with Gnostic theology, clearly the great threat to orthodoxy two thousand years ago. She flooded her senses with the intriguing Gnostic creation story of the wisdom goddess, Sophia; Lucifer; and the demiurge, the lesser god Yahweh. *Was Jesus a Gnostic? Was Paul? Was Marcion, even?* The more she studied the original documents, the more distraught she became about the loss of ancient wisdom. What if Jesus had been the central player in a Gnostic cosmic drama, a liberating breakthrough figure awaited for thousands of years? Was Jesus a divine being who incarnated on Earth to bridge our world with the spiritual realms? *If that was his purpose, suppressing the truth about him was criminal. It still is. Imagine how the world could transform if the truth was revealed.*

Later, while relaxing at a small outdoor cafe near the Fountain of Four Rivers in the Piazza Navona, she thought more about the early Church. Her studies had finally started to coalesce in a way that made sense to her. Finally she felt she could see the whole picture. Before 200 BCE, the ancient world had participated in an exciting and complex, global, spiritual, and magical culture. Prophets and great teachers were communicating with each other from Egypt to Persia, from the Middle East to the British Isles, from Greece to Rome, and all this wisdom was gathered in the Alexandrian Library. The fragments Sarah had studied indicated they accomplished a great synthesis of global knowledge, evolution, sacred science, cosmology, and art. Sarah believed this knowledge went back more than ten thousand years.

She crossed her legs and looked across the piazza, feeling someone's eyes on her. Unable to find the source of the gaze, she returnd to her thoughts. She couldn't escape the ugly truth anymore even if it meant she would lose her faith: During the fourth century in Rome, early Christianity had aligned with the emperor Constantine to create Roman Catholicism, a murderous religion. Ancient wisdom was deemed heretical, and the faithful were forced to worship the Jewish god, Yahweh. Marcion had become the big threat because he wanted to base Christianity on Jesus and compassion, a New Covenant. *I'm having a crisis of faith! I know Jesus came to teach us about love to awaken our hearts. Finding my own love may be what my journey with Christ is about from now on.*

Armando sat behind the fountain, rendered invisible by the thick misting rainbow pouring out of the Nile god's mouth. As he watched Sarah, he pondered the question that had been weighing heavily on him: whether or not he wanted to marry her. He'd never thought seriously about marriage before. Yet he thought it was time to pass on his lineage, and that she might be the perfect one for him. *But how can I be sure? One thing is for certain: I won't find one more beautiful.* He watched her cross her legs and hesitated again. *What if she's an ice queen? Seems strange that such a beautiful woman may be a virgin at age twenty-five. I suppose it's because of her exceedingly unpleasant father.* Armando had always thought that someday he'd pick an eighteen-to twenty-year-old virgin to be the mother of his children, but his conversations with Sarah had made him realize how bored he was by such women. He could talk to Sarah, really talk to her. *So perhaps this is to be the woman, the mother of my children. Perhaps it is my time.* As he thought about it, he was stirred by the desire to father Pierleoni sons. He had been watching long enough; it was time to act.

"How marvelous to find *you* here today!" Armando said, strolling casually around the side of the gleaming rococo Bernini fountain to approach her table. "May I join you? May I order us a glass of wine to enhance the sunshine and rainbow waters?" Warmth flooded her body as she smiled up at him. He sat down very close to her and waved at a waiter. A wise woman with silver hair sitting at the table behind them looked Armando over, wondering if the beautiful girl was a fool.

"Have you had lunch? Would you like a salad?" Armando asked. Sarah felt like she was in the middle of a movie.

The outrageous Bernini fountain was alive with dancing ecstatic children splashing their hands, faces, and arms in aquamarine water. Sarah loved their joy, and she loved the sensuality of Bernini's sculpture. Armando laughed when the periodic sprinkles made her bare legs sparkle. She shivered when his insistent hand grasped her left arm firmly while his other hand softly brushed over her breast as he reached over to stroke her exposed neck. Staring intently into her green-flecked eyes, he said in a low voice, "Sarah, have you ever wanted to feel the ripples of an orgasm moving through you and blinding your mind? Have you ever thought of me with longing? You are as exquisite as this wild fountain with sun filtering through the mist. You have captured me with your beauty; I want to know what you *feel*."

This early summer day was truly ecstatic, his knowing touch thrilling, so she lost herself in his dark seeking eyes as her cheeks blushed from his closeness. *What did he just say?* She felt like she was going to faint when his words registered, and Bernini's orgasmic sculpture of St. Teresa in the Church of Santa Maria flashed in her mind. Dense pulsing in her sacrum dulled her mind, and a knot tied in her brain as if his hand had reached into her skull and made a fist. As his voice penetrated her consciousness, it felt as though the rushing scene of color and sound was inside her head instead of out in the world.

The woman behind them thought the girl looked like she was about to fall out of her chair. Armando broke in, "Are you all right? Did I scare you? Are you okay?" She'd turned ghostly pale, as if she were about to pass out, just like St. Teresa fainting in ecstasy.

Sarah was staring at Armando. *This is so bizarre I can't register it.* In a quick flash the skin on his brown and toned arm had transformed into iridescent green scales. For a millisecond his tongue was slithering, and his eyes had turned amber and were glinting under a strange protrusion on his forehead. She struggled to regain her composure, thinking her vision was an overreaction to his provocative words. *How Italian of him, really. I'm old enough. We know each other well enough for him to say that.* Once she had absorbed what he'd just said, a great welling stream of hot fire moving through her body made her feel thick. Spontaneously she rose out of her seat and kissed him on his quivering mouth.

He closed his eyes, savoring the touch of her delicate and searching lips while he lightly touched her ribcage, moving his hand under her breast. The elegant lady behind them stood up and marched inside to pay her bill. *Typical Romans, such damned exhibitionists!* Sarah sat back down and tried to slow down her breathing while Armando paid the bill. They decided to take a short bus trip to the Spanish Steps, where eventually they made their way to the lower terrace traditionally favored by lovers.

Positioning her so her back rested against an alabaster railing that had weathered into encrusted oyster shell, he pressed his groin firmly into her body and ran his fingers through her hair. This time he kissed her, and she melted into hot rushing waves. She gasped, "Armando, I think we'd better slow this down. I don't know what this means to either of us. I need time; I need to go home and pull myself together."

"So do I," he said breathing heavily. He was delighted by his progress. "There is no hurry." Somewhat reluctantly they went their separate ways.

An old man standing a few steps up on the rising stairs above the terrace wished they'd stay all day just for his own entertainment. *Ah, Rome! The city of romance!*

Sarah had planned to go to the library to do some research, but she could not think straight. *Now what am I going to do? I'm doing things I thought I didn't want to do, but I've never felt like this before. After all, I don't even know what his intentions are. I have no idea! I wonder if this could be love? If it is, it feels like the flu coming on!* Tortured by these thoughts, she uncharacteristically gave up on studying and called her mother. Her mother, Mary, listened carefully while Sarah expressed her feelings, and then responded in her truthful way, "Of course, I'm sure he is a very lovely person, but is he interested in your work? Do you share your thoughts with him? Does he really know you very well? What is he interested in?"

Mary's questions jostled Sarah's besotted mind. She had to admit that Armando had no idea what she thought about, no idea about her quest. Worse, she didn't know what Armando thought about, not at all. Maybe understanding his love for painting is enough? Regardless, I'm just so physically attracted to him that I don't care about telling him about my research. Maybe I don't care because I have Simon to talk to?

She replied, "Mom, I'm very confused because I'm so attracted to him! I've never had feelings like this. Now I see how women get attracted to the wrong person. He is handsome and sophisticated, alluring and charming, and he pursues me relentlessly. It isn't what I ever thought I'd want, but he is sweeping me away! It's early summer and everything is so sensual in Rome. People fall in love every day in the Piazza Navona. Maybe it is time for me to just surrender and be a woman?"

Mary switched on her inner eagle eye. Armando is fifteen years older and very rich and sophisticated. He could easily have his way with her because she's fascinated by his lineage and his status as an aristocrat. Sarah has always sought perfection. I worry this is her blind spot. Mary replied, "I think you should come home for the month of June, maybe even July too. It will be hot in Rome, you can read at home, and I miss you!"

Sarah hadn't even considered going home, but with Simon gone and Armando pursuing her relentlessly the trip might be just what she needed to balance herself. "Yeah, Mom, I think you're right. I will come home as soon as possible. It is getting hot here in Rome."

After a going-away dinner at the Doria Pamphili, Armando took Sarah home and pulled her close to his body, pressing her against the garden wall. Roiling desire enveloped her and his cologne fogged her mind. Water rushed audibly in her brain when he lightly stroked her bare back. She felt like screaming when hot energy shot up her spine, into her neck, and up into her head. As he softly kissed her neck, he felt hard nipples pressing through her blouse and said breathlessly in her ear, "I haven't felt this way before, Sarah, not with anybody. This is not a game; it is much more serious than that. I will be here when you return; I will be waiting for you in Rome."

After taking her to the door, Armando strolled away into the warm evening air. She went inside and hugged her body in the hallway, feeling delicious pleasure and joy. *This is real desire! It feels like a spiritual breakthrough.* Armando dialed up the doorman and walked back to his club. A seventeen-year-old darling from Milan would be waiting for him in the parlor by the casino.

Sarah was all packed when the phone rang at midnight. When she told Simon of her upcoming trip, he responded excitedly, "No kidding! I'm leaving Jerusalem and going to New York to do some work at the *Times,* maybe for the whole summer. This is great, Sarah, great! I can come see you in Boston to meet your mother and see William again. Maybe you can come to New York or to my parent's summerhouse on Shelter Island? Will you?"

Sarah said she would love to see him over the summer. After falling into bed, she fell into the twilight zone. *Will I feel such strong sexual desire with Simon? Maybe this is all happening just because I am ready to have sex? Am I going to start reacting this way to any man? I'm not sure I like these feelings. What if I'd rather remain as I am?*

Sarah's mother had been right. It was so good to be in her old room, take familiar walks, and read on the porch in the oak swing.

William was relieved she'd come home after hearing from Mary how Armando was overwhelming Sarah, seducing her. He was taken aback by how much he hated the thought of it. *Maybe I'd feel different if Armando wanted marriage and not just sex? But I don't even like the idea of Armando marrying her. Of course, I'd accept it if it was what she wanted, since Armando is Catholic and Pietro's oldest son.* Meanwhile a Jew was coming for dinner! Before he had any idea what was up, Mary and Sarah had it all set up. Mary couldn't wait to meet the courageous reporter who'd written great articles about priestly sexual abuse and the school and church closings in Boston that angered her so much. This was a young man she was sure she'd like.

Simon strode up the front walk of the Adamsons' large nineteenth-century house, admiring the wide porch filled with comfortable chairs and swings across the front. *Just exactly the house I imagined she'd grow up in, so comfortable and warm.* He bounded up the stone steps wearing tennis shoes, broken-in jeans, and a lime green seersucker short-sleeved shirt. Sarah opened the door and gave him a big, friendly hug. She looked fresh and rested, healthy and relaxed, a girl he'd take a second look at any day.

William came up behind her to take Simon's extended hand, expressing his pleasure at seeing him again. Mary came down the stairs wearing a light blue shift and sandals. Simon thought she looked just the way Sarah would look in thirty-some years except her hair was redder, her eyes more blue than green.

"Hello, Simon," Mary said. "It is so nice of you to come all the way from New York. William has told me so many nice things about meeting you in Rome." She smiled at him with Irish eyes crinkling with fine wrinkles. She liked his shy and respectful manner and his healthy, relaxed body. She warmed to his deliberate clear brown eyes set in a kind face. Spritz, the Adamsons' floppy golden retriever, sniffed Simon's thigh and then turned and walked away, wagging his flowing tail.

After a drink and crackers and cheese on the porch, they moved to a large dining room with golden oak beams, milk glass sconces, and gleaming butterscotch wainscotting. Mary brought out coq au vin with potatoes, salad, and asparagus, and they all felt very comfortable while they enjoyed dinner. Simon felt right at home when the conversation moved deep into the difficulties and scandals in the Church, the pernicious confusion and pain in American parishes. William had gotten over his initial anger at Simon and admitted he wondered if the Vatican was ever going to do anything about the abuse. If they didn't, why would the clergy change? How could Catholics trust the Church anymore? It looked like the pope wanted the faithful to just shrink back into hard-core believers who would obey the rules. But who would pay for that?

"It was amazing to be in Jerusalem," Simon volunteered.

Yeah, sure, William was thinking, *especially since you're a Jew.*

Simon guessed what William was thinking and said, "You know what? It's as much of a shrine for Christians and Muslims as it is for Jews. The ancient city is filled with the sacred sites of all three major religions. The most amazing one I visited is Mary's Tomb, a site you'd never hear about unless you went to Jerusalem. There's a Greek Orthodox Church above the tomb now. Over hundreds of years a series of churches were built on the site to guard this significant tomb. Muslims and Eastern Christians believe it is the tomb of the mother of God. The Muslims revere Jesus as one of the fourteen prophets before Muhammed."

"I'd never heard about that, had you, Mary?" William said, amazed.

Simon continued. "The Persians destroyed the early church next to Mary's tomb in 614 CE, other churches were built there and destroyed, and even the Crusaders built a church there in 1130 that Saladin destroyed. But no one has ever disturbed the tomb of the mother of God, which has been intact for two thousand years! I went down into it and it has a very special feeling."

"Imagine that," said Mary. "Imagine being able to pray in a place where the mother of Jesus may be buried."

After her parents went to bed, Simon and Sarah sat out on the porch listening to peepers, crickets, and frogs in a pond nearby. He said, "Your home is exactly as I imagined it, and your mother is so lovely. You take after her. Are you happy to be home for a while? Do you miss Rome?"

Sarah's mind went to Rome and Armando, and what came out of her mouth surprised her. "I don't know why, but I feel I have to say something even though we are just friends. I saw a lot of Armando Pierleoni while you were in Jerusalem. I've come home to assess my feelings. He's interested in me, and I don't know how I feel. I thought you should know."

At first Simon felt alarmed and shaken, and then he got angry. He was in for a battle, a battle that he intended to win. The only question was how to do it. He tapped into his intuitive, persuasive element and volunteered in a slightly sarcastic voice, "Well, how fascinating," as he snuck a covert glance at her long bare legs resting on the porch rail.

"Fascinating?" she replied.

"Well, yes. You are in Rome studying sources that suggest true Christianity got derailed right there. So, now you are dating a guy who is a classic Catholic Roman aristocrat, a guy from a family that produced a few popes." While saying that, he realized he had to get her to Shelter Island to meet his mother. He didn't know why; he just knew. "Sarah, you and I are very close in our own way. You mean a lot to me, probably more than you think. I'd have to meet this guy to see what he's like before I'd have anything to say about him. But while we're here, I wonder if you'd do something special just for me? I want you to meet my parents. Can you come to New York, and then I will drive you out to our summerhouse on Shelter Island? They'd love to meet you, and it would be like a small vacation for me. Will you come?"

They made plans on the spot. After he left, she had some time to think about it. *I really do want to know what his parents are like. I feel like I am caught in a great riptide. Simon just makes me feel good; he always has. I love his quiet strength. He seems to know himself so well.* Sarah was happy he cared about what she was doing while he was away.

12

Shelter Island

The cab exited off the Brooklyn Bridge to Brooklyn Heights and dropped Sarah off in front of an ivy-covered brownstone—35 Pierrepont Street. She caught her breath when she realized she was breaking her promise to her father by visiting Simon alone. She'd been so focused on what to wear for meeting his parents, and as she rushed to hop the morning train from Boston and then to check into her hotel in New York, she had forgotten her father's admonitions. *Well, better than visiting Armando alone. I suppose Simon will just take me out to dinner after I see the house.*

The heavy iron knocker on the shiny dark green wooden door echoed within. Simon opened the large door. "Welcome to the house where I grew up!" He hugged her affectionately, pulling her close. Noticing reticence mixed with anticipation in her face, he gently released her and said, "I do hope you won't mind, but I couldn't resist cooking for you. This is a wonderful house, better than any restaurant in the city. If you love old houses this one is a gem. Welcome!"

Sarah scanned the elegant hall with appraising eyes. It was about twenty-four feet long and ten feet wide with twelve-foot ceilings. A tall, narrow staircase on the left rose way up to a landing and then turned to hook onto an open second-story balcony. Staircase and balcony were both edged by an ornate iron and brass railing. Spotting closed gleaming wooden doors upstairs, she was hit with a sudden urge to go up and explore. *This is like walking into a temple.* A brass, gas-electric fixture on a long stem subtly illuminated the ceiling in the lower hallway, which was decorated with ornate plaster-raised geometrical designs. Craning her neck, she could see a partially visible oval mural of an azure blue sky with fluffy white clouds around an oval skylight of thick feather glass in the coved second floor ceiling. The building was from around 1860 and beautifully restored. To Sarah, it was like walking into Mrs. Manson Mingott's mansion in *The Age of Innocence,* her favorite Edith Wharton novel.

Her father's rules went out the window the moment she entered his house, and Simon knew it. Gently, he guided her into the parlor, occasionally brushing her back with warm and subtle touches. He loved seeing Sarah, dressed casually in a beige silk blouse over loose black pants, in his home. He snapped a picture of her in his mind's eye as a dreamlike daguerreotype image, and then placed it on the mantle.

"My mother, Rose, supervised the restoration when I was a toddler. She is a decorative arts fanatic, so she researched the original décor and then copied it as closely as possible. It was a wreck when they bought it more than thirty years ago, but most of the original features were still there, hidden in grime. The work was constant for a few years. We treasure it because she did it so well. It is aging gracefully like fine wine, and all we have to do is repair the exterior occasionally. Would you like a tour?"

Warm and inviting feelings flooded her heart as she looked around the front parlor. Highly polished dark woodwork and bright blue-and-white Minton fireplace tiles carried her back to the nineteenth century. Afternoon sunlight dappled the wavy glass set in high round-topped windows and framed by mauve velvet drapes. The mantle was crowded with intriguing photos. One was Simon when he was around twelve with thick and wavy chestnut hair, standing by a friendly-looking border collie; another an old white yacht with a blue Norwegian flag; another of a happy young couple by the beach; and one a picture of a strikingly elegant young woman in front of Notre Dame in Paris. Simon loved seeing the curiosity and excitement in Sarah's face as she examined his family pictures.

"What a wonderful house," she exclaimed as he took her arm again and led her into the library behind the parlor. The small, intimate room was suffused by soft light coming in through tall windows above a green leather window seat. The windows admitted good light even though the red brick building next door was quite close. Dark wood bookcases lined the walls, and the fireplace was tiled with small red-and-blue checks. She asked, "Were the original owners Dutch? Were they early New York Dutch aristocrats?"

"Ah, very astute of you, Sarah. But how do you know?"

"Well, anybody might have Minton tiles on a fireplace like yours back in 1860, but I think only a Dutch person would have chosen red-and-blue checks in New York at that time."

Simon grinned. "Boy, are you and my mother going to get along or what? Sounds like you two have been dipping into exactly the same books! Actually, my parents had a fight about these tiles because my father thought they were corny. So she dug up an original pastel drawing of this room that was sketched by the architect," he said, laughing. "And there they were, just as she said they would be!"

He led her through the library into the dining room with more rounded tall windows, a room in the back of the building with a view out into a small walled garden. A gleaming dark cherry table for eight was set for two at one end with china, crystal, and silver. "I really had fun getting this stuff out for you, and now you are in for a treat, the kitchen garden." They passed through a door into a small galley kitchen and then out the back door and down a few steps into a walled patio with an outdoor brick oven. "As you would know, the kitchen would have once been in the basement for servants; however, my mother designed a small butler-type kitchen in a maid's room on this floor for convenience to the back patio where we pretty much live when it is warm enough. We'll see if we ever make it back into the dining room tonight!" He led her to a seat by a small table and went back inside for a moment.

She crossed her legs and settled back in the chair, letting her senses take over. Slightly acrid aromas exuded from old brick walls still warmed by the fading sun. Irises and daffodils in a mason jar on the table blended their scents. He returned with a martini shaker and an ornate Portuguese clay dish filled with cheeses, crackers, and olives. Proudly putting it all in front of her, he sat down. "This sure is more relaxing than the daily chaos and rancor of central Jerusalem!" Simon held the shaker aloft and tipped it, its contents cascading down into two long-stemmed glasses. As he handed her a brimming glass, she reached for it with both hands. He sat down and reached his hands out to encircle her fingers on the glass. "First you drink, then me because I'm so happy you are here right now."

She tasted it while his fingers enveloped hers. Then he tipped her glass to his mouth, drawing in the cool intense liquid through his lips while looking into her startled eyes, thinking *I feel like a satyr.* He put her glass down, and then picked up his own.

The silky coolness of the garden stimulated Sarah. She knew he was eyeing the lines of her neck. He asked, "Do you ever view a garden as time-lapse film growing through the spring, summer, and into fall? Do you ever feel like you've been in a place just like this before, a hint of times long ago? Of course, it is a primordial garden."

A subtle shift is occurring, she mused. *Tonight his eyes reveal his feelings instead of just his thoughts.* He scanned her face as she thought about what he'd just said. *I could sink into his eyes.* His voice settled down lower into a new intimate tone. "I will just say it. I have missed you so much this past month that I've forgotten who I am or ever was."

As he spoke, she moved backward through a tunnel that opened out into a landscape of dry yellow soil and ancient medium-green dry trees, a pale blue sea visible far in the distance. Her inner eye sought the meaning of this scene as her lips became sensitive, and she absentmindedly touched her lower lip with her index finger. *Where is it? I see this place again, southern Portugal.* Snapping back into current time, she felt his hands firmly cupping her face as he rose up and kissed her for the very first time. She did not resist him, yet she saw him through a distorted-looking glass. Warmth suffused her lower body. Her face tingled as his fingers lightly stroked her cheek while his lips sought hers. She drew back wryly, smiling, and said, "Do you remember our agreement in Rome?"

"Don't worry," he said. "I intend to keep it, but first . . ." And before she realized what he was doing, he firmly stood her up and drew her to him. "You need to know what my body feels like with yours, just like this first kiss. Whatever happens with us, we must know what our bodies feel like together." He held her very closely but respectfully as he carefully fitted his body to hers while enjoying her long back with his sensitive hands and arms.

Sarah was amazed by his gentle control, not knowing that just before she arrived he'd stopped time by sitting at this very same table and visualizing this exact embrace. Feeling the joy of his touch, she cascaded rhapsodically back through a wall of water edged with warm flames. The exquisite early evening summer breezes fluttered through the long hair falling down her back as she surrendered to his hands exploring the back of her waist and moving down. She felt free because she felt his respect for her; he would not invade her. *He's worshipping me just for the sheer joy of it! He's asking me for my feminine power from long ago.* Then she laughed and said, "Well, now do you feel like you know my body? I hope so, because I'm serious about our agreement."

She needs to draw away. I don't mind, since I have gone where I intended to go. I'm surprised she has so much self-control. He ran his right hand through her hair while kissing her forehead, released her, and they sat down. Eventually they went inside and enjoyed steak and salad in the dining room. Before she knew it, she was back in a cab driving into Manhattan to her hotel where she drifted into the twilight zone. *What is it—the cork forest in Portugal with the blue sea in the distance?* Once asleep, she dreamed of a stocky, well-formed man wearing leather overalls and a rough linen shirt walking up a hill carrying an iron tool that was used for scoring the year dates on cork trees. As she drifted into deep sleep, she saw he had Simon's dark eyes.

During the long drive to the eastern end of Long Island to reach the ferry to Shelter Island, Simon and Sarah talked and talked. As if nothing unusual had happened the night before, they shared all their experiences of the past couple of months. While she prattled on, he was thinking about something else. *I want her. We became lastingly connected last night and she won't go away. She knows my body. I've planted a garden in her heart.*

Walking off the ferry, they saw his parents standing there. Sarah first noticed Simon's father, David, who was exceedingly distinguished and urbane with silver hair, an animated angular face, and quick movements; his darting incisive gray eyes drew her right in. His wide smile, showing even teeth, was genuine. He extended his hand to Sarah while Rose stood back watching. Sarah responded warmly to his handshake and avid welcome. Rose was surprised Simon had brought home such a beauty. *I'm amazed by his deep intention. I've never seen this look in his eyes before.* Discreetly appraising Sarah's white sandals and loose blue dress, she thought the attire complemented her long, beautifully-shaped legs. Rose felt challenged by Sarah's startling grace until Sarah turned to her, smiled tentatively, and shyly offered her hand. Her warmth and strength grabbed Rose, and she found herself welcoming Sarah with her own genuine warmth.

As they drove out to the Gardiner's Bay side of the island in an old gray SUV, waving tufts of sea grass bent against the salty wind flooded with noisy sea gulls, herons, and crows. Simon told the story of Rose and David finding the house more than twenty years ago, and how they spent every summer here. "Appel" painted on a driftwood sign caught Sarah's eye as they turned into a crushed rock driveway snaking through small pines that struggled to grow in the sandy soil and constant wind. They pulled into the back of a weathered gray-shingled house with medium blue trim and went inside. Rose showed Sarah to a large airy room on the second floor with a balcony looking out to the sea and made her comfortable by telling her to enjoy the run of the house and rest for a while.

A few hours later, Rose found Sarah in the library buried in a pile of large books. Sarah was so absorbed that she didn't even hear Rose's footsteps in the hallway, which gave Rose a moment to stand quietly and observe her. Sarah had pulled out a pile of out-of-print, nineteenth-century decorative art books, and she was engrossed in one of Rose's favorites—*Lost Examples of Colonial Architecture: Buildings that have Disappeared or been so Altered to be Denatured* by John Mead Howells. Rose studied Sarah's face in its most concentrated mode. Her eyes danced and gleamed, and her mouth moved expressively while she read, drinking in the compelling images. Rose was charmed by Sarah's total absorption in a subject that meant a great deal to Rose. *Now I see why Simon is so taken with her.*

Sensing Rose's presence, Sarah looked up and said, "Simon made dinner for us in your Brooklyn Heights home, and I love your restoration. It is one of the most authentic and charming that I've ever seen. I also love beautiful old buildings, although I'm concentrating on ancient history right now."

Rose responded, "Nothing gives me more joy than saving something from the past, houses and antiques that express the true essence of a period. I feel like we'll lose touch with each other and our family lines without retaining our feelings for the past. These days, things are going so fast that nobody seems to care about beauty. So, maybe it is even more important to save things than it ever has been? The intensity of the destruction is ferocious with developers consuming material reality like carnivores. When I can't take the modern world, I sit in this library poring over my collection of books for hours. I time travel with them, which restores my hope in the future. Or at least it keeps me from going crazy."

"I know *exactly* what you mean, Rose," Sarah responded. "Maybe you can empathize with my need to study the early Church? Instead of wanting to save antiques or old buildings, I want to salvage and help restore the real story of the life of Jesus. I know it may seem like an odd and futile quest, but the Catholic Church is just as bad as a developer that trashes old treasures for money. Because of modern scholarship and remarkable archaeological discoveries, we can now reconstruct the true story of Jesus. Many people want to recover what was lost two thousand years ago." She gestured to the book in her lap, where she'd been paging through photos of the Boston Custom House, the Franklin Crescent, and daguerreotypes of front doorways. "I've never seen this book before. These photographs show what we've lost—the remnants of America's early days. The lost voices of people who believed in Jesus long ago speak to me as the haunting buildings in these evocative photos do."

Rose perched on the edge of a leather settee. "What an intriguing comparison, one I never would have made. Of course, I haven't thought much about Jesus, but I've always felt something big must have been going on in his life because his imprint is still so potent. Actually his imprint *is* very much like the psychic imprint of destroyed buildings; one just knows he was important." She paused, searching Sarah's eyes. "Do you ever feel like a house, building, work of art, or an antique actually emits personality, memory, and presence? This is not something I discuss with most people. But from what you are saying and your response to *Lost Examples,* I think I can ask you."

Sarah studied Rose's strong Middle Eastern features, a prominent nose and an expressive mouth boldly accentuated by red lipstick. Her body was strong, forceful, and slightly stooped. *Simon's delicate facial features and physique came more from his father, but Simon has his mother's dark eyes. I see the same mysterious deep blue flashes in her eyes. And, like Simon, when she's making a point, she moves her hands in wide sweeps.* Searching for the right words to describe something she almost never shared with others, she said, "When I go to an old neighborhood, such as lately in Rome, I stand in front of old houses or buildings that still have many original features. By relaxing my hold on current time, I can feel my way back into the probable timeline of the structure; this is palpable. Then something amazing happens: a whole movie unfolds in color of it being built, families living in it, the history of time flowing through it. When I've researched a building, I've found I *did* see the correct season and year of the building and the flow of events that came in time. My read on events is so accurate that I must be detecting past imprints. In other words, I think I read buildings similar to how some say they can see ancient battles at battlefields. I volunteered for a local historical society in Boston when I was a teenager, but I spooked them! This skill is quite useful to me now because I use it in my historical research. I *feel* past events. Have you ever felt anything like this?"

Rose nodded. "Yes, I have, Sarah, and I've used these feelings to guide my restorations and to figure out where to put things. I've found objects that were in houses in the past and then put them back where they were before! Luckily, there were a few relics in the attic of the Brooklyn Heights home, and I had some uncanny experiences with them. Look at the daguerreotype of the West Gate of the Salem Common by Samuel McIntire on the opening page of the book you are holding."

Sarah flipped to the front of the book and looked back up at Rose.

Placing her finger on the page, Rose continued, "I found that same daguerreotype in the attic. I suppose it was a popular tourist souvenir in its day. I just knew it had been on a certain wall in the parlor of our home, so I put it there. A year later, I found an early photo of our furnished parlor in the Peabody Museum in Salem." She gestured excitedly with her arm. "There it was on *exactly* the same wall!

"Then one day when I was alone in the parlor on a rainy afternoon, I studied it for a long time, feeling energy being drawn to it from around the parlor. The thoughts of people looking at it in the past came into my mind as if they were reaching me through a veil while I enjoyed the image. So I invited them back into the parlor for a visit and they came!" She smiled broadly, and then her face grew thoughtful. "It was wonderful to feel connected with the people who had lived in our home in the past, yet as their thoughts precipitated in my mind, I found myself overwhelmed with how different I am from them. I'll never know them or their times, never understand their minds. Knowing this has reduced the intensity of my quest to recapture the past, which was getting obsessive. Maybe this primary realization might be useful for you? What I mean is, millions have tried to figure out who Jesus was and what he meant to the world. Seems like the more people go down that road, the more he recedes. How can we ever bridge that gap, the great chasm?"

"Your experience sounds fascinating!" Sarah replied. "And I understand what you mean, but that gap is exactly what I'm trying to understand. Have you thought much about how quantum physics might explain what's *really* going on in our world, especially regarding time? For example, what if potent feelings and beliefs imprint photons or light particles in places and things? Do they switch back and forth between particles and waves according to whether we tune in to them or not? What if ancient things that people feel so strongly about are especially loaded with these photons? Maybe we liberate particles when we access memories? What if we can, in a sense, bring things back into the current moment or field if we have the capacity to feel things like this, such as you and I do?"

"It is intriguing to hear you put it that way," Rose replied. "I do know that nobody ever feels alone in our parlor. It's as if presences from the past are all around."

Simon walked into the book-littered library to find Sarah and Rose engaged in animated conversation. *I can't believe I've found a woman my mother likes so much.* Sarah didn't notice Simon was there as she said, "I think that's why I don't like new buildings. What I feel in Tuscany and Rome is amazing, the glow of antiquity. We don't have these profound feelings here because we are such a young country."

Simon cleared his throat, and the ladies realized he was in the room. "Dad is waiting for us on the porch. It's almost six o'clock!"

13

Simon Magus

There was something unique buried deep inside Simon, and his father was the only person who knew the whole truth about him. Simon and David shared their deepest thoughts during times together on Shelter Island, a tradition that had begun when Simon was seven years old.

After both Sarah and Rose retired to their bedrooms for an evening of reading, Simon and David took a walk on the beach and then went into David's study, his very private and favorite room off the back hall behind the kitchen. Before David had chosen it, it had been the summer cook's suite. The cook's suite may have seemed an odd choice for a study, but it had a large window with a view of the sea. David loved looking over the tall yellow grass and through the scraggly pines out to sea. Years ago Rose had lain out there on the sand in a faded denim dress with her rich brown hair blowing in the wind just like the young woman in the sand dunes by Andrew Wyeth. What could be better than a window where he could sit at his desk and gaze out to the sea, a lovely contrast to the intimate interior with its cozy fireplace.

They slipped into two dark green leather easy chairs arranged around a Sibley oak table subtly lit by a dogwood stained-glass Tiffany lamp bought by Simon's grandfather in 1912—a family heirloom that would someday be Simon's. David got up to get two crystal brandy snifters from the oak sideboard, a sign it was time to talk. He noted Simon's brooding eyes while he fingered his glass, capturing the green glow of the Tiffany lamp in the facets. He wondered what was troubling Simon. Was it something to do with the disturbing subjects he'd been writing about? David respected Simon for going out on his own as a journalist and making it.

David was a third-generation businessman. The original Appel ancestors had come over from Flanders in the 1870s and become merchants in the booming American economy. As soon as they accumulated enough capital, they became manufacturers of various metal parts for the Gilded Age, such as household hardware, plumbing, and lighting parts. Back in those days they were clannish and discreet, since you had to be careful about being marked as a Jew. Thankfully this onerous discrimination was largely gone from the American scene by the time David came into the family business and eventually the family had become very respected. Now here is Simon with a lovely girl, one who may be the first non-Jewish bride in our family. It doesn't matter to me because I like Sarah so much, but we've got to talk about it at least once.

He began, "Simon, Sarah is charming, and I think you're quite taken with her. Tell me all about her family."

"The relationship is not that serious yet," Simon replied, hoping to avoid the discussion.

"Well, that may be the case right now," David said in a crisp, persuasive voice. "But out with it! I can see how you feel about her. I think she has totally captivated your heart, mind, and soul, and we can see why. You've met her parents, so tell me about them."

"Her mother, Mary, is pretty the way Sarah is but more domestic, a woman who loves family life. I don't really know her very well yet, but I have gotten to know her father, William. I met him when he came to Rome a few months ago to visit the Vatican. Sarah was sure it would be a rough go because he's not partial to Jews. Worse, he was really angry about my article on priestly sexual abuse in the *Times*. In fact he came to Rome to meet with Church dignitaries to discuss the crisis. You've always encouraged me to just go for it if I really want something, so I took them both out to dinner at Alfredo's. It took him twenty minutes to figure out who I was, and then he almost turned into a steaming teakettle. But he is too well-mannered to gore his host, and we instantly liked each other! I'm still amazed that it was so easy. Last week her parents welcomed me to their home, which was diametrically opposed to how I was treated by the non-Jewish families of the girls I used to date. I think it's because her father is a hard-working construction engineer, not an effete blueblood."

David took all this in very thoughtfully. He was a little surprised Sarah's family had been so friendly. *This girl must be strong and managed to maneuver her father into a favorable mood.* "Of course, it makes me happy to hear you are being respected. Do they know very much about your background? You're the effete blueblood!"

Simon listened to the wind driving soft rain against the big window to the sea while pondering his situation. *Funny how it is when you're successful in your own right. To Sarah, being an Appel is merely a sidebar, and her parents probably have no idea how prominent my family is. They'd be the types just to think of my work and how it aligns with hers. Hell, Sarah probably hasn't thought much about the importance of my family but she's probably catching on now.*

There was a long pause while Simon tried to figure out how to probe his father on some issues that he knew would take him by surprise. *Oh well, the only thing to do is just do it.* "Dad, do you remember when I was a kid and you talked about Isaac Luria, everybody's Ashkenazi mystic?"

"Isaac Luria? What in hell does that have to do with romance?" *What on earth is he after?* "Is Sarah into the Kabbalah, like Madonna?"

Simon smiled. "Nah, I'm the one who is into the Kabbalah,

and you started it. Do you remember telling me stories here in this room about Luria exploring many dimensions? You said his unusual ability to see things on so many levels started a whole new mystical phase of Judaism?" Simon wondered if his father had any idea how much that conversation had influenced him. Maybe not, since he hadn't said much about it after he grew up. Maybe in his father's day, these were good ideas for living day-to-day life and doing business, however, Simon had been using the knowledge to navigate reality. Simon saw himself as more of an adventurer than his father, but despite their differences, he knew his father was the only one he could talk to right now.

David looked puzzled. "Well, sure, but so what? I'm genuinely perplexed by what Isaac Luria might have to do with getting the girl you want! Please elaborate."

"Okay, I will try. I think I'm having some experiences that only you can relate to. When you told stories about Luria and explained his Kabbalah model—the Tree of Life and many dimensions—I thought it was how reality actually functions. Maybe you were teaching me these ideas because Luria is our famous ancestor? Whatever the reason, I've found practical applications for these ideas in my life. I've put them to use, they work, and maybe that is why I've gone so far and fast as a journalist?"

David was shocked. He remembered how serious Simon had been when he shared the esoteric models with him. David had talked about it for hours because Simon had seemed so fascinated, but Simon had never said a word about it since. "What are you doing, Simon? Are you having séances with Sarah?"

At this point Simon felt like laughing and blowing it off. But he had to find a way to frame a question that would get him an answer. His father had influenced him in two main ways—mystical sharing and firm moral values, the reason why it was not difficult for him to respect Sarah's sexual boundaries. He'd been taught morality came out of respect for another person's needs and rights, an approach that was second nature to him. As a result Simon had earned the deep respect of his friends and colleagues, even Sarah's father. *My father taught me respecting others is what causes them to respect me. Then does he really think it's okay for me to use mystical methods to get what I want?* "Dad, have you ever used manifestation techniques, like visual skills, to successfully conclude a business deal for the most favorable outcome? Do you do that when you think it would be a good outcome for all involved?"

David put his brandy glass down on the table so abruptly that it made a high-pitched ping. *Is he nuts? Does he think the way to get this girl is to use the Kabbalah? Who in hell ever did that? . . . Come to think of it, probably a lot of guys!* David was quivering because something was calling him to full alert, so he just let some words flow out. "Well, we don't talk about these things in business, but I've heard that some successful men use rituals, even sexual rituals, to influence people's minds. Stanley Kubrick explored this in *Eyes Wide Shut,* a great film showing how the elite use sex rituals to control the world. Regardless of what other men were doing, I have noticed that when I want something to happen in business, if I believe in it strongly enough it tends to happen. This is especially true when I visualize a desired outcome. People often said I get the things I want by my will, but I think it is because I see things before they happen. I've never, however, related my success to Isaac Luria!"

"Well, why not, Dad? Why were you so successful when other guys were not? Hell, you don't even work that hard. When you taught me how to manipulate reality, I took you seriously because I thought you used visualization to get what you wanted. You are ethical, so you would never do it without believing others would also benefit. Amazing! Maybe this Luria lineage is ingrained in our blood as an unconscious force in our family, especially in the men."

"Simon, I learned the business from your grandfather, and I did okay. Visualizing positive outcomes seemed to be second nature, and we always made plenty of money. But what in hell does this have to do with Sarah?" David responded, feeling confounded.

Simon took a deep breath. *Oh man, here we go!* "Okay, Dad. Do you remember when we used to talk about the Fallen Angels, angels coming down to Earth and taking women? I was fascinated and concluded a bunch of extraterrestrials were hanging around here thousands of years ago. Now this issue has come back for me. Look, unfortunately I'm not the only guy who's after Sarah. An Italian aristocrat from Tuscany is also seeing her, and I've been having dreams about the guy as a Fallen Angel who has come to take her. I dream of him with wings! I brought her out here to meet the two of you because my dreams are so alarming. I've been using some of our mystical techniques to bring her closer to me. I'll do anything because I care about her so much. I love Sarah! But is this right; is it moral? The facts are, these things work, which sometimes gives me the creeps."

He raised pleading eyes to his father. "I need you to know about my struggle. I need your help. I want her and I need her. I am on the verge of a really nasty battle with the Leviathan, a modern-day dragon, when I get back to Rome. This is a battle that I intend to win. I just know that this other guy is a real threat to her. The skin on the back of my neck bristled when she told me his name— Armando Pierleoni."

David got up slowly and went over to his desk to pick up a strange black object. He came back to his chair and sat down, holding the object in his left hand where it filled his palm. His fingers closed over it. "I don't know if you remember me showing you this when you were little. It is a petrified whale's ear that is millions of years old, and it has always been in the family. Probably it comes down from Isaac Luria, and someday it will be yours. My father gave me Levi as my middle name to honor our magus lineage from Luria, just as I gave you Isaac as your middle name. My father did battle with the Leviathan in business after WWII, so I am sensitive to what you are facing," He sighed. "There is so much evil in the world. When I hold the whale's ear, it gives me answers for how to deal with these potent forces. Maybe it works because I'm sensitive to the sea—maybe there is information in the waves? So let's see what the whale's ear has to say."

Simon watched his father close his eyes while holding the whale's ear. *I always wondered what he was doing in this room alone for many hours.*

Like film stills moving on fast forward, a blur of images poured into David's inner eye. He struggled to pick out forms, faces, and landscapes, trying to slow them down enough to see them. Unlike when he tuned in to the whale by himself, he had to describe what he saw, but the images were coming so fast that they passed before he could describe them. Keeping his eyes tightly closed, David said in a thick and slow voice, "Ask me a question about what you want to know."

Simon stared at his father's slightly frozen face, his eyelids quivering as if in REM mode. Pulsating blue light flashed in the whale's ear. *Where is my father right now?* He spoke the first thought that came into his mind. "Is Armando Pierleoni a threat to Sarah?"

The question went right into the deepest part of David's forebrain where an answer was already ringing. A high-pitched disembodied voice came out of him, seeming to originate from the center of his skull. *"Sarah is a rare daughter of the divine feminine, a woman with a great heart, a very advanced soul. Her pure frequency has drawn a very dark being to her; instinctually he wants her because he senses she could save him from doom. He easily gets any woman he wants; he has never been denied, and boredom is his worst enemy. He does not feel what he does to others, the pain he inflicts on them, because he is a sociopath. You'd better be careful because he will get violent if he's thwarted. He is a threat to Sarah, not you."*

David was breathing deeply and regularly, as if he was almost sleep.

Simon remembered from childhood that he could only ask

three questions, so he said in commanding voice, "Should I protect her?"

"You can only protect her by winning her over," David said very softly. *"And you have to win her over before he does, which you already know. The time in the States before you go back to Rome is critical. Sarah must be your main goal now. What happens between the two of you during this time could save her."*

Simon had already figured that out, but the answer afforded him the chance to ask the last question, the one that would matter. Clenching his fists as he looked at the whale's ear in his father's hand, he said, "She is a virgin and very naive. Should I seduce her right away to protect her from him?"

David felt a sharp electromagnetic disturbance in his brain, almost like a minor ischemic stroke. As he breathed even more deeply and continued to finger the whale's ear, his brain electrified, generating palpable magnetic fields in the room. His voice now became deeper and more distant. *"She is an ancient sacred virgin like the Vestal Virgins of Rome or the temple priestesses of ancient Judah. The Vestals were used to keep evil away. She has no idea why she is so watchful and virginal, why she feels she would be breaking a vow if she has sex. Her father wants her to be a virgin until marriage, so he put a lock on her. As for Sarah herself, she is very lusty, very ready for sex. This man is dangerous because he is so experienced, and she is very passionate. She is so confused by her ancient vow that you cannot seduce her or propose to her until she's ready to renounce virginity. She wants to go beyond the vow of chastity her father imposed because it locked her into the old, the past. She needs to break through to sexual love without all these rules, especially religious ones, or she will never be free. If the man in Rome plays it right, he could easily convince her that he is the one who can liberate her."* Then his voice trailed off as if he had fallen asleep.

Simon sat back in the green glow of the Tiffany shade, pondering what his father had said and scribbling detailed notes on a pad on the table. Glancing up at his father, whose eyes were closed and body slack as if he were napping, Simon noticed the whale's ear was about to fall on the floor and he reached carefully for it. The touch of his hand caused David's eyes to fly open. David blinked, clearly disoriented, so Simon asked, "Do you remember what you said?"

"It's very strange. I honestly don't," murmured David. "I feel like I enjoyed a nice nap. I can remember something from when we first started, some comment about Sarah being a very spiritual person, but that's it. I know one thing: this is yours." He reached for the whale's ear on the table and handed it to Simon. "My time with it is complete. Now it's your turn. It will help you focus and figure things out, as it always did for me. Maybe it *did* belong to Isaac Luria?"

Later Simon lay on the top of his blanket while the evening was still warm. He put his fingers on the back of his skull, pressing the place where his skull connected to his neck while he visualized the inner structure of the house, the halls and rooms and the things within them. Once he had a total scan, his light body rose slightly above his body, and he floated down the hallway into Sarah's room where she was sleeping deeply in the moonlight. He hovered over her body, sending waves of light into it.

Meanwhile, Sarah dreamed of walking on the beach wearing a sheer white gossamer tunic. Feeling drawn to a shadowy figure in the distance, she felt like flying to it but wasn't sure what it was. A white egg of vibrating light enveloped her body, reducing her to a tiny nucleus in the egg.

Simon floated back down the hall, into his room, and back into his body to sleep.

Simon and Sarah had to go back to the city in the morning. He had an appointment, and she had to catch the train to Boston. After saying goodbye to David and Rose at the ferry dock, they were on their way. Sarah thought Simon was strangely quiet. Finally when they were on the road again, she said, "I had such a lovely time. I'm so impressed by your parents; they're so warm and welcoming. Thank you for bringing me out to meet them."

Clenching the steering wheel while trying to figure out what to say, what to do, he just said the first thing that came into his mind. "Sarah, they can see that you aren't just a friend, that you mean more to me than that. This is serious business, and we may not have all that much time or opportunity to have what I think we both want. It was not an accident we met by the House of Cumae in Rome. Certainly my parents won't oppose us getting closer. Help me. How do you feel about me?"

"Whew!" Sarah exhaled as she sat back rigidly in the passenger seat, a million thoughts cascading through her mind. *How lucky am I? Simon means a great deal to me, but something is holding me back. Is it Armando? Am I more sexually attracted to him than to Simon?* As that thought came into her mind, she felt heat between her legs and nausea in the pit of her stomach that made her dizzy. She had to say something, so she said, "It's the classic line—I need more time. We have been apart for a month, and we didn't spend that much time together in Rome before that. I have very strong feelings for you and I adore your parents, but I need more time. Luckily we will have it in Rome, time just to get to know each other better."

The traffic was building, and he cursed himself for bringing it up in the car while driving. But it was his last chance before racing to a difficult editorial meeting, so he tried one more thing. "Will you consider staying an extra day in New York to have dinner with me at home again in Brooklyn Heights?" He watched her out of the corner of his eye as she pushed back in her seat and crossed her legs in lotus position, leaving her sandals on the floor.

Looking straight ahead into the weaving traffic, she said, "I have to be the sensible one: I can't be alone with you again in your house because I'm afraid I would break our agreement. It isn't time yet. I don't know why, but both of us need more time. If we are meant to be together, you will not lose me. If our relationship is meant to go deeper, it will happen. We have to trust; we can't hurry it. I have very strong feelings for you, Simon, but I have to leave it at that for now."

"All right," he replied. "I think we should see each other again in Boston before we both go back to Rome, if you agree." She did.

14

Summer Giulia

In late June's rising heat, Tuscany smells heavenly. Armando's favorite day—summer solstice—had arrived! He was in his studio poised like a dancer waiting for the sun to attain its maximum strength. *As soon as it goes into Cancer, I will paint Sarah.* A large blank canvas with a photo of Sarah by the side awaited his brushes. She reclined on the light tan leather divan, wearing a loose medium blue dress that revealed a good portion of her right leg. Her delicately arched ankle drew his eye. Smiling enigmatically, she seemed to be gazing off to an etheric view. *Her fine and prominent neck bones framed by the long hair falling down over her left shoulder onto her breast are exquisite. She is the long-forgotten Etruscan beauty, Giulia.*

He'd photographed her on the divan in the foyer below the curving stairway of her building in Rome between one of their daytime walks and evening dinners before she went home. With the ornate stairs rising gloriously like a Fibonacci spiral above the divan, it was the perfect composition. He had rushed madly back and forth, snapping shot after shot. "You will be the return of the remarkable goddess portrayed in white marble by the front entrance of the Villa Giulia! This way with your arm; your leg up slightly more; relax your lips!" Click, click, click! in rapid fire. When he developed the film, she glowed like a woman ready for love. This was his first contemplation of her face with an artistic eye. *The dress's cerulean hue brings out the subtle contrast between the color of her skin and the tan divan. Her face glows like ivory silk with a subtle emerald cast in her solemn green eyes. Huh! Never noticed the yellow flecks near her pupils. Her proud aquiline nose draws out that ancient look in her eyes. She watches through the centuries; she knows.*

Glancing at the clock, he saw the sun poised at the very top of the Tropic of Cancer. He felt the urge to paint her. *It is turning south again. I'm ready!* His eyes narrowed to alert snake slits while he studied the long curve of her exposed leg. He detected energy lines in her groin flowing up the midline of her body and rising between her breasts, connecting with a strong line of light on her throat. Each side of her face reflected this centerline, which drew attention to her eyes. Gazing into Sarah's enigmatic emerald-green orbs, Armando's fingertips began to tingle and pulse. *The light shimmers on the canvas.* His whole body surged with orgasmic waves as he brushed on lines and points with medium blue to create a geometrical form—the lines of light between the stars of a new constellation. *I see connections between the stars.* As he brushed on more lines faster and faster, the form crackled in his brain and became three-dimensional. After adding touches of paint here and there, he used a thicker brush washed in gray to flesh out the form. He lowered his paintbrush. *It is done, can't touch it again. I must let it rest. My god, this took only an hour and the solstice is already past.*

Armando was electrified as he walked away from the canvas. He sat down at a small round table to drink Bordeaux and appraise the abstract image. As he responded to its power, a palpable magnetic field surrounded his body. *I'm ready; I will have sex with her, the only reason to paint a beautiful woman.* He brought out his larger palette of flesh tones, umbers, and reds while sucking air deeply into his lungs. Returning again to the table with the wine, he placed her photo on the table, studied it for a moment, closed his eyes and then fell into stillness. Once his awareness was centered in the deepest recesses of his cranium, his eyes popped open to stare at the photo, blurring its outline. Using his knowledge of color and anatomy, he visualized Sarah nude on the divan. *I want the unabridged essence—rose-pink skin, hard dark nipples, deep brown and red flowing curls, soft brown hair between her legs, deep red lips and vital green eyes. She is a miracle of vibrant flesh colors. She glows slightly redder than the dewy sheen of the leather divan.* The blue dress crumpled to the floor.

The curves of the staircase sail her body into motion as she quivers with desire. My body presses on hers—the two of us on the divan, my penis like the curve of the spiral. Armando was so aroused that his chest heaved while his diaphragm sucked in and out. He was tempted to go over to the door and masturbate at the same place where she had stood some weeks ago when he first kissed her, but then he would lose the painting. Like a dog in heat, he stood up with a throbbing erection and went back to the canvas to begin painting furiously. Making love to her with each stroke, Armando watched the gorgeous nude body on the divan emerge within the initial geometrical form. As he brushed her with his fingers, caressed her with his forearms, and touched his thighs, she impregnated his mind.

Three hours later he finally calmed down and was able to finish the soft detail lines by adding light accents. *No wonder I need to be alone when I paint.* Exhausted, he sat back down to study his creation, one of his greatest nudes—Summer Giulia.

Sarah was on the wide porch in Boston, enjoying the balmy warm night while peepers and bullfrogs sang to the stars in the nearby pond. Her cell phone rang.

"Hello, Sarah. I've just gotten my schedule and I will be back in Rome by mid-July. Can I come up to see you before I go, like weekend after next?" Simon said.

"Of course! Come to our summerhouse in Western Massachusetts near Sheffield, since I'm going out there to see my parents in a few days. It's closer to New York and is a very special place, the office building of an old quarry my mother's parents restored. Would you like to come up? I don't have to check with my parents. You are always welcome and we have plenty of bedrooms."

Simon said an enthusiastic yes.

A week and a half later Simon was exiting the highway for the private road leading to Sarah's house. The road ran alongside a quarry pond with steep granite sides dripping with green vines. Every turn in their relationship was a new chapter of a mysterious unfolding story.

What an intriguing place. How in hell did they ever find it? The quarry office was quite small and very close to the side of the drive, just like old stone houses in Wales or Cornwall. They'd transformed the old factory road into a private drive shaded by large pines. The result, Simon thought, was everybody's dream of a hidden place. The house was fashioned of granite blocks from the quarry, which was now filled with clear rainwater. Rays of light barely penetrated the tall trees, filtering through to sparkle on the water. Simon guessed that there were large bass down there and maybe trout lurking under the ledges.

Parking by the side of the old office, he stopped to admire an enormous and vigorous ancient oak shading the drive. Sarah rushed out to greet him. *I've never seen her smile quite like this—so eager to see me!* She took his hand and drew him through a simple narrow door that admitted light through distorted glass circles in the upper casements. The smooth-cut granite walls were cool and damp, and air moved through the main room out to a screened porch, refreshing the house. Typical of a simple early industrial office, small low-ceilinged rooms opened from one into the next, and deep-set, original twelve-over-twelve windows drew ambient light into the rooms. These rooms would be very dark during the long New England winter, but today they felt cool and refreshing in the summer heat. *This house is naturally air-conditioned,* he thought as he admired the rough-cut stone floors smoothed by the boots of hard-working men. The old stone floors also reminded him of walking in ancient temples. The décor was complemented by early New England country-style antiques upholstered in beautiful fabric with small flowers and animals. Gleaming old leather books were scattered about. *This is a special place.*

Sarah studied the sexy outline of his upper lip while he surveyed the cottage, and then she led him back to the large screened porch. "My grandmother restored this in the late 1940s because my grandfather just had to have it. She hated it here at first, but once they dead-ended the road by offering the people behind us better access to another road, she grew to love it. It was a welcome retreat, an escape from the oppressive Catholic social pressures in Boston after the War. It became my parents' retreat in the 1980s. My grandfather did a tremendous amount of work on the building, which was worth it because it's all made of hand-cut stone. Let me show you your room to drop your bag."

She led him up a steep stone staircase to a narrow upper hall that was open up to the rafters. The rooms were framed on one side only. "This part of the house is not a full story like where my parents and I stay, but it's cozy up here and guests like it." She opened the door into a spacious room under the eaves with a dormer as wide as the room. Rusty orange chestnut floors gleamed in the sunlight pouring through the dormer casement windows. Fresh air flowed in through large screens in the window.

"It's perfect," he told Sarah. "I'll sleep very well in this room." He put his bag by the dresser and followed her back downstairs.

"Well, fancy seeing you here, young man." William grinned and extended his strong right hand while holding a gin and tonic in his left. "Who'd ever have thought you'd make it all the way from Rome to a quarry house in New England?" he said, laughing and indicating a canvas chair for Simon. "One rule around here is no serious talk, especially about the damned Church. Especially about the pope! You agree, Mary?"

Mary smiled warmly. For a second time, her cornflower blue eyes triggered "Irish Eyes Are Smiling" in Simon's brain. Gallantly taking her hand, he held it to his lips and softly kissed it.

"Oh, how charming!" she said. "I'm so happy to see you again, and happy to have you visit us here. We are here most of the summer because we have to close it for the rest of the year. We cherish this place. You'd be shocked by how much stone came out of this quarry to supply New England for two hundred years. Will you be taking him swimming, Sarah?" Sarah nodded, so Mary continued. "Ours is the most exquisite swimming I've ever experienced. It is the most beautiful and clear swimming pool in the world!"

After they ate a tray of sandwiches and salad on the porch, the afternoon heat became oppressive. Simon changed into his swimsuit and met Sarah to head for the other side of the quarry on a path through the woods. At the edge of the quarry were deep rock ledges that functioned like stairs into the pond. Sarah explained that they had been carved out during the final phase of the stone cutting. She stood on a ledge and stepped out of the loose beige cover-up she wore over her bikini. *She is like a fine, tawny gazelle.*

Simon was so busy trying to cover up his own peeking that he didn't notice she was boldly studying his body. *Simon is fit, wiry, strong, graceful like a well-bred racehorse—a male body I like.* As they dove into the cool water, their heated skin shivered and contracted. Daringly they swam and dove deeper into where it was really cold. "How refreshing," he said as they drifted toward the middle where they could see the house on the other side.

She swam with strong, sure strokes, stretching her limbs to warm them as her body temperature cooled off in the icy water. "Yes, I've never found a better place to swim in my life. Nobody knows about it except the local kids who sneak in when we're not around. It has been a favorite swimming hole for a hundred years, so we don't mind, since the 'No Trespassing' signs protect us from liability. Every summer my parents have a party and invite the members of the Sheffield historical society, who appreciate them because they saved it. Imagine if a developer had gotten it."

They swam for a long time in the delicious water, but they eventually got cold and returned to the ledge. She climbed out ahead of him and warmed her back in the sun while rubbing her hair with a towel. He strode up the rock stairs, took her right arm to get her attention, and then gently turned her so that she faced him. "Don't worry, I am not going to say anything but I'm going to do something."

Water drops glistened on his face and chest as she engaged his determined dark eyes. *I really like his ways.* In slow motion, he moved both hands up to her face and kissed her for a second time as she allowed her body to slide into his. This time she felt the energy in his lower body when he pulled her very close. Her nipples hardened in response.

She became acutely conscious of her skimpy bikini and dripping skin, so she moved her hands and arms to his chest to gently separate their bodies as he caressed her lower back down low. Achingly stimulated by his bare arms and chest covered with black curly hair, she laughed joyfully, feeling palpable vibrations coursing through her warming body. She felt free. *I'm wildly attracted to him.* Her excited eyes challenged him as he struggled to keep his eyes and hands off her incredible body. She said sweetly, "You make me so happy!" Then he watched her turn to walk up the path, remembering what his father had said about her search for freedom, freedom from sexual restriction. Right now, he could tell she felt free, but how long would it last? What if she got hurt?

After dinner, William said, "You like to play games, like Monopoly or bridge, Simon? Or would you like to work on a puzzle that has me stumped?"

Simon was in a great mood after the swim and a languorous

afternoon nap. He was feeling closer to William, who was the key to protecting Sarah, so he was willing to play any game. Mary broke in, "We play a lot of games out here because there isn't much else to do in the evening." *I can think of a few other things I wouldn't mind doing tonight,* he mused as Mary went to get the Monopoly set. They all moved to the dining room table and soon were throwing dice, pulling cards, watching the bank, buying property, and laughing. William said, "People have been playing this game since the Great Depression when this quarry finally closed." A few hours went by and then the poignant call of a loon echoing off the quarry walls and a night owl hooting in a nearby pine tree reminded them it was time to sleep. As Sarah drifted off, she could feel Simon's nearness in the house and wished she could hear him breathing. *I like having him nearby. I wonder if he's thinking about me? I'm tempted to sneak down the hall and open his door.* Just as that thought passed through her mind, William knocked softly on her door. "Good night, Sarah."

"Good night, Daddy."

The next morning as Simon came quietly down the narrow back stairs, he heard loud voices coming from the kitchen. *I wonder if somebody is having a fight?* He slipped noiselessly out to the screened porch and sat down in a rocking chair. William was ranting in a loud and exasperated voice while Sarah was cooking eggs. "Have you seen the *New York Times* yet? I can't believe *both* things happened on the same day!"

"And right after the solstice, I might add," Sarah muttered as she flipped eggs over easy.

Her father fumed, "This is total crap! It's one thing to convict the perpetrators, but another thing to convict a Church official, a Monsignor no less, in one of the largest archdioceses. Philadelphia no less! Why should Monsignor Lynn get all the goddamned blame, since Cardinal Bevilacqua was the one who passed the buck around. Of course, the cardinal conveniently died before he got blamed for anything. I feel sorry for Father Lynn. This is crap!"

My god, Simon thought out on the porch. *They must have found Monsignor Lynn guilty of allowing that abuser priest back into a parish.* Simon knew the story. A priest had been reinstated by Monsignor Lynn after he had been suspected of abuse; he cornered a terrified ten-year-old boy and then went after more kids. His conviction would be a milestone, the first time American courts convicted a prominent Catholic prelate for allowing known sexual predators to have access to children.

"Ahhhh! What in hell was going on yesterday—solstice schmolstice?" fumed William. "Jerry Sandusky convicted on the same day, almost at the same time for multiple counts of sexual abuse of young boys at Penn State! Who would believe that? I'm sure you're thrilled about it, Sarah, Simon too, but, this is a simultaneous breakdown in our best institutions—sports and the Church."

"Well, Daddy," she retorted, cutting him off. "The situation in the Philadelphia Archdiocese was horrendous for years; you know it as well as anybody. It was a seething sex pit, a virtual torture chamber. The parishioners were terrified of the clergy, and the clergy didn't care. They still don't care! Something had to happen, somebody had to blow the whistle. And as for the coach, I've been so sickened by what he did to a little boy in a shower that I can't sleep at night. The reports have gotten to be so graphic that hideous visual images are stuck in my brain. His wife acts like a pious zombie, yet obviously she knew what he was doing. One of his adopted sons claims that Sandusky abused him for seven years! It looks like they adopted kids so he could use them! This guy was a monster, and somebody had to stop it. The torture of innocent children must cease; I don't care what it takes! I'm happy to hear this news. They should revive Alcatraz and put them all in there together!"

Their voices drifted to a halt while Simon stayed out on the porch. *The solstice part is what intrigues me, since the solstice is reputed to be the awakening of the goddess. Maybe women have finally gotten enough power to end this torture. Solstice 2012—maybe this 2012 end-of-the-world thing is about ending sexual abuse? What a wacko idea! When deep abuse is exposed, we are getting someplace! William must be very worried about how this will affect his archdiocese.*

Sunday was not easy at the Adamson quarry house, but they all got through it. By evening, both Sarah and Simon had read the article that had set William off. Mary and William were having wine on the porch, so Simon and Sarah went for a long walk on the back quarry road behind the town.

Simon took her hand and said, "Justice may come! I didn't think exposing the truth would matter. I thought the best I could do was help some people see what was going on and protect their kids. Really, this is an amazingly positive outcome, the sort of thing that renews my hopes. How about you?"

Enjoying his firm grip while their shoes crunched on the gravel, she replied, "Well, I really think Lynn might get it because they have a lot on him and know the public was watching them. It's odd that this is happening at the same time that football coach Sandusky's abuses are being uncovered. Such synchronicities may be signs of a field shift, a change in the thoughts of a large enough group of people to turn events in another direction." Gesturing with her free hand, she went on, "Take last year's Arab Spring in the Middle East. Suddenly many people fought to throw out dictators. The battle for basic rights was contagious. You and I have a lot of work to do as writers. Now that a monsignor is being held accountable, Church scandals creep closer to the Vatican and you will be called to write about it. To be frank, I am so sickened by the graphic descriptions of what these men are doing to children that I wonder why anybody would want to have sex! There is a stinking pestilence in the air, an evil distortion of physical integrity tainting the world. I don't know how to mature in this environment; It's the reason I'm how I am with you." She stopped in the road, wrapped her arms around his neck, pulled him tightly to her and said, "Here's a hug for hoping that the world will be safe for children for a change."

He nuzzled into her ear and kissed it, holding her close and enjoying her warmth. "We have plenty of time, and I can't wait to be with you in Rome again." They just stood for a while in the safety of a warm embrace. Simon hadn't had sex with a woman in months and didn't care. *Time stops with Sarah. Whatever is happening between us is so much bigger than any of my petty needs and desires. I never thought I'd feel this way but I do.* "You know, it has been a long time since you've said a word about your research. What's happening with your work right now?"

Turning down the dark road, she said, "For me, Jesus's heart opens with these convictions, the vindication of children who suffered who are now men. They were wounded and forgotten until now. Something is happening in the world, Simon, a turn to the good after so many years of intensifying evil. Abuse happens when hearts are dead, yet now hearts are coming alive. The eternal quest for light in the world is coming forth in our times. Divine infusion was diverted two thousand years ago, yet the seeds were planted that are sprouting now. According to quantum science, past, present, and future are not real, so the potential for divine infusion is always there." She paused for a second. "There's so much coming together right now. I'm ready to get back to work."

On Summer Solstice 2012, grown men and women who had once suffered in the hands of priests and others in positions of authority came to new conclusions about fairness. Some were beginning to feel sane for the first time in many years. The public's refusal to believe them often damaged and confused them as much as the abuse itself. Now they could heal. As for the perpetrators, the victim's pain had never mattered. This was a reckoning and past conquests didn't feel so exciting anymore. For once the perpetrators were afraid instead of the other way around. Those who dared to tell the truth were the heroes, not the smug and pompous lying hierarchy or the leering and slavering coach who loved to smear his face all over the TV until he got caught. Finally the loss of inno-cence mattered.

As broken victims went to sleep that night, for some their souls returned to enter their battered bodies; they could feel again! Others were not able to respond to the truths being revealed. William Adamson, who was sleeping alone because he snored in the sum-mer, drifted off. His soul took him back to that sickening afternoon in the rectory when he was nine years old. Father Rafferty grabbed him from behind and rammed his stomach against a prayer kneeler. As he lay in bed, the sticky sweet smell of stale incense awakened him, but he fell back into a dead sleep. As usual, his unconscious again blocked out every detail of that day in the summer of 1962.

15

Sister Hildegard

Sarah felt free as she settled into a small room in an old house near the university for the month of August. Instead of flying back to Rome with Simon in late July, she had gone back to England to consult with her thesis advisor. Sarah worried she was losing her sense of direction and felt she needed to refocus and deepen her priorities. The attention of two extremely unusual men was confusing her. Time flew while she read and took notes all day in the university's Victorian library while dusty summer light filtered through tall windows and warmed the creaky old wooden floors that groaned under the feet of heavy nuns passing by her cubicle to go to nearby study desks. Observing them, Sarah thought what she always did, that they were species from another time. When it was cooler she went to meditate in a pristine Norman chapel, her sanctuary for clear thought. *I have to find the answer. I have to know why Jesus burns in my heart. When I seek you, I see Simon's face. Are you reaching me through this good man? Is this how I will know you? Is falling in love my way to be with you?*

Raising her eyes slowly up to the only object in the chapel—an exquisite Italian Renaissance-style ivory Jesus carved in perfect anatomical detail nailed to a rosewood crucifix—she noticed the aging ivory was slightly yellowed and his body glowed in the soft light as if he were alive. In the past, the deep lines and agonized eyes of his suffering face had evoked peace in her mind, but not anymore. *Why are you on the cross yet not in the eyes of children? I have seen you in Simon's glistening body on the quarry rocks. I need to know you not just as one who suffers. Why have you abandoned my religion, the Church stained by the sins of priests who say they carry your cross? Will you ever return to the Church?*

By the middle of July, Simon was back in Rome after visiting his parents at Shelter Island. Before he left, his father gave him a substantial income out of his inheritance and some advice. "Live a better life now that you're thinking of having a wife. Don't get used to being a lazy bachelor. Good women notice things like that, since how you live indicates how their life with you would be. Sure, Sarah likes our home in Brooklyn Heights, and our home here on the island, but what about *your* home? What about creating something that shows who you are? Seems like the place to start is with a good apartment in Rome, since you will be there for another year or two." Simon, who liked the good life as much as anybody, accepted the money gratefully. He was deeply touched that his parents cared about him so much and hoped his father was right and that Sarah would become his wife.

Rents were high in Rome, but with his improved circumstances he found a very special apartment. He couldn't wait to say goodbye to his room with a kitchen above a noisy tailor shop in favor of the furnished one-bedroom apartment on the Via Frattina, a few blocks west of the Spanish Steps. It was on the fourth floor of a small building with trendy shops on the street floor and a private entrance out of the courtyard garden for the twelve flats upstairs. The street was very quiet because cars were not allowed, and the garden had old trees and felt peaceful.

I feel like pinching myself. It's too good to be true—a dream!

The owner lived in the building because he loved it, and he'd furnished all the flats with charming antiques. After the owner had proudly shown Simon around, Simon had paid the deposit on the spot. The building was five hundred years old and had been updated more than once. The façade above the shops had been redesigned during the Art Nouveau period when an architect had added ornate rococo plaster carvings and rusting ironwork balconies. The interior still retained the Renaissance style with handsome original woodwork with many layers of soft white paint. The wacky facade reminded him of Gaudí's buildings in Barcelona—distinctive, slightly decadent, and very sensual.

The plaster walls were painted in subtle pastels, and the kitchen was charming with deeply worn white marble counters that glistened when the afternoon sunlight streamed in through deep casement windows that were perfect for plants. The casement windows with their worn deep slate sills accentuated the thick walls, giving a feeling of security and depth to the kitchen. Subtle light from the inner courtyard warmed the bedroom. Simon could imagine a Vermeer painting of Sarah looking out through the deep windows. The front door opened into the living room, which had a gas fireplace with a large and ornate marble mantle decorated with carved griffins and vines. The fireplace would be very cozy in the winter when he entertained Sarah, and it had not escaped his notice that the apartment was located a mere twenty blocks from the Vatican and Sarah's apartment. The four-poster double bed afforded a view out to the balcony through tall French doors that made the room feel breezy and magical. A hallway with large closets led into a sensual bathroom with a Victorian copper bathtub in an alcove tiled with evocative burgundy and deep blue fleur-de-lis tiles bordered by fading golden lions that sparkled in the sunlight. *What an incredible find!*

He got right to work after moving in boxes of books and files. He was amazed by how much had gone on in Rome the past two months. It was as if the Vatican had been hit by a tornado. They had thought the irksome scandal regarding Cardinal Anthony Bevilacqua, Archbishop of Philadelphia from 1988–2003, would just melt into the past once he died in early 2012. When an American civil court convicted Monsignor Lynn after the solstice, however, the ugly reality of the corruption during Bevilacqua's reign was thrust into the limelight. The truth about the bizarre sexual free-for-all could no longer be hidden. The Vatican quaked during summer 2012 as the scandals edged closer to Saint Peter's dome, and Simon was thrilled to be back in Rome to cover the escalating scandals. Thomas Doyle, the priest who'd cast the spotlight on Cardinal Bevilacqua and Monsignor Lynn, testified at Lynn's trial that Bevilacqua ordered the shredding of the list of thirty-five abusing priests in the Philadelphia Archdiocese. Doyle, already a well-known whistle-blower on priestly abuse, successfully exposed the depth of the corruption in Philadelphia. Simon knew it was a game changer and viewed Doyle as a hero. Simon had been following Doyle's activities for years, ever since he had stated publicly that the pope had to have known what was going on in the Philadelphia Diocese. Rechecking his sources, Simon read again what Doyle had said in 2010: "Pope Benedict is a micromanager. He's the old style. Anything like that would necessarily have been brought to his attention. Tell the vicar general to find a better line. What he's trying to do, obviously, is to protect the pope." The vicar general who had tried to protect the pope was Gerhard Gruber, who worked under Ratzinger when he was the Archbishop of Munich. In 1981 Ratzinger was appointed to head the Congregation of the Doctrine of the Faithful, an insider group that searched out heretics and operated in total secrecy and autonomy, the modern-day version of the Inquisition. Then in 2005 Ratzinger became Pope Benedict XVI. Now in 2012 settlements for victims were more than $2 billion and rising. The scandal spread to Ireland, Italy, and Germany, edging ever closer to the pontiff.

Sitting out on his balcony at 10 p.m., watching the last glow of the setting sun behind the Vatican in the western sky, Simon was in deep thought, strategizing. He knew the hierarchy would say it was an unpleasant phase in Church history, one that would soon pass. *This papacy may be a rotten nest of sexually deviant secrecy freaks, but as soon as Benedict is gone there will be another pope and another reality.* What was going on seemed much bigger than that to Simon, big enough to set up a second Reformation. Based on the excellent data gathered by Doyle and others, at least ten percent of priests and bishops had abused children during the past sixty years. It was outrageous, since most pederasts had multiple victims. The Church's response was simply to say sexual abuse by clerics had always been a huge problem. What kind of answer was that? Did the hierarchy shield abusers because they were directing a long-standing systemic Catholic program that serves deeply hidden purposes? What was the real reason for this shocking amount of deviance? Simon knew he had to dig deeper, but at least the laity now knew the rectory was dangerous for children.

Back in England, Sarah entered the office of her advisor, Sister Hildegard Brennan, a renowned author on early Christian sects, a Discalced Carmelite who had come out of seclusion twenty years ago. This was only Sarah's second meeting with her, but she had been greatly impressed with Sister Hildegard's wisdom and compassion and looked forward to talking to her again. Warm summer air wafted in from the rose garden as Sister Hildegard embraced Sarah and pointed her to an old comfortable chair. Sister Hildegard settled into a seat facing her.

"How have you been, Sarah? What's it been like to study in Rome, the center of our Catholic world?" She spoke softly while looking deeply into Sarah's clouded green eyes.

Sarah studied Sister Hildegard's delicate features, soft skin with just a trace of wrinkles, and steady gray eyes. She was still very beautiful in her seventies, with inner grace suffusing her face. Her white-collared periwinkle blouse was tucked into a demure gray cotton skirt that went down almost to the top of black, mannish shoes. Sarah noticed a print on the wall in a faded gilt frame, depicting St. Teresa of Avila praying by a huge rock with light shining down on her from above. *I wonder if she misses the life of total seclusion away from the sins of the world? I see her in sandals and a long gray robe walking in walled gardens during daily meditation.*

"Thank you for taking time with me," Sarah said. "I'm progressing well, but the deeper I go into early Christianity, the more I am confused. Can we talk about that? Am I free to express what is really on my mind, or would you prefer to discuss only academics?" She'd carefully composed these lines in advance so she could observe Sister Hildegard's body language and facial expressions. Sarah was beholden to her father's generous financial support, and she wasn't going to risk her status by being too open, but she hoped to share her crisis of faith with Hildegard.

Hildegard detected deep worry in Sarah's eyes, a subtle fear masked by her sweet virginal purity. *Whether she's a virgin or not, she's very pure in heart and soul. She would have been a great nun.* "Sarah, I'm not your spiritual advisor, yet I am here to guide you. You can feel absolutely safe with your confidences, since your personal and spiritual welfare affects your studies. I've discussed early Church doctrinal issues with many students, and the early period often brings up a crisis of faith. We accepted you because you are deeply thoughtful and dedicated, so I'd be surprised if you *weren't* disturbed by these topics."

Relieved, Sarah blurted out, "Sister Hildegard, I feel like I will be thrown to the lions if I follow my thoughts to their logical conclusions! Back in the second century, early Christians were not the same as Christians after Constantine. They lived in simple communities and practiced Jesus's message of love and compassion, which was lost when the hierarchy went in the opposite direction. The original way of life mostly vanishes after 400 CE except in some orders, such as the one you lived in for so many years. Today the Church struggles with rampant sexual, financial, and power abuse, and I want to know how this happened. Many second-century Christians said the Church would eventually destroy itself unless it confronted some difficult theological issues, such as questions raised by the Gnostics." Sarah watched Hildegard's face very closely when she said the word Gnostic, but Hildegard didn't seem to react at all to the word.

Hildegard crossed her long-fingered hands. Sarah's eye was caught by the thin gold band that identified her as a bride of Christ.

Hildegard said, "As far as I am concerned, *nothing* could be more important than investigating the early period to determine what the first Christians really believed. If the Gnostics were right about what Our Lord intended, then the suppression of their beliefs could explain why we are having a crisis in the Church today. As we both know, male theologians scream *Heresy! Gnostics!* Yet the sins committed by the male hierarchy over a thousand years are beyond belief! They invented Absolution as a way to clear the path for the next sin! Frankly, I don't see how you *could* look deeply into this period without seeing that Our Lord's intentions blew away in the winds of history. So would you like to be more specific?"

Sister Hildegard's blatantly heretical comment about Absolution—forgiveness granted during Confession—stunned Sarah. It unknotted a tight coil in the center of her body, causing a tingling spin in her brain. It had been a relief to share these ideas with Simon, but it was an even greater relief to share her thoughts with a knowledgeable female theologian. *I'm not the only one.*

"Sister Hildegard, what are your thoughts about Marcion of Pontus? Considering the size and spread of his early episcopate, a tremendous number of Christians must have thought our Bible should not include Hebrew scripture. Marcionite bishops were once in the line of apostolic succession, but their authority was stripped away when Marcion was excommunicated in 144 CE by Peter's church.

Then it claimed all powers of succession, allowing them to absolve themselves, just as you've said. We can't alter early history, but in light of recently discovered sources, we see *why* Marcion advocated a fresh start, a *New* Covenant. Reading what the Gnostics actually said, not just what the early Fathers said about them, means we can examine their stance on evil in the world. For example, the Fathers said the Gnostics hated the world. But now we know the Gnostics said they hated evil in the world, not the world itself. Well, I *detest* evil in the world!

Encouraged by Hildegard's supportive nod, Sarah continued, the words tumbling out one on top of the other. "Ironically, rampant evil possesses the Church today. As soon as a priest or bishop is accused, the faithful are instructed to forgive him in the name of the Lord. But what if these horrific sins reflect a struggle with demons, the forces the Gnostics feared? Why *were* the Gnostics so concerned about the sins of the Fallen Angels and the cruel god Yahweh? Possibly this arcane esoteric drama is being played out day by day, parish by parish because the early Fathers *didn't* confront the problem! If that is true, are we going to keep on absolving abusers and sending them out to do it again? How can the Church tell a mother to forgive a priest who attacked her child? Demanding forgiveness for unbridled lust is a hierarchical power play! During the fourth and fifth centuries, early synods hammered out the doctrine of original sin—Christ came to die for our sins so that we can be saved. Well, what if Christ actually came to found a new religion of love and compassion, a religion that could not thrive and grow if people feared the old evil god, Yahweh? Jesus himself said he came through the domains to free us from the grip of the powers and principalities, the throne of the jealous and angry god. I know my statements are blasphemous, but the Church is making arrogant and obscene demands! Gnostic beliefs about the evil, jealous god may explain why so many priests indulge in such evil acts. The Church commission reports say priests have abused children as young as *two years old!*"

Suppressed tears enlarged Sarah's eyes, which flashed with images of children being abused. *I see broken small bodies on the floor wrapped in crumpled clothes, in the fetal position on cots, others being penetrated when they kneel in the rectory. Shrill cries echo down deserted hallways where doors are quickly closed, and it happens again.* Sarah could not block the horror flashing in her mind.

Because she saw that Sarah was truly suffering, Sister Hildegard probed her inner mind while running the beads of her grandmother's ebony rosary through her fingers. *Mother of God, this crisis has to be faced. Now that the works of the early Christians who truly loved the Master and followed his way have been found, the real truth about the Church is coming forth. People struggled to have safety and comfort amid historical chaos. By offering some comfort and beauty to them, the Church got away with too much arrogance and dished out deceit to people. Now that people have some comfort and safety in the world, they can no longer tolerate the Church's arrogance.*

Hildegard said slowly, "I think you are meant to be a voice for the early Christians who believed evil would take over the Church if it became an institution that claimed divine powers, especially absolution for sin and infallibility. The Church is based on an earlier culture, Judaism. Yahweh as Lord probably did elevate the primitive tribal people four thousand years ago by making a covenant with them as the Chosen People. But what does that matter for our Church? We are having a horrendous crisis. It would be bad enough for secular people to commit such grievous sins, but for clerics it's an abomination. Great potential exists in your desire to speak for early Christians who had a pure vision. I've read what the Gnostics said about the evil god in the world and that we should be wary of worshipping him. Considering what's been happening to innocent children—meta-bestial acts—Gnostic beliefs challenge me too."

Sister Hildegard and Sarah locked eyes, two Christian women who understood each other. Sarah said, her voice determined, "Birmingham is not a Catholic institution but it is Christian. If I go out on a limb and base my thesis on Marcion, will I be denied a degree for a thesis that raises such heretical issues?"

Sister Hildegard considered Sarah's question. The only problem she could foresee was with one close-minded Dominican. Regardless of him, Sarah's academic credibility would be the deciding factor as long as she was her advisor.

Interpreting Sister Hildegard's silence as hesitation, Sarah continued, "Sister Hildegard, I must have some sense of the playing field. I am really lucky to have my father's financial support. I can't play with that and just throw it away. Really, how safe *am* I taking such a radical approach?"

Sister Hildegard said firmly, "I think you should expose things in the early Church that may be the source of the present moral degradation. A solid critique of apostolic succession and the hierarchy could offer new perspectives for where we are now. After all, anybody is entitled to a mistake, except, of course, a pope," she said with laughing gray eyes.

Sarah said good-bye to Sister Hildegard feeling totally supported. But as she returned to the Norman Chapel, she started to wonder, *How can I ever do this? This is so much work. I have Hildegard's support and even her enthusiasm. But how can I do it?* Seated in the deserted chapel, Sarah fell into a state of deep meditation and first saw Simon's shy smile. Next she saw Yaldabaoth—a peculiar Gnostic image of the father of Yahweh—with Armando's rakish eyes. Scanning her sources, a deep knowing came into her mind from a faraway place: *The events and synchronicities that occur in my life will show me the path of spirit. Life is my source for truth. I can't find these answers in my mind anymore. I have to find them in my life even if I have to experience evil.* She came out of meditation when a thin prelate lit a beeswax candle on the simple soapstone altar. When she rose to leave the chapel, she chuckled over what her father would think of what Sister Hildegard had just said.

16

A Home in Rome

During early September cool morning breezes from the Umbrian hills north of the city swept down to the waking city and cleared the sultry air that had pooled on the Tiber from the previous day. Dragging slowly across the floor in her robe, Sarah went to boil water for coffee. She had flown in from London the night before. Curling up in the window seat, she listened to early street sounds while noisy birds splashed in the garden fountain below. The night before, she had forgotten to remove the gold chain holding her grandmother's diamond, and rainbow rays of light flashed from it as the morning sunlight penetrated the diamond. The black-and-white floor squares bordered by delicate gold filigree lines seemed even more ancient than they had before she'd left. *I'd forgotten about Donatello's rich coffee beans, and I'd forgotten how much I love beginning my day here. I wonder about the life of Luciana Amelia, the favored daughter who lived here long ago. Was she cherished? Did she marry or go into a convent to avoid giving birth?*

The rising sun penetrated the ancient leaded glass circles dappled with trapped air bubbles. It created shimmering spheres that resembled distant galaxies when the universe was born. She was foggy and dreamy when she took out her cell phone to dial up Simon at his new apartment. *I wonder if he's there? I hope I'll see him today.* Just when she was ready to dial, the phone rang, startling her. She answered thinking it must be him—*what a synchronicity*—but instead she was greeted by a lilting and crisp high voice with a strong Italian accent. "Hello, Sarah. This is Matilda Pierleoni!"

"Oh, hello," Sarah responded tentatively.

"Ciao! I hope you have recovered from your flight? We are all so happy that you have returned!"

"It's so thoughtful of you to call. I am quite well, but how did you know I just arrived?"

"Well, I must confess that I called your home in Boston to see when you were coming back," Matilda replied. "I reached your father yesterday and was delighted to hear you were coming last night. I do hope you will not think I'm presumptuous, but I just had to call to tell you something very exciting. Armando has painted you! I have not yet seen the portrait because he wants you to be the first to view it. I have, however, seen the photographs he worked from. They are very lovely, my dear, very captivating. So the painting must be marvelous, but he just won't let us see it until *you* have seen it first. I can't imagine why, since he has always been anxious to show us his work as soon as possible. But, anyway, I'm so anxious to see it myself that I hope you will come to Tuscany this weekend to see it? I am anxious to see you again too! Our weather is exquisite right now, while it is still so hot in Rome. Armando is here now, too. Will you consider coming as my honored guest? My driver has errands in Rome today, so he could easily bring you up here tomorrow morning. We'd just love to see you!"

Sarah hesitated. This rather demanding request made her aware Matilda knew she'd been seeing Armando, and Sarah wasn't at all sure she was ready to see him again. *I feel so connected to Simon, and I've got to get to work right away. I almost forgot about being photographed by Armando; it was so much fun and so natural at the time. Regardless, it was an aberration on my part.* As she was thinking these thoughts, she stroked the left side of her neck and fingered the old diamond, remembering Armando's scent when he touched her while posing her on the divan. Sarah wanted to see Castel Vetulonia, the venerable old library, and the Tuscan countryside again. But she felt ambivalent about seeing Armando and his painting.

"Well, Matilda, thank you so much. I suppose this is possible because I can't get back to work until next Monday when some tractates arrive. Are you sure Armando wants me to see the painting now?"

"Oh, yes! *Prego!*" Matilda replied with an audible sigh of relief. As a lady born to the Duke of Lucca who ended up as a count's wife near Siena, she wasn't accustomed to the possibility of her invitation being denied. "Armando says he can't wait to have you see it, so then hopefully we can also see it. He is not up yet because he was working late last night, but I'm at liberty to invite you as my guest. He will be surprised and delighted. This is perfect! Guido can pick you up at nine o'clock tomorrow morning and you'll be up by one o'clock, just in time for lunch. The tomatoes are just in, and we will have made antipasto. Oh, how delightful!"

Sarah felt she was being pushed by a strange wind, but so far that was how things had been since the beginning of 2012. She never knew what was coming next until it hit, and then she reacted. Once she had accepted the invitation, however, she began to recall luscious images of the family chapel, the inviting library, the ancient tower, and the view of the castle from the lower road. By appealing to her fixation on being a dutiful and perfect daughter, Matilda had made it impossible for Sarah to refuse. She made Sarah feel like she was standing in the way of Matilda's viewing of her own son's painting! Regardless, Sarah finished the call with real enthusiasm. "This will be wonderful, the perfect way to spend my first weekend back in Italy. I am very curious about the painting. I'd love to spend more time with you, so I will see you tomorrow afternoon! Thank you so much for such a lovely invitation!" And that was that.

She slumped down into the squishy plush velvet cushion, releasing air from her constricted lungs. The bubbles in the ancient glass sparkled in her pupils like faint stars. She felt peculiar. *It must be the late flight. I do want to go to Tuscany again, but something feels odd about getting back here.* Sarah's body was sending disturbing subliminal signals from the knot in her sacral root Armando had deftly implanted there months ago. *I'm not so hot to see him now that I have grown so close to Simon. Yet I want to see the painting. Sometimes the energy in Rome feels very strange.*

She forgot about trying to reach Simon until the phone rang again. "Oh how lucky! I wasn't sure you were back yet, but I thought I'd just try," Simon said in a happy, light voice. "I can grab some time today, so can we have lunch? And would you like to see my new apartment? I'm all moved in!"

Scrunching deeper down in her window seat, she felt waves of relief. *I always feel secure when I hear his voice. I always know things are right when I'm with him.* "I would love to have lunch and see your apartment. Can we meet at Luigi's near the Cumae site? That will give me enough time to unpack and relax. A walk would be good after the flight."

The morning flew by and soon they were eating salad and sharing pasta primavera at Luigi's, just down the road from where they had first met. As Simon held his wine glass to his lips, savoring the aroma, he took a moment to study Sarah's face while she told him about her last conversation with her father before leaving Boston. Her sensual yet slightly thin lips were glossed with soft, shell-pink lipstick. He noticed for the first time that she used very light eye makeup, just a touch of emerald-green eye shadow and light mascara. *I wonder why I didn't notice this till now? Did she always wear makeup?* His journalistic side always dissected things, so a more intriguing possibility came into his mind: *I've been so taken with her naturalness, her stunning elegance, that I didn't even notice things like this. Sometimes she doesn't seem human. And what's the cool distance I sense in her today? I suppose it's the late flight?*

"So my father had some advice for me," he heard as Sarah's voice drew him back to their conversation. "Simon, are you listening to me?"

"Yes, of course. What did he say?" Simon responded quickly. He possessed an ability to snap back from his private thoughts into conversation when somebody uttered anything that called for his attention. He was naturally an exceptionally keen listener, a quality his profession had enhanced.

"He lectured to me about getting down to business this year in my work. I think it was because he'd gotten a call from Matilda Pierleoni, who called him because she wants to see me. I suppose it made him think I'd be up playing in Tuscany like when he visited. But he was really funny because he's never hounded me about studying before. If anything, I've always thought he wished I were less bookish." Watching Simon's face, she detected a veil in his eyes when he heard the name Matilda Pierleoni. *I wonder if he's jealous?* She did not mention her weekend plans.

Walking to his apartment, they lingered for a moment at the bottom of the Spanish Steps so he could point out how great his neighborhood was, the Via Frattina beginning at the lower end of the Piazza di Spagna. On his very first morning at the new apartment, he had gotten up early and walked to the Piazza to see the sun rise. She glanced up at the twin towers of the Trinita Dei Monti and said excitedly, "I've always loved the view of that old church by the side of the Hassler Hotel. Let's go visit it someday, maybe even have lunch at the Hassler?" Actually she was remembering the day Armando had kissed her up on the stair landing just above and how intense that day was. Of course, she didn't mention the kiss; it seemed a lifetime ago. Yet recalling it made her realize she felt distanced from Simon today.

They came through the front door and walked into his living room, and she was thrilled. A large archway led to the kitchen, where ivory lace curtains waving in the breeze from open casement windows caught her eye. The space was light and airy, and the moldings and the elegant mantle were stunning. "Simon, a cardinal might have lived here or any aristocratic Roman. It's elegant yet so cozy!"

"All for you, my darling," he said as she noticed his cute wry smile when he teasingly touched her lightly on her back. She shivered as he grazed his fingers lightly over her strong shoulders. He was keeping his distance because of what was to happen next. It was time for Simon the seducer. "Come with me into the kitchen to see my plants and my new set of fine Italian porcelain dishes."

She followed him eagerly, admiring the soft white marble counters backed by cracked eighteenth-century brown-and-white French tiles with thin blue borders. Sarah thought the color tones were marvelous—cupboards with blue porcelain pulls that matched the tiles, and a delicate, ornate brass gas-electric fixture with lacy topaz shades that hung from the high pressed tin green ceiling.

Slightly salty air blowing in from the balcony rustled her short skirt, something that did not escape Simon's notice as he poured two glasses of white wine from a bottle resting on the marble counter. Clicking his glass with hers, he penetrated her eyes and jolted her. Wispy images of scenes from long ago merged in her mind—watery glimpses of lime green and yellow cork trees on a hillside in southern Portugal. *Who are you? Who are you?*

Gingerly he took her left hand. "You have not yet seen the best part!" He led her from the kitchen into the bedroom and touched her fingers to mauve velvet drapes embossed with trellis patterns that covered the French doors out to the balcony. "Don't they feel exquisite?" he said as he watched her eyes slyly noting his double bed covered with a white coverlet. "The owner has such excellent taste! I didn't even have to buy this stuff myself." She started to feel like a cornered doe ready to bolt but stood there obediently. Simon knew exactly what she was feeling. *She can't help being polite. I haven't had this much fun in my whole damned life!* Taking her hand again, he said, "Come through the hall to see the tiles in the bathroom. They are fantastic."

She followed him through a hallway elegantly finished with built-in drawers and closets—a dressing room for a gentleman. She felt naughty glancing at his red paisley silk robe. Walking into the bathroom, she was taken aback by its outrageous high-Roman décor. The copper tub on claw legs with a high, raised back was perched like an emperor in the tiled alcove. The marble sink set with pewter faucets and porcelain hot and cold knobs was perfect. The porcelain bidet with raised vines and flowers made her feel uncomfortable. Over-the-top burgundy tiles with gilded lions gleamed in the glow from the sconces. Thick butterscotch towels were draped over clear glass rods that ended with glass balls that turned the bathroom upside down. "This is just marvelous, Simon. It's fit for a count!"

"Yes, I agree, and the count is me!" he said in an amused voice. Going back through the hall and the bedroom, they walked out onto the balcony to a small table with a plate of cheese and nuts. Sarah welcomed the salty air. *Whew! I'm glad to be out of there!*

Sarah put her wine glass down beside Simon's, preparing to sit but suddenly he was standing very close to her. Turning her slowly toward himself, he said in a husky tone she'd never heard before, "We are going to have wonderful times here. There is no hurry about anything, but the time is coming when you will know me." Then he pulled her sinuous trembling body close, tilted her face up to his, and penetrated her eyes. He kissed her passionately, penetrating her lips with his tongue for the first time.

She went limp, not resisting because his erotic demand took her totally by surprise. As he kissed her while provocatively massaging her lower back and hips and moving his pelvis subtly against her, waves of intense desire rose in both of them. Feeling dizzy, hot, and helpless, she realized her skirt was barely a handkerchief over a lace thong. The sensations in her sacrum and solar plexus were so strong she could have triggered an earthquake; all she could do was surrender. Simon knew exactly what was going on in her body; so just when she started to stiffen as she always did, he gently disengaged his hold. She'd never resisted any move he'd made, and that's how he intended to keep it. Also he was getting hard in spite of visualizing William's face to control himself.

He brushed his lips lightly on her forehead while he mastered his breath by clenching his hands into fists. Then he just held her while she rested her head in the crook of his taut neck. She detected what he was trying to hide and wanted to reach for it. Without saying a word, they both sat down at the little table.

In a voice so quiet Simon had to strain to hear it, Sarah said, "You will never know how much your patience means to me. I have so much to do right now, and I have to focus. It is a joy to think of the wonderful times we're going to have here." For a third time, he penetrated her eyes with new intensity, then his mind snapped with an insight, as if something had reached into his brain and grabbed him. *I knew her a long time ago! But when, where? Why am I so determined to protect her, to watch over her?*

She looked away into the courtyard. *I'm beginning to think I will marry him. In fact, I think I will. Maybe I will marry him just because he knows how to let me have my own time, my own space.*

The air was sultry on Shelter Island that September. The beach smelled of rotting kelp and salty clams after three days of dead calm—hurricane weather. Close to midnight Simon's parents relaxed in Adirondack chairs with firm canvas cushions. Rose enjoyed a tart 2004 Malbec from Chile while David smoked a small hand-rolled joint, rather unusual behavior in the Appel house in recent years. Excessive humidity and the mirror-flat sea were boring, but tonight's conversation was not.

"I heard from Simon late this afternoon, and he seems to be very happy," David said, expelling the sweet smoke from deep inside his lungs. "He loves his wild apartment; Sarah does too. It sounds too Baroque to me, too gushy, high Italian, but the balcony over an interior courtyard would make the place for me."

"I still can't believe what you told me about your conversation with Simon. Knowing my son, I'm surprised he's so enamored with a virgin. Who did you even know who was a virgin past age twenty-one? Anybody?" Rose said.

"Certainly not you! But I wasn't looking for that by the time I found you. I don't think that has anything to do with why he is so taken with her. In fact, I think he wishes it *weren't* an issue. But I think this is the first time he's fallen deeply in love. They have a lot in common through work, she's lovely, he enjoys her family, and we both like her. That's a pretty good score these days." He took a deep drag on the joint, feeling a warm, fuzzy tingling above his eyebrows. "I mean, hell, she could have pewter nose rings, purple hair, a dragon tattoo, and black mesh stockings with a skirt up to her ass!"

Rose chuckled, wondering whether David had told her everything about his conversation with Simon. She was happy her son and husband shared frankly with each other, but he often left her out. "Do you think she's frigid? Or maybe she's a lesbian and hasn't figured it out yet? She didn't seem cold when she was here, but, I mean, she is twenty-five years old! She should have had at least three good lovers by now, especially considering her looks! Come on, David, you've talked to him. What does he say? I am going to get worried if Simon is this much in love and then gets rejected over sex they haven't even had. Is this the way Catholics act now? When I was in college, most of the Catholic girls were more sluttish than the Jewish girls, and that was saying something! The Jewish girls really liked sex once they started. The Catholic girls were easy lays, then they felt guilty until the next time."

David was really stoned, a great way to feel on a sultry evening in late summer. Images of hot sex flowed through his mind while he listened to Rose. He replied, "Wellllll, maybe she doesn't want the guilt; maybe that's why. But she is human and he's a very hot guy, a man that any smart woman would love to have. So now that he has his own apartment, I bet this won't last long. I'm sure you haven't forgotten how it was with us. You behaved a lot better than most of the girls I dated, didn't give in for weeks. I was impressed by that and thought you must be somebody." He smiled lazily. "But I know your story. You used to get laid on the first night if you liked a guy, but then you changed when you wanted to get married. You wanted respect when I met you, so you caught my attention in the middle of a string of easy girls. But you didn't hold out once you were sure about me. And all these years later, I'm still hot for you, which shows how great good sex can be."

David always talked a lot when he was stoned and Rose was all ears. Even after all these years, she still found out new things about him. He went on, "You made me wait until I was thinking about fucking Margaret Mary McGuire just to offload my horns. I think you sensed it because I will never forget the night you just led me upstairs when everybody was gone in the house you were staying in for the summer. I can still remember every single moment of that night, the night when I went deeper and deeper into you until I lost myself. It must have been hours!"

He was making her feel warm and fuzzy, as did the wine and the aroma of marijuana. "Yes, something just came over me. I just had to have you even if it meant you'd drop me. All my strategies ended when you kissed me in the hallway. As soon as you embraced me that night, it was over. It was a wonderful first love with you, an incredible way to find the person you want to spend your life with. I want Simon to have that. I want him to have a woman he loves."

While Rose spoke, David was seeing a slim woman with long hair walking down a long stone hallway with a man at the end watching her approach. Simon was standing in a round temple with large columns. The woman was very young, just a girl. She walked to Simon with her eyes raised up to his face and handed him a sprig of laurel tied with a soft red wool tie. She knelt, then rose and turned around, and he watched her go back down the hallway. David knew the girl was Sarah. "I think she's the one for him, Rose, I really do. I can feel things. She isn't frigid. She is very spiritual, so she struggles with the ugliness and tawdriness of the world. Something in her is keeping her from giving herself. Maybe she's afraid of losing her spiritual qualities, and Simon doesn't want to take anything from her.

He carefully snuffed out the joint and placed it in a nearby ashtray. "What I haven't told you because I didn't want you to worry is that Simon is worried about another guy, a Roman aristocrat who is hot after her. He feels like the guy is dangerous because he's older and very sophisticated. He's afraid the guy will do anything to get her. That's why I wanted to support him by releasing some of his inheritance, to let him start making a home to show Sarah he's ready to settle down, be in things for the long term. I think he's right about that guy, and I also think he is going to be in a battle over her very soon."

"Well, if that's what is going on, Simon will win. He always gets what he wants when he's determined." Rose sighed. "If she were Jewish, I'd feel better. I know he's had trouble with the families of non-Jewish girls he dated. Her family really seems to like him though, so I think he will win out. Any girl who gets him is lucky. Some other guy is not going to outfox Simon," she said emphatically.

"Only time will tell," David replied. He eyed her wickedly. "Let's go to bed."

17

The Lady of Villa Giulia

Once again Sarah admired the Tuscan landscape as they came up the drive to Castel Vetulonia. She felt peculiar as they drove through the arched entry. *I wonder if I'm making a mistake?* Guido parked in the back and said she could go right to the library for refreshments before lunch. Not quite ready, she first went up the wide staircase to her room, relieved not to see anyone right away. As she quietly closed the bedroom door, the beautiful old room welcomed her again. She splashed cold water on her face, touched up her lipstick and eye makeup, smoothed her pants, and then went over to the tower window to see the view she remembered so well. A bouquet of white roses dusted by a touch of pink perched on the dresser. She went to smell them and noticed the card signed, "Joyful to be with you again, Armando." A sense of unease spread through her. *Was he in my room this morning?*

When Sarah came into the library, the family was in front of the tall mantle. Noting her arrival with a catlike knowing smile, Armando had already registered the exact moment she'd stepped into the back hall. Standing by his father, he appraised her as she approached his mother for greetings. Pietro took in her beauty as an experienced gentleman. Her fair Celtic skin had a becoming touch of summer color.

Armando's dark eyes caught hers as she went to Matilda to take her hand. *There is a new complexity in her face. What happened this summer?*

"Oh, Sarah, how kind of you to come," gushed Matilda. "Was the drive comfortable? Guido always gets people here on time. You look lovely as always. You glow."

"Thank you, the drive was easy and comfortable, and I'm so happy to be here in Tuscany with you." She kissed Matilda lightly on each cheek while Matilda sniffed the aroma of summer roses. *I must ask her about her perfume.* Matilda and Sarah turned to Armando and Pietro by the fireplace. Sarah took Pietro's wizened hand while he kissed her on both cheeks, dusting her face with his mustache. Then she turned to face Armando. He grasped her bare upper arms firmly, saying, "Welcome to our home again, Sarah. It is so kind of you to come visit us on such short notice."

As he held her below her shoulders, she glanced into his intense dark eyes. *I have forgotten how handsome and striking he is, so magnetic.* He projected fire into her groin, outrageously violating her. She experienced vertigo as the room swirled wildly around her body. Matilda stared at them, thinking, *What a well-matched attractive couple; they will steal the show in Rome.*

He wore a rumpled honey-colored linen suit with his fine white linen shirt casually unbuttoned half way down to a black Florentine leather belt. She glimpsed blue-black, shiny chest hair and detected the pungent odor of patchouli and lavender as he smiled an enigmatic, partial smile.

Sarah blurted out, "I've come to see the painting. Can we all see it before lunch? Oh, Armando, thank you for the lovely roses."

This uncharacteristic demand and abruptness intrigued Matilda, but of course the painting was the subject at hand.

"Ah, Sarah, my darling, not so easy yet," Armando said, reaching for a crystal tumbler of scotch on the mantle. "First, what will you have before lunch?" He signaled to a maid as soon as she said white wine, and then he replied. "Since you are my subject, first you must view it with me alone and then we will see it with my parents. These are my rules."

"Oh, Armando, you are giving us all such a difficult time," his mother broke in. "I can't imagine why we all can't just see the painting!"

"Mother, dear, as Sarah has discovered, there is a hidden reality in my work, and she is one of the few who sees it. I don't want anyone else to see her likeness before she discovers its hidden reality. Then anybody can see it," declared the artist. "After lunch, Sarah, will you come to my studio with me?"

Of course there was nothing else she could do but agree, so Pietro offered a toast to the first viewing to come after lunch, and they clicked their glasses in front of the fireplace. They shared a wonderful lunch of slightly warmed fresh vegetables right out of the garden and milk-fed veal in a white sauce spiced with rosemary. After finishing with lemon sherbet and Pietro's aged grappa, the time had come. Walking into the great hall entrance of the castle and glancing up the curving stairs, Armando said, "After such a long drive, would you first like a nap?"

She felt really peculiar. She could just say yes, go up the stairs, and lie down to collect herself. But she was so curious about the painting she replied, "No, thank you, Armando. I really want to see it now, so may we?"

They climbed the many stairs to the top of the ancient tower and pushed the heavy door open. It was hot, so he took off his linen jacket while indicating a chair for her by a small table. He got up on a ladder to open the dormer windows to the north while she looked around the studio. She noticed an easel holding a covered canvas. That must be the painting. There was a dark red velvet divan to the far right of the painting that resembled a psychiatrist couch. I wonder if he uses that thing for posing nude models? He walked past the canvas and sat down on the second chair by the little table.

"I have some really good Chianti up here. Would you like to share some with me before I pull the cloth? Perhaps you will be less nervous if we have wine?"

"No," she said. "It would be too much for me since we had grappa after lunch." He brought a ruby red bottle with a single glass as she said, "Should I close my eyes?"

"First I want to talk," he said, putting his glass down and leaning back in his chair. He was breathing deeply while tensing his fine arm muscles. "Sarah, this moment means more to me than you may realize. I cannot do this unless you understand that I care for you; I care for you very much."

Sitting primly in the rickety old wooden chair, Sarah felt heat rise in her lower spine into her middle back and warm her chest. Armando was intrigued by the subtle shades of pink flushing her cheeks like the touch of pink in the white roses in her room. She turned to him, looking boldly into his eyes as if she wanted an answer from him. Putting one arm on the table with her hand turned up as if she had something for him, she asked, "Exactly what do you mean?"

After a long pause, he said, "Well, I did not paint you exactly as you were in June; I painted you as a woman. You have to understand this before I show it to you. When I say I care for you, I, ah . . . " As he struggled to express himself, her anxiety grew. *Why doesn't he just say what he wants to say? I can't imagine what he is getting at. Why is he so nervous?*

Armando went on. "I care for you, deeply. I'm old enough to know what I want and I can offer you more than most women could ever imagine—a life of outrageous beauty if it is what you want. But for now, this painting and what you find in it is important to me, my first attempt with you. Forgive my poor English. Because this matters so much to me, will you grant me one important request, only one?"

Hmmmm. I forget that he speaks four languages, no wonder he expresses himself so awkwardly sometimes. Still, I can't figure out what he's after. Something odd is going on. It seems silly to be afraid of him, especially since his parents are so nearby. Funny, sometimes he seems so immature. Though she sensed she could be making a mistake, she replied in a firm voice, "Of course I can honor one important request before we view the painting."

"All right. Will you promise me that no matter what you see, you will study the painting long enough to detect its hidden meaning? That is all I ask of you."

"I will. After all, that is what I am looking for. But before that, you still have not answered my question. What are you trying to say about caring for me? How can I grasp the hidden meaning in the painting without understanding what you are trying to say? If you care for me in a way that I cannot return, then this adventure ends right now and I should go." Her muscles were sending flight signals into her brain.

"Then I will tell you something important," he said, drawing her green eyes into his.

Sarah shifted in her chair. His intensity and neediness were making her nervous.

Armando continued, holding her gaze. "If you can see below the surface of this painting and I believe you can, then you will discover your essence. Finding this pearl will mean more to you than anything in your life. I found you by painting you. I found something you will never discover without me showing it to you." As he spoke, he pulled his male power into his root by flexing his inner thigh muscles. This power penetrated her sacrum, making her feel caught.

Poised on the tightrope suspended between her long-forgotten feminine mystery and the self-control she devoutly practiced, she was ready to fall into a dark zone of awareness that was much richer emotionally than anything she'd ever felt. *I am Persephone in Hades.* This pulsing, throbbing dark place resonated in her parasympathetic nerves when she detected the hook in her groin. *Armando's eyes rip me open, revealing corridors of dark broken mirrors that reflect moon-light. Danger!* She replied in a shaky low voice, "I don't know what to say; I really don't." *I'm vacant, my mind isn't working, and something is being taken away from me just by sitting here. My father is right, my father is right . . . My brain is oceanic, my body thrashes.*

His sensual Italian accent crept into the back of her skull, "Sarah. Do you know how beautiful you are, that every man in the room wants to see as much of you as they can? That is my enigma, my, ah, intrigue. When I paint a home, a woman, or a tree, I show its essence, but only if I have grasped its true beauty first. I have to strip away everything to find the center. You've discovered this in my work, which is why I want to offer my life to you. But first I had to find your center, your essence. Your surface beauty made it nearly impossible to get into that deeper part of you, but I did. I found the place you can discover only with me. To find you, there was only one way I could do it. I ask you to accept it, otherwise, you will judge me unfairly."

The relationship between surface beauty and pure inner spirit had always intrigued her. As he spoke in a soft, mellifluous voice, she knew she was being seduced. When he pulled back and appealed to her highly developed artistic sensibilities, her mind engaged. *This afternoon is so tense and difficult. He keeps pulling me down into deep emotional layers, special places I only share with those who allow me to feel safe. But I don't want to misjudge him. This odd conversation would be over without this shrouded canvas, his bargaining chip, the third person in this conversation. The painting probably knows all about what Armando wants!* Her response to his question about her beauty took him completely by surprise. "Armando, I know a lot of people think I am beautiful, but I do not think of myself that way. I am not identified with my surface. I am lucky to have beauty as God's gift, but I care only about what is in my heart."

He realized she believed what she said, so he replied, "Well, then, maybe that is why I knew I had to strip away your surface. Maybe your beauty won't shock you; I hope so. Are you ready to see your-self?" She nodded in assent as he got up to go to the easel. She had expected to be brave and nonchalant about how he'd portrayed her, yet now she found she was afraid. Grandly, like a matador taunting the bull, he whisked off the cloth and stood beside his creation with his cape lowered, waiting for the charge.

Sarah stared at the image of the nude on the divan as if she were viewing a bold painting of a beautiful woman by a great artist like Goya. Her mind, with its deep understanding of art, took in every detail while every cell in her body electrified as if she'd been struck by lightning. Pink excited nipples, seductive luscious curves, soft brown hair at the base of her thighs, and her commanding radiant face with green eyes revealing the wisdom of the ages blinded her. Armando stood next to his painting with his hands at his sides, the artist waiting for approval.

Her cells screamed. *Whatever this image is supposed to be, I am not ready for it.* Then a deep and angry voice growled through her strangled throat, "How dare you, how dare you? Why have you done this to me? I did not agree to this!" She stood up and lunged for the door.

Desperate, he rushed to cut her off as she rose. He was so used to doing as he pleased that he had never truly considered that she would be angry—judgmental maybe, but not *angry*. Clutching her right shoulder roughly, he pulled her body to his and grasped her with both hands as he pleaded, "You caaann't go! You promised to study this painting to find its essence. You are not being fair; you *promised* me!" Then he pulled her to his tense body with desperate flashing eyes.

She smelled sulfur, and paralyzing fear swamped her mind. *Maybe he is crazy. What am I going to do?* "You don't understand," she snapped. "I can't look at the painting because I cannot get past the surface, the conjuring of me in the nude. I can't see anything beyond that and neither will anybody else."

He clutched her closer, hurting her arms as she struggled to jerk herself away, but he was very strong. Snarling into her face, he said, "That is *exactly* what I mean. *That* is the surface beauty everybody sees. They strip you nude with their eyes to do whatever they want, like when I took you to the Doria Pamphili. That is what you don't understand, sexual desire. You torture men just by being in the same room; they rape you with their eyes. Welcome to the real world, Sarah. It's ugly."

Oh god, I feel weak, like a victim in the claws of a monster. I've got to keep my brain going to avoid total panic. Armando glanced back at the canvas and felt his penis get suddenly hard from a shocking inner explosion that blinded him with white light. Power surged in his groin, shooting hot energy up his back as he became a rod and his shoulders grew great black wings that turned into steel. Struggling to escape his grasp, she twisted violently to see his face. Blood flooded the whites of his eyes; his mouth distorted. He grabbed the sides of her face and pulled her face to his, crushing her lips, plunging his tongue into her mouth. More fire hardened his penis when her breasts touched his partially bare chest. He gyrated his bursting erection against her soft pelvis and pubic bone, out of control with the most potent sexual desire of his life.

Gasping for breath, she struggled with the pressure of his pelvis jamming her backward toward the divan. She clutched for his hair, but that turned him on even more as he rubbed his rock-hard penis more forcefully against her pubis and began moving it up and down. She fell backward on the divan, nearly cracking her head as the blur of the nude painting flashed by. Pinning her with his pelvis, he rose up triumphantly with his outer thighs pushing her legs painfully open. Stretching her legs open even more violently with her back flattened against the back of the divan, he tore at her blouse. She tried to knee him, but he had immobilized her legs with his own. Wrenching the blouse off her right shoulder, he pulled off her bra and pressed down harder on her groin. Pinning her wrists with one hand, he massaged her bare breast and tongued and sucked her stiffening nipple. *Oh god!* Sarah thought with a rising mixture of panic and shame. *I'm getting excited!* He was biting her while his rotating pelvis rubbed her inner thighs. "You are hurting me," she cried desperately.

"Don't worry; it won't last much longer," he growled into her neck. "I'm going to take you, take you all the way because I want you. If you resist, I will hurt you more, hurt you a lot. If you allow me, I will make love to you. It's your choice."

"You can't do this," she cried angrily. Armando put his free hand over her mouth and shoved her face back against the divan. She felt like her neck was going to break. Pinning her tightly with his legs and pushing her face harder, he rose up and arched back to unzip himself with his right hand. She was terrified because she couldn't get out of his strong grip and couldn't breathe. When he pulled out his huge throbbing erection, she bit his hand hard, causing him to release her face as she screamed, "You are a Fallen Angel!" The thought had come subconsciously from the deep recesses of her faith and her feminine intuition—the same intuition that had been giving her warning signs since Matilda called the previous day, and even before that. Suddenly she was not helpless. With her chest heaving, she wrenched her pelvis and cried out, "Jesus! Jesus! Jesus, help me!"

As she named Armando for what he was and cried out to Jesus, weakness flowed into his legs, the blood sucked out of his penis, and his reptilian wings receded. As he softened, she shoved him hard on the chest, pushing his legs off with her knees, kneeing him contemptuously. Collapsing down, grabbing the side of the divan and holding his crotch, he gasped, "What did you say? What did you say about a Fallen Angel and Jesus?"

Sarah pulled her blouse back together, stood up, and stumbled out of the studio. "You will never get a chance to try that again, and you are never to show that painting to anyone. Destroy it immediately."

———

Pulling the rest of her clothes back in order as she went, she ran down the stairs to the back of the castle, relieved she did not run into anyone on the way to her room. She went inside, shut the door, and locked it. She drew a hot bath and soaked in it, scrubbing off his smell and tenderly washing her violated breast. Massaging her pelvis erased his imprint, and she reflected on her own part in the drama. *I am not innocent.* She slipped into a white bathrobe, crawled into the enveloping canopy, and stared at the tendrils of vines, leaves, and delicate flowers. *This room comforts me; beautiful rooms have often sheltered violated women. I will be all right. I've had a few tussles like this before but nothing went as far as this one. Thank god he didn't rape me.*

She considered talking to Matilda. But Armando was her oldest son, and Sarah knew Matilda hoped she would marry him. *How can I get out of here?* Looking over her arms and legs, she only found bruises on her inner thighs. *Maybe I can manage to be a decent dinner guest,* she hoped as she drew herself out of the tub. Just then there was a quiet rap on the door, and a maid's voice said, "Miss, miss, I have a note for you." She took the note and opened it. On white paper embossed with the family crest, it said:

> *Sarah. All I can do is apologize. I was taken over by an evil force that I don't understand. No one will ever see the painting, I promise you. I hope you still can attend dinner with my parents tonight? I planned to ask you to marry me today. Perhaps knowing that, you can forgive me someday? I know you will never be my wife because I do not deserve you. But I hope you can continue to be our family friend, especially in light of my mother's fondness for you. Please don't break her heart.*
>
> *With absolute respect and humility,*
>
> *Armando*

Sarah let the note fall from her hand and left it on the floor where it fell. Despite the comfortable temperature of the room, she began to shiver. With mechanical motions, she set the alarm for dinner time and crawled under the soft covers. It seemed like only ten minutes later when the alarm sounded. Still in shock, she was determined to go to dinner and do her best to act normally. She slipped into a demure gray dress with a high square neck that she always wore with her aunt's long pearls. They met again in the library, and this time she joined Pietro in a double scotch, hoping he could charm her.

Matilda noticed Sarah seemed to be nervous. *Something must have happened that was too intense, something negative.* When Armando came to join his father, Matilda took Sarah's arm and asked her to come sit in the window seat. "My dear, tell me, did you see the painting, and do you like it? I feel like you are upset about something. Is it the painting?"

Sarah stared at the ground, her mind blank. She had no idea what to say, but Armando, who was listening with his fox ears, hurried over after handing his father another drink and said, "Well, Mother, I have bad news. Sarah does not like the painting! That is her prerogative since I altered it from the photo." Matilda eyed him ruefully, noting he looked like he'd been crying. *What is going on with these two? Something, but I cannot ask.*

"Well, that's too bad, Sarah. Why don't you like it?"

Armando was about to break in again when Sarah volunteered, "It's not a painting of me, not at all. I don't want anyone to see it, not ever."

Dinner was quiet and intense, with food being consumed amidst strained conversations that would not go anywhere. Neither Pietro nor Matilda could imagine what was going on. After dinner, Armando asked Sarah to speak with him in the library in private. Sarah agreed reluctantly, reminding herself that his parents were in the next room. As she followed him into the library, she noticed he seemed diminished. Dropping into the bay window seat with the rising moon behind him bringing silver light to the deep blue night sky, Armando said, "I will never see you again. My only hope is that you will forgive me. This is very sad for me. I want to show you something to prove my sincerity. Sometimes I just get out of control and become a rake, but I am not a liar. May I?" She assented by nodding her head as she looked at his sad, resigned eyes. *He has been crying.*

He brought out a small velvet ring case and opened it. Her eyes fell on a ten-carat deep emerald set between two diamonds. "I have never thought of marriage until I met you. This is what I wanted to give you today if you appreciated my painting and wanted to share life with me. I have abandoned that hope. We must say good-bye, yet is there anything you want to say to *me?*"

She sat in silence, thinking these circumstances couldn't be further from what she had imagined for a proposal of marriage. Like most girls, once she had dreamed of being a princess who grew up to become a queen. Why did her first proposal have to be so tainted? The thought of how this could have gone if Armando hadn't acted the way he did passed through her mind. *What would it be like to wear a ring like that? What would it be like to be sequestered in the Tuscan aristocracy and be loved by a man like Armando? He would have loved me if I became his wife; he would change. What would it be like to bear children in this ancient lineage? I am partly responsible for what happened today because I was attracted to him and what he offers and I didn't listen to my instincts.*

Sarah was troubled by what she saw as her own complicity in the terrible scene in Armando's studio, yet no matter what had happened there, she kept coming to the same conclusion. *I would never marry him because I don't trust him. Having sex with him would probably be incredible but dangerous. I wish I'd done it with somebody by now so I'd know what it's like and how to handle these feelings. If he hadn't attacked me I might have surrendered, forgotten my misgivings and fallen into the folds of the deep past. It would be nice to live here in this castle, sheltered from the ugly world, but that's not really possible, not with him.* She brought her gaze to meet his, seeing that he still held the box open in his right hand in case she'd take it. "You have become selfish and immoral over many years, and I hope this experience will be the last of it. Even if you change, I will not be in your life. I hope I will be able to forgive you someday because I understand you didn't want to act like that." She dropped her gaze down to the bruised thighs hidden underneath her dress. "But not yet."

Sarah raised her eyes to his again. "You're right, though. There is one thing I want to ask you. You are the artist, so what is the hidden meaning in the painting?"

Armando responded eagerly, "Oh, that's easy, Sarah. I found the part of you that is ready to surrender as a woman. The exquisite nude expresses your readiness, the beauty of a woman on the threshold of love. I captured you though I've never seen you. I lost control and panicked when I realized you would go away forever. Like the rape of the Sabines by my ancestors, I tried to take you. If I had succeeded, you would be wearing my ring tonight. The first man who takes you will have you forever. I captured your desire for love in the painting, a masterpiece. Do you know that about yourself?" he wondered as he slowly closed the box and put it back in his inner jacket pocket.

Sarah broke through her shock to respond emphatically, "I wish every woman could be safe enough to surrender to love, but the way you acted today is the reason we have to be so armored. Women are taken easily and then discarded before they have any idea how special they are. Armando, this is the twenty-first century. You would not have me if you had succeeded today. Nobody is going to take me away from myself."

Pietro's and Matilda's quarters were in the castle wing over the library. It had been built in the fifteenth century, a time when

Tuscany was peaceful. The worn stone floors were covered with thick oriental rugs. Damask drapes on the great canopy bed could be closed to ward off the damp and penetrating cold. Moonlight shining through ancient lead casement windows cast geometrical patterns on the velvet settee in a small sitting area in an alcove under thick ancient beams. Matilda spoke quietly and reflectively, "Something is wrong, Pietro. She is perfect for him; he wants her, yet I feel like it will never be."

Pietro said sadly, "I think it is the times. Armando can have anything he wants, any money, any body, any thing. Not realizing how precious she is, he probably didn't woo her with the long haul in mind. He probably hasn't even thought about the children we need in this family. She is younger than he is, but she is much wiser. She needs an old soul with great character, and that just isn't Armando. I am sorry about it. I am afraid our generation is one that is to have few, if any, grandchildren because people have forgotten how to live."

18

The Ruby Crystal

Sarah stared listlessly out the car window, trying to forget about the medieval tower as they crept along in the snarled traffic of Rome's perimeter. *I feel disembodied.* Massive old stone buildings—unmemorable ghosts like the meaningless and repetitive thoughts running through her mind—passed by, reflected on the hazy glass separating her from Guido in front. *How many millions live here who barely get through the day? I am empty, broken, trapped in someone else's nightmare. All I want to do is get to my apartment and go to sleep; I want to sleep.*

Simon had been calling Sarah constantly all weekend. By Sunday afternoon he was frantic; he knew something was wrong. *Where is she? It isn't like her to just disappear.* Could she be in the library? But even then, he reasoned, she'd have her cell phone with her. He decided to call her number once more before concluding something serious was going on. This time she answered.

"Where have you been all weekend?" he asked, his tight voice betraying his anxiety. "I have been calling you five times a day. I was beginning to get seriously worried."

"I'm sorry, Simon," she responded. "As soon as I got back after seeing you last week, Matilda Pierleoni called and persuaded me to go up to Tuscany for the weekend to see Armando's painting, the one he made of me during the summer. Armando wouldn't let anybody see it until I saw it first. So I agreed to go even though I wasn't sure I wanted to see Armando again. I rushed out and forgot to take my cell phone with me."

She had been with Armando! "Well, that will have to be that," Simon said, trying not to sound as crushed as he felt. "So how is the painting?"

"I did not like it at all. It horrified me, so I want to forget about it," she said, her voice flat and peculiar.

I just want to sleep, she thought.

After a twenty-second silence, Simon was alarmed. "Sarah, is something wrong? You don't sound quite like yourself. Did something happen this weekend that upset you?" He waited.

She was sitting in her window seat, completely unaware of any light or beauty in the room. *My lower body aches; my mind is dull.* She was so devoid of feeling that she came close to clicking off the phone. Simon's voice sounded like it was coming through a metallic tube. "Sarah, what is the matter? Tell me what is wrong?"

She is like a gray shroud floating away to a distant shore. He said in a firm voice, "Sarah, listen to me. I am coming over to see you right away. I have never been up to your apartment, but I expect you to ring me in when I get there. I will be there in fifteen minutes. Wait for me, stay there, and answer the bell. Make sure you answer the bell when I ring it." Then he hung up and rushed out to grab a cab in the Piazza Di Spagna.

Sarah dropped the phone. *I am turning to stone.* She barely heard the bell ringing in her head. She recalled Simon telling her to answer it when he arrived, so she muttered the number and opened the door. Simon rushed in, scanning her eyes. She seemed to be barely aware of him as she vaguely indicated the window seat. *I wonder if he drugged her? Bastard!* He sat down next to her and pulled her close under his arm. "What is the matter? You must tell me."

His cradling touch released her tight breath. *He's in my room; it doesn't matter. Just hold me while I sleep.* Relaxing back on the plush velvet pillow, Simon pulled her closer so that she snuggled into him with her head resting on his chest. He pulled a small blanket over both of them and they curled into each other. Then she said in a flat voice, "Armando tried to rape me after he showed me the painting."

Simon's adrenaline rose, but he controlled himself because he knew he had to handle this exactly right. He said in a level voice, "Just talk to me about it. I only want you to be okay. Tell me what happened and maybe I can help you with it, whatever it is."

A distant part of her came back, a small fragment. *It is the part of me that jumped out of my body when he slammed me against the divan and was pushing on me.* Her hands reached out as if grasping for something as he held her. He wondered if she was having a vision. A magnetic form that he could not see was floating in front of both of them, a form of herself that she could feel. *I see my room and my window in the kitchen, so I can tell him.* Her voice got stronger as she said, "Just before I left Rome at the beginning of summer, he photographed me on the hallway divan wearing a blue dress so that he could paint me. But, when he pulled the cloth off the canvas, there I was as a nude! He has never seen me; it wasn't me. He used his anatomical genius to concoct a shocking, lurid form of me. I never agreed to that! The painting raped me! I should not have gone to his studio. Then things got very scary, very fast." Her vocal cords tightened; her hands went to her throat.

"Sarah, just keep going. I want to know exactly what happened and you must tell me now. You have to share everything so that it doesn't go deep into your consciousness, especially into your heart. No matter what you had to do, you must share this with me." *That rotten bastard. How dare he pull something like that and then attack her. The guy is sick, a psycho. Oh my god, what did he do to her?*

She spoke in a low but determined voice while gazing fixedly at the blue-white image of her spirit suspended in front of them. "He is really strong and crazy. He has always gotten whatever he wants, so when he's stymied he goes off like a madman. I saw this tendency once before, but this time I was terrified. I felt like a weak lamb about to be flayed when he shoved me back onto a red divan next to the painting. He forced my legs apart and it hurt! I started screaming, so he shoved his hand over my mouth and kept spreading my legs apart. I bit his hand. He jerked and winced, and then he crushed my face harder with his hand while he unzipped his pants with his free hand. He tore my blouse and bra off and I got mad. My back was screaming, yet my body flooded with hot energy. It sickens me now to recall that feeling—lust was pulling me down into hell." Her voice lowered to a whisper. "I looked at him as he exposed himself; I wanted it." She started to sob quietly, her hands twitching.

Angry blackness boiled in Simon's heart. *I only care about one thing. I want her to get through this and not be damaged by it; my father sure knew what he was talking about.* She began to shake as he pulled her closer while softly stroking her hair. She paused to breathe as he said, "Just tell me. What happened does not matter to me, only whether it hurt you. It's normal to feel desire; many women do. You should not feel guilty about it. You are a sensual woman and sexual urges are primal. Please continue, Sarah."

She relaxed against the wired tension of his body and thought about Simon for the first time. *This must be terrible for him.* When she thought of his feelings, her magnetic double merged with her. *I know where I am now; I can see my room.* "He bit my bare breast and it hurt," she said, her voice hard and disgusted. "He pushed against my crotch, using his hardness as a weapon. He snarled and said he was going to take me, and my only choice was to have it hurt or enjoy it. He growled at me and tried to force me to look at his face by gripping my jaw, saying he liked it either way. Then suddenly I saw his face, the contorted face of a possessed demon! My desire went away and I named him as a Fallen Angel and screamed for Jesus to help me, and he stopped; he just stopped! Maybe I kneed him; I don't remember. His strength sucked out and I got away from him. I got out of there and crawled back to my room.

She was speaking more normally now. "I bathed and slept and tried to recover because I didn't want to leave the Pierleonis abruptly. I have known them for so long. I did not want to make a scene. I didn't know how to act or what to do, except to try to act as normally as possible. I almost feel sorry for them that their oldest son acts this way. My manners barely got me through dinner—I was like a zombie—and I left early this morning. I started to feel peculiar while driving into Rome. All I wanted to do was come here to sleep. Armando proposed to me after dinner. The whole thing is a blur in my mind. He said that was what he planned to do in the studio, but he lost control when I got angry. He is sorry and I accepted his apology. Of course, that is the last time I will ever see him. He needs professional help."

A great wave of relief overcame Simon, since he had prepared himself for the worst. *The creep would've drugged her to get what he wanted, the bastard.* It horrified him to think how this monster could have hurt her, since he knew plenty about what guys like Armando do. He said softly, "I am so relieved that it wasn't the worst. But you know what? I love you no matter what happens to you. You handled this so well and now it is over. I've been worried about this guy ever since you mentioned him on the porch in Boston. It doesn't matter you responded! You are very sensual because you're ready for sex. This readiness has been growing since the day I met you by the Villa Cumae. It doesn't mean you wanted it to happen that way or that you are to blame.

He gently stroked her forehead. "Even if he'd gotten away with it, you'd still belong with me and we would work it out. We are going to be together for the rest of our lives; that is what matters. I've been so worried about this creep that I told my father about him! My father could feel the danger. But now he's gone and you will never have to deal with him again. You are my delight, and I am patiently waiting for you. As soon as you are ready to be my wife, we will marry. All you have to do is tell me when you are ready." As he gently stroked her forehead, he could see Sarah was becoming drowsy. *She probably didn't hear me say I want to marry her!* While she was still slightly awake, he said, "If I put you to bed, will you be all right if I go home? Or shall I stay with you and sleep in the window seat?" She told him she would be okay, and she was fast asleep in her small bed when he slipped out the door. *This is her sacred space, her sanctuary, for as long as she needs it.*

Simon walked very fast through the dark Roman streets. He didn't like being out late in the city when the streets and alleyways were filled with prostitutes. As he walked by the Via Condotti his eyes were caught by the sultry gaze of a young prostitute in fishnet stockings, tall boots, and a miniskirt barely covering her crotch. Gorgeous large breasts visible almost to the nipples in a tight red low-necked sweater glowed shockingly white under the streetlight. Her hungry dark eyes and sensual red mouth easily lured him. As she caught his glance, she slipped her hand down to her crotch. All this happened in slow motion, and Simon felt a sharp cringe in his balls. Sucking in his breath while turning away from her knowing eyes, he pulled out a bill and tossed it to her and moved on at a faster pace. The bill distracted her so she didn't follow him. *Oh god! I am too horny!*

The next morning Simon called his father to share what was going on in case he had any advice. David was not surprised, since he'd been plagued with dreams of Sarah in a painter's studio. When Simon finished, David said, "I have an engagement ring for you, and I have been waiting for the right time to send it to you. It will come by special courier in case you can use it. I think you should propose right away. I won't tell your mother because she'll get too excited, but you should waste no time. You can have a long engagement, but I think this is what you should do now. Watch her carefully to see if she is still upset, but I think she will be okay because he didn't get away with it. That crummy bastard! Damned lecherous Italian men!"

The family heirloom arrived just before the fall equinox, and Simon was intrigued. *My dad is really something; I never know what he'll have up his sleeve.* He sat down on the small couch in the living room while the lace curtains in the kitchen rustled in the breeze. Before opening the box, he read the note:

Dear Simon,

This ring belonged to my grandmother, Emily Levi, the first very wealthy woman in our family back in the 1880s. It is a ten-carat star ruby. She obtained it in India and set it in twenty-two-carat gold with small diamonds. It will guide Sarah. It has been waiting for a long time, so it has very special energy. I do hope Sarah will accept it.

Love, Dad

Simon stared at the ruby for a long time. Its purple-red color reminded him of fine port. Light refraction formed a small spinning spiral that sent out six lines of light like a blue star. Staring into the spiral, he heard a whispery voice say *The Ruby Crystal*. He looked more intently at a vision in the tiny light: white flashes swirled into a mist around a golden Buddha in an ancient rock shrine, the Adi Buddha of the Himalayas twelve thousand years ago. The Buddha looked back at Simon with an enigmatic smile. *I see it! This ruby was the third-eye stone of the ancient golden Buddha! Somehow this precious gem has come down through our family.* Holding it to his forehead above his eyebrows, his brain imprinted his intention: *this is for Sarah and she will be mine for the rest of my life while we live in the golden world.*

As the 2012 fall equinox approached, world events became truly chaotic. New Age fanatics ranted about the end of the Mayan Calendar, Christian fanatics predicted the end of the world, and normally rational people joked nervously about both. Many thought the ancient Maya really had forecast something catastrophic in 2012.

Yet how could *that* be? The world seemed to be holding its breath. Eurozone financial tension reached agonizing levels with huge demonstrations against banks and governments in many European cities. Angry crowds of unemployed and desperate people clashed with police. Middle Eastern tensions intensified to frightening levels. Four members of the U.S. consulate were murdered in Benghazi, Libya, while a civil war ravaged Syria that many feared could ignite a wider war in the Middle East. Western economic sanctions destabilized Iran while Israel threatened to bomb Iran's nuclear facilities. Catastrophic droughts and terrible fires exacerbated the great tension. In Rome amid severe economic tension, scandals intensified around the pope's butler, who'd been arrested for stealing private papal documents. People wondered if these documents were about the pedophilia scandal and Vatican Bank corruption. The butler was known to be very loyal to the Pope so common gossip speculated somebody else in the Vatican was behind the scandals.

On September 18, Harvard theological scholar Karen L. King presented her translation of a fragment of a fourth-century Coptic papyrus. In it Jesus refers to Mary Magdalene as "my wife," and more significantly, Jesus says Mary is worthy and can be his "disciple."

Sarah was ruminating about King's announcement while walking over to Simon's apartment for a special dinner he was preparing in honor of Mary Magdalene. Since King was an eminent scholar, Sarah hoped the public would get the message, which significantly backed up her research. Dan Brown's *The Da Vinci Code* and many other books had hypothesized Jesus and Mary Magdalene were married. The implications for the Church of such a realization were huge. The male priesthood and apostolic succession were based on the premise Jesus was celibate and all his disciples were men. If the hierarchy crumbles because people realize Jesus was a fully sensual man who loved women, good riddance! This was Sarah's frame of mind when she arrived for Simon's special dinner, her stomach rumbling in anticipation.

With a grand gesture, Simon swept open the front door of his apartment, and she laughed. He'd blown up renditions of Jesus and a Mary Magdalene with wild red hair and hung them up over the mantle. Below the happy couple, he had fashioned a tacky "Just Married" sign with old soup cans hanging on it, American style. Sarah grinned and wondered what Simon was up to tonight. He led her out to the balcony where the table was set with a white tablecloth, beautiful porcelain dishes, and etched crystal from Roman antique stores.

"Oh how thoughtful!" Sarah exclaimed. She was Grecian tonight, wearing a sheer ivory top draped over narrow gray pants. The old diamond graced her neck, and gold earrings enhanced the color of her pronounced cheeks and eyes. Her lips were slightly glossed and moist but he restrained himself from kissing her yet, even though he knew she hoped he would.

She stood by the kitchen window while he finished an unusual sauce, steamed some vegetables, and grilled two small steaks. He observed her closely. "You really are beyond Armando, aren't you?"

She replied, "Yes, I can't even remember what he looks like! I'm more interested in Karen King's announcement. I hope now more people will realize Jesus was as human as any one of us. He was not like that pack of thin-lipped weirdo eunuchs, the simpering hierarchy."

Go, Sarah, go! Simon cheered inwardly as he turned down the flames to let things simmer for ten minutes. He handed her a glass of wine and said, "This way!" He looped his glass under her wrist to mimic a wedding toast. Raising his glass, he offered a mock toast. "To Jesus and Mary!" After they touched glasses and drank, he put her glass on the windowsill next to his and turned to embrace her. The aroma of fennel, garlic, mint, chili, and olive oil mixed with the heady aroma of the wine, opened her senses. He explored her lower waist while kissing her neck, and then he kissed her so passionately that her boundaries dissolved with the pressure of his lower body on her pelvis. Her top slid off her right shoulder when he kissed her on the neck

again and gently touched her breast for the first time, causing a deep
shiver to run down her spine. Then he pulled her top back over her
shoulder. "I have to put dinner on the table because it's perfect right
now, just like you."

As they carried their plates to the table on the balcony, she realized she had never imagined she could feel this happy. *And it's only
just beginning.*

While savoring steak tagliata with summer squash and spinach,
his eyes lowered to her breasts, which sent delicious sensations into
her center. A mysterious wiring system was waking up in her body, a
map of delicious sensations.

"How will we get through dinner?" she asked.

He replied, "Considering your beauty, maybe we won't. Remember,
William said you are not supposed to be here without a chaperone."

Sarah laughed. Boldly she took his hand and put it under her bra
to reach a nipple and said in a soft, low voice, "Imagine if William
saw me do this."

Taking his hand away with reluctance, Simon went inside to get
warmed apple pie with vanilla ice cream and cognac, her favorites.
While she tasted the cognac, his hand massaged her thigh, which
was aching with dull energy. "Well," he said. "I have something more
important to do than feel you up!"

Pretending she was insulted there could be anything more important, she said, "Yes, what?"

Withdrawing his probing hand, he put it into the inner pocket
of his jacket. Her eyes widened when he held out a small velvet box
and opened it. She stared at the large ruby set in diamonds while he
watched her eyes. He said very soberly, "Will you marry me, Sarah?
Marry me as soon as possible?"

"This is so beautiful. It must be a family antique?"

Simon's raised eyebrows and pleading gaze made her realized she
hadn't answered yet. "Oh!" *What do I say? How do I say it?* "Yes, I
will marry you as soon as possible. I knew I would the day I first

saw you only five months ago, the most special day of my life. We are meant to be together; we always were. Yes, yes, I will marry you!" Sarah's heart beat fast as the smile on her face broadened.

He took the ring out and slid it shakily onto her finger. The large ruby, a ring for a queen, was just the right size on her slender and elegant long-fingered hands. "It was my father's grandmother's ring. Her name was Emily Levi, and she was a grand dame back in the 1880s. My father sent it to me after I told him about Armando. He had nightmares about you in a painter's studio."

A slight furrowing of Sarah's brow alerted Simon that he had been tactless. "I'm sorry," he said quickly. "I shouldn't have brought that up at this moment. I just wanted to say that my father is going to be very happy when we call him."

With the ruby crystal on her body, Sarah saw the clearest vision yet of the man in Portugal who carved the harvest dates on the cork trees. Looking deeply into Simon's eager, dark eyes, she saw the man gently disrobe a woman and tenderly lay her wedding dress over the back of a simple old chair. Wind from the sea swirled curtains in moonlight. She looked down into the stone, and strong energy pulsed into her heart, activating her psychic eye. She met his gaze boldly. "Now that we are engaged, I can enjoy having sex with you."

Just her words made Simon suddenly hard. They both had waited for this moment for so long. Trying to control his body and his breathing, he led her slowly into the bedroom and handed her an exquisite antique lace gown.

Sarah raised her eyebrows. "Was I that much of a sure thing?"

Simon smiled. "Hey, a guy can hope. After I got the ring, I went to a little boutique and picked that out for you. Do you like it?"

Sarah stroked the delicate ivory lace and nodded. "I love it." She disappeared into the bathroom, where she quickly slipped the gown on. She looked at herself in the mirror, patting down her hair and noting with a smile the way her cheeks had already flushed pink. Then she opened the door to go to her fiancé.

He lay on the bed with his body fully displayed like a reclining Roman god. Sarah swallowed. Her eyes met his, and then she looked down to his thick black hair where his penis stood erect. It rose even more as he beckoned her with his hand. She sat down by his side. "I have never touched a penis before. You need to be gentle with me."

She turned to him while he unlaced the ties that held the front of her gown. Slowly lowering it over her shoulders and down over the rest of her body, he took in her beauty fully for the first time. Her breasts had an exquisite contour above her long and strong waist, and the slope down to the soft hair between her legs was unspeakably erotic. Determined to pace himself, he stroked her gently all over her body.

The size and hardness of his penis surprised her. *It has a life of its own.* It got larger when he licked her nipples. She leaned back, delighting in the sensation of his tongue. Carefully, holding her gaze all the while, Simon positioned himself above her and slowly entered her. As he moved in deeper, she uttered a small cry of pain, and then she clutched his shoulders to encourage him. With a groan, he moved deeper into her than into any other body he had ever known as she rose to meet him and then drew him in even more.

As their bodies came together that night, something was going on in a cosmic realm. As Simon moved deeper and deeper while seeking to prolong himself, an earthquake rose in Sarah's body and shot energy all the way out her fingers. Her ring vibrated like a communications device. I see a pathway up to a temple of fluted columns. A woman in the temple sits on a bench, a goddess. "Who are you?" Sarah whispered in her mind. A voice came thundering out of the goddess when Sarah convulsed in an all-body orgasm that was sparked by thick electromagnetic pulses coursing all the way through her body and limbs. Struggling to hear the goddess as she melted, she looked up at Simon moving above her. Ecstasy convulsed the muscles in his face and the goddess said: *I guard the library; Simon is your twin.*

PART TWO

Armando's Redemption

19

The Parents' Dinner

The lovers woke up at 11 a.m. Sarah wondered what she'd gotten herself into when Simon jumped out of bed, screaming, "Shit! I forgot to ask William for your hand!"

Clutching the silk sheets around her shoulders, she said, "We can call him in a little while. William is up really early. Besides, there's not much he can do about it now."

After a few hours spent snuggling, reliving the details of the night before, and relishing in the awakening of the power of their relationship, Simon geared up for his phone call. He perched on the couch in the living room with the phone. "Well, here we go!" His genuine nervousness touched and delighted Sarah. *I have really gotten myself a good one. He's worried about not asking my father first. This is how I want it. I don't give a damn what Daddy has to say about it. I have found the best husband in the world, and Daddy already knows it.*

"William?" Simon began in a deep and serious tone of voice. "This is Simon calling from Rome. Is this a good time to speak with you?" Hearing a grunting assent, he proceeded nervously. "Sir, I would like to marry your daughter. Will you give me her hand?"

There was a short pause, and then William said, "I have to talk to her mother about that. I will call you back in about an hour. I am honored you've asked me, and as always it's good to speak with you."

Simon and Sarah exchanged glances. They'd just have to wait. To pass the time, Simon disappeared into the kitchen to make a very late breakfast, and Sarah sat back on the couch in delicious anticipation. What a cook she'd be living with! He popped homemade cinnamon buns into the oven, and then he brought her a plate of raspberries, strawberries, and sliced bananas with a dollop of cream. As they sat together on the couch waiting for the phone to ring, she said, "If it's over an hour, he's going to give us a hard time." It was not; the phone rang in exactly twenty minutes.

"Hello, Simon, this is William," he said with a hint of pride in his voice. "I assume Sarah is not with you in your apartment this morning?" Since Sarah could hear his loud Irish voice, Simon looked at her. She shook her head. He replied, "No, sir, of course not."

"Well, good," William bellowed into the phone, enjoying his big moment. "Well, have you already asked her yet?" Again Sarah heard what her father said and shook her head. Simon replied in a crisp voice, "I am asking you first, sir, as is proper."

There was a pause. "Well, good. Her mother likes you very much, Simon, and she is happy you want to marry Sarah. As you know I'm very impressed by you. That's great and all, but what about the basics? Do you think you can make her happy? And what about the inconsistency of your profession? Do you think you can provide for a family?"

"To be honest, William, I haven't thought that far because I'm so hopelessly in love with her, have been since I first laid eyes on her. I just want to marry her right away if she will have me. I assume you may wish to help her finish her education, but if you don't I can support us fully. I have plenty of money from my family as well as from my work. Money is not a factor in this proposal."

Remembering the risk Simon had taken in setting up their first meeting at Alfredo's and the way Simon had looked at Sarah when he visited them in Boston, William trumpeted, "Well then, young man, I'll honor you. As your generation says, just go for it! Why not? I wish you success with Sarah, as does Mary. Call us as soon as you've gotten up the nerve to propose. I was going to call her this morning but now I won't. It's still early here, so maybe we'll hear from both of you later today?" *I know Sarah. I bet she's sitting right there with him in his apartment.*

Sarah called her parents later that day to tell them she'd agreed to marry Simon. When Simon called his parents, they received the news joyously.

But as Sarah began to think about their wedding, complexities soon came up, such as how to do the service and whether to be married in the Church or not. Sarah began the conversation, knowing she might have the biggest problem with her staunch Catholic parents. "Simon, do you have any desire for religious elements in our ceremony?"

"Since you are not Jewish, there is nothing to worry about on my side," he replied. "A Jewish man who marries a non-Jewish woman rarely has a Jewish wedding, and I don't want one anyway. What about you with the Church? I'm okay with marrying you in a Catholic ceremony; however, I am not okay with raising our kids Catholic. I've heard I would have to agree to that if we were married in the Catholic Church. Is that true?"

She nodded in assent while she turned things over in her mind. *I never thought about my kids not being brought up Catholic. Yet how could I raise them in the Church? In fact, I think I may soon leave it myself.* She replied, "I do not want to be married in the Church; it would betray my beliefs. I cannot raise my children in the Church—I couldn't even leave them alone with a priest! I can't believe I just said that, but other Catholic women must be saying the same thing; the Church has betrayed us. It's going to be very hard for my parents, though. I know they have looked forward to my wedding in our church."

He cleared their breakfast plates while thinking about what

she'd just said. *I'm amazed she's come this far in such a short time. She will have to handle William on this one.* Sitting back down, he said, "So what do we do? I want my parents to meet yours because they will like each other, and we need their support. We need to come up with a viable solution of our own and present it to them. I think if we know what we want, then it will be easier for them."

"I think you're right," Sarah replied, shifting closer to him on the couch.

"I have a good friend at Harvard who is a Quaker and a justice of the peace, and now he's a dean in the theological school. He is a great guy, you will love him, and I'm sure he'd marry us if I ask. That way our wedding could be spiritual, but on our own terms. Maybe we can be married at this great old meeting house in Boston on the Charles?" Simon suggested.

Sarah liked the idea, and together they worked out the details of the ceremony, deciding they would combine the silence and community participation of a Quaker ceremony with some elements of a more traditional ceremony for the sake of their relatives. They both only wanted close relatives and friends. And they set the wedding date for the weekend after Thanksgiving—only two months away.

The opening overture between the parents came from David, who called William immediately after Simon announced his engagement. "Hello, William. I am Simon's father, David Appel."

"Hi, David. Nice to hear from you so soon!" a surprised William replied.

"We are utterly delighted with your daughter Sarah and thrilled they have decided to marry. It is rather sudden and I think they will rush their engagement, but you know how things are when people are in love!" David said.

"Yes, I know Mary and I couldn't wait to be married once I had proposed, and we were younger than Simon and Sarah. So I can't blame them for wanting to move things along."

"Since we may have very little time before the wedding, my wife Rose and I would like to invite you to dinner as soon as possible at our home in New York. Can you join us on September 21, this coming Friday night?"

William and Mary climbed out of a cab at 35 Pierrepont Street, Brooklyn Heights, and climbed up worn brick steps to the front door of a very elegant brownstone with a shiny dark green door. William lifted the heavy brass knocker, making a loud thump. As they waited, he said, "Whoa, Mary, I think Simon's family may be better off than I thought."

Mary stood on the top step, feeling very happy that she'd worn her favorite beige suit and good pearls. She replied, "This certainly is a lovely home, very elegant."

The heavy paneled door swung wide open, and David greeted them with a friendly smile as he ushered them through the door and took their coats. Mary was delighted by the soft light, warm wallpaper with touches of gilt, and highly polished dark wood. She especially liked the spiritual feeling of the staircase rising up to the open second floor hallway. Taking David's proffered hand, she noted he was debonair and handsome like Simon.

She spoke up, since the opulence of the Appel home had temporarily silenced William. "David and Rose, it's a delight to meet you. What an exquisite home, the very best of the late 1800s when people still celebrated beauty. It feels like time stopped in this foyer. If only it *had* stopped then!" Her eyes twinkled, and David could see Sarah's beauty and charm in her face.

She's delightful! he thought, already picturing Simon's and Sarah's beautiful children.

Rose had stood slightly back by the entry and was pleased to hear what Mary said about her house. She walked up to William and took his hand. "Welcome, and thank you, Mary. I am so happy to meet you *finally*. I can't even begin to express how much we like

Sarah, and I know we will grow to love her as Simon does. We're so happy to have you visit us."

"This is an amazing house," William exclaimed. "You'd never know the ugly modern world is out there. What is the story with this place? Did you buy it like this? It is totally old world, yet so comfortable."

Rose led him into the parlor, responding warmly, "As you can see in the photos, we have lived here for over thirty years. I did the restoration when Simon was a little toddler before his sister Jennifer arrived. She lives in Paris right now, but you will meet her at the wedding."

Mary followed closely behind them because she knew William would not know what to say. Mary understood that William felt diminished by the thought of Sarah marrying into a rich family, genuine old New York aristocracy. At heart, William was a simple construction foreman who'd become a very successful builder. Mary's family had been very prominent in Boston banking for a century, however, so she was totally at ease.

"Rose, your home makes me feel so happy. It is such a joy to see everything done exactly right," she said as she walked into the library with Rose.

William decided to let the women discuss the restoration as he joined David, who led him back through the house to hit the bar. William's eyes rolled when he saw dark paneling, gleaming antiques, and gorgeous oriental rugs. *Hell, this joint reminds me of the archbishop's house!*

Back in the library Rose said to Mary, "Thank you so much. It was a wreck when we bought it and required research to restore it correctly. We found some tinted drawings of these rooms in the American Room archives at the Metropolitan Museum, and these new tiles are exactly the same as the original ones."

"My favorite place in the world is the American Wing!" Mary exclaimed to Rose's delight. "I've never had the opportunity to do a restoration because we have a wonderful well-preserved old house in Boston." Rose showed her a few more special features before they were seated at the dining room table, which was elegantly set with china, silver, and crystal.

Mary was having a great time, but William didn't know what to say when a cook wearing a white apron presented the meal. Before William retreated into total shyness, David took a champagne bottle and lavishly poured bubbly into William's glass. "A toast to the happiest couple in the world, Simon and Sarah. We are honored to have you here tonight! We never imagined that our son would find such a lovely partner!"

William sucked down champagne while casting furtive glances around the room, and then he sprang to life. "David and Rose, I begin with you! Congratulations for raising such a fine son, the ideal husband for our special daughter! This is the night to celebrate our good luck, the night parents hope for. A toast to Simon and Sarah! They have found each other at last, and may they be blessed with children and a good life together!"

The dinner was excellent; they concluded it with very warm feelings toward each other and genuine joy for the new couple. The complexities would come later.

The fall equinox was the day after the parents' dinner in New York. Sarah loved the equinoxes because they made her feel harmonic and balanced. As the sun rose, she relaxed in her window seat with her legs crossed and eyes closed. She still hadn't told her parents about their plans to marry in only two months, or that the wedding wouldn't happen in the Church. She knew the news would shock and devastate them. As Sarah asked for divine guidance, her consciousness moved into her heart and her mind fell into a quieter place to receive ideas. *What I must tell them will not make sense unless I tell them the truth about my faith. I have to tell them that I am leaving the Church when I begin my life with Simon.* Sitting quietly with the idea for a long time, she resolved to call them as soon as they were back from New York. *I have to face it; I have to do it.*

The next day was Sunday, so she called her father when she knew he would be home from Mass. "Daddy, I am calling you to share some painful things. This is hard for me, but I have to tell you now. Simon and I don't want to waste any time. Taking the time to get married is difficult for him because of his responsibilities at the various papers, and I need to write my thesis this winter. We want to get married right away, at Thanksgiving."

"Well, yeah, your mother will go ballistic, but I don't care," William said. "What the hell is so painful about that? Hey, we like his parents a lot, and you hooked a big fish. Sure you can handle all that money? His family has the big buckaroos! Some house too!"

"I don't care, Daddy. Since we both want to write, it is great not to worry about money. Simon showed me his apartment after he gave me the ring. It's cozy and perfect for two, so we will be happy there."

"Well, why are you in such a hurry, Sarah? You hot for love?"

She giggled into the phone at the suggestion sex might be the reason they were hurrying. If she could just keep him in this silly frame of mind, maybe he wouldn't get so mad when he heard about the Church. So she said, "Well, it *is* because of love. I'm twenty-five and he's thirty-five, and you can't expect a guy to wait forever. Certainly the Irish guys never could."

Chuckling William said, "So answer me, what's painful?" Then a light bulb lit up in his brain as he put together the big hurry and something painful. "Damned, Sarah!" he howled. "You can't be . . . you're not pregnant! You didn't do *that!*"

This is perfect. For him, my getting pregnant before marriage would be even worse than my leaving the Church! She replied in a huffy voice, "Of course not! But, what I have to say may be just as bad. We do not want to be married in the Church. We've asked a Quaker theologian to marry us at a meeting house on the Charles."

I can feel shock waves coming through the telephone lines. How am I going to keep him from having a heart attack?

The long silence was horrible. *I can't attack her. I never have, I won't now.* But the news was devastating. Sitting rigid in his study surrounded by tributes from Opus Dei, William gazed up at his simple crucifix from the old family chapel in Ireland. Once he got over the wrath of God, a wave of sadness that closed his heart moved through his body: *I will be alone.* His stomach churned, tears filled his eyes, and his throat closed, making it hard to speak. Finally he uttered in a choked and resigned voice, "I have to talk to your mother; that is all I can say. I never thought you would do anything like this." He hung up the phone.

The receiver clicked off and Sarah felt tears prick at her eyes. She had always hoped she'd never have to do anything to hurt her father, since she knew him better than anyone except her mother. The Church was her father's passion, literally his life. He was nothing without his faith. William's great-grandparents had watched three children die during the Potato Famine in 1849, and they nearly died themselves on the passage from County Armagh to Nova Scotia. Eventually they made it to Boston to start another family and thrived. These horrible memories were written into their genes and passed down to their children. Sarah understood that for William, going to church literally warded off starvation. He stuffed his fears of starvation and death by serving the hierarchy. *I am his beloved daughter—educated by him so that I can serve in Opus Dei—and now I am leaving the Church! His grandchildren will not be Catholic, which to him is anathema. I feel like a heretic. I hope my mother can help him get through this.*

Mary called her that evening. "Thanks for calling, Mom."

"Are you sure you will not be married in the Church? Are you going to leave the Church?"

"It wasn't an easy decision. I've been thinking of leaving the Church for a while, and this marriage forces the issue," Sarah said.

"Tell me what is going on, Sarah, because William is listless, swilling Scotch, and muttering to himself in his study while walking back and forth and crossing himself. Even the dog won't go into the room. Can you tell me more so I can make this easier for him?"

"Now that I have deeply examined events in the early Church, I have to leave. You will see why when you read my thesis, which I'm about to start writing. It's a long story, but maybe you can help Daddy now. The real reason I can't stay in the Church is not just because of priestly abuse or Simon or anything else like that. I am leaving to save my communion with Christ. I continue to have profound feelings for Christ as always, but Church dogma separates me from Him. The last place I can find Him is in the Church, so I have to leave. We could argue about it ad infinitum. Maybe if Daddy realizes I have not lost my faith in Christ, only the Church, then maybe he can accept my choice?"

After hanging up with Sarah, Mary walked into William's study, taking note of an empty Scotch glass on his desk. His feet were propped on the desk while he leaned back in his office chair looking completely disheveled. "Well?"

Mary sat down in a nearby rocking chair and said softly, "She says she has to leave the Church because her studies make her feel like Christ is not in the Church. Since she has such a profound communion with our Lord, she cannot marry in it because, for her, the Church is devoid of our Lord."

William was quite tipsy. "She would look at things that way, wouldn't she? She was always a damned idealist and thinker, and now she had found an intellectual guy. There they will be, the smarty pants. I would rather have my faith than my reason. The Church comforts me in my hour of need. Just wait till she loses one of her children like we did when Patrick died. Then she'll find out what it is like to have no God to pray to."

"William," Mary retorted pleadingly. "I think she will always be able to pray to our Lord. For me, Christ *is* in the Church as He is for you. But if that is what she feels, I think we have to respect her. I think we are going to have to tolerate the way they want to plan their wedding."

William gave himself a week to adjust. He consulted with several spiritual advisors, who mostly said the same thing: most people lose their faith when they investigate the heresies that stained the early Church. That's *why* the heretics were condemned! People often lose their faith when they consider different ideas.

There was something about this that didn't sit quite right with William. To one priest he commented maybe the Church would drive everybody out eventually if they couldn't handle more points of view. That priest shrugged. "Well, so what? This is *our* faith, which is open to anyone. We intend to keep it the way we want it."

When William finally called Sarah he was resigned. "As your father, I hope you will never lose your faith in Christ. If you do, you will be alone in this world. No one should be alone in the world. I will give you away in the chapel at Harvard."

20

A Stormy Night

Wednesday was Sarah's and Simon's favorite day of the week, the day for late afternoon meetings to keep up with wedding plans and a delicious dinner prepared by Simon. On one such Wednesday evening in early October as they sat in Simon's living room, he said, "I bet you loved it when the Vatican pronounced Karen King's fragment mentioning Mary Magdalene as Jesus's wife a fake?"

Sarah laughed. "Yes, it is circuitous reasoning in top form! Since everybody knows Jesus did not have a wife, therefore the fragment is a fake. That is so typical of them!"

With a burst of excitement, Sarah suddenly changed subjects. "I found a wedding dress, a really simple Edwardian ivory lace gown. I looked online to see where to go and it was easy. It is exquisite; you will be charmed." Simon smiled and looked into her eyes intently. *He has a way of focusing just on me. When he deepens his eyes, he looks so intentional and serious. He makes me feel like he knows something about me; he studies me.*

Steering the conversation back to his interests, Simon said, "I'm sure I will. At the Vatican today, a guy told me to keep my Jewish nose out of the pope's affairs. Shit, you'd think we were back in the days of Olimpia Maidalchini and Pope Innocent X!"

"Did you say Olimpia Maidalchini?" she practically screamed. "What does she have to do with the pope's affairs?"

"Well, I am kind of joking. The butler in the Vatican slammer guarded the pope the way Olimpia guarded Innocent X, so now he has pissed off the inner circle. The butler controlled access to the pope to protect him from all the intrigues. I'm thinking about writing some columns describing the historical intrigues and rumors during the reign of Innocent X to satirize the current drama, since little has changed in a thousand years," Simon explained with a smug smile.

As they sat down at the table, he continued, "It could be very funny and suggestive, and my editor at the Italian newspaper likes the idea. There are so many parallels: to this day high positions in the Vatican are doled out to the pope's relatives. There is always a scheming relative who is either a financial wizard, or a promiscuous fool, or both." He gestured excitedly with his wine glass. Vatican insiders would gobble up every word! Romans just love quasi-historical fiction and satire, so it could be good cover. I don't want to make direct accusations, even though I know my instincts are right."

"I like it, Simon, using humor to get your point across," Sarah said.

"Yeah, it's the best way to change things. This could get steamy since many historians think Olimpia was Innocent's mistress. So far few think that's what's up with the butler though. Anyway, why the reaction to Olimpia's name?"

"When I was dating Armando, he took me to his private club, the Doria Pamphili, below the Hotel Circus Maximus. During our first dinner there, he went on and on about Olimpia Maidalchini. Otherwise, I never would have heard of her."

"Sarah, you are joking! He took *you* down into the Doria Pamphili? Are you serious?" He watched her nod with wide, curious eyes. "Do you have any idea what that place is? It's the most notorious sex pit in Rome. It's rumored there is a tunnel from the club to an aqueduct juncture where perverts go to conduct Black Masses and orgies, some say Satanic rituals!"

"We just went there for dinner twice, and the first time I didn't know where he was taking me," she answered as her eyes got even wider. "The club is in a large limestone grotto that was part of the ancient aqueduct system. The food there was great except I did notice some peculiar people around the room, but I always do in Rome."

A file opened in Simon's brain, always the sign something was brewing. It was the same feeling he got when a story or scandal was breaking through; then he followed the leads. *The connections that keep coming up between Sarah and me always seem to lead somewhere. What if the butler discovered something really dark going on in those tunnels? What if he got wind of some nasty undercover stuff? Is Sarah in any danger from dating Armando Pierleoni? After all, his parents are known to be big players in Vatican politics. Why would Armando have taken Sarah down in the Doria Pamphili?* He said, "How seriously do you take synchronicities?"

"Well, I do notice them sometimes, and I wonder if they mean anything," she replied, wondering what he was getting at.

"Have you ever tried to follow a synchronicity to see if it led to something hidden?" he asked. Inadvertently, she found herself staring into the ruby crystal with her eyes widening. "What is going on, Sarah. What do you see?"

She was staring into the stone where she could see the entrance grotto of the Doria Pamphili. She felt herself getting smaller and smaller, just like Alice in Wonderland. Simon's living room transformed into the grotto. Sarah closed her eyes and began speaking in a hollow voice that did not sound quite like her own. *"We are in the Doria Pamphili and we can go anywhere we want; come with me."*

Closing his eyes and feeling cool limestone touching his skin, he said, "Take me down into the grotto with you." Immediately he fell down through a long tunnel. She said, *"Can you see it? Are you with me?"* He was in the middle of a large cave with four caves or tunnels at right angles to where he stood. His first thought was, *I wonder if they're oriented to the four directions?* He answered, "Yes, I am under the Bernini altar in St. Peter's Basilica! There is a large flat altar in the center. Energy swirls in a vortex over a crude and bare stone altar, and a screen floats above." Her voice penetrated his mind. "I can see this too, but we cannot look anymore. Maybe we can't ever look at this; maybe it is dangerous?" Then he felt her hand on his arm and he immediately shot back.

Sarah's face was white. "What's going on, Simon? This ring is making me psychic. I can see things in it like movies, especially when I'm with you. I am afraid."

His logical mind knew some things, so he put his hand on Sarah's reassuringly. "You're right, Sarah. The ring is making you psychic. But since you've been given this gift to penetrate hidden things and I can go with you, I think we should explore this way to find secrets. We need to know what's going on before we can imagine what we could do about it. That's how I write my articles. Often I know ten times more than I can put in print. Because I have deeper knowledge, however, readers sense it. This is how a journalist can reveal secrets. My father gave me the ring because he sensed you were in danger for some reason. After all, you are investigating heretical ideas and your father is in Opus Dei. You shouldn't be scared; the ruby crystal will protect you. I will protect you. My father and I both think you've been chosen to use it."

Sarah turned the ring this way and that, admiring its depths. "So you knew when you gave it to me that the ring was more than a family heirloom?" Sarah asked, her dinner temporarily forgotten.

"My father told me it was special," Simon said. "And we have this incredible opportunity now. I keep noticing the synchronicities between your research and the various stories I'm working on. The whole world is in a vortex of change right now, the time when the Vatican may finally be exposed. The whole Middle East where the three main Semitic religions interface is exploding. Many people are penetrating ancient secrets and testing all religious beliefs. For some reason, we found each other in Rome during 2012. I think we are destined to explore the real truth about dark secrets that mind-control the public."

In his study one mid-October night, William was deep in thought. It was nearly midnight, and sheets of icy rain battered the copper roof above his window seat. He respected his oldest daughter's choices for her marriage, but her desire to leave the Church had shaken him to the core. *I want this to be a joyful time for our family, but I can't shake something in my mind. What is it? What is eating away my edges?* In an abstracted frame of mind he was rummaging through his files for the text of the homily the pope had given for the June 2012 Eucharistic Conference in Ireland. *What was it that he said? It was deeply meaningful for me a few months ago.* Finally he pulled it out and read the part marked with red ink where he had underlined what Pope Benedict said about priestly abuse: "How are we to explain the fact that people who regularly receive the Lord's body and confessed their sins in the sacrament of Penance have offended in this way? It remains a mystery. Yet, evidently their Christianity was no longer nourished by a joyful encounter with Jesus Christ. It had become merely a matter of habit."

With his big feet propped up on his oak desk, William found that this time the sentence about the priests not being nourished by a joyful encounter with Jesus Christ really caught his attention. *That is exactly what Sarah says about Jesus not being present in the Church. She says she has to leave because Christ is not there. I admire her for being so honest. Now it is time for me to face what I feel, since I have not felt Christ in the Church for years myself. Long ago I felt Him in the blessed sacrament and around the altar, but not in many years. I have tried to get the feeling back by serving my parish and Opus Dei. When did I lose it?*

The wind was blowing so hard he was afraid big trees might

come down. Regardless, he stayed at his desk and forced his mind back, back, and back. *When I was nine and a new altar boy, I loved being close to the priest. I loved casting my eyes piously up to his hands as he raised the Host. I saw light above the altar fill with the sweet presence of our Lord. I loved receiving Communion before the people during Mass and then standing by Father as the people lined up to receive. I loved the light in their eyes, their tears of joy. What happened to those feelings? Soon after that everything was gray and boring. I was dull and felt disgusted by something. I didn't want to be there . . .* Suddenly his mind was blinded by a flash and a push. *I can still feel the place on the side of my arm where I got cut and bruised.* Rubbing his arm to make it go away, he was jolted by shocks deep in his solar plexus. *I am the great oak by the porch ready to crack!* He felt his young body with the priest behind, jamming him against the prayer rail and pulling up his cassock, and he also caught a flash of the obscene moment. But he stopped the distant movie in his mind. *I can't go there, it won't help. It won't help anybody.* He slouched down deeper into his chair, expelling air from his clenched diaphragm and cramping stomach. *Oh my God, my God! I will not think about this, not ever again. Now I know the truth; now I remember. But I don't want to remember any more of it, ever. I have to admit the truth to myself, the ugly truth.* To keep his sanity, he had to block the recovery of any more details. He blanked his mind, a skill he had learned when he had to take care of a worker who had fallen off a ledge on a construction site and spilled his intestines.

He hadn't wanted to tell anyone of the horrible thing the priest had done, but he was bleeding so badly when he got home that his mother insisted on taking him to the doctor, and the doctor knew exactly what must have happened. William could still remember his mother sitting by his side hugging him and brushing his hair softly with her fingers, the pitying look on the doctor's face. *When I came back home, I hid myself from the grave expressions, all the sadness.* His parents were prominent parishioners, so the priest had been sent off to a far-away parish in the middle of the night, and soon a young priest fresh from Ireland replaced the old one. *That was the end of being an altar boy, the end of feeling like a good little boy.* Eventually he became a beer-drinking carouser in high school and was in a serious car accident that had killed one of his friends. Luckily he wasn't driving, but that sobered him up. When he met Mary in college, he fell in love, forgot everything, and began to heal. *I will never tell her what happened to me, for shame! I was lucky. The priest got sent away, so it only happened once. I'm sure other guys had to deal with that priest over and over again; they must be wrecked for life.*

He sat there for two more hours listening to the wind while occasionally tapping his pen on the desk. Around 3 a.m., as he was nodding off, he had a vision of Sarah's face when she was only a few hours old. Great light surrounded her little body, like a golden halo! A triumphant voice said, "This is my beloved daughter, and I am well pleased." *When I first saw Sarah, I felt the presence of our Lord again. Just briefly, but it was enough for me to keep my faith and raise my family in the Church. As the pope said in his homily for the Eucharistic Congress, "It remains a mystery." If the pope could say that, maybe he didn't know what was going on? Either way, evil lurks in the Church and I want to know why, but it is not Sarah's fault.* Finally the terrible wind abated after he fell asleep on his couch.

The next day he dialed Sarah's apartment at 7 a.m. Rome time. "Sarah? It's Dad. I want to talk to you about something."

She hoped it was something good. She was so happy just to hear his voice again and hoped he was getting over his anger. She responded, "Yes, Daddy, what is it?"

"Well, Sarah, I have remembered some things, some things that go way back to when I was a young altar boy. I don't want to discuss all of that with you, no need to. But I want to tell you that all my sadness and resistance about you not being married in the Church is gone. Remembering some things helps me see that you and Simon know how to begin your marriage. The only reason for remembering anything in the past would be if it could help us now. Now that I understand myself better, I am really ready to give you away at your wedding. We are all ready here to celebrate with you and Simon."

Sarah knew that key events like weddings often get people to remember deep things and she didn't want to lose this opportunity. *Obviously he is alluding to some kind of abuse, and I wonder if I should probe him. But it doesn't feel like this is the right time.* She said, "It sounds like you have recalled a childhood abuse trauma? Sure you don't want to talk about it? You can, you know."

"Sure, I know I can, and if I wanted to, I would. I think I could even talk to Simon about it, if you can believe that. That tells you how I feel about your intended. But it is the past. I know it isn't that way for everybody and I can understand why."

"Okay, Dad, as long as you are okay."

"But there is something I want to share with you. You brought all this up for me because you said you can't find Christ in the Church, which kept eating away at me. That's blasphemy, yet it is the truth for you. And the pope said something similar at the Eucharistic Congress in Ireland this summer, which caught my attention because it was the most honest thing I ever heard him say. I wonder whether he knows what is really going on?" William paused. But as neither had an answer to this question, he went on. "Anyway, because of what happened when I was young, just like you I couldn't find Christ in the Church anymore. Yet I found Him again when I saw you after you were born. The real presence came in with you, Sarah, and I admire you for refusing to let it go. Makes me wonder whether all newborns come in with a halo, which makes me question original sin. You must never let Christ go. If that light isn't in the Church for you, then you should not stay."

Her throat muscles tightened and thickened. She managed to squeak out in a small voice that William could barely hear, "Daddy, your words give me so much happiness that I need to get off the phone and cry for hours. I *never* thought you could understand; I had not even hoped. This is the sweetest gift a father could give his daughter. You are the reason I have not lost the light, and now you are letting me go to love Simon. The way you responded to Simon has been so touching."

"It wasn't hard, Sarah; just look at his family. He was raised well."

"Regardless, when you met him, you welcomed him. This meant everything to him because he didn't expect it. He loves you simply because you accepted him."

"You have chosen a really extraordinary person, a man who will make his mark, a man strong enough to challenge even you! I could not possibly be happier."

"Well, maybe someday you will share more with me about what happened to you. Now it is time for happiness and celebration. I've had a few traumatic experiences of my own, and my faith has supported me. Maybe I will share these things with you someday, but now is not the time. I understand not needing to process it. Some don't have to because not everybody is crushed by these kinds of things. But I stand tall for the ones who need help with these matters because the abuse they suffered arrested their growth."

"You're right, Sarah. And I'm proud of you for standing up for what you believe in. It's exactly what we raised you to do."

"You should call Simon's parents in a few hours to start making arrangements; I'm sure they'd love to hear from you. Bye, Dad. I love you."

"Love you too, sweetie."

William waited a few hours and then called David. "Hello, David. This is William, Sarah's father."

"Hi, William. How can I help you?"

"I wanted to call to thank you for having us for dinner and to tell you again how happy I am with your son. You haven't heard from me because I've been having a hard time with Sarah's decision to marry outside the Church. It took me a few weeks to accept it, but now I have."

"How thoughtful of you to call," David responded in a warm and crisp voice. "I've been wondering how you felt about that. I have stayed out of the plans because they are both old enough to know what they want. However, I thought it might be hard for you; it would be for me if I were in your shoes. I am happy you've come to a resolution. I'm sure Simon's work didn't make it any easier for you to get used to the idea of them together."

"Well, when I first met your son, I had just read his priestly abuse article in the *Times*. I can assure you I was pissed off! When I realized Simon was the writer, who by the way was adeptly hosting me for dinner in Rome, I almost tore into him. But I'll be damned, David! That kid knows how to get along with people! He completely disarmed me and he's been doing it ever since. He has stolen my daughter's heart! I am just plain one hundred percent happy about this wedding. I don't care where they have it."

David was smiling into the phone. "We are too, he replied. We could have used a few more months before their wedding; I'm sure you could have too, but their wedding will be simple and meaningful without a lot of folderol. Every time I go to a big wedding, I feel like it is the worst way for the couple to begin. Judging by how things often turn out, maybe it is. So we all get to have a really good time and see a few special people. I very much look forward to seeing you and Mary soon."

That night William went up to their bedroom where Mary was sleeping soundly. He slipped off his clothes and went into the guest room to avoid waking her. Crawling into bed for a few hours of sleep, he was afraid he might be plagued by painful memories or bad dreams. Instead he recalled the sight of Sarah's light at her birth while drifting off to sleep. *Whenever I am troubled, I will bring back her light.*

21

St. Peter's Bones

It was Wednesday and Sarah was headed to Simon's for a roast chicken. She strode briskly along the busy Via del Corso, then through the Piazza di Spagna to Simon's street. She slipped into the vestibule and smelled scintillating aromas.

"You will be so happy to hear about the conversations between our fathers," he said, pulling her close and giving her a passionate kiss.

How did I resist him for as long as I did?

"Oh, I *know*," she said, leaning back and pressing her pelvis against his. "I am amazed by my father. I never thought he'd accept our plans. I can't believe it! He's going through some of his own things about the Church, and really it is about time."

He moved toward the couch and Sarah followed. "I agree, but I think our parents will continue with their respective religions because of their friends and their communities. Lots of people from our generation are dropping out though, especially Christians."

Sarah frowned. "Why Christians in particular?"

"Maybe monotheism did inspire people to evolve three thousand years ago as the so-called Chosen People, the Jews. But the lies about Jesus and the disciples retard the average Christian; it is a religion for naive children. The Church's denial of Father Bagatti's discovery of Simon Peter's ossuary in Jerusalem infuriates me! Sometimes Catholics are just stubborn and stupid! Excuse me!"

"May we have an afternoon glass of red wine in honor of the Host while you tell me all about St. Peter's bones?" Sarah said, laughing.

He stood up, announcing, "*I am the host so I will serve you whatever you like.*"

Seeing Simon so wrought up amused her. "Since I'm still a Catholic girl, let's have our first big fight over St. Peter!" *What is it about men when they get disgusted? Maybe men get wrought up when they're horny.*

He stood up and went into the kitchen for the wine, calling back as he went, "Perhaps we have been getting along too well, my dear? Maybe we need to have our first fight?" *Truth is, I just need to get laid. What a week!* He'd been reading Olimpia Maidalchini's letters for three days solid.

Returning with two glasses of wine he said, "Do we have any wedding details to worry about before I rant? As far as I know, everything seems pretty taken care of. The guests are being invited as we speak, and our parents are planning various social gatherings." She nodded as she geared up for his intellectual diatribe. *He's so earnest when he goes off. He retreats into his mind when he's frustrated just the way I do.*

"What have you read about Father Bagatti?" Simon began.

"I've heard of him, but I don't know much," Sarah replied.

"Well, he was a Franciscan archaeologist who researched an early Christian tomb at the Mount of Olives after discovering it in the 1950s. He found the ossuaries of many early Christians including Mary, Martha, and Lazarus, as well as the probable remains of St. Peter correctly inscribed *Simon Bar Jonah.* The Catholic archaeologist J. T. Milik verified the inscription as St. Peter's, and they co-wrote a book about it."

Sarah sipped her wine, and nodded at him to continue. "In it

Milik says there's a hundred times more evidence that Peter was buried in Jerusalem than in Rome. But of course Catholic tradition says St. Peter was the first pope in Rome and is buried under the Vatican, so Pope Pius XII met with Bagatti to ask him to be quiet about his discovery. But the remains were stored in a semi-private museum by the site of the Church of the Flagellation, and Bagatti refused to obey the pope and published the book with Milik in Italian a few years after his discovery. Two years after that, a Christian researcher, F. Paul Peterson, wrote a book in English about the discovery. When I tried to get Peterson's book, the price on Amazon was over eight hundred dollars. The Vatican probably burned the copies!"

Simon paused to emphasize the injustice, and Sarah couldn't help but smile a little at his exuberance. It did seem crazy, though, that in this age of technology information could be so easily suppressed.

"The Vatican has made various claims that Peter's bones are under the Bernini altar, but *none* have ever been substantiated," Simon continued. "It wasn't until *Newsweek* ridiculed the Vatican claims that people even heard about the Mount of Olives discovery, possibly the greatest Christian discovery of all time! For Jews it would be like finding Solomon's tomb! The fact is Bagatti's discovery undermines papal succession and *could* bring down the Catholic Church, since the hierarchy's power comes from the lineage of popes from Simon Peter. Constantine built his Basilica in Rome believing it was over St. Peter's tomb, yet there is absolutely no archaeological, historical, or biblical evidence for *any* of this. The real truth is the Roman Church came up with this cock-and-bull story during the eighth century when it broke free of the Eastern Church, and still this bald-faced lie commands the obedience of the faithful! The location of this tomb on the Mount of Olives is extremely significant." Simon was beginning to sweat as he got more and more worked up over the topic. With his hands wildly gesticulating he went in for the kill. "It is said Jesus met with his disciples there, and prophets say it's where Christ will return in the Second Coming.

A series of chapels have been built there over two thousand years. Muslims worship there too because they believe it is where the mother of Issa is buried. Yet when a top-notch Franciscan archaeologist authenticated St. Peter's remains there, the papacy silenced him and announced *their* discovery of St. Peter under the Vatican Basilica! It's ridiculous!"

He ran out of steam when he realized Sarah was ready to burst out laughing. She inched up her skirt to sit cross-legged, offering a view of her inner thighs. *Maybe she's not wearing panties; that blouse really shows off her cleavage.* She moved closer and his face melted. He reached between her legs, stroking her, breathing deeply as her head fell back. *I can't believe how hot I am for her.* He lifted her skirt higher while he ripped off his shirt and plunged in with half their clothes still on. He fumbled with anything in the way as she fell back and coursed with waves of joy, her left hand gripping his shoulder.

She loved his desperation. *I don't want him to stop.*

He groaned from the depths of his whole body. "Goddess, I love you."

Simon dozed off, but Sarah found herself wide awake. *Sex is a strange thing. Physically, the way this happened isn't all that different from what Armando tried to do. Our urges were just as animalistic, but without the evil undertones. Simon knew I was giving myself to him.* Sarah was amazed at how wonderful it felt to just be taken with abandon by a man who had her trust and permission. When he woke up, he fingered her ring as it reflected the last rays of light. "You are mine and I adore you."

Later they sat quietly on the sofa while the chicken roasted in the oven. As the sun fell down behind the top of a nearby building, the ruby on Sarah's finger began to vibrate. She looked at it in wonder. *It's like a central computer device that can access anything as it picks up vibrations from deep in the Earth.* "Simon, my ruby responds to our emotions. How did you feel when we went down into the caves below the Vatican? *Why* do you want to go down there?"

Simon peered at the ring. "It's interesting you detect emotions in the ruby. My father and I think it came down to us from Isaac Luria. My father never gave it to my mother because she's not psychic. But you are, and my father knows it. He thinks the ruby is a sacred talisman that reads the records of time."

"Why didn't you tell me all of this before?" Sarah asked.

Simon hesitated. The truth was that there was a lot more his father had told him about the ring that he had yet to tell Sarah. He was waiting for her to be ready. "I wanted you to discover how to use it so you would believe in its powers. You have to build your confidence; information from a powerful talisman requires constant verification."

Sarah bit her lip. "I think I would like to go back into the caves under the Bernini altar by sharing what I felt when we both began to see the central chamber with the large flat altar and the four tunnels opening into it," she said hesitantly. "I felt intense dread, yet there is something I am supposed to find down there. Maybe we can get more of a reading now in this liminal light."

"Okay," said Simon. He watched as Sarah moved her hand over the stone. A hollow and faraway voice emerged from her throat, *"I see the scene in the stone and I touch it to access its vibrations. I get more information by feeling it."* Her voice dropped deeper into her gut. Almost growling, she muttered, *"Watch it, Simon Magus. You have no business being down here, and you know it. You know that you are involved in what goes on down here, both you and Sarah, so watch it. We know who you are."*

A cold, serpentine shiver moved through Sarah's body. *I must take my fingers off the ruby and pull myself back into the room.* She opened her eyes, seeing a haze in the room and asked, "What is this, Simon?"

Simon hesitated before answering. He threw his arms back behind his head, stretching his body. *What a trip. She went right to the next stage—vibrations and sound. She must know about this stuff from past lives. Maybe she was the Sibyl of Cumae, but I have to be very careful because she is so young. She could go too fast and end up with too much energy in her body. She's such a loving and willing being. She'd do anything for me, just as I would for her, so I have to be very careful with her.* Finally, he said, "Do you feel okay talking about it some more while in a conscious state of mind?"

"Yes," Sarah responded immediately. "I want to understand. What do you think that threat was all about? It's so strange hearing those words come through me, and sometimes when I'm speaking through the ruby I can't even remember what I've said."

"May I hold the stone to see if it will give me an answer?"

She took it off her finger and handed it to him. He closed his eyes and started to breathe deeply. In a firm voice, he said, "I resent being told to watch it, somebody telling me what my business is." Then he quieted and said in a silvery voice very different from his own, *"You are destroying our mind control; you and Sarah can do it."* Simon felt something grip his shoulder blades and he snapped back quickly. *Go away back to where you came from, now!*

He opened his eyes and handed the ring back to Sarah, observing her closely. He thought she might be ready to hear everything he knew about it. "You've figured out so much for yourself, so I think I can tell you more about the ring now."

Sarah lifted her chin. "Yes, tell me!"

"Okay," said Simon, "Sensing sound vibrations is a more direct way to see things because the vibrations open high dimensions. Sound activates very high mental and spiritual knowledge. Are you afraid of that?"

"No, not at all as long as I know what it is," Sarah said, and she turned her body toward him so she could look deeply into his eyes. "I want to know your depth." Sapphire lights moved and shimmered in his eyes, like the flashing of the aurora borealis.

"If you really are not afraid, then I will tell you more about what I know. I've been talking to my father a lot lately and remembering things he taught me as a child. According to him, we are up against a gatekeeper, a spirit that has been appointed to guard the site under the Vatican. We can ask it to open the gates and it either will or will not. That is not something we want to do right now, not before we are married. We need to be very careful. Judging by the synchronicities that are leading us, we will access this site, but not now."

Sitting with her legs crossed and light flashing in her eyes, Sarah was having such a powerful vision that she barely heard his voice. *I see the simple room in Portugal with my wedding dress on the back of the chair, and I'm curled up in bed with him. But I feel such pain, such sadness. He loves me so much, this simple man, but I feel so sad.* Then she flashed farther back and felt nauseous. *I'm held down, smothered and ripped within my body. What is that? I see sapphire blue velvet, an ermine strip, and a gold ring stamped with the Maltese Cross. He is pushing me, cramming me, then he shoves me away.* "Enough; I had you first." Sarah gasped at the realization. *The local duke took me by first rights when I was a virgin, only fifteen; maybe he impregnated me.*

Simon stared into her eyes and what he saw scared him. He beheld the eyes of Eve's wise serpent, a cobra poised to strike at one false move.

As Sarah pulled herself back into the room to Simon, she said, "You're right that this is not the right time for us to go deeper into these visions. I sense that we will be safer once we are married, but nothing is going to stop me this time. Not now that we have found each other again!"

Once dinner was on the table, Simon said thoughtfully, "Sarah, I thought we were just having a love affair, but now I see the extraordinary potential of us working together. You are unbelievably adept. It's as if the ruby waited for you to claim it. That's why we met at the Cumae site when you were staring at cats attacking a rat. Why were you so fascinated?"

"Hmmmm," she murmured as she cut into a tender piece of

chicken encrusted with crushed macadamia nuts and topped with mango sauce. She put it in her mouth. "Delicious, Simon. I don't know how you do it. You are a cook!"

"All Jewish guys are. We are good in bed too because we get more sex if we cook. Come on, Sarah, what attracted you to those cats?"

Sarah hesitated. "At first I was just curious because I think cats are the guardians of Rome," she replied.

"They are," he interjected.

"Okay. Well, what drew me was the main cat torturing the rat, like the Christian martyrs were tortured in the Coliseum."

"You must know by now that it was the Gnostics getting knocked off?"

"Well, that is probably true, since so many early Christians were Gnostics. I guess I was thinking about how much courage it took to stand up for your beliefs, and how much pleasure the torturer took in punishing those who thought differently. It all seemed very relevant to my studies and the way my faith was changing."

She took another bite of chicken and chewed it thoughtfully. "Also, even that first day, I felt a strong connection to that place. Tell me what you know about my connection to the Sibyl of Cumae."

"Well, in some ways you *are* her. Maybe that is what happens to all women when they access the goddess? But you must be part of a lineage or you would not be so naturally adept. My father and I shared our little secret for years, the lineage of Isaac Luria. For my father, the value is pragmatic; these tools *work* in business. Where do you think *you* get this psychic ability?"

"Now I will make you laugh," she replied. "I get it from sex! This ability came once I had sex. You like that answer?"

"Come on, Sarah, I'm not letting you off the hook. There is more to it than that," he persisted.

Sarah rested her hand on her chin. "Well, I suppose my relationship with Christ might be a factor; I know Him, I call to Him, and

He answers. The Gnostics said we all can do that, and they used talismans and magical techniques to reach him. My psychic ability awakened when you gave me this ring, yet I have always believed I can access anything I want. In that sense I am a Gnostic. Let me ask you the most important question," she said, capturing his gaze with intensity. "You seem to want to use me for something. What?"

Simon moved his head to the side and his neck cracked; he was cornered. *What the hell, I'll just be truthful because it seems only fair.* "Look, I would marry you and give you my life and never follow these leads, but I think we've come together to explore how and why evil got into the world, especially in the Catholic Church. Look at what you're studying and writing about; look what I'm paid to investigate. Look at how we met and what we've been led to. My father, a real magus, recognized you. This is more than a marriage; we are a psychic team."

"Yeah sure, but *why?*" she interrupted.

He paused a bit, then said, "I want to give you a child. But look at the world! The U.S. embassy in Benghazi, Libya was attacked, and a truly great American ambassador was murdered. The war in Syria pushes refugees into Turkey, Lebanon, and Jordan; and Israel threatens Iran while strangling Gaza. Fanatics gunned down a young Pakistani girl in a school bus because religions obscenely foment death and misery. Before we have our child, I want to know the real source of evil; I want to describe it so it can be eradicated."

"Simon," she interjected quietly, "that is the eternal quest."

"No, it is not," he retorted looking her straight in the eyes. "Or maybe for women it has been the eternal quest. It is time for men to join them! Both sexes must unmask these black forces together. Our world *can* be better, and then I can imagine bringing a child into it. Maybe that is the essential difference between Jews and Christians. We Jews believe the world can improve, yet Christians believe they must suffer."

The last piece of sweet mango chicken slid down her throat

as she said, "I think Jews are more into suffering than Christians! Many Jews feel even more guilt and that's saying a lot. Maybe we do need to have a good fight?"

Simon grinned. "Nah, after sex like that on the couch, forget it. Besides, we are two lone souls who both think Marcion was right. History is a pile of crap—Christian bullshit piled on top of a really stinky pile of Jewish bullshit. And Islam has piled its fair share on as well. If sex *has* made you psychic we should call it a draw and have lots more of it so we can have fun while penetrating dark secrets. Why not?"

After enjoying Simon's apple brown betty for dessert, they crawled into his cozy bed and marveled at how easily they'd traveled into deeper waters. They were destined to.

22

Caves under the Vatican

Leaves made scratching sounds in Roman piazzas in mid-October as strong winds from Umbria buffeted the ancient city of seven hills. Dry branches scraped Sarah's garden walls, and yellow leaves floated like tiny origami sailboats on the fountain bowl's surface. Her wedding was only five weeks away, so she was cherishing her last moments alone as she snuggled in her window seat. She couldn't, however, stop processing disturbing thoughts about the fourteen-year-old Pakistani girl, Malala Yousafzai, an activist for girls' education who had been shot in the head by Taliban gunmen. *Why so many children, really remarkable and good children? As more light comes in, darkness is closing in all around us. What is happening—really?*

The morning dew glistened on her windows as the first rays of sunlight came over the garden wall. As the sunlight illuminated the leaded windows, she wondered what would happen if she tuned into the images forming in the bubbles. Why not?

She touched the ruby as the air bubbles transformed into miniature spherical worlds of birds, flowers, sunlight, and garden. *Everything that exists vibrates on curving inner surfaces! Other dimensions flow into the garden on the edges of the color spectrum.* She stared into her favorite bubble, green eyes reflected back to her as the ruby vibrated beneath her fingers. *It worries me when Simon talks about the "gatekeepers." I want to see what goes on in the cave system under the Bernini altar.* Sarah wanted the timeline of the Vatican Necropolis.

Forms appeared within thick mist swirling in the bubble. *Oh! I see Paleolithic images from maybe fifty thousand years ago. Way beneath the Vatican, there is a cave that was on the surface during the Ice Age. I see Neanderthals scraping away the soil with antlers. In silence they place the body of a very small girl wrapped in rough woven cloth inside the cave. Her face is painted red. Her body is surrounded by wildflowers.*

Sarah continued staring into the bubble as color spectrums illuminating the inner surfaces formed miniscule rainbows. Another scene unfolded. *Now the walls of the cave have large paintings of wild animals, trees, and plants. People are playing flutes and drumming and gathering—Magdalenian people fifteen thousand years ago! They go on visionary journeys by assuming a special posture with their legs crossed and hands holding their knees.* The bubble became a round jewel of light like a small crystal ball. Another scene opened. *A circle of people stand with their hands clenched at their sternums and their eyes closed. A drummer beats very fast on tight skin; the staccato force makes them sway. They wear finely woven tunics and have braided hair—Etruscan people three thousand years ago. They just buried someone.*

The bubble lost its intensity and glowed from within like the last embers in a fire. *I see a small hut on the surface above the cave entrance. I see crude graves marked by wooden headstones or crossed sticks. I wonder if the people buried here knew about the cave?* Her ruby began to vibrate very fast and felt hot. As the bubble lost the last light, she could still see more images. *What is this now? Five men in dark tunics with hoods gather around the place where the hut once existed over the buried cave. One man draws a four-sided cross in the clay. I feel very strange, but I have to see this.*

Erotic force welled up in Sarah's body. *One man says to the oth-*

Sarah's eyes reflected in crystal planes

*ers, "Now!" Two other men approach, holding a struggling young girl
with long red hair; the circle parts. "Put her down!" the man says to
the men holding the wild, writhing girl. They hold her down on the
ground at her shoulders, and another man wrenches her tunic above
her waist to expose her shockingly white and vulnerable young body.
"Ah, she is good," the man says as he pulls up his robe to expose his
throbbing penis coursing with angry blood. "We defile her to take
our power!" The other men leer, saliva coming out of their mouths as
they watch this man, the bishop. He gets down on his knees, parts her
small legs, and then lowers his body down onto her, piercing her as she
screams like an animal being killed. Her cries excite them. The more
she tries to move, the harder he thrusts into her small bleeding body.
She passes out and can't feel the hot slime as she lays there helpless and
unconscious—out of her body. They line up for their turns. The bishop
announces, "Now we have consecrated this sacred ground, the portal to
Earth's center, the great library once known to ancient man. Here we
will build our Church over St. Peter's bones."*

Sarah came back into the room with electric waves flowing through her body wondering what she'd witnessed. *More sexual energy harnessed by the Church. Why am I aroused by this scene? I don't feel guilty or tainted in any way since it is only energy, but is this the power that binds the Church? Why am I being drawn into this? Am I that girl in some way? Have I just seen the original rape of myself? Or is this an image that is constantly projected into our planetary fields by beings from another dimension?*

Simon reached David on the phone while he was in his study on Shelter Island watching heavy rain pelt the old glass, deep in thought. *I feel other dimensions through a veil as water slices the wavy glass. I wonder if Hurricane Sandy will be that bad?* Jarred out of his reverie, David picked up the receiver and heard Simon's greeting. "Yes, Simon, glad you called. I was just thinking about you as I watched the rain on the window. You must be getting very excited about the wedding?"

"Yes, of course I am, but I really need to talk to you about something else. Is this a good time? I wish I could come to see you, but I can't leave Rome right now."

"You can always talk to me, Simon. What is it?"

"As you thought would happen, the ruby engagement ring is making Sarah psychic and we have used it to penetrate veils by remote viewing. But when we try to get into the area under the Vatican, we get blocked. Something or someone tells us to keep out. You once talked about gatekeepers, and I think that's what we're running into. How do we get past them?"

"Well," David responded, "if ever there was a place that would have gatekeepers, it is down there. Begin with the premise that you have the absolute right to know, and then they cannot stop you. How far you get depends on your courage and patience." David paused. "But Simon, with your wedding coming up so soon, do you think this is the best time to pursue this?"

"Sarah and I are doing very little of this before the wedding. But my job never goes away, and I feel there is something else I should know. What do *you* know about the forces we're up against when we try to penetrate the Vatican?"

There was another brief pause as David tuned in and then spoke more slowly in a higher pitch. "Simon, you are asking about the fourth dimension, the dimension just beyond the solid world we inhabit. This is the quantum world of collective thoughts and emotions that are somewhat tangible and nearly visible. Many people think that things going on in that dimension are happening in our solid world, but they are not. Systems like the Vatican extend their power way beyond their true size by projecting patterns from the unseen realm into the real world. We must be very respectful of this interface because guardians that work for both sides maintain these zones."

David leaned back in his chair as he continued. "For example, you and Sarah might see a weird ritual going on under the Vatican that many other people have seen—the Black Mass. Many people think it actually goes on; it might or might not. You may be picking up thought forms or movies concocted to mind-control people, or possibly people are detecting the shadow of the Mass."

Simon hung on to every word. *So if we see a vision, we can't know if it's the real thing? Are these movies concocted to influence events, even free choice?* "Dad, how can I tell the difference? How can we know whether something is real or not?"

"Ah, that's the crux of the matter. A concocted scene, say, a bizarre ritual, actually is real, but not in the same way things are real in our solid world. Often these things are *probable* events, unfulfilled desires that play out. These desires influence people's minds and often cause people to act like robots or maniacs, the same way violent movies can trigger violence. Entities like the Vatican project potent images that run their programs, such as claiming consecrated wine is the body of Christ to hook people into ancient blood sacrifice. They are masterful mind controllers."

"Well, then," Simon interjected, "Does it *matter* whether things are real or not?"

"Of *course* it does!" David practically shouted, surprised by Simon's pessimism. "It sounds like you and Sarah want to find the real causes *behind* things, for example what causes a priest to abuse a child. I am suggesting that some of these priests may not even realize they are doing the things they do because they are hypnotized by these programs. A program that incites *many* evil acts is worse than any individual who carries them out. Meanwhile, what they do is real and has consequences."

Simon felt a little bit of hope rise in him. "Dad, lately I have been thinking we may be on the verge of figuring out why people commit evil acts."

"I have waited my whole life for that moment—the public exposure of other-dimensional influence. You and Sarah seem to be instinctually drawn right into decoding these central programs, the ones that cause so much confusion."

"I feel like a little kid again, but I have to ask you," Simon said in a quiet voice. "What in hell can anybody do about any of this?"

"Now, Simon," David replied, sitting up straight at the sound of the rain beating loudly on the surface of the fragile glass he loved so much. *This barrier between my warm place and the ferocious elements is like the gossamer shield between dimensions.* "*That* is the essential question! These programs do not control everybody. People who understand how this influence works cannot be incited to act out these programs. These days, many people get sucked into evil actions because they are over-stimulated by communications technology; they live in virtual reality. However, each person must figure out what is real. We can't go on being dodo birds stumbling around in the solid world, getting knocked over by the desires of evil! We just can't! We each have to learn the difference between living by our own intentions or acting out someone else's desires. Each one of us has a clear choice at some point; it is the great human mystery—free will. Anyone with great integrity is impervious to this sort of thing."

David shifted in his chair as Simon pressed the phone tighter to his ear as though it might bring him closer to his father's powerful presence. "Simon, I've been tempted to say this for months: You and Sarah are serious writers with potent pens. It is your responsibility to help uncover these secrets. Great writers flavor their sentences with traces of other realities. You are writing about forces that *are* detectable in collective events. Events function according to complex probabilities that offer us choices. Your priestly abuse article was very influential because you accurately described things that are very real. People have a nose for the truth, and lies pop like soap bubbles!"

"I was just talking to Sarah about that the other day—the importance of the underlying presence of what I know but cannot say outright in my writing," Simon exclaimed.

"Listen carefully," his father said. "At this point a growing number realize they cannot expect to know how reality is constructed without mastering many dimensions. Look at what people are discovering in quantum physics! Your job is to figure out the master program of the Vatican—to see *how* their programming incites priests to abuse children. For some reason the higher-ups need the pure energy of children, as if they are half-dead vampires."

Simon was in deep thought while listening to his father. *I wonder if the space under the Vatican is a fourth-dimensional media chamber, a virtual reality machine?* He interjected, "Well, you seem to be saying that if we see a vision of something, it may be a thought projection somebody is using to incite mindless behavior?"

"Yes, *exactly*, Simon. You can identify the projections by examining repetitious events, such as what has been going on in the rectories. Question is, why are the priests sucked into mindless lust? Seek the intentions that drive the actions, things that just seem to come out of the blue. Something very nasty is going on in the Vatican that is beyond their control, an arcane primal possession. By figuring out exactly what these guys are doing based on observable events, code patterns emerge. Exposure emasculates the perpetrators! I used to think the world was divided into black and white, but now I know it is mostly gray. What's black and white is the virtual reality dimension, like checkered Masonic floors.

"Using visions to project realities into our world requires absolute secrecy. The minute *anybody* figures out what they are really doing and gets the word out, they can't do it anymore. Never underestimate the power of your mind! Good psychics can read the plots of the secret programs inserted into our world; Sarah can do this or she will soon be able to. In the coming years, this ability will become more important, something that should have happened when Isaac Luria was alive. Instead it is coming now. When you combine the exposure of secret influences with effective action in the world, such as protecting children by watching out for them, ancient patterns that limit our species break down. I think most people influenced by the patterns would rather opt out, maybe even the pope! Yet the higher up a person is in the hierarchy, the more the patterns entrap them. Ordinary people, on the other hand, can instinctually clean out these old forms because our solid world feels more real than virtual reality. Angry men have been running the world and abusing everybody for at least five thousand years and I believe this is shifting. If I didn't, I wouldn't get up in the morning.

"You and Sarah have work to do because you are brilliant seers with fine creative minds. You *feel* what's wrong, so you follow what you know. Lucky for you, you figured out how to get paid for it. But you have to be very smart and careful and never blow your cover."

"I know not to blow my cover, but what I don't know is how to access this information," said Simon, his shoulders feeling literally bowed with the load of what his father was proposing.

"Use the tools that the men in power use, such as employing gates and guardians, astrology, seership, and sacred sex. Keep that part of your work to yourself. As for our conversations, now that we have gotten this far in your training, you and I can't speak over the phone anymore about these things, only in person. I advise you to adopt that practice with Sarah. If somebody tries to block you, just castle and go after it from a new direction. This will be especially fun in Rome, the checkerboard home of the global mind controllers."

David paused for a brief moment. "But never forget one thing. First, detect things that are real in the solid world and differentiate them from what exists in the thought realm. If you can do that, you will avoid trouble. I can't really tell you *how* to do that; you have to learn it by living. These two dimensions, the third and the fourth, feel *very* different, so once you can feel that difference, you will be shocked by how easily you can read people and events. It becomes child's play, and if you watch children carefully, they know all about these two different worlds."

"I know what you mean, and I have a lot to learn," Simon replied. "You've trained me well though—when I encounter a person, I can sense whether they're acting fully of their own free will. It's almost like I *hear* the program that is running them when they talk! Now that you've explained this I think I'll be able to tune into it even easier."

"Good," David responded. "Impeccable ethics, a clear mind, and a wise heart will protect you. Your mother has always simply loved you as you are, so you are protected by her love as well as my wisdom. I have noticed the same with Sarah. These influences must be exposed to the light of day for greater happiness in this exquisite world. We are nowhere if we refuse to see the truth, no matter how unpleasant it may be."

Both men hung up with a sigh—David's for the burden he knew he was placing on his son and Simon's for the weight of the journey he had ahead.

23

Old Friends

Just before Thanksgiving, close relatives and friends began gathering in Boston for the wedding. Simon and his sister, Jennifer, moved into the Algonquin Club with David and Rose where they would host the rehearsal dinner on Friday night through reciprocal arrangements with their New York club.

The Adamson house vibrated with anticipation. Sarah's sister, Susan Marie, was to be the maid of honor, and Sarah's best friend, Felicity Wallace, was to be the bridesmaid. All three women had their dresses fitted at the house Wednesday afternoon while Mary began preparations for Thanksgiving dinner the next day. After a light supper, Sarah spent some time alone with Susan and Felicity. Neither had seen Sarah since she went to Rome, so they were dying for the chance to find out all about Simon.

"How'd you meet him?" Susan Marie asked. She and Sarah were sitting cross-legged on Sarah's bed, while Felicity perched in a nest chair by the bed.

"I'll tell you the truth, but you can't tell Mom and Dad. He picked me up in the street in Rome!" Sarah said. She hadn't quite planned to tell them that part, but she was so nervous about the upcoming events she just blurted it out.

"In the street, Sarah?" Felicity retorted. "How *could* you?"

"It isn't as bad as it sounds, but it is the truth," Sarah said, remembering the first time she saw Simon. "This will sound like a cliché, but I knew he was the one when I first laid eyes on him. You hear about things like that and that's what happened to me. There was another guy on the scene for a while. Do you remember the Pierleonis, Susan? Dad's Italian friends who came to visit a few times when we were growing up?"

"Of course I remember them," Susan said. "When I heard Daddy took you to visit them in Tuscany, I was so jealous."

"You would have loved going to their castle. It's hard to believe that anybody lives that way anymore, but they do," Sarah said with passion. "Matilda Pierleoni took a fancy to me and introduced me to their oldest son, Armando, a really sexy guy, who almost stole me away from Simon! I can't believe I was so cavalier, dating both of them at the same time. Last summer Simon got sent to Jerusalem on an assignment, and I was left alone in Rome with Armando."

"Dating two guys at the same time?" Felicity broke in. "That does not sound like the Sarah I know. When's the last time you even dated one guy? I haven't met Simon yet, but from what you've said, he's impressive and perfect for you. So why'd you date this other guy?"

Sarah leaned back onto her pillows. "Now that some time has gone by, I've had a chance to think about it. Under normal circumstances, I wouldn't tell anybody, but you are my sister and my best friend. You've known me all these years, and you may have thought of me as a woman above it all?"

Susan watched her sister, surprised at Sarah's forthrightness. Usually she was so guarded. *I wonder what she's getting at,* she thought. *It's as if she wants to confess something.*

"Well," Sarah went on. "I found out that I knew a lot less about men than I thought. I'm about to be married to a man who offers me a very happy life. I need to talk about Armando with both of you because I need to warn you about some things, especially you, Susan."

Sarah smiled at her sister. Twenty-two-year old Susan was very beautiful and more delicate than Sarah; she more strongly resembled their mother. When they were growing up, Sarah had felt like she was too big, too athletic in comparison. Susan was the pretty one with sky blue eyes sparkling in her avid and demure face. Also, she was deliciously fleshy like a yummy baby with dewy and translucent skin. Felicity was twenty-five, a tawny beauty with intense brown eyes, high cheekbones, and a strong classic jaw. She was a champion tennis player who moved with the grace and awareness of a jaguar. Felicity had always been the meeting point between Sarah and Susan Marie, and she wanted to know what Sarah was getting at. In their teens, the three of them had made a pact to remain virgins until they married and promised to tell each other all their experiences with men.

Felicity said, "Come on, Sarah, 'fess up."

"Armando is a painter, a very good one, and he is very charming," Sarah began tentatively. "He photographed me reclining on a divan so he could paint me. But before I explain, I have to tell you that even before the photo session we had kissed several times. I was very attracted to him. It was the first time I ever really felt desire! He is handsome and sophisticated, and as the oldest son, will someday be a count. His parents live in the perfect castle in the perfect setting. I think I fell in love with the idea of living there. Old European glamour snowed me and I'm not proud of it; I was under a spell. If you ever run into someone like this, I hope you will be able to resist better than I did! Frankly I wasn't sure which man I wanted, but I noticed Simon always made me feel strong and safe, while Armando always made me feel nervous and excited. Armando was debonair with seductive manners, while Simon was safe and sweet.

Sarah sighed. It was harder than she had thought to admit her mistakes, even to her sister and best friend. "I was incredibly naive and should have listened to my instincts. The first time I was in Armando's studio alone, he put the moves on me. I made him stop, but I should have been smart enough to never see him alone again. He apologized so convincingly that I went on to date him, and he behaved himself. The truth is I was so physically attracted to him that I did not see how dangerous he was."

Felicity and Susan stared at her, engrossed in Sarah's story.

"His mother, Matilda, invited me back to Tuscany when the painting was done, and . . ." Sarah paused. "I'm lucky I'm sitting here in one piece before my wedding. When he pulled the cloth off the painting, I saw he'd painted me as a nude! I was horrified! I felt like he'd raped me. Once he saw I was angry, he grabbed me and threw me on a divan where he *did* try to rape me." Susan gasped, bringing her hand to her mouth; Felicity frowned, her hands curling into fists at her sides. Seeing their reactions, Sarah hastened to add, "He didn't succeed, but he was strong and it went very far. It was a terrifying experience that could have ruined me. Worse than that, once he got going, I started to feel turned on. I'm telling you, lust is dangerous."

Felicity shook her head with eyes wide and reached over to the bed to take Sarah's hand. Susan reached for Sarah's arm to stroke it while she thought about what Sarah had said. She felt terrible for her sister, but at the same time she couldn't quite understand her actions. *I don't think I would've seen this guy alone if I had feelings like that. Sarah has always been the strong one, the adventurous one. I always figured she'd get herself into trouble.* Her thoughts were interrupted by Felicity. "Damn it, Sarah! What is wrong with that guy, what's *wrong* with him?"

"I think he's crazy. He loses control of himself when life isn't served to him on a silver platter. But regardless of that, I should have known better, and that's why I am sharing this with you. Things are so meaningless these days that most people think the kind of rules we three adopted are passé. Hardly anybody looks at dating the way we do. I just wish I'd been able to pay attention to the part of me that knew better! I was wishy-washy because I felt foolish about my morals and my instincts, the things our parents taught us."

"*Really?*" Susan interrupted. "I never do because of my faith and the things Mom and Dad have taught me. Kevin is very understanding of the vow I made. He never pressures me because of our shared faith." Kevin was Susan's boyfriend, an older computer programmer she had met at church.

Sarah was just about to tell Susan about her crisis of faith, but Felicity broke in again in a heated voice. "You want me to be honest with you, Adamson sisters, you naive Catholic goody-goodies who will someday find out about the real world? The dating scene is so bad I've considered being a lesbian. I made this pact with the two of you to keep my personal freedom! It can be *dangerous* to go out with guys these days! If they don't get what they want, they can force you, slip you a drug, or both. I am surprised Armando didn't do that to you, Sarah. I figured you two would be old maids and live at home. But you went to Rome and ran into the real world. Thank goodness you handled it as well as you did. You don't feel guilty about this, do you? If you do, you shouldn't!"

Sarah shook her head. "I don't feel guilty partly because I told Simon about it right away and he really helped me get over it. Like you, Felicity, he knows how it is out there because he's had a lot of experience. So it is not about guilt, it's about how weird things are with sex. The three of us have never talked about other dimensions, but this experience changed me. I think dark forces flow through Armando from other dimensions, forces he's not aware of. When he tried to rape me, he was demonic; I've seen the face of evil."

Susan's eyes were as wide as saucers; she'd never heard of anything like that before.

Felicity ran Sarah's comments through her mind. *Wow, has Sarah changed! I can't wait to meet Simon.* She'd known the Adamson clan for years, and she'd always thought Sarah was like her father, a jolly guy on the surface who was sad inside.

Felicity gazed intently into Sarah's green eyes. "You're leaving the Church, aren't you? You see how complex things are and don't believe the patriarchal story anymore? I wondered why you're getting married at a meeting house, but I thought it must be what Simon wants. Are you finally exiting the Catholic guilt program?"

Sarah smiled, but none of this was funny to Susan. "Sarah, you're not, you're *not* leaving the Church? I can't believe it!"

"Susan," Sarah responded. "I think Mom and Dad must want me to tell you, since they haven't yet. Yes, I'm leaving, and do you want to know why?"

Susan stared at her sister with her mouth open, her pupils reduced to small points in recoil. *I don't know if I want to know. I suppose it's because he's a Jew.* "Yes, I would like to know. Why? Because of Simon?"

"No, not because of Simon," Sarah answered. "In my studies I've learned that the Church has done more to suppress the story of Jesus than spread it. My deep relationship with Christ remains regardless of what the Church has done to His story. For me, the Church is devoid of the divine, so I can no longer be a part of it." Seeing Susan's wide, shocked eyes, Sarah took her sister's hand. "It doesn't mean things have to be different between us. Even Dad accepts my feelings."

I cannot believe anybody could change this much in a year, both Susan and Felicity were thinking from opposite perspectives. Felicity said, "*William* has accepted you leaving the Church? I think everybody is nuts these days. What is going on, Sarah?"

"Felicity, I'm amazed by my dad's latitude. Maybe it's because he likes Simon and his family; maybe it is because I dropped Armando. He met him in Italy and couldn't stand him—even though I thought he would be happy about us dating at the time. Maybe it's because he's changing too. All the articles Simon has been writing about the priestly sexual abuse crisis have really shaken Dad up and forced him to face it."

Felicity's eyes narrowed as she observed Sarah and Susan. *I never thought I'd see so much change in this family, never.* Her parents were both anthropologists, more interested in studying and analyzing religious beliefs than in practicing them, and she took an interest in Sarah and Susan to study how religion influenced them. Felicity had never had the same rules imposed on her because her family was more liberal, yet her closeness with Sarah influenced her thoughts about sexuality. When all three girls were teenagers, however, Felicity had sometimes resented the way Sarah and Susan were protected from the world. Believing in the obsolete teachings of the Church seemed to make life so simple.

"Sarah!" Susan screeched. "I just can't believe you're leaving the Church. Dad would never do what you're doing, Mom never would; I never will. I just have to say that. I'm happy you are getting married, but you've ended up where you are because you broke the rules and dated someone outside the Church. Just think if Patrick were here today. What would he think?"

Felicity wanted to tell Susan to watch it. "Susan, don't you think you are being too hard on Sarah?"

Before Susan could answer, Sarah interjected, "We can't know how Patrick would've lived his life. I'll share something with you if you'll promise me you will be more patient and understanding with me, especially now." Susan took a deep breath and looked into Sarah's soft eyes and nodded her agreement. "For me Simon is like the return of the older brother we lost. I missed having Patrick in our childhood, and often I've wanted an older brother who would watch out for me and love me. Maybe you are the same? Or maybe you have not needed an older brother because you always had me. I think that is partly why I fell in love with Simon—he's so nurturing. Now we've grown up and you'll probably keep your faith and marry in the Church. I sure hope so because then somebody will make Mom and Dad happy! This is not easy for me, marrying outside the Church, but I have to follow my conscience."

Felicity was glad that the sisters had made peace for the moment, but she couldn't help but think: *wait until Sarah meets Kevin!* Felicity quickly added, "Good, I'm glad you two won't have a cat fight. I hope I won't lose you as a friend, Susan. I think it doesn't matter whether anybody is in the Church, but even you will have to face the corruption; I'm happy I don't have to deal with it."

24

Thanksgiving 2012

On Thanksgiving Day, Kevin McCarty came early to meet Sarah before the arrival of Simon's family. Susan stood proudly by Kevin as he took Sarah's hand and said with bumbling enthusiasm, "I can't believe it, Sarah. You are as beautiful as my Susan, but in a different way. How'd you pull it off, William, two such gorgeous daughters?" William smiled and went to the kitchen for a Scotch.

Sarah looked him over as if appraising a horse, which put him on guard. Kevin was thoroughly Irish with reddish cheeks, recessed blue eyes, a small pot belly, and large teeth. *He looks like he just got off the boat from Dublin! A computer programmer slapped over a jolly gnome like a cheese sandwich wrapped in Saran Wrap. How old is he, forty? He sure is easy with Daddy.* "Thanks for the compliment, but you have the prettiest daughter."

Sarah tried to be conversational as they followed her father into the kitchen. "Susan says you met at church and you program computers?" she began while continuing to examine him.

"I'm a programmer for IBM and we did meet in church. That doesn't compare with meeting a hot reporter in Rome and snagging him quick!" As Susan walked away to help her mother prepare the meal, "Susan and I have no plans yet, but I am serious about her. That's why I was invited today. Weddings often spawn proposals, so perhaps your wedding will be the final push?" He smirked and turned himself slightly to get a better view of Sarah's chest. "You are wearing a beautiful diamond. Is it a family heirloom?"

Sarah felt very uncomfortable and invaded. Whenever he spoke her ruby vibrated with the warning of what was really being said beneath his words: *I've waited a long time to find a virgin! I've got Susan if I want her, but I'd rather have you, babe. You better not stand in my way.* Sarah winced and tried to maintain her composure. "Yes, it was our grandmother's. So you are thinking of proposing? If you'll forgive me, since she's my only sister, how old are you, Kevin?"

Kevin flushed and sat up straighter. "I'm forty-one and in *our* tradition the man being older is best. I'm established and can support a family, so she'd be well taken care of. Seems to me I heard Simon is quite a bit older than you?"

At this point, Sarah was so mad that she couldn't detect the weird double voice. She replied curtly, "I think I hear someone at the door. Thanks for the little chat." As she walked away, he checked out her ass undulating under her black skirt. *That's one thing they both have, a world-class ass.* The front hall was filling when she saw Simon hanging up his trench coat. As she went to him, a tall, intense, and striking woman touched her shoulder, a feminine version of Simon.

"Jennifer?" Sarah asked.

The woman smiled broadly, her dark eyes warm and open. "You must be Sarah. I am so thrilled to meet you! Simon has told me all about you. I never imagined he'd fall so deeply in love! Now that I see you I can see why. You're absolutely beautiful. He's told you I'm a Parisian high-fashion photographer? You're beyond anyone I have done. Wow! Go, little brother, go!"

Sarah laughed and then blushed, which made her even more becoming. Simon took her hand and kissed her on the forehead. "See what a beauty, Jen? That's not why I love her, but it sure helped me pick her out of the crowd in Rome." He looked at both of them. "Sarah, Jennifer's wedding present is to do a study of us this year. Maybe in Paris, maybe Barcelona."

Jennifer nodded. "I would love to do that whenever it works for you. But for the next few days I want to be the sister and not the photographer for once!"

The three of them walked into the living room where David and Rose stood with Mary and William. Simon said to Jennifer, "Our families really like each other, have from the first even though we didn't give them much time. Come meet Sarah's parents."

Simon brought Jennifer to Mary, who pressed her shoulders, looking warmly into her eyes. "Jennifer, I'm so happy to meet you. We've been looking forward to it. You're lovely; you resemble Simon so much." Mary noted Jennifer's intriguing beauty, her poise and presence and clear, magnetic dark eyes.

William said, "Hello, Jennifer! I'm William, Sarah's father! Welcome to our home, welcome to a day of good food! What'll you have?" he asked, pointing out some glasses of wine and water. "If you want the hard stuff, just say so." Jennifer happily accepted a glass of wine.

Sarah slipped away from Jennifer and her parents to bring Felicity to Simon. "Simon, this is my best friend, Felicity Wallace. She's been anxious to meet you. She's staying with us here, so I've told her *everything* about you. She's likely to say almost anything to you, so be prepared."

Simon turned to smile at Felicity, yet he was so overwhelmed with happiness he hardly saw her. *Here I am in the house of the woman I love and we are about to get married. I never thought this would happen.* "Hello, Felicity," he said, training his laughing brown eyes on her. "Since Sarah loves you so much, I hope we'll be very close. It's wonderful to meet you."

Felicity was not prepared for Simon. *Now here is a man, a man any woman would love to have. I hope Susan will wake up when she meets Simon and his family. I'm so afraid she will fall for that hairball. Once she gets into it, she'll never get out of it, the whole Catholic thing.* "Simon, I'm thrilled to meet you. I've never seen Sarah so happy. And of course, you're lucky to have her."

Wandering into the big dining room with the table set for ten, Felicity discovered she was seated between Simon and Mary. He smiled warmly as he pulled out her chair. "Excellent! We'll have a chance to get to know each other better," he said.

Mary had carefully planned the seating arrangements, and once they all sat down she was satisfied. Conversation flowed while they ate roast turkey, cranberry sauce, rice stuffing, potatoes, squash, and rolls and honey. Sarah felt trapped between Jennifer, whom she truly wanted to know better, and Kevin, the person she most hoped to avoid.

Jennifer looked discreetly across at Susan, intrigued by her lack of resemblance to Sarah. Susan strongly resembled Mary, and Sarah looked more like her father. *Sarah has a strong masculine side, which will be good for Simon, since he's ambitious.*

Sarah broke into her thoughts. "If you don't mind me saying so, Jennifer, I can't believe how like Simon you are! You're impeccably polite, but below the surface you seem to be always studying people. Simon functions like two entities, one acting in the world, the other with a built-in radar system that watches every detail. Maybe that's why he is a superb reporter. Am I right? If so, I bet this helps with your photography too."

Jennifer was uncharacteristically drawn right in. *Oh thank god he didn't pick a dry intellectual too much like himself.* "Funny you say that because I had to develop that ability. When I'm photographing someone, I have to be aware of comfort zones and boundaries. I use my artistic eye to capture what is beautiful, nasty, powerful, or insecure in them. So yes, I am always doing two things at once, two tracks running in my head, always." Jennifer was discreetly observing Sarah's strong neck and lovely skin. *I can't wait to take her picture.*

"There is something else that I've always wondered about photographers," Sarah said. "Do you care whether your subjects like their photos once you've really captured their true essence?"

"That question opens many possibilities," Jennifer replied, feeling easily intimate with Sarah. "If I'm sure I've captured them, I don't give a damn whether they like it or not. However, often they make me into a psychologist because they haven't come to terms with how they look. You would be amazed! Absolutely beautiful women who look exquisite on film are sometimes as horrified as if I've made a mockery of them. I never know how they'll react! I don't try to make them look a certain way; I just record what I see. The more beautiful they are, the harder it is to capture them because they've learned to obscure themselves." She studied Sarah again. "Possibly you are that way?"

Just then William clicked his glass with his spoon for the first toast. "To Simon and Sarah, two young people perfectly suited for one another, to a long and happy life together. And welcome, all of you!" Sarah raised her glass to her father's. Kevin clicked hers, which enabled him to peek at her right breast when she raised her arm. His invasive eyes burned into her neck as she looked across the table to Susan Marie's vacant, glowing face. *How can I get her to start thinking? This guy is a sleaze.* She turned toward Jennifer, but Kevin took his chance to break in because he'd run out of things to say to William "You have such a great father, Sarah. You both are so lucky. That's the best kind of girl, one with a strong and responsible father," he said.

Sarah was appalled by his glazed eyes and slurred words. *He's already loaded. What a klutz he is! Why can't Susan see? Is she confused by desire? She didn't say anything last night when I was so open about my struggle with lust. What do I say to this ass?* She turned her eyes away from Kevin's flushed face to see Simon gazing at her. Searching his eyes, she made a mental note to remember what she had just heard Kevin say beneath his surface words, *When I get your younger sister, we'll have a bunch of good Catholic kids.*

Felicity said to Simon, "You have a wonderful family. I had a moment with your father and he is very astute and cultured. Your mother seems strong and wise. She adores Sarah. She told me that she knows Sarah is the right person for you, which was very forthright. Maybe Sarah won't have a mother-in-law problem."

Is she worried Sarah might get a cloying Jewish mother-in-law? Taking note of Felicity's incisive face and inviting hazel eyes, Simon said in a clear voice, "My mother took to her immediately because they both love the decorative arts, my mother's great passion. As for my father, he adores her, pure and simple. Once he met her, we had to get together."

Mary stood up to toast. "To Simon, the perfect partner for our oldest daughter, a partner who will be with her through life. We lost our first child when he was a baby, and Sarah missed out on the companionship of her lost brother, Patrick. We welcome Simon to our family as a son. Please, no one hear what I have to say as tinged with sadness. So with my toast, Patrick, come to the table to share Sarah's joy with Simon."

They all toasted, then Felicity turned to Simon and said quietly, "As far as I know, that is the first time she's spoken of Patrick in public. Maybe she is beyond her terrible pain? Your arrival may be opening her heart because she wanted a son so much. Since I'm Sarah's best friend, I want you to promise me something. May I ask?" He tilted his head respectfully to invite her to continue. "When the bride and groom have their wedding, everything is love and light. Then they go out into the world and often end up hurting one another. Promise me, Simon, that you will never hurt Sarah. She is very special."

This is what I'd expect from Sarah's best friend. Felicity is dead certain of her opinions, just like me. He laughed. "Are you always going to grill me like this, Felicity? I've waited thirty-five years to find my partner and I will never hurt her. My father has not dishonored my mother, and neither will I betray my love. I am very much aware of her high spiritual nature. Your best friend is in good hands." They clinked their glasses together discreetly.

Sarah looked on, understanding exactly what was going on. She smiled at Simon across the table as another clinking glass called for attention.

David stood up, tapping his glass a few times, and gestured to Rose to stand up with him. He looked into their waiting faces. "First, I toast Sarah, the beautiful bride, a woman of strength, intelligence, and kindness. Simon, I salute you for finding her and not letting her go, no matter what was in the way. To Mary and William, we toast you for bringing her into the world so that our families can enjoy her. We hope someday we will have grandchildren. Blessings to their love." Rose smiled and bowed as if she had nothing to say beyond this.

The Friday night rehearsal dinner in the Captain's Cabin room at the Algonquin was warm and joyful, with all the guests enjoying great food in the understated elegance of the old traditional club. After dinner Susan tapped on Sarah's door, hoping she was still awake. Sarah was in a chair by the window in deep contemplation. The extreme potency of what was about to occur had dawned on her for the first time. Struggling to pull herself out of her reverie, she let Susan in.

Susan came in and sat down on the bed, her eyes wide and anxious. "You don't like Kevin, do you, Sarah? You have to tell me what you think because you are going away again. I have to know what you think."

Sarah sighed inwardly. She loved her sister, but Kevin was the last person she wanted to think about tonight of all nights. And what

could she possibly say? "It's not that I don't like him, but is he right
for you? You are still so young! Do you love him? Are you attracted
to him? Are you sure you want someone who is twenty years older?
Do you like his family? Do you like being with his friends? I really
don't know him well enough to say much about him, so I can only
help you if you will tell me how you feel."

Susan felt irritated with Sarah. Sarah always had it all; she was
the beautiful one, the smart one, and now she had found a husband.
Still, Susan had been extremely impressed by Simon's warm family
and his comfort with her sister. Kevin wasn't comfortable with her
that way, not yet. "I've met his parents, a sister, and a brother who is
a priest. They're very nice. As for how I feel, he has swept me away.
He takes me everywhere, the best restaurants and front-row tickets
for games, I . . ."

"But, how do you *feel* about him? Have you kissed him, held
him? Do you like his body?"

"Things have gotten physical," Susan admitted. "When I'm
alone with him, which isn't often because of Dad, he pushes me further. I want him but I'm trying to keep my promise. I think I should
marry him so I don't do it before. If he asks me, I'll say yes. Does
that answer your question? Dad likes him a lot, and Dad should
know."

"But do you love him? Do you want to spend a life with him
and have a pack of kids? That's what he wants. What do *you* want,
Susan?"

Susan looked puzzled. "I don't know what I want," she said
slowly. "I think I want a husband and kids, but I've never really
asked myself before if that's just because I'm *supposed* to want those
things."

"Don't rush into anything, Susan," Sarah urged. "And don't settle for anyone, especially not because you think other people like
him. I thought Daddy liked Armando, but I couldn't have been
more wrong."

Susan still looked confused, but she accepted a hug from her sister and went back to her room.

As Sarah dropped off to sleep, she visualized the old meeting house with light pouring in through tall windows. Her last thought as she moved into the twilight zone was that she hoped Susan wouldn't get stuck with Kevin just because she, the older sister, was getting married.

25

The Wedding

Finally it was the day. Sarah and Simon's wedding was scheduled for 11 a.m., November 24, 2012, at a simple meeting house on a deep bend in the Charles River, a beautiful setting sculpted by wild and potent wind. The home of Henry Wadsworth Longfellow was across the street, so a few guests parked and strolled in the famous gardens of the serene yellow Georgian mansion before coming into the chapel. Others went quickly inside the meetinghouse to escape the bitter north wind blowing down over the icy cold Charles River.

Simon stood by the front door waiting for his family. The bitter wind ruffled his thick black hair, brought tears to his eyes, shrank his skin, and bit his cheeks. He was ecstatic. He was glad to see David and Rose approach as his father always had a calming effect on him.

"I'm so proud of you, Simon," David said gripping his son's shoulders and staring into his eyes. *This is right.*

His mother gazed at her son in his classic black tuxedo and said, "I shouldn't ask, but I will. Have you seen her dress?"

"No, that's bad luck for the Irish," Simon replied. "I won't see it until her father brings her to the altar. Let's go inside so we can sit quietly for a while." They entered through the west door. High multipaned windows on the north and south sides brought in the light.

Late November sun sparkled through the wavy, distorted glass, casting watery and crystalline shapes on the soft pine floors. People chatted in hushed voices as the ushers led people to their seats. The room was full of magnetic energy. It was as if angels were flying under the high ceiling.

"This is a lovely meetinghouse," Rose whispered. "It is absolutely original, so pristine, a good choice."

Simon sat quietly with his parents and used yogic breathing to stay calm and in his body. He was suspended on the edge of an unknown world, feeling like his head was going to spin off his neck.

David sensed his anxiety and put his hand over Simon's hand, thinking, *He's still four years old and discovering magic.*

Simon snapped back to what was going on around him when his old friend Marc Sinclair walked into the altar space wearing a navy blue suit. He smiled at Simon, who got up and walked into the altar space to face Marc. Simon turned to gaze at the smiling people while David and Rose came to stand by his side. An audible rush of whispers suddenly swept the room. Simon's knees wobbled, and his eyes flooded with salty tears. *I'm afraid I won't be able to even see her!*

A whoosh of powerful wind from the Charles swept in when the inner doors opened for William and Sarah. Wavy-glassed windows undulated as the guests turned to face the middle aisle to view the bride. She came slowly forward, an angelic vision in ivory silk, lace, and pearls. Her hair cascaded over her shoulders, barely obscured by an ivory lace Portuguese mantilla that fell down over her arms. Her hands were covered by white lace gloves embroidered with pearls. She wore a low-necked empire waist bodice that glowed with countless iridescent pearls gleaming against ivory silk. Flushed with anticipation, she was from another century.

Proudly she approached Simon and Marc with her arm in her father's. She held a simple bouquet of yellow jonquils with dark green leaves, the yellow vibrant against the ivory, pearls, and Sarah's luminescent face. William guided her by her elbow as they approached the altar.

Simon stood patiently, beholding his bride. *I'm afraid I'm going to levitate! I was not prepared for this heavenly sight.* He felt small in the face of her beauty. *No matter what everybody tries to think these days, this is her ultimate moment, and I am humbled.* He smiled shyly, realizing he'd never seen her before as his moist eyes showered her with love.

Sarah's heart pounded in her chest. She gave her bouquet to Susan, and then her father placed her hand in Simon's. William stood by her side as Mary came to stand by Susan. The altar space was not elevated, so the guests stood on their toes. Simon was grateful they were all on the same level as a great force from deep in the Earth rushed into his body through his legs.

When the bride and groom and attendants had all assumed their places, Marc spoke extemporaneously. "I am here today to guide the union of Sarah and Simon, and spirit moves me. I have known Simon for many years, and I testify that his heart is as true as the pristine light in this sacred space. He has found a home for his heart in his bride, Sarah." He turned to search deeply into Simon's dark eyes looking for the realization of the import of this union; Simon's body jerked involuntarily in response.

Marc turned to Sarah and said, "I've only shared time with you a few times while we prepared for this moment. You are the mother of Simon's soul, the one he began seeking when he was born. He tells me he knew this when he first saw you. Therefore, Sarah, know him in all ways as only a woman can know a man. Take his heart and hold it in yours!" Looking benevolently into her green eyes, he touched her lightly on her left shoulder, and her spine buzzed and vibrated in long waves. She was afraid she'd faint.

"Now," Marc said in a louder voice for the gathered people. "Soon it will be time for you to speak because you are here today to support Simon and Sarah. In our sacred space, we do not ask if there is anyone who objects to this marriage. Instead, we ask you to express your thoughts about these two people choosing to be one. We will observe ten to fifteen minutes of deep silence, going into our hearts to seek the essence of what Simon and Sarah desire. Then, those who wish to speak to them before they marry, speak. If you wish it, Simon and Sarah, you may hold hands during the silence."

Sarah relaxed when she felt Simon's hand firmly grasp hers. Strong earth energy was making her dizzy. *I had no idea it would be like this. Everything feels unreal to me as if I am reliving an old time. I know the truth to my visions, I have stood with him before.* The silence felt like seconds while she gripped his hand.

When he took her laced hand his strength returned, a new balance. *She is mine, really mine!* As they stood silently connected by delicate touch while people in the old pine pews meditated, the cold north wind crackled tree branches, falling leaves scraped against the glass. The sun flashing in and out of clouds transformed the meeting house into a kaleidoscope of rainbows. The silence deepened when slapping waves on the Charles brought the water element into the room. Then a tiny bell was rung; it was time to speak. Mary said in a low but clearly enunciated whisper, "Come, Patrick, come into this room. Be with us now!" The old pain stabbing William's heart melted in quietude.

One by one, the people uttered a word at a time: "Joy." "Peace." "Happiness." "Home." "Children." "Good food." "Gardening." "Plants." "Lace." "Coziness." "Dogs." "Beauty." Marc waited a few minutes for their voices to subside; it was now time for the marriage.

Sarah and Simon faced each other, holding hands. He released a hand and brushed aside the veil; she looked frail and flushed. While Marc led them through their vows, Simon's voice kept cracking while hers was strong and clear. After exchanging their vows and the rings, she looked expectantly into his eyes. Marc asked them to go down and face each other on their knees. They looked at each other, wondering what was going on, since this had not been part of the rehearsal. Marc placed his large hands firmly on the top of their heads, took a deep and audible breath, and said loudly, "Spirit, now come into them and bless them!"

A force came through his hands that made him rigid; Simon and Sarah were electrified. The people could see a vibrating rush of blue light flow into the couple like a strike of cosmic energy in a painting by William Blake. The rush was greater than the fierce wind outside that exploded when Marc humbly blessed them; the great blast moved the old wooden structure. William felt a shock, and David steeled his body in proportion to the force. Mary and Rose were filled with joy, their hearts completely open with their son and daughter. Marc grinned ecstatically and pronounced in a joyful and triumphant voice, "*Now* you may kiss the bride." Simon pierced the great force by pulling Sarah to his body and planting a lusty kiss on her lips. She'd lost the sense of where she was, but his kiss brought her back. She was laughing when he released her, and they turned to face the people together. Everyone who was there on that windy November day knew something very special had happened. They would always remember the wedding of Simon and Sarah Appel.

The reception was wonderful and joyous, and after the long day was concluded, Simon and Sarah were finally alone in a bridal suite at the Four Seasons Hotel on the Common. Tired and drained, they were grateful for this gift from David, especially since they had to get right back to Rome. The little parlor burst with fresh white and yellow roses from Mary and William. Little sandwiches and a plate of cut vegetables were set out for them.

"This is so perfect, Simon. Just what we need. I'm wiped; this day was wonderful, but exhausting." They sank down into comfortable armchairs around a low coffee table where a bottle of wedding champagne was chilling in a sweating silver bucket. "This is so thoughtful of our parents, like a mini-honeymoon."

"Yeah, my parents really know how to do things right. You'll find they are very frugal, but they always celebrate lavishly at the right time. My father completely shocked my mother by whisking her off to Paris on a first-class flight right after their wedding reception! He even packed everything she needed. This hotel feels like heaven right now. I love Mary's flowers." He reached for a chicken salad sandwich. "What happened today? What *was* that at the end of the ceremony? Did you feel that huge force going through us like a lightning bolt? How'd Marc do that?"

"I felt like I was completely out of it until you kissed me. I don't know what happened."

"That's funny. In my case I was hyper-conscious, hyper-aware as if I could see the essence of everything, jazzed with energy. Where do you think you went?"

Instinctually she moved her fingertips over the ruby crystal to go back to what she had felt when Marc put his hand on her head. "I felt like I went to another planet, someplace that rules marriage. Until today, I had no idea that marriage could create high energy. I've always felt that becoming part of a new family was the point, not that there was something more. I never witnessed *anything* like this in the Church. The nuptial Mass is the central focus when supposedly you are married in heaven." She paused. "I'm having trouble expressing this. I had the feeling there is a place somewhere in the universe that's in charge of marriage. Isn't that weird?"

Simon reached for another sandwich. "Yes, it is weird, yet something happened today. I felt a force greater than anything I've experienced before. I wonder if everybody who gets married feels this, or did we feel it because we are sensitive to this kind of energy? Marc never mentioned doing it, so I have to assume that he wasn't going to do it unless he detected something special between you and me. Quakers always wait until they are moved by spirit. I suppose I'll always wonder about it. Maybe Marc will tell us. Meanwhile, what matters to me is what we felt. We're really married now, which is a mystery in itself. Everything will be different from now on. It's time for champagne!"

26

Sarah Meets Claudia

An icy wind off the Tiber in early December rattled the doors to the balcony; meanwhile, the gas fire in the living room was delightfully warming. It was Sarah's first day alone in weeks. Simon was out probing some of his Vatican contacts and having lunch with a few reporters. Roman gossips twittered over Vatican intrigues, while the world wondered about Benedict's involvement in the sex-abuse scandal. Were the ancient veils of secrecy actually lifting?

As soon as they got back to Rome, the newlyweds had become obsessed with trying to ascertain the truth, and now Sarah needed to think by herself. *Why do priests do these things?* She wondered if sexual deviance, a common flaw of people in power, was beyond greed. After all, the hierarchy had all the money it wanted. Unless they outright robbed the laity, nobody really cared about what they spent. She concluded that the extent of sexual abuse in the Church must instead be caused by celibacy, which distorted the animalistic aspects of sex. Sarah didn't know where she went when she was having sex with Simon; sometimes that made her feel insane. But violating children was another thing! They were so vulnerable to authority figures. It was the *why* she was after, however, and she continued to have the sense that the hierarchy somehow used the children's energy to invigorate themselves. *Like vampires.*

Simon came home just before dinner—Sarah was doing some cooking for a change. "I made a simple meal—baked potatoes, veal cutlets, and salad," she called from the kitchen.

Simon sat down on the couch and began reading *La Repubblica*. Sarah brought him a glass of wine, and he thanked her.

"I can't wait to sit down with you and eat. I spent most of the day talking to other reporters about whether Benedict is at the top of the sexual abuse pyramid. I vacillate between thinking he's only a pawn and wondering if he's been the director of the priestly abuse program for years. We know he read all the abuse reports when he headed the Congregation for the Doctrine of the Faithful, the modern form of the Inquisition. When he became pope, he focused on damage control. Sometimes I think he's trying harder than the bishops and cardinals have in the past to clean up the mess. But he looks like the personification of Satan with those creepy dark shadows around his eyes and glittery salivating thin lips."

Sarah stroked his hair. "Leave that for now. Let's have dinner."

Since it was wintertime, the small patio table was now in the kitchen by the window. She lit the candles. "I hope this is spicy enough for the Malbec. After all," she said with a self-deprecating smile, "I'm just a simple Irish cook."

He rose and kissed her before sitting down. "Everything looks perfect. It's so nice to have you cook for me; I escaped bachelorhood just in time!"

Today he'd been reminded of his bachelor days during lunch with some of his colleagues. Claudia, an old lover, had sauntered over to the table wearing a loosely knit cotton sweater over a tight suede mini-skirt stretched over black fishnet tights. "Ciao, Simon," she had said, managing to sound bored and demanding as only a Roman woman could. "I hear you got married? When can I meet her? I'm hoping we can have a few minutes together? I have some information about the Vatican that might interest you."

Hmmm, he had thought to himself as he introduced her to

the other men, watching one of them look over her catlike body. Claudia had never lied in the past; maybe she did know something. "Is your phone number still the same?" She nodded yes. "Then I'll call you. Thanks." She had walked slowly away, while they all gazed at her magnificent proud ass pushed up by outrageous spike heels. Noting one man whose mouth had literally dropped open, Simon had said, smiling, "You horny, Donatio?"

"Not like the priests, thank God," he had replied while the others chuckled.

"Sarah," Simon said, emerging from his thoughts. "Have you thought about whether we want to meet each other's old friends?" Seeing Sarah's open and questioning look, he continued. "Specifically, are you open to meeting one of my old girlfriends, the one I stopped seeing when I met you? I ran into her today, and she says she knows something about what's going on in the Vatican. She gave me some tips last year that led to some valuable insights. Her name is Claudia Tagliatti, and she hears things in her shop from customers who are in the know. It's gossip, but often gossip points the way in Rome. I think I'd prefer to see her with you, but of course I can also meet with her alone?"

Sarah wasn't sure how she felt about that. *I've had his undivided attention, yet he did have another life before me that he hasn't told me much about.* She was curious about this Claudia, and of course Sarah was also penetrating Vatican secrets. "I'm interested in what she has to say, too. I'd like to meet her with you, if that's really okay with you?"

Now Simon wondered whether Claudia would be as forthcoming if Sarah came. "When I call her about a meeting, I'll ask her if she will share what she knows if you are there. If she says she wants to see me alone, will you be okay with that? Of course, I'd meet her in a public place."

"That's fine with me, Simon. I'm not worried about an old girlfriend. I don't want to interfere with what she has to tell you. But what does she look like?"

Simon almost laughed. He was so used to the new, strong Sarah that her vulnerability was a little charming. "She's beautiful, a world-class model type, tall and statuesque, very fashionable and intelligent." He smiled at Sarah. "But she doesn't have breasts like yours, and I dropped her when I met you. Actually, I hope she feels she can speak to me while you're there because I think she'd like you. I can imagine the two of you becoming friends. In fact, now that I think about it, she might say even more if you're around. Sometimes women respond better to other women. I want to hear what she knows; I sense it is something."

Simon called Claudia the next morning to set up a meeting. "I've missed seeing you, and can my wife, Sarah, join us? If that won't work for you, I can meet you for lunch somewhere near your shop. What do you prefer?"

There was a long pause that felt strange to Simon, and then she responded slowly. "What's the deal, Simon? Is she the jealous type?"

Simon chuckled. "No, not so far. She's in Rome working on her Ph.D. in early Christian studies. We became friends because we share a lot of the same interests. Then one day we fell in love and I didn't see you after that. She'd like to hear what you have to share if you can handle it. If not, she is perfectly okay with us seeing each other alone, so what do you prefer?"

"Your question is not so easy for me to answer," she said, rolling her voice in a thick and ponderous accent. "First of all, with what I want to talk about, you'd have to come over to my place. Maybe she wouldn't like that. She's American? Hmmmm, perhaps you will understand better if I tell you that this is about Armando Pierleoni among other things."

Simon reacted to the mention of Armando's name first with shock, then anger. "What!? What on earth are you getting at, Claudia?" he snapped. "What would you know about him?"

"Plenty, darling, perhaps more than either one of you could

guess," she replied. "He was my lover years ago, but of course I didn't mention an old lover to you before." Abruptly she changed the subject. "Don't you feel weird now that it's the end of 2012, the end of the Mayan Calendar with all the apocalyptic fear? The rumors are that a comet or the dark star Nibiru or lightning is going to strike the Vatican!"

"I can't believe you pay attention to that shit, Claudia!" he said in a high, tight voice. "Have you gone nuts or something? And if that's what you want to talk about, I don't think either one of us wants to see you!"

"Thanks a lot for your usual charming frankness. That is not what I want to talk about. I just wondered if you also feel strange, like everything is about to hit a wall?"

"I did feel that way, but I just got married a few weeks ago, which took me outside of time. Sarah, too." Simon paused. "Did you know Sarah dated Armando Pierleoni before we got married? If you know something about Armando, she might want to hear it. Are *you* dating him?"

"Well, not exactly," she said in a low, sexy voice, "Ummm, I think you should both come tonight after dinner. But how liberal is she? Is she a typical American uptight snoot like the girls I dress all day? You know, darling, we *can* speak the truth to each other."

Typical Claudia. "She's not a snoot but she is young and rather innocent. Can we agree we've forgotten about our past, Claudia? If so, we can come over around 8? Actually, you will like her a lot even though you are older than she is."

"I will *never* forget our past, darling, and thanks for reminding me that the younger girl always gets the guy. See you tonight, Simon." Click.

Walking with Sarah up the wide marble stairs to the entrance of Claudia's suite, Simon wondered if he should've warned her that Armando might come up in conversation. He hadn't mentioned it because he had discovered he usually found out more if things just unfolded. He looked over at Sarah's beautiful, eager face and wondered how she'd react to Claudia's dramatic personality.

Large double doors swung wide open.

"Ciao, Ciao, Sarah, Simon's lucky bride. Thank you for coming!" Claudia greeted them both with extravagant cheek kisses and led them through the front foyer.

Claudia astonished Sarah: she was a ravishing, mature Italian beauty made up to perfection, more jaguar than human. Sarah blurted out, "Claudia, you are beautiful. A paragon of Roman perfection! I'm delighted to meet you."

"No more beautiful than you, darling, and you have the advantage of youth. But surely that is not why Simon chose you? He tells me you have mutual interests?"

Claudia swept them into her favorite small parlor with a bay window on the street. Sarah took it all in—marble columns, Grecian statuary, elegant fabrics, and fabulous antiques. Claudia's décor was beautiful and exotic, an extension of her magnificent catlike body and strikingly animated face. The women settled onto a charming small love seat while Simon took a leather chair opposite them. "I can't resist," he said. "How could any man not enjoy the opportunity to gaze at two exquisite and wonderful women? You look marvelous, Claudia. You are my first Roman friend to meet Sarah. It was so good of you to invite us."

Claudia nodded vigorously. "Ah! Then I can forgive you for not inviting me to the wedding, darling, or for not calling me up right away to tell me. Did you hurry? It seems so sudden?" She stopped herself before revealing she'd seen him less than six months ago. Sarah was actually wondering when he'd last seen Claudia. *Seems like any woman would be jealous of her, yet I'm not! Actually, I like sitting next to her. She makes me feel warm.*

Claudia poured grappa from an etched decanter into three small glasses. "What I need to talk to you about is not easy to get into, not easy at all. I promised you I would not talk about the 2012 thing, but I must begin there." She looked at Simon imploringly. Reluctantly he nodded his head. "If things were not getting so weird," Claudia continued, "none of us would be here tonight. You will not be able to understand why I feel compelled to share some coveted secrets with you unless I can make a few short comments about the so-called end of time. I don't obsess about things like that, but there *is* a feeling of catastrophe in the air, a feeling of impending doom. It's this very feeling that compels me to talk about some things that are normally hidden. I *must!*"

Sarah was riveted. She'd noticed many people in the media sniggering about the mysterious end of the Mayan Calendar. Regardless of the media acting like the idea was a joke, the U.S. government had become completely dysfunctional after Hurricane Sandy devastated New York, mass shootings were increasing, the Church was collapsing, Europe was in financial tatters, and a nasty civil war was brewing in Syria. There *was* a weird feeling of end times. She hadn't said much about it because Simon found talk of the Mayan Calendar New Age silliness. Regardless of what he thought, Sarah broke in now. "Claudia, I agree with you. I think the world feels very peculiar, very much on edge right now."

Simon interrupted. "Claudia, are you going to share some things about the Vatican or not?"

"You bet I am. I just want you to know *why* I'm doing it because if you don't, you won't believe what I'm about to say. Sarah, this is about Armando Pierleoni." The breath sucked out of Sarah's lungs as Simon watched her face like a hawk. *Nothing like getting right into it; well, that is why we came to see her.*

Claudia took a deep swig of grappa, leaned forward over her crossed legs, and exhaled deeply. "In Rome, we enjoy the ancient pagan ways and we only endure the modern world. One of the things we enjoy the most is reversing the ways of the world because we miss early Roma. We play a vast and complex game that's been going on for millennia. In pagan times the Vestal Virgins—pure women who honored the sanctity of marriage—guarded Rome to protect the family, and needy men went to the temple prostitutes. In modern times, selected Roman women carry on the custom as vestal whores who guard Rome's pagan virtues in secret. *I* was one of them, ever since my early twenties when I was chosen for my beauty." She fixed both of them with a stern glare. "I expect both of you to *never* reveal this without my permission. I am telling you because great changes are coming. You will not understand these changes without this information from me, changes it sounds like both of you long for."

Sarah shifted in her seat. How did this woman she had just met know what she longed for?

Claudia continued. "All of us know the greatest threat to human happiness is the Roman Catholic Church because it is demonic. We Italians have struggled more than others with these forces because the power is centered here; we do things that only Romans understand. No matter what anybody does to us, we are pagan and one with earth. Before I describe *my* part in this, I want to share some things I have discovered while playing my role, things that may interest you, Sarah."

Claudia locked her gaze onto Sarah's green eyes as her wide-spectrum aura narrowed down to laser beams coming out of her slanted eyes. Sarah felt even more uneasy. "Do not worry, Sarah," Claudia said warmly. "You are beyond fear of these things. When you came down into the place down below the Bernini altar with your ruby crystal, I was with you."

"What on earth are you talking about, Claudia?" Simon interrupted.

"Just be quiet for a moment, Simon. Surely you are not afraid of anything I might say to Sarah?" Claudia turned back to Sarah. "When you played out the timeline of the most powerful sacred site in Rome—the vault under the Basilica—I watched the movie with you. I saw things unfold over tens of thousands of years until the

Church took over a few thousand years ago. It was the vision I have sought my whole life. Because you opened this vision, I want to give you information about what goes on down there now."

Sarah looked over to where Simon stared at her with accusing eyes. She had never told him what she'd seen. In a determined voice, she said, "I did some psychic archaeology on my own a few weeks before our wedding and got some amazing information that Claudia obviously also got. I didn't share this with you because just after I had the visions, your parents called from New York during the hurricane. Then travel and the wedding, more important things, took over."

Simon understood and visibly relaxed, so she turned back to face Claudia. "I know you saw what I saw, but how did you know it was *me* seeing the visions?"

"I saw green eyes reflected on glass watching the visions with me. Your eyes," Claudia said.

"Can you tell us what goes on there now?" asked Sarah.

Claudia nodded. "There are four altars to the directions that open into a large cave area beneath the Bernini altar. This central area was a necropolis that Constantine desecrated to construct the First Basilica in the fourth century. Recently the graves were excavated and rearranged by Vatican archaeologists who also closed off the four passages into the necropolis. This work was the first major change down there since Pope Julius II tore down Constantine's basilica in 1506 to build the current one, the greatest destruction of a sacred site of all time. Julius tore down a thousand-year-old temple that was in constant Christian use! Some say Constantine is so furious he haunts the Vatican!

"Somebody made the four caves accessible to the Basilica through tunnels from behind. Who knows how long those caves have been there? In the caves priests serve continual Masses—one every hour for twenty-four hours a day. These Masses focalize Roman Catholicism to generate papal power to run their mind-control programs. When Catholics go to Mass anywhere in the world, they plug into this sacrificial vortex. I discovered this system by accident down there many years ago when I stumbled onto a Jesuit serving a Mass in a cave. He told me this had been going on for more than a thousand years; nobody really knows how long. I'm sure both of you have heard rumors about things going on down there? Everybody has."

After her visions Sarah had thought these rumors must be true. But with Claudia's confirmation she thought she and Simon might be able to delve even deeper into the mind-control of the Church. She looked over at Simon and his nod indicated their thoughts were aligned.

"We Roman pagans must defuse this vortex because they'd take over our city if we didn't. We do it by constantly mocking them, but much more goes on in secret." She drew her body back, making herself very tall like a cobra and cleared her throat. Then she said proudly, "As a vestal whore, my ceremony was the Black Mass. Our cave temple is accessible through the back entrance of the Club Doria Pamphili, where Armando told me you had dinner together, Sarah.

"You were wise to get away from him as quickly as you did because he is not what he seems to be. Now that I see you, I imagine he probably had big plans for you. He is a wizard, a high priest of the Black Mass, and I was one of his celebrants. This is shocking, I know, but for hundreds of years our cult has kept the Vatican at bay by transforming dry celibacy back into lust for the goddess. If it weren't for us celebrating the sexual rites of the Earth God with the Goddess, the priests and the hierarchy could terminate human reproduction. Who wants to have children when the world is this way? Will people have children just so priests can rape them? If you've ever wondered why the Church is against birth control, now you have the answer: they need children for energy. These days others serve the Black Mass; I have not for more than ten years. I wouldn't be telling you about this if it weren't for the crisis in the Church and the urgency of the end times. The Vatican's power is coming to an end because we are going back into balance, and repression and abuse will cease. You both have a big role to play in this."

The silence in the room was palpable. Simon and Sarah could barely breathe; they knew Claudia was telling the truth. Sarah was thinking, *This is the clue I was looking for, the missing piece—the use of sex to get power.*

Simon's investigative reporter took over. "I assume that the Jesuit who reported this to you demanded your silence, so we can't have his name. But *how* did you run into him?"

Claudia drained her glass of grappa. "He was serving a Mass in the East cave when I stumbled into it after attending a Black Mass and going out the wrong way. It is a labyrinth down there. He was in the Consecration, so I sat on a stone bench awaiting Communion and hoping he would tell me about the ceremony. He was so shocked to see me that he told me all about it. He was an American Jesuit, a Lakota Indian, visiting the Vatican. Maybe he told me because he himself was amazed by what goes on down there."

"Okay. Are there other men who play the role Armando plays, which I assume is a typical Black Mass—sexual intercourse with the goddess lying on the altar?" She nodded. "How big is this cult, this group? Is this the same thing as the ancient Greek *hieros gamos*—sacred marriage—which probably goes back thousands of years?"

"There are always twelve priestesses and twelve priests in Rome. I'm happy I am done with it. Armando has told me he is done with it too. But I still believe in what I did," she said to Simon in a strange pleading tone. "We had to neutralize the sacrificial energy generated by the constant global Masses. Perhaps knowing about this can help you better understand Armando, since getting involved with all this sexual energy when he was young may have screwed him up? Ritual combined with sex, sacred sex, is too much for most people.

Meanwhile, priests have been doing rituals with innocent children for fifteen hundred years!"

"Claudia, I do not judge you in any way," Simon said. "But have children or adolescents been involved in your rituals?"

"Never!" Claudia exclaimed in horror. "Our work was dedicated to using sex for energy based on conscious choices between mature adults. We believe this ritual has gone on for maybe ten or twenty thousand years or more because traces of it exist in many ancient sacred cultures. We believe the sacred marriage ceremony was created to avoid perversion. We think Christianity spawned the weird perversions we see now by substituting carnal pleasure with power abuse. You've probably heard children are abused in the confessional and the rectory, even that priests seduced their victims by inviting them to 'private Masses?'" Claudia was really animated now, waving her empty grappa glass around as she spoke. "And it's not just the children who are harmed. Repressing female sexuality *causes* perversion; when men and women are balanced, they don't violate children or each other. You have been exposing this perversion, Simon. Maybe 2012 is the time of revelation?"

Simon looked at both Sarah and Claudia. "What did you mean when you mentioned a 'timeline' under the Basilica?"

Sarah felt guilty. She knew Simon didn't like being the only one in the room who didn't know something. "Simon, I will tell you all about it when we are alone."

Simon nodded. "Well then, I think that you've given us quite a lot to think about, Claudia. Do you want to meet again after we've had some time to digest all this?" It was late and they agreed they all had plenty to think about before they met again.

27

December 2012

Simon and Sarah's first separation came barely a month after their wedding when he went to Jerusalem before Christmas to investigate tension between the three Semitic religions. Although he was annoyed at having to leave his new bride, the trip would give him the chance to revisit the Tomb of Mary Theotokos.

"I wish you didn't have to leave so soon," Sarah said in a wistful voice the morning of his flight. "But you'll be home for Christmas. We have to get used to separations at some point, so maybe this is a good thing for us. And I'll have time to get a handle on my thesis. I've outlined it in detail, and now the fun starts—the writing. I do really need concentration time."

Simon waved goodbye as he climbed into a cab, and then she was alone. She cleansed the apartment by putting Simon's things away and shutting his closet door. She rearranged books and decorative items. No breakfast or lunch because she'd put on a few pounds since the wedding. It was delightfully freeing not to have to prepare food or clean up afterward. Her thesis outline took over the kitchen table, and she moved the plants off the thick slate ledge to create a shelf for reference books. She poured herself a glass of water and prepared to dive in. She turned to Tertullian's tractate on Marcion and G.R.S. Mead's *Fragments of a Faith Forgotten,* a spiritual work on the Gnostics that included Marcion.

No sources for Marcion's original writings had ever been found, so the best point of access to his theology was Tertullian's refutation, *Contra Marcion.* Previous scholars such as John Knox used it to extract Marcion's thought. With Mead's *Fragments* on top of Tertullian's *Contra Marcion,* Sarah fell into intense concentration. *Tertullian refuted anyone who said the Hebrew god was not the same god as the god of Jesus. Why? Tertullian said Marcion said there were two gods—one just and one good. Meanwhile, Mead notes that Marcion said one was a god of the law and the other a god of love. Marcion insisted the Jewish god was inherently destructive and inferior to the god of love revealed by Christ. Grafting Christ's ideas onto Judaism—a limited creed of one small Semitic cult—was a grievous error that limited the universal glad tidings of Jesus.*

Her meditation complete, she began writing:

The son of an early Christian bishop who probably knew Paul of Tarsus, Marcion was born around 70 CE at Sinope, the main port of Pontus on the Black Sea. He became a wealthy sea trader and a theologian. Contrary to Church dogma, Marcion was not a Gnostic; first and foremost he was an evangelist—an early devotee of Jesus. He believed Christianity must be a new religion divinely inspired by love and compassion, which was a threat to the newly forming Church of Peter in Rome because the Jewish god, Yahweh, was their god. The Petrine bishops excommunicated him around 144 CE, calling Marcion the first and greatest heretic. Original sources for his work have never been found, even though his church was more extensive than Peter's church in the second century. Historians find references to Marcionite parishes as late as the sixth century, and there were lingering remains of the sect as late as the tenth century. Regardless, the Church succeeded in almost completely erasing Marcion from history.

Ever since the Gnostic literature was found at Nag Hammadi in

1947, the Gnostics have been the best source on first-century beliefs about Yahweh, since discussions about the Hebrew god were central to their own theology. Many Gnostics said Yahweh was an invasive force that enticed humans to rape, murder, and sacrifice. Marcion, however, was not a Gnostic; he was an early evangelist! If he had been a Gnostic, Tertullian would certainly have castigated him about it in his refutation to Marcion's lost tractate Antitheses. *Instead, according to Mead, Marcion said Yahweh was the god of justice and law, while Jesus was a teacher of love and compassion. Marcion made the most important point:* the old god must go for a new god to come.

That's the crux, she mused as the ruby ring on her finger got hot. *It is time to rehash early Christian concepts of deity now that two thousand years have passed by. Human models of god transform as humans evolve; however, two thousand years ago we got stuck!* She looked out the kitchen window, listening to dry leaves rattling around in the courtyard like old bones. *Well, what do we have now from adoration of law? Corrupt courts and crammed jails, frozen Church dogma, control by the rich, and maniacs on legal drugs going on killing sprees using legal weapons. It's one thing to honor justice and law, but when it's deified, it is demonic! The truth is, Christianity is trapped in an atavistic demonic vortex. Marcion was right!*

She stopped to make a light supper and switch on BBC. Demonstrations against government control were raging in Spain and in Tahrir Square in Cairo. *Regardless of what Simon wants to think, people are desperate; they are willing to die for freedom. They do act like it's the end of the world!* The phone rang. She expected Simon, but it was a female voice with a thick Italian accent. "Hello, Sarah! This is Claudia, and I hope you won't mind I call you?"

"Hello, Claudia. How nice of you to call."

"Can you and Simon come to visit so we can continue our explorations?"

"I'd love to visit again with Simon, but he's in Jerusalem for three weeks on assignment."

"Oh, darling, hmm, you are lonesome? Will you come to see me anyway?" Claudia asked in a buttery, persuasive voice.

Sarah wasn't sure she wanted to see Claudia without Simon, yet she sensed their discussion could accelerate her thesis. *Since she saw my visions while I was having them, we might be able to access amazing things together.* She also wondered if they might get further without Simon around. Despite the fact he had encouraged her psychic skills in the first place, Sarah felt he was slightly skeptical about them. Plus she was dying to talk to somebody about 2012 given what was in the news.

"Sure, Claudia! I *will* get lonely, and we do have things to share. Is evening best for you since you work at your boutique? I need a few days to concentrate on my thesis, but knowing we will get together will give me the incentive to work harder. How about Thursday evening after 7? But just the two of us, okay?"

Claudia frowned. *I wonder if she thinks I'd spring Armando on her? I wouldn't think of it!* She replied, "That is perfect for me too, darling, and do take a cab please. It is dark at 7, and there are a few sketchy areas between your apartment and mine."

Sarah worked diligently until Thursday afternoon. She was very productive knowing Simon was busy in Jerusalem. When he called he told her how excited he was about his upcoming visit to the Tomb of Mary in a few days. She was so wrapped up in telling him about her progress on her thesis she forgot to mention her pending visit with Claudia.

"Oh, hello, darling," Claudia said as she swung the door wide and gave Sarah a forceful peck on each cheek. "Stunning, just stunning," she said, admiring Sarah's robin's-egg-blue-and-taupe patterned tight pants and tan Ferragamo shoes. Turning her around to see the entire outfit, she said, "The way your black silk blouse flares slightly over your hips is gorgeous. Someday, darling, I will dress you; your figure is perfect for my lines."

Claudia's perfume was divine, and Sarah asked if it was Noel du Nuit.

"No, darling, it is an essential oil, rose oil. I love it."

"It's my turn to admire you, Claudia. You have such a gorgeous body, and your face is so elegant and patrician. Are you from an old Roman family?"

"Of course, we all are around here. Our task is how to avoid being decadent, as with our friend Armando. Will you mind if I mention him?"

"Of course not. I'm a grownup." *But I will never tell you or anyone else what he did.* But Claudia knew all about Armando's seduction attempt; there were few secrets between Armando and Claudia.

They sat down in the same intimate parlor. Sarah sat in the leather chair while Claudia relaxed on the loveseat and said, "Perhaps we should have some wine or grappa a bit later since we want to have clear heads?" Noting Sarah's agreement, she plowed ahead. "You seem to be so happy, Sarah. *I* will never marry, so I can't imagine how it is. Is it delightful to have a future you count on? Your engagement ring is exquisite. I looked at it carefully when you were here the last time. It is an extraordinary ruby, a very powerful stone?"

"Yes, Claudia. Would you like to hold it and tune into it?"

"Oh, my *dear!* Yes, I would! May I?" Sarah handed it to Claudia, who took it and cupped it in her hands. Her amber eyes sharpened as she gazed into it. Sarah took a moment to study her face. Claudia's skin rippled with small twitches as she sucked in her cheeks and tilted her head down. Her jaw was long and elegant like the edge of a bass viol. Angular cheeks accentuated its curve framed by absolutely straight medium brown hair that turned slightly under, making a perfect edge. When she moved, this edge brushed the bottoms of her jaw dangling in line with large, gold hoop earrings.

"Sarah, this stone is ancient, cut and polished more than twelve thousand years ago! This is a talisman, the third eye stone of an ancient Buddha later hidden away in Himalayan caves. It holds the ancient records of Earth in multidimensional planes. *Where* did Simon get it?"

Sarah wasn't sure how much she should say. But Claudia was describing many things she'd already found in the stone, so she decided to be forthcoming. "Simon's great-grandmother on his father's side obtained it in India during the late nineteenth century. That branch of his family is descended from the Jewish Kabbalist, Isaac Luria, and they think it came down from him. But the grandmother finding it in India does not square with this, since Luria lived a few hundred years before that. I also feel it is thousands of years old. Possibly there were family records that told his great-grandmother where to find it?"

Claudia continued holding the stone, which heated her hand. "I see the face of a great magus, very old with a long beard and hair and wearing a coarse robe. I see him hold the stone, which takes him into other dimensions. It *must* be Isaac Luria!" When she spoke his name, the stone gave her an electric shock. "Oh my, it *is* Luria's energy! Simon told me his father was part of the magian lineage. Those kinds of Jewish families keep records and old letters. They have ways of passing information down, so it would make sense the grandmother could have retrieved it for them. The question is what are *you* doing with it?" She handed the ring back to Sarah.

Instead of putting the ring back on her finger, Sarah held it in her palm. She met Claudia's gaze. "Claudia, tell me my visions of the timeline under the basilica. Then I will tell you more about the stone."

Claudia raised her eyebrows slightly in an expression of respect. She understood Sarah was giving her a test. "Well, see the patio out there on the other side of the dining room? I was sitting out there on a Sunday morning when my body began to buzz. I knew a vision was coming, which by the way is unusual for me. Luckily I was alone with no distractions." Claudia got up from her seat and walked over to an exquisite Renaissance cabinet enameled in ornate gilt, ruby, amethyst, and emerald. "This cabinet belonged to Olimpia Maidalchini, the consort of Innocent X, who was a vestal whore," she said pointedly, watching Sarah's eyes widen. Claudia opened the mysterious cabinet, reached in, and drew out a large crystal ball around six inches in diameter. She set it down on a pink alabaster stand on the coffee table in front of Sarah.

"On that Sunday, I got out the crystal ball and took it to the patio with me, stared into it, and waited. The first thing I saw on the quartz planes in the ball was a beautiful face with limpid green eyes. When you came here with Simon, I recognized it as your face. I was astonished when I saw you. Within this crystal ball, your face passed into a mist, and then I saw the visions like a book of short stories moving through time. Your eyes darkened and became emeralds lingering in the mist around the crystal like the cat goddess of Atlantis. I could tell we were seeing the same time sequence. It was the dream of my life to see visions of human interaction with the Vatican power vortex going back fifty thousand years! Maybe we can figure out how they control the world. They do, you know, with their mind-control programs and global banking system."

Sarah studied Claudia's earnest face and knew she was speaking the truth. Sarah asked, "But why would I see this? Why would you see it? I have to know because I intend to work more with this stone."

"I am sure you do; I'm sure Simon would not have given it to you otherwise. Just imagine what a treasure it is in their family!"

"Yes, and actually Simon's father, David, gave it to Simon so that he would give it to me. You say he is a magus. But what do you have to do with this, Claudia?"

Claudia leaned forward. "That is why I tried to talk to Simon about the end of the world and the Mayan Calendar, but he wouldn't listen. He does that. You will become accustomed to him. Until he figures something out himself, it's not real to him and certainly not credible. He took Harvard way too seriously. Regardless of what *he* thinks, something is going on with this crazy end-time thing, and you and I both know it. Sometimes I think the Maya held a secret that was not available to Europeans and Asians. But I don't want to divert to that now; it is too complex. Perhaps we will talk about it when the time comes, maybe even be together on December 21, 2012? Now I answer your question about *us*. I am the dark and you are the light; I am a vestal whore and you are a vestal virgin. You were pure until you had sex with Simon, weren't you, darling?"

Sarah laughed a deep throaty laugh. "Yes, but that is long gone. So what?"

"It is nothing, really," Claudia replied. "But I want you to understand the way we balance each other. You will discover that you can totally trust me because I am the dark. We are twinned archetypes that resonate through many lives. I penetrate the dark side of things; you see the light. We are both blind without each other. Armando triangulates between the two of us, but that is for later. Armando is not a lost soul, not yet. We are all vessels for dimensions that extend when light penetrates the underworld. You are not superior, though some people think light is better than darkness. One cannot exist without the other. The interesting thing is the edges—the field planes between the dimensions. See the planes inside this crystal ball? Visions can be viewed on these planes like the ones you saw. Your ruby crystal opened you to the second dimension below this one, and you detected its timeline. Once you accessed the second dimension, then you watched fourth-dimensional movies generating forbidden rituals in our solid world. After December 21, 2012, these visions will be seen by many people, which will make them crazy.

Claudia held Sarah's gaze. "I participated in rituals to discharge their control over innocent victims, people who are possessed by them. But until *you* ripped open the Vatican timeline, I was never able to observe these rituals, only to partake in them. These things cannot be understood without seeing them, so your vision has freed me. I have been tortured by demonic forces because I got pulled into darkness by Armando when I was only nineteen. Armando unleashed demonic forces just like those I later tried to neutralize through the Black Mass. Now that I see what's being replayed over and over again during the Black Mass, I see the only way out of this circular game for me. These fourth-dimensional movies will continue to control our planet until enough people see how this works. It is so difficult to explain. What I am trying to say is the second dimension can be *felt* in rituals, but the fourth dimension must be *seen*, very much like television images."

Sarah frowned, trying to understand what she had just heard. "Okay, Claudia, this is a complex way of thinking for me. I am going to be very open and frank with you. I don't understand very much about what you're talking about but it resonates with me. I do sense layers of influence in what goes on around me; they vibrate at different frequencies, like stations on a radio band. Maybe the planes in crystals access these layers? I sense I'm getting in touch with the second dimension when I have sex with Simon. So what is this second dimension, or fourth dimension? Are you talking about Einstein and the quantum?"

Claudia crossed her legs and gave Sarah a knowing smile. "Darling, I'm *sure* you are in the second dimension when having sex with Simon, but going any farther with that is indelicate at this time. If you'd had sex with Armando, you would have gotten *stuck* in the second dimension, like Persephone taken by Pluto down into the underworld for half the year. The dimensions are easily defined, and Isaac Luria was famous for doing it very well. No wonder this stone works so well; it's his tool! Anyway, here are the basics: The first dimension is the iron crystal in the very core of Earth. The second dimension is the world below the crust of Earth down to the first dimension. The third dimension is our solid world, and the fourth dimension is above the third dimension. The fourth dimension is the realm of the collective mind, the thoughts and feelings of all humans, the archetypes. We are all plugged into it, so when you say you *resonate* with something, actually you are detecting the thoughts of others.

Claudia noticed that Sarah was hanging on her every word. "People in power use the fourth dimension to manipulate our thoughts and feelings. Think of a master computer used by game masters in the sky. They project them onto the refracting planes in crystals, and if a crystal is made into a sphere, such as with this crystal ball, seers can watch the movies. Also when ordinary people stretch their intelligence, they can detect the programs. *Stopping* them, however, is very difficult since most people just give in and go with the programs. Around 85 percent of our species are sheep—dumdums who wander out of their keep in the morning, chew on grass all day (compulsive shopping and eating), and then go to sleep drunk on the media after stuffing themselves. The fourth-dimensional control programs tell the masses what to believe; then they do not have to think. They gratefully pay the elite for the latest inventions they believe can save them, such as medical testing and guns."

Sarah thought Claudia was getting a little far afield. "Claudia, excuse me, but anybody with half a brain cell knows about the global elite game. But what I don't get is the power vortexes under the Vatican, the rituals, and the second-dimensional influence, that is, *how* they play it."

Claudia stared into the crystal ball for geographical information. She couldn't see what she was looking for, except she noticed a silvery crystalline plane that sliced the exact middle of the ball. *I wonder why it didn't split into two halves long ago?* She brought herself back to answer Sarah's question about the second dimension. "As I said, the second dimension is the realm of tectonic forces under the crust that are stronger and weaker in various places around the globe. Sacred sites and temples are located to access the special energy that exudes from the tectonic realm. They are strongest in places where the crust is thin, such as Rome down to Naples. Notice Italy is a mountainous ridge that lies above the ocean mostly at 9 to 16 degrees East longitude, and there is a division line of Earth's mental plane located at 12 degrees East. The ridge accesses the second dimension, the tectonic." Claudia now saw rainbow spectrums when she glanced at the dividing plane in the crystal ball. "The fourth-dimensional programmers have been using this division line to control people's beliefs for over five thousand years. This line is the key to freeing the people from hierarchical control systems, such as the Roman Church."

Claudia tapped her long fingernails on the crystal ball. "I tried to tell Simon about this line last year when he was harping about East/West tension, but he laughed at me. Regardless, scientists finally described the geophysical attributes of this divisive structure of our planet a couple of years ago. This 12 degrees East line runs through Gabon in Africa, up to Tunisia, through Italy, Germany, and up through Sweden, and the most powerful section is right through Rome and the Etruscan sites. *That* is why Constantine built the original basilica here, where we now have the Vatican! The tectonically active section is Naples, close to Mt. Vesuvius and Lake Avernus, the cave system used by the Sibyl of Cumae to prophesy."

Sarah was mesmerized by the rainbows flashing on the planes in the crystal ball; Claudia could see her face and green eyes again reflected there. But the mention of the sibyl shocked Sarah. She lurched forward and her knees struck the side of the table, almost knocking the crystal ball off its stand. Claudia was about to say something about Sarah's reflection on the crystal plane when Sarah said in a husky voice, "The Sibyl of Cumae? What do you know about her?"

Now Claudia was truly challenged. *What do I say to an innocent vestal virgin who intuits her own past lives but hasn't woken up yet?* Claudia could see a person's past lives roll by like a movie on a misty screen behind their head if she looked. "Sarah, how much do you want to know about these things? I must be careful with you. Maybe you should just be normal, get pregnant, and focus on family? You are on a fast esoteric learning track, but this knowledge could be too much. Perhaps you need time? The Sibyl of Cumae is no big deal. Everybody knows about her, so why did you react so strongly? You almost crashed my crystal ball!" *I do wonder what she really knows.* "I must understand such an extreme reaction on your part before we go further. After all, we cannot endanger this lovely crystal ball."

Recovering from her surprise, Sarah replied, "Well, Claudia, who are you to say I must take time when December 21 is only three weeks away? Who says anybody has time? You and I both know something is going on that means something important. But I don't know what it is, do you?"

Claudia laughed her throaty laugh, stuck a cigarette in a long ivory holder, and lit it. She sucked it until the tip burned hot, then stood up, took the crystal ball, and put it back in the cupboard. She sat back down and tapped her cigarette into an obsidian ashtray carved with Maya hieroglyphs. "Let's do a trade. If you will tell me what the Sibyl of Cumae means to you, then we can have a drink and share what we know about the end times. By the way, that ashtray you're staring at was carved in 750 CE and was used for burning copal. It was found in the Courtyard of the Nine Bolontiku at Palenque."

Claudia offered Sarah a glass of wine and she took it, shrugging her shoulders. "I wish I *could* tell you! You startled me because I met Simon at an archaeological site reputed to be the Sibyl's family home in Rome, that is all."

Claudia laughed again. "How funny, how interesting, and how *synchronistic.* I'm sure you realize the importance of synchronicity?" Sarah nodded. "Then since the Sibyl's oracle is near Baia and Lake Avernus near Naples, we must drive down there. I'd like to see what you *feel* there, and it's only a two-to-three-hour drive. Rituals have been conducted down there for at least three thousand years, probably more. Sometimes I think it is more potent than the area under the Vatican. It may be the antidote to Rome's poison. Do you think Simon would mind if I took you there?"

"Even if he did, I'd go if I wanted to," Sarah said indignantly. "So what do *you* think about the end of the Mayan Calendar? Or are we just too tired? Should we save the discussion for the drive to Naples? I would love to go to the Sibyl of Cumae's oracle! If we go in a few days, it will be around the time Simon is visiting the Tomb of Mary in Jerusalem, a meaningful synchronicity."

"Darling," Claudia said, expelling a thin wisp of cigarette smoke after sucking down a huge cloud and flicking the ash into the Mayan artifact. "Synchronicity is always meaningful, especially our connection—the vestal virgin and the vestal whore. As Simon visits a place of great light, you and I explore the darkness."

28

Lake Avernus and Baia

While packing a small suitcase for the trip to Naples with Claudia, Sarah thought about her thesis. She felt like she'd finally found her voice and her ideas were flowing. Meanwhile, she wondered what Simon really thought about her trip with Claudia. Sarah had been reluctant to mention she was going because she wasn't sure how he'd feel about her getting so friendly with Claudia, but when he called last night, she had told him their plans. His reaction took her by surprise. He was excited about the prospect of visiting the Tomb of Mary and was happy to hear she had such a wonderful opportunity while he was away. *Simon is such a great partner! He truly wants me to be free. It was silly to think he'd feel Claudia is a bad influence. I'm sure Daddy, however, would keep his eye on Claudia.*

They left for Naples at the end of the rush hour at 10 a.m. "Oh goddess! It is great to drive south," Claudia said as she accelerated her vintage silver Fiat and pushed back deeper in her crackled forest-green leather seat. "I hope you will like my plans. I've reserved at the Lago D'Averno Hotel, the best place to feel the vibes of Lake Avernus. It can be risky to stay there because the lake is a volcanic crater surrounded by smaller craters. The region often smells of sulfur. Around thirty-nine thousand years ago, a supervolcano exploded and the whole region is still very seismically active.

Pompeii, just south of Naples, erupted only two thousand years ago. The nearby town, Pozzuoli, is located in the center of the huge caldera, the Campi Flegrei, which in English means 'Fiery Fields.' Last year, a big flap occurred between British and Italian seismologists because the British wanted to test the magma chamber. The mayor of Naples forbade drilling because he thought it could explode the fabled monster. Pozzuoli slowly sinks when the magma chamber lowers and rises when magma flows in, causing days of earthquake swarms. Lake Avernus means 'Lake of the Underworld'; the whole region is a gateway to the underworld. So I thought we should sleep on the edge of the lake, the crater. I hope you will like this? I'm always amazed anybody lives there, although the beaches are wonderful and the views out to sea are spectacular."

Sarah vaguely listened to Claudia going on and on about seismic activity. *It seems bizarre to go down to sleep in a hotel on the edge of a crater over a supervolcano a few weeks before the Mayan end of the world! Oh well, if everything is going to blow, this could be the perfect place.*

"How did the Mayan Calendar end date get calculated?" Sarah wanted to return to their unfinished conversation.

Claudia smiled broadly. "Oh, Sarah, I'm so glad you want to hear more about the Mayan Calendar! Most of what we hear in the popular media uses the traditional date from scholars, the GMT Correlation—December 21, 2012. People got very curious about the Calendar during the 1970s because they wondered whether this end-date indicated catastrophe or enlightenment. A slightly different end-date—October 28, 2011—gained prominence around 1999 based on the writings of Carl Johan Calleman. Have you ever heard of him?"

Sarah said no, so Claudia went on. "Calleman writes about a fascinating series of nine calendar cycles that track the evolution of the universe over 16.4 *billion* years. His ideas attracted widespread interest because he related the Maya cycles to Darwinian epochs and extinction events. Well, how *could* the Maya have known about these evolutionary cycles a thousand years ago? But what really interests me is an intriguing sub-theme in his books—the divisive force on the 12 E longitude line we spoke about last time we were together. This hypothesis caught my eye because it runs through my city. I took the idea more seriously in 2011 when revolution ignited in Tunisia exactly at 12 E longitude! I think your visions were generated by this strange, potent underground vortex. Calleman says this line generates what he calls 'the winds of history,' cycles of historical tension between East and West. His analysis is very detailed and complex, and I find it fascinating. How could a geographical division line generate historical patterns? How *does* the inner Earth influence our minds?

Claudia was growing more and more excited and gesticulating dramatically, so much so that Sarah began to wonder if she should offer to grab the wheel. The car's trajectory remained steady, however, as Claudia continued. "I think the ancient people—Neolithic and Paleolithic—were very aware of this force and intentionally used it to enhance our planet and their lives. Also, thousands of years ago, Earth's magnetism was much stronger than it is now, so they probably felt it much more than we do. Global evidence exists for an ancient earth science that archaic people used to live in harmony with Earth, for example, the megalithic system of Carnac in France. When history emerged around five thousand years ago, the global elite figured out how to use this force to control people by building temples and pyramids on ancient places of power. Now we've come to the point where their recklessness and greed could *destroy* our world!" As Claudia's voice sped up in her excitement, so did the car. Sarah discreetly clutched her seatbelt as Claudia turned to her. "And here, Sarah, is where the Church enters the story! Christianity joined with the elite to take this earth science away from the people by demonizing them as pagans. Meanwhile, in secret they use this force for their agendas. We're down south where this force is free and uncontrolled. The Sibyl channeled during the Magna Graecia when the early Greeks came to Italy. Mysteriously, somebody constructed sacred earth portals, such as near Baia, *before* the Greeks came, then the Greeks enhanced these portals, such as at Cumae. In those days, the whole world venerated sacred sites with female oracles. We need her voice more than ever! The Gnostics venerated the wisdom of the goddess Sophia, and I think the Sibyl of Cumae was a version of Sophia!"

Caught up now in Claudia's enthusiasm, Sarah forgot to be nervous about her driving. She nodded vigorously. "You're right; the Gnostics did venerate Sophia, and I have thought the Sibyl could be a version of Sophia. All this information about longitude and earth science is fascinating, but please don't tell me any more specifics. It could enhance my sensitivity, but at the same time I don't want to taint my intuition before I visit the oracle. I'm impressed with your knowledge, though. You've obviously spent a great deal of time studying science."

Claudia laughed. "Darling, once a priestess, always a priestess—the primal scientist. I am a devotee of the Sibyl and Sophia because they revered Gaia. The suppression of feminine wisdom is destroying our species and all living things. I embody her powers as an initiate; they were my gift. The knowledge was given to our clan, the Stone Clan. We already know all about Earth's midline, so we wait for the scientists to discover these things and report to the public. For example, last year a group of scientists announced that the eastern and western hemispheres are separated by sharp asymmetrical boundaries in the same place we know these midlines to be. There is a string of crater lakes and volcanoes on this line through Italy, and the greatest turbulence is in Campi Flegrei. Of course, scientists do not consider the possibility that such measurable systems affect human behavior, but they do!"

As they rounded a bend, the lake came suddenly into view. Claudia continued, "For example, the eruption of the supervolcano around thirty-nine thousand years ago corresponds with the downfall of the Neanderthals, the takeover in Europe by Cro-Magnon man! These forces are detectable intuitively, as you well know. I want to know how the elite uses these forces, since the people in power today are so destructive. The public must wake up to what evil science is doing, for example governments are researching ways to control the weather while scientists distract the public with the global warming rant. In the ancient days, men and women listened to the Sibyl, who taught them to care for our planet." She braked suddenly and turned onto a side road. "Ah! Here we are at the hotel, so let's go in and settle."

They checked into two small bedrooms that opened into a central parlor with a balcony out to the lake. The doors were closed and a small gas fire was already burning since it was chilly.

"Claudia, this is lovely," Sarah said, looking out at the mirror-calm golden lake.

"Yes, this is how I hoped it would be. We will not have problems with sulfur odors since it is December and our windows are closed. Let's rest for a while and have an early dinner. I will take you to Cumae early in the morning."

Sarah lay down on a pristine pine twin bed covered with a Greek cotton cover embroidered with poppies and lilies. The sun-warmed terra cotta floor exuded an earthy aroma, and heavy corbelled ceiling beams were cozy. She fell into a deep sleep, losing all sense of time as curling swirls of gray clouds spun above her body. Her eyes were twitching as she saw herself in the midst of an enclosure where moist ferns grew in wall cracks the color of peach skin. Light flooded her cranium. Her hand wearing the ruby crystal flopped heavily over the edge of the bed while her body floated in thick density. *I am turning to stone.* Tingles in her cells rushed through nerve pathways, making dormant muscles quiver. *Oh, I am so sleepy, so sleepy. I have been here for thousands of years. Where am I, what is this aqua-blue water? What is this constant shaking in my body like a*

swarm of quakes? The fire melts the rocks into hot liquid, a murder-
ous force that reverses and cools, cracks, and congeals, making fossils
through the ages.

How long ago is this? "Long before the Romans, my dear." How
long ago is this? "Long before the Greeks, my dear. We are the ancient
people of the lake. You are to remember one thing: if you detect the
feeling of men in my oracle, push yourself further back in time before
they cloud your eyes."

Claudia and Sarah were famished when they sat down for an early
supper of tagliatelle, salad, bread with local olive oil, and red wine.
"Now, darling," Claudia began, "we will discuss *The Marble Faun*
by Nathaniel Hawthorne. I assume you have read it, since you are
an American from New England?"

"My goodness," Sarah replied. "That's the last thing I thought
you'd bring up. I read it when I was around twelve, so it may be hard
to remember. . . ." Sarah paused and closed her eyes for a moment.
"Oh, now I remember, it's about nineteenth-century travelers in
Rome."

"Yes, Hawthorne explored the strange energy in Rome better
than any other novelist," Claudia replied. "Do you remember a character, the Count of Monte Beni, the scion of a really ancient family
that goes back to the early sylvan days, the time of the Etruscans
and earlier, rather like Armando? Possibly he fascinated you because
you read about the Count at such a tender age?"

"Well, that's always possible, but that isn't the most interesting
thing about *The Marble Faun*," Sarah replied, preferring not to discuss Armando. "The scene I recall best is the one in the catacombs
when the heroine is seized by an evil spirit."

Claudia was disappointed. Even though Sarah had read the
book, she didn't seem to have a strong impression of it, so perhaps
this discussion was a dry well. She persisted, "Hawthorne danced
around the idea Rome was trapped in layers of time by power

intrigues, the battle between the dark and the light. Since the city is on the midline, people who travel to Rome *would* tend to constantly repeat archetypal dramas like the ones Hawthorne describes. Rome was the perfect place to sink the goddess into a hole and drag her down into the Underworld! Now that we have come to the end of history—his story—we *can* see that the goddess has been whipped back and forth between East and West on the midline for thousands of years! Hawthorne knew nothing about the midline, yet his characters display its influence."

"Claudia," Sarah broke in, "honestly, I don't know where you're going with this. I'm confused."

"Actually, darling, I struggle for words. I've pondered *The Marble Faun* since I was thirteen when I first detected the possessive force. Soon after that Armando took me down into the Underworld. I've always thought foreigners like you in Rome could feel this force, but I've never been able to talk about it with anyone. You are my guest and you may wonder why I chose you? May I surprise you?" Claudia reached across the table and touched Sarah's hand. "In *The Marble Faun,* the two female characters are strong and independent women who don't get neutralized by men. You and I are the same, Sarah. Do you realize how unusual you are? It takes guts to explore Marcion, the first and greatest heretic. You are snooping into what blocked the incoming light two thousand years ago when Christian revelation was distorted, history piled on it, and Jesus was lost. Hawthorne also went after the burial of truth in Rome, but he didn't have the information we have. Hawthorne said Confession encouraged priests to become sociopaths because Absolution relieves them of guilt, an amazingly advanced insight at the time. There's a reason Hawthorne made guilt his primary theme in *The Scarlet Letter;* he knew guilt is the basis of human manipulation. Do you know about the Fatima Prophecies?"

Sarah, absolutely baffled by Claudia's constant changes of direction, murmured, "Just a little," so Claudia hammered on. "A hundred years ago, the Virgin Mary gave three prophecies to three little Portuguese girls. The first two, about the world wars, were revealed in 1941, and then the third one was partially exposed in 2000. Our current pope, Benedict XVI, Cardinal Ratzinger at the time, has been behaving in ways that guarantee the Third Prophecy, which is reputed to say Satanic infiltration of the Church will cause clerics and laity to abandon the Church, an apostasy. That *is* what's going on! Financial and sexual abuse *is* emptying the Church. For god's sake, the pope's butler is in the Vatican prison because he tried to leak information about the corruption! Rumor has it the Third Prophecy says Islam will defeat Christianity, which *will* happen if the Church goes on as it is!" Claudia brought her hand down on the table, causing the silverware to rattle and Sarah to jump. "Think what Rome will be like if *that* happens!"

Sarah shook her head. "It makes sense to me that there is some sort of power in the Earth that enables the Vatican to divide and conquer the world, but I don't quite know what to make of the idea that the West will be defeated because it's the elephant sitting on the fault that's ready to crack. To me, though, the *real* shift is the resurgence of the goddess, the reemergence of her wisdom. When she returns, the priests will love women passionately, off go the burkas, men will mother children, and war will cease." Sarah stopped and massaged her temples. "I'm getting a headache just talking about the midline. Leave me alone so I can embody Sophia. And do I get dessert?"

"Oh, yes, darling. But I want you to have a rudimentary sense of the midline because its tectonic power is so potent. There are signs the supervolcano is going to explode again."

Sarah laughed as she ordered tiramisu. "I enjoy you, Claudia, just because you are so *serious*. Simon is about to lighten the mood on all this Church mystery: his first column satirizing Olimpia Maidalchini and Innocent X will be published next week, 'Between the Sheets in Roma.' All the Roman gossips are going to crack up over his thinly-veiled satire of the pope, his butler, and the dashing personal secretary. And as long as Romans are laughing, the supervolcano will not explode, not even at the end of the Mayan Calendar next week!"

"Now you are in for a treat, darling," Claudia said early the next morning as she drove into the Sibyl's Grotto. "This is one of the most serene and beautiful sacred sites in the world, yet few people come here. We can tune in without being interrupted. We'll walk slowly through a long corridor that leads to Sibyl's chamber. If you feel yourself picking something up, just go ahead. I will be doing it myself, and I will not disturb you. Once we've gone down the corridor, I will take you into her chamber and we will sit down and I will not interrupt you. If someone is around, ignore it. Women come here to meditate all the time."

Sarah looked around her in wonder. *This is a dream come true. My new life started at the Sibyl's home in Rome and now I am here.* They walked very slowly, enjoying the distant sound of thundering waves and twittering birds. Sarah moved over on the path when a snake slithered under a bush to escape a twitching golden feral cat. Another cat, black, raced across the path, its fur brushing against her legs. At the bottom of a steep cliff Claudia indicated a cavelike entrance to a tunnel. Sarah looked up to the left side of the opening, and her heart stopped because facing her was a strong web with a large wolf spider as big as her fist in the center. Ugh. Spiders were her phobia.

Once in the tunnel, however, Sarah forgot all about spiders. She could hardly believe what she saw! Ahead was an extremely long, beautifully-fashioned trapezoidal corridor with light coming in on the right around every twenty feet like a progression of receding mirrors. The corridor ran parallel to the hillside and contained many slit openings on the right side that admitted light and sound.

Cumae passage to the Sybil's Oracle

The sidewalls fit perfectly to the eight-foot-wide smooth stone floor. The walls rose to a deep rock ledge at shoulder height, creating the side cut of the trapezoidal support for the upper walls that rose up to a three-foot-wide flat ceiling fifteen feet overhead. The trapezoid excited Sarah's skull as she felt wings growing out of her shoulders while she moved slowly forward. Passing by one slit after another, the light on her right side stimulated her right brain, which quieted her left side. *I have seen this pentagonal shape in the corridor to the Tomb of Pacal Votan at Palenque. This form supports me up to my neck and the tipped-in upper sides make me feel like I'm flying! Certainly my mind is. I have been here before, many times.*

Sarah came to the end of the corridor, where it opened into three chambers. Claudia gently nudged her to the left to the Sibyl's chamber. The round-topped room was about twelve feet high; the back rock walls were encrusted and serrated by snail trails and lichen, nature's hieroglyphs. Standing in the center, Sarah turned around to face outward and spread her feet apart, closing her eyes.

Claudia sat on a stone bench to her left. The silence was total, the peacefulness absorbing. Sarah turned the key in Gaia's heart. Losing awareness of where she was, she felt energy course up her body through the soles of her feet. A crystalline aura sparkled in dappled sunlight waved around her body. *I am safe with Claudia; I trust her. Yet this is not the place. This place was chosen after the Etruscans. Men blocked the energy here. There is another place, maybe Baia, but this place connects to it.*

She breathed in to find the link to the real place, and then a hot poker like a branding iron stabbed her in the heart. She propelled further back in time. *Before the Greeks, before the Etruscans, back to the forest people of this place . . . Oh my, even further back, back before the explosion, back to the time of the great crack, the rift that tore the line from south to north, the time when the core expanded the planet. Now I see people. Oh the pressure, the pressure on my body is so intense! Who are they? What is happening to them?*

Claudia was watching her very carefully, occasionally closing her eyes for a moment to ground the electric energy coursing through Sarah. She glanced at her watch and realized Sarah had been standing rooted in the same spot for almost an hour! Nobody else was around, so Claudia said, "Would you like to speak? Would you like to share what you see?"

To Sarah Claudia's soft voice sounded like it came out of a tunnel deep in the Earth, the soft whisper of the Goddess. A voice rose in Sarah's body, and when it came out of her mouth it was full-bodied like a roaring lion. Claudia checked the corridor once again to confirm there was nobody there and then closed her eyes to listen.

"OH THE WRENCHING PAIN OF THE SPECIES THAT GUARDS EARTH— NEANDERTHALS! YOU GROVEL IN CAVES TO ESCAPE THE FIRE IN THE SKY, THE SICKENING WAVING MOTION IN EARTH. THE SUN IS GONE, THE RIVERS DRY, ANIMALS SHRUNK TO NOTHING; THERE IS NO ESCAPE. EARTH ROLLS AND STRETCHES IN PAIN; SHE CRACKS TO EXPAND!"

Claudia's eyes flew open and she saw that Sarah's face was contorted in agony as she clenched her hands and swayed.

"IT IS LATER NOW; THE NEW PEOPLE COME. THE OLD PEOPLE HAVE LOST THEIR HABITAT. FOR THE NEW PEOPLE, OPEN LANDS FREED OF HEAVY BURDENED ICE ARE A BOON. NEEDY MEN TAKE THE FEW WOMEN OF THE OLD PEOPLE AND USE THEM FOR RELIEF. OF THESE UNIONS CHILDREN ARE BORN BUT THEY ARE WEAK AND NOT WANTED; THE MOTHERS WHO BEAR THEM DIE. THE NEW PEOPLE KILL THE OLD PEOPLE IN THE WAY. THE OLD PEOPLE ARE LAID OUT FOR VULTURES.

"THE NEW PEOPLE DO NOT FEAR THE EARTH FORCES BECAUSE THEY WERE FAR NORTH AND EAST DURING THE GREAT EXPLOSION. THEY FEAR THE GREAT ICE, BUT IT DOES NOT RETURN; THINGS GREEN, LIFE BLOSSOMS. BUT THE NEW PEOPLE DO NOT WANT THE WISDOM OF THE OLD ONES. IN FACT THEY DON'T NEED IT. THIS LOSS WILL HAUNT THE SPECIES—MAN—IN THE FUTURE."

Sarah slumped, and Claudia stood up quickly to support her. She brought her over to the bench and cradled her like a mother holding her child. Sarah sobbed softly. "Oh, Claudia, how will we ever get anybody to listen? I saw the Neanderthals dying out after the volcanoes and earthquakes forty thousand years ago. Cro-Magnons came from the East in a wave of dominance; this was the first genocide. They did not value the ancient Neanderthal wisdom. They refused to learn the ancient ways of the planet, so the new race flowed mindlessly back and forth over Earth's new crack. This hot fissure goes all the way down to the core that turns at a different speed than the mantle. I saw a vision of it! I heard a horrible grinding sound down there that will haunt me for the rest of my life, the cries of the Fallen Angels. The new people forgot about the incredible force in the center, the keeper of all living things. They began the process of using life instead of aligning with it. Then I saw the Sibyl! She said the time has come to learn how to remember the intelligence in the core."

Sarah sat up, her tears drying on her cheeks. "We've come to the logical end of one dominant species. If the one-species will not remember how to listen to Earth, the crack will widen and the inner forces will expand the planet. This dominant species cannot travel out into space after they've destroyed Earth."

Minutes passed in silence. Sarah was calm now and felt complete, her message shared and embodied. The two women walked slowly back down the corridor. The trapezoid with light on their left balanced their brains as they departed.

29

Between the Sheets in Roma

The new moon of December 13, 2012 was an ideal time to discover new things. Simon left his hotel moments before sunrise and walked quickly through Jerusalem's Old City to pass out through the east gate—Lion's Gate. The chill penetrated his bones, so he crammed his hands into his vest pockets as he wondered which way to turn to cross the Kidron Valley. He was glad he'd worn his wool sweater. His previous visit had been on a tour bus, so he wasn't sure exactly where to go on foot. He hoped it would be easy to find his way across the valley over to the Mount of Olives. His cash was zipped into the inner pocket of his canvas vest away from the hungry eyes of beggars. He passed quickly by souvenir hawkers outside the gate and jogged west across the valley. When he made it to the Garden of Gethsemane, the parking lot was already filling up with tour busses so he slowed back down to a walk. *This is where they say Jesus shared his anguish with his disciples just before he was crucified. Christians come in droves to wallow in his agony.*

The morning sun casting long shadows behind the Dominus Flevit felt warm on his back. This eye-catching church was shaped like a teardrop to express Christ's sadness when he saw a vision of the Second Temple's destruction. Simon decided to come back later. It looked interesting, but he needed to get to the tomb. He slipped through a stone gate to an olive grove and read the historical plaque: "The Romans cut the original trees in 70 CE and then planted this grove sometime after they destroyed the Jewish Temple." He breathed in cool, refreshing morning dew. The lovely grove thrived and grew quietly while history rolled along. Before the Romans came, it had been the garden of Ashtoreth, the old goddess.

A huge gnarled olive tree with a trunk easily three feet in diameter beckoned. Simon wondered if the healthy new sprouts breaking through the old dry bark would actually produce olives this summer. *They stretch like yogis in the sunlight trying to calm the tense city of Jews, Muslims, and Christians.* An old Arabic man with a stubby brown cigarette in the corner of his mouth watched him. Simon checked out his eyes, intensely brown like tobacco leaves, then smiled at him and looked down respectfully. He walked out of the garden looking for signs to the nearby Tomb of Mary Theotokos. As he approached the small white stone church over the tomb, he realized it looked very different from what he'd remembered. It was so simple, almost stark. *No one would notice it if they didn't know what's down below; it feels guarded here.* After passing quickly through the arched entry, he was at the top of forty-seven wide stone stairs that descended into the dark tomb.

As he walked slowly down, light coming through high narrow slits in the top of the stone sidewalls barely illuminated the dusty worn stairs. Magnetic heaviness constricted his lungs. *Thank goodness I came back. I could not feel this place with a group.* At the bottom, the street level two thousand years ago, there was a palpable shift. A sign said "Remove Shoes," so he took them off and set them down. As he stepped gingerly through a large and ancient round stone archway, the back of his skull began to tingle.

He was in a vibrant sanctuary glittering with reflected light that flashed in his dark eyes. Exquisite Greek Orthodox icons painted bright red, royal blue, deep purple, and lime green—saints with radiating gold auras—gleamed in the lamplight. Their soulful eyes grabbed Simon. Crabbing his feet on worn stone floors, he felt hot energy rise through his legs, into his torso, and then a flame ignited his chest. *What is that?* He was able to calm himself because the sanctuary felt cozy and domestic, a little home for saintly monks, apostles, the Madonna, and Jesus all shining with heavenly golden halos. *They judge me!* He released that idea when his logical mind flowed out in a hot filament that disintegrated in cosmic space. *I am empty!* This feeling terrified him because he was so used to clinging to his intellect. *These eyes know everything about me; wizened hands grasp for me.*

To avoid passing out from the strange sensation and the sticky incense, Simon made his way to a kneeler. He was mesmerized by staring beings undulating with their edges transforming to shimmering waves of light. *Man! This is like acid! I am afraid I'm having a heart attack! What if somebody sees me?* Since he'd become a reporter, he worried about public displays; he preferred being seen as cool and neutral. *My god, I've never felt a force like this; it could kill me. No wonder few people come down here, especially Christians.*

A heavy, out-of-breath Arabic man came in and slammed onto the same kneeler with aloud crack, almost hitting his head on the altar rail.

Here we are, a Jew and probably a Muslim praying together while my heart is liquefying. I see Sarah! She had materialized right in front of them in a white gown standing by the primitive entrance to the tomb. *What a vision! This is crazy!*

The man beside him sobbed quietly as Simon's heart opened. *Oh, my god, I'm shrinking into a tiny seed—the homunculus conceived by my parents. Sarah! We will have a child! I am turning to stone. I see a great blue egg surrounded by deep burgundy flames, the inner egg fertilized with shining gold stars. Does the man next to me see it? Is this what the icon painters see?*

The stars within the blue cosmic egg burst and emitted rays of golden light like the great flash at the beginning of time. A new universe descended from the sky, blanketing Jerusalem, heaven's goddess. Simon's eyes blinked open to see a primitive stone entrance to her tomb. He'd never been in such an altered state; he wondered if he could walk. *It's time to go into the sarcophagus. Incredible. This burial was two thousand years ago and never disturbed!* The man poked him, so he turned to look into his eyes—dark bottomless pools of infinity. *I'm dizzy. These are the most soulful and loving eyes I have ever seen. His heart pulses in his large careworn hands.* They both looked back to the tomb entrance where a new vision materialized: A four-year-old girl with wide, beautiful blue eyes and golden curls floated through the entrance. Her bare feet brushed the floor as ethereal light glowed in the ancient entrance. Simon touched the man to see if he saw it too. Yes, he smiled joyfully. The little girl—she must have been real—wended her way to them. She touched the man on his shoulder and transformed into a feather!

They both knew it was time to go to the Mother of God. The man pulled his long robe off the kneeler, and they both went through the entrance to kneel by the tomb together. Crystalline light reflected in their eyes from gypsum specks that pocked the stone lid of the tomb. As their retinas adjusted, a shaking blue light formed above the sarcophagus. It swirled into a frenzied quantum field of billons of tiny blue-white vibrating forms—elemental spectrums spinning information out to spiral galaxies *Oh my god, I see the vibrating strings—a miracle!* For one incredibly long second, they became one with the magnetic power of the feminine. Then Mary Theotokos spoke.

She said to Simon in a childlike musical voice, *"It is time for you to embrace me. Men of good heart come to me here. I want your absolute trust in* spite of evil. Evil will expand until it removes its mask. I am goddess keeper of Earth; I say keep finding and describing evil plugs—nexus points used by the elite to destroy the feminine heart, the home of the child.

"As for you, Abu, I have my eyes on Moloch, eater of children. Possessed by the evil god, here Solomon built Moloch's altar. He also built an altar for Ashtoreth, the Canaanite goddess. Solomon died and Yahweh split the Kingdom. The Jews try to put it back together again, but their efforts are futile. Yahweh said Ashtoreth was the evil one, but it is Moloch, who wanted to eliminate the goddess of the Pleiades. The time is coming again when she will rule with Gaia. Abu, you mothered your children. Soon you, Simon, will mother your children. When enough men mother, they will sever the generational chain of abuse."

When Claudia and Sarah arrived back in Rome, insiders all over the city were agog at Simon's column. Despite the darkness of the moon-less skies, new light was being shed on St. Peter's Dome! The first installment of "Between the Sheets in Roma" shot a hole through the layered Vatican cover-ups:

All right now! Why was Olimpia Maidalchini stuck in the Vatican pris-on? Even those who knew her best could never figure it out. How could she have made a disastrous mistake after mastering so many games? What coveted secret incurred such disfavor? Did she complain too much about Pope Innocent X's randy obsession with his secretary, the blond and dashing pretty boy who went past the cardinals and climbed to the top? We've heard that Innocent laughed at his secretary's lurid descrip-tions of priests raping boys in the school for the deaf where nobody could hear their cries in the night.

Or had Olimpia discovered something else she could not stand? What would she have thought when she heard about priests fondling young nuns in the confessional and hoarding money in secret accounts? Well, Olimpia got rich by embracing a man rather than the nunnery. But which man did she prefer? Look through the "double doors" between Olimpia's private quarters with her husband, Pamphilio Pamphili, which led to the inner rooms of future Pope Innocent X, her husband's brother, Gianbattista Pamphili.

It's so hard to imagine the true rewards that come with controlling the pope's time, being the one who opens or shuts that holy door. Regardless of the exact facts, we've heard a few things that are worth mentioning while hanging around in the back halls outside the confessionals. Rumor has it Olimpia lost her mind when she was young, poor thing. Maybe it stemmed from the same patriarchal disobedience that got her in the end?

They say, once a pope always a pope, since once the mantle is donned Satanic power possesses the holy mind. In those days nasty rumors leaked out like sewer gas in the Vatican. Truth be told, the poisonous vapors that rise from Hell corrupt all those who breathe them. But why did Innocent X incarcerate Olimpia of all people? Why? What did she do to incur such horrid displeasure? Did she withdraw her favors when she saw the evil serpent? Perhaps the heady joys with blond and dashing Monsignor Matthew Boffonini outclassed Olimpia's golden aura? Or was it Monsignor Bertonini?

Yes, Roma, we know: even you can't keep the names straight; nobody ever could. Of course if we knew what they were really doing back then, perhaps we could know what's going on now? Then getting the names right would be a piece of papal cake. It's all very nuanced but I'll take a stab!

Olimpia mastered the game when she got Gianbattista Pamphili made a cardinal and later a pope. Once selected to rise in the hierarchy, Gianbattista was appointed to the Holy Office of the Inquisition. His qualifications? The same in his day as now: appointments are offered to those who most enjoy the sins they must detect! Gianbattista's great flaw was his obsessive love for Olimpia, a woman! You've all heard about the homosexual underground in the Vatican? So can't we see why Olimpia lost favor long ago? We think Olimpia would have done better with the rest of the clergy if she had a longer appendage!

In our global world, we must examine all patterns, since each new *trend goes everywhere and takes over everything. Innocent's loss of in-nocence was no isolated incident in the clergy then and we know it isn't now. It is an open secret that the priesthood is filled with adulterous love affairs and active gay men, so what does that mean for the Church? We think it important to ask whether sexually active men are qualified to be priests? What happened to practice what you preach? The workings of the gay underground in the Vatican will be the focus of the second "Between the Sheets in Roma: What's Up in the Vatican?"*

Tune in February 2013 for the next juicy installment, and remember to keep an eye on the secret passages! We need your eyes and ears. What about the tunnels below the Vatican that go under the Tiber? Whisper, whisper: the clergy use them for trysts in the Trastevere on the West Bank of the Tiber, and the night of the full moon is the best time.

Sarah tried to read Simon's article, but her Italian wasn't good enough to catch the satire. She headed right over to see Claudia, who promised to explain it to her.

"Darling!" Claudia expelled a mouthful of smoke. "I *can't* believe Simon dared; he has struck exactly the right tone. Finally people are laughing about this three-ring circus—The Holy See. 'Between the Sheets in Roma' is a thinly veiled spoof on Ratzinger, his butler, and his hot private secretary! Simon is revealing the truth about today's cast of characters through the lens of Innocent X's love affair with Olimpia Maidalchini. I always wondered how Monsignor Ganswein, 'Gorgeous George,' got so far with Ratzinger back in the old days when they both worked for the Inquisition! Nobody will ever know what really went on, since now the pope is old. I'm sure Ratzinger was selected by Vatican insiders because they could blackmail him. He was the nasty hit man behind the scenes for John Paul II, who ran around the world kissing babies and smiling. John Paul II died and Ratzinger was the perfect choice."

"Okay," said Sarah. "I did see that Simon was alluding to Vatican snakes like Cardinal Bertone who actually said the pedophile crisis has arisen because too many priests are gay. And that 'Boffonini' was for Dino Boffo, the journalist who's said to be a voracious gay stalker. I don't really care whether someone is gay. But it's too much for me to have priests sleeping around with men or women at the same time they preen and strut around as pious celibates. Still, that's nothing compared to the priests who prey on children in the confessional."

"Sarah," Claudia went right on as usual, "of course, darling, now you realize the way to figure out the game is to know what goes on between the sheets?"

Sarah found Claudia's words and tone more than patronizing. She had had enough of that in her life. "You know what, Claudia?" Sarah said, narrowing her eyes and leaning forward. "I hope we will be friends after our trip to the oracle. But I am sick of you always railroading our conversations and treating me like a ninny, especially acting like I'm innocent. I am the one who married Simon, not you."

Claudia was so surprised by Sarah's words that she almost choked on her cigarette. "Ooohhh!" she expelled in a hurt voice. After a moment, though, she got mad. "Let's get one thing clear. I didn't want to marry Simon, even though he *was* great in bed."

Sarah took a deep breath, suppressing the thought of Claudia in bed with Simon. *So what. I knew he had a past. Of course he slept with her; who wouldn't? But I can't stand being treated like an idiot.* "Claudia," Sarah retorted, "I'm not threatened by your past relationship with Simon, and I certainly do not want the details. I'm trying to get through to you because you limit our communication by being so dominant and knowledgeable. I have just as much to say as you do, if you would only listen. "

Claudia listened carefully. She was hurt, yet she knew Sarah was right; she had been patronizing. *I want to talk deeply with her; I really do. I don't want to be an aging bitch.* She took a deep breath. "Sarah, I'd like to tell you about my experiences with Armando. I think it will help you understand me better, and then perhaps we can be closer. I haven't told you this before, but I know all about what Armando tried to pull on you, and I don't think of you as a prude. Can we talk about that? Maybe the end of the Mayan Calendar is forcing us to be more honest?"

Sarah barely heard Claudia because suddenly her inner eye was back at Sybil's chamber. What had come through in words was a small part of what she'd seen. She recalled the message she'd gotten on the first day in the hotel: if you detect men in my oracle, push yourself further back in time before they cloud your eyes. While Claudia droned on, Sarah recalled a delicious time before she was controlled by men. I'm sexually free! We do not marry, and we do not keep men unless they cherish us. If they restrain us, we discard them like old rotting vegetables in the compost. We leave the children with others, sometimes with the men. The old world was like swimming in the Caribbean in silvery blue salt water amongst colorful tropical fish in bright coral.

This vision of a time when women worked together with the help of men still dancing behind her eyes, Sarah responded. "Claudia, I'd love to have a conversation with you about Armando. I want to know why you loved him, maybe still love him? Even though I didn't love him, I care about him and his family. I wish I could understand him better, but I know Simon worries about me ever seeing him again. Simon had to help me afterwards when I almost went crazy." She gazed off into the distance, relieved that the thought of Armando now brought her more pity than pain. "Judging from what I experienced, I think Armando needs a lot of therapy. I had this insight about him at the time." She looked at Claudia, who was watching her intently. "I thought that maybe Armando was a Fallen Angel." Sarah was quiet for a moment, remembering the cries of the Fallen Angels she had heard during her vision in the cave. Then she shook her head, ridding herself of these unpleasant thoughts. "Anyway, I'm sure I was just one more potential seduction in a long line. At any rate, I would like to be able to see his parents again."

Claudia stubbed out her cigarette. Sarah understood more about Armando than she had realized. "We should talk about these things, but it is late and I am tired. Yes, darling, it will be our next talk, perhaps on December 21? And it's too bad his parents didn't like *me* better twenty years ago."

"Yes, Claudia, and will you please stop calling me darling?" Sarah said in a low voice as she went out the front door to catch a cab. *Thank goodness Simon will be home soon!*

30

The Shadow of Moloch

Sweaty sheets gripped Simon's waist as he wrenched himself over by the nightstand to grab his ringing cell phone. *Where am I, in Mary's Tomb?* When he came back to his room last night, he had thrown his dusty clothes off and collapsed, no dinner, no set alarm. Now he groggily answered his phone and heard his father's voice. "Hello, Simon. It's Dad. I have news to share with you, news I don't want you to hear from anybody else. It's not about Sarah or the family. It is about a tragic massacre of small children. Are you ready?" David's voice was very strained, almost taut. His father almost never called him about the news, so Simon steeled himself for the worst.

"A mentally disturbed twenty-year-old shot and killed his mother in their Newtown, Connecticut home. Then he drove to the nearby Sandy Hook Elementary School with an arsenal of guns and multiple-bullet magazines. He crashed through the doors, and murdered twenty children and some teachers. Then he shot himself in the head and died obscenely among the children on the floor. Your mother is mumbling incoherently and staring off into space, and I can't fathom how such a thing could happen. I've seen a lot of terrible things in my life but this is incomprehensible. Can we talk? Can you help me with this?"

"Dad, this is the first I've heard of it. I don't know what to think," Simon said, taking a deep breath. Then he spilled out the first thing that came into his mind. "Oddly, yesterday I was thinking about Moloch, the early Canaanite king in the Bible who made his people offer child sacrifices. It made me think of Columbine, which made me wonder whether anything is getting better. Human behavior is going backward, barbaric behavior is growing."

"The shooter must have been on meds. Did you know that most mass killers are either on meds or trying to get off them? I think I've told you reporters aren't allowed to say anything about medication issues since the 1996 Medical Privacy Act. So the public doesn't realize legal drugs are nearly always a factor. If people knew doctors summon Dr. Jekyll, wouldn't they put the blame for these crimes on the doctors and the drug companies? Would parents allow them to put their kid on meds? Doctors who don't fathom the depth of the human mind are legal drug pushers! They open their patients to possession by robbing them of their free will! The slaughter will escalate until people go after the cause—legal guns and drugs. Sorry to rant, Dad, but reporters are *muzzled!* Drives us nuts! I'm sorry Mom is so upset. Tell her I love her. I'll call Sarah in Rome. She'll be utterly devastated." He paused and then said quietly, "Dad, we want to have children."

"I am sure you will, Simon, because you and Sarah can contribute in the world. But," David's voice was dead and metallic. "Imagine if you raised a baby and your adorable small child was butchered after going off bright-eyed to school! This is an abomination! Most of the kids who died were in the first grade. How could anybody kill them? The media wonders if the shooter was bullied in school, but I think you're on the right track. He probably was on stimulants by age six, anti-depressants as a teenager who raided the parent's liquor cabinet—booze, drugs, computer addiction, and guns by age twenty. Ironically, the kid began with murdering his mother, the one who should have done something about his arsenal. The neighbors say she used to take him to the shooting range where they both practiced. Will the NRA still have their way after Newtown? I suppose so, since it happened in Connecticut where gun manufacturing has enriched the state for a few hundred years. I don't know what else to say, Simon, I'm numb! Have you heard some people say the world is coming to an end December 21? The Newtown arrow of doom feels like a harbinger. How can we go on when little children are murdered in school?"

"Hmmm, Dad," Simon responded thoughtfully, "the incident is like a Greek tragedy—matricide by a young man who slaughters small children. I can see why it's upset you so much: when things like this happen, Americans are told by their pastors to pray and ask for forgiveness, but what good does that do? When terrible things like this occurred in the ancient world, people wrote about it to inspire people to seek the causes and meaning in the human mind. Instead, I'm sure Newtown will be the perfect inspiration for Hollywood movies and sleazy crime novels."

He gazed out the window at the ancient and troubled city then continued, "When Sarah and a friend talked about the Maya end of the world, I teased them and said they were acting like New Age airheads. Well, here I am in Jerusalem for the tenth time since 1999, and I feel a death grip. Desperation pervades everything, stark meaninglessness. The Israelis don't give a damn about peace as they cynically grab more territory and transform the Palestinians into chained dogs. Syria may be the next tinderbox in the Middle East or maybe Egypt. I haven't shared my feelings with Sarah lately because I don't want to worry her. Your call reminds me we have to talk about these painful things. We *must* share our feelings. I wish I could come home for the holidays; instead I'm stuck here alone. Madness is breaking out everywhere that is collapsing our world."

"Yes, I know, my only son. You remind me to start every day with blessings. I'm glad you and Sarah have each other's support. Thank goodness Sarah is safe in Rome doing her work, and Rose and I can go to Shelter Island to find peace. I am happy to hear your voice right now. Just think," David said as his voice cracked, "Newtown parents will never hear the voices of their children again. I can't imagine not hearing your voice. Here is something I've always wanted to say to you: The world has been deteriorating since you were born and now it's getting radically worse. I am grateful for every moment I've had with you, with Jennifer, and your mother. I look forward to many more. When I go into my heart in the morning to find my center, you are there. No matter what happens, I love you beyond time. It's impossible to understand the world, yet we always have love. We will call Sarah too. How terrible this happened so close to the holidays, so soon after your wedding, how terrible. I hope you can be home soon."

"Sarah, it's me," Simon said, waiting to hear by the tone of her voice if she knew what had happened. When she began to speak, he could tell she'd been crying.

"Simon, did you hear about it, the children? I didn't want to wake you up. I'm in such a state of shock that I can barely move. What's going on in the United States? Other mass killings shocked me, but this is incomprehensible! I do feel like the world is ending. Oh, I'm sorry, I know you hate that. When innocent children are murdered in school, it strips hope away! But forgive me," she said slowing herself down as she imagined his deep brown eyes flashing with blue. "How are you? How are you handling this news? Can you come home? Oh, I'm sorry I said that. I'm okay. But maybe some people will change their plans after an event like this?"

"As much as I would love to, when the world goes mad, reporters can't change their plans for personal reasons." He paused. "Sarah, let me apologize for ranting about that end of the world stuff. I have been thinking about it myself! An event like this turns my mind to conspiracies, and I can be crazier than either you or Claudia. Newtown's timing is very suspect. What if someone triggered this guy to *make* people feel like the world is ending? It's too sinister:

psychologically disturbed young people on meds unleashed as killing machines using weapons provided by Mom to kill at key moments. Way-out conspiracy theorists say these killers have chips in their minds that program them. Maybe that's true, yet the alarmist blood-soaked media is just as guilty. When I examine mass murders since the 1980s the timing always gets my attention; they often happen at the ideal moment to traumatize the public. The more sinister and bizarre they have become, the more people react by turning in to zombies. Are you surprised to hear me say things like that? When my dad told me about Newtown, the first thing I thought was that it is the perfect elite drama designed to keep us in fear. *How* do they insert these violent films into our world?"

Sarah felt a great sense of relief hearing Simon's words. "Simon, I'm glad to hear about your change of heart! This means I can talk to you about my feelings about the end times. I'd feel like this even if I'd never heard about the Maya, never talked to Claudia. Speaking of conspiracies, the media repeats *twenty children, twenty children*. It grated in my ears and then I got it! *Twenty* is the big Mayan number, since the Calendar is composed of twenty symbols for the days—twenty primary archetypal paths in life. I wonder if the massacre cast asunder the primary archetypal elements of reality? Is it a tipping point? I can imagine what this event means to you, since we both wonder how evil enters the world. The ultimate abuse, child sacrifice, frightens me. It's too dark for me, so it helps to verbalize it. I can't hold this horror inside anymore; something is wrong, *very* wrong."

Simon hated hearing the pain in her voice; he wished he could be there to hold her. "I have more to say, lots. We have to counter the dark by celebrating the beauty in our lives. My father always does that, and he just reminded me of it again. I'd like to share something that happened to me just before I heard about Newtown, and thank goodness it was *before*. Yesterday I went to the Tomb of Mary and had what I'd describe as a full-blown mystical experience.

It changed me; I saw things. There is more going on in this world than I ever imagined. Confronted with evil, maybe our world will not end if we widen our perspective? I think you already have." He mused. "Maybe women do it more easily?"

She responded slowly, her voice low and rueful. "The world of those children just ended, the joy of their parents gone, the return of the slaughter of the innocents. I'm happy you had a mystical experience because I know there's more to life. It doesn't have to be that way in the U.S. We will be happier together if we can see and share more. "

"Then I'll share more about it," he said very softly, his breath barely audible on the phone. "My experience at the tomb has made me know we will have a child—soon, I hope. If I'd heard about Newtown first, I'd be going in the opposite direction. An event like this would convince me to never have a child. But life is about life and death. If I have a god, it is personal courage. It's time to put myself on the line."

Sarah smiled, even as tears blurred her eyes. She too knew they would have a child.

David and Rose usually stayed in the city during the holidays to be with friends, but this December was different. They endured a few days of trying to avoid TV, but their friends called constantly to talk about Newtown, so they decided they had to get out of the city. As they drove across Long Island to Shelter Island, the proximity of the Connecticut shore reminded them of the crime scene. The only way to avoid hearing people talk about praying to God was to avoid the radio and TV; the crucifix hung over the entire Eastern U.S.

As they rode the ferry, wind blasted the old boat, which cracked and strained as if it was dying. Rose looked eighty, her deep red scarf only accentuating the dark circles under her eyes, and David worried about her. *I wonder if she's thinking about the gas ovens and Jews being loaded on trains?* She was. They arrived at the house and traipsed into the cold hallway, wrapped themselves in blankets, and shared some brandy by a struggling fire. Radiators creaked and groaned as they began to warm up the rooms, and the old well-built house sheltered them from the angry wind. When the main room attained sixty-two degrees, Rose went to snuggle upstairs, and David went to his study to set another fire.

He made a kindling nest under a huge oak log in the soft light of the Tiffany lamp. He lit crumpled newspaper with a long match and blew on the small flame, which exploded. Poof! *If only I could change the world as easily as I can make a fire. I have to think this all the way through. If I don't, the world is going to unravel and the whirlwind will come. I know the meaning of the murder of twenty innocents. Global elite bastards. You think I went away long ago, but I haven't. I've been watching every god-damned one of you every day of my life: I wondered whether you'd dare bring Moloch back to service your desires, you blood-thirsty curs. You won't get away with this—I am here.*

The oak log crackled when the flames turned the bark to fire. Watching out for sparks, he pulled a slim leather case out from under the base of the Tiffany lamp and removed a key. He walked over to a tall and narrow, nearly invisible cabinet in the corner. Carefully he inserted the key into a small brass keyhole. The narrow door unlocked when he turned the key. It looked empty; however, he deftly stuck his index finger into a round hole in the back. The back was hinged and moved to the side, revealing a hidden chamber. *It has been so many years since I've seen it, so many years.* A fist-sized quartz crystal skull with deep eye sockets and big teeth nestled in a wreath of lime green and orange parrot feathers grinned at him. *Ah, it is the same, the skull of Dzibichaltun—keeper of nine dimensions.*

He lifted out the icy-cold skull and cradled it in his hands to warm it while caressing its large cerebellum. Golden firelight flickered in the center and generated electrical signals, brain waves. The last time David had held it was before Simon's birth thirty-six years ago, yet he was always aware of it. It was given to him by his teacher, don Alejandro, when he went to Mexico to study spiritual teachings forty years earlier. As he held it up to the firelight to study its planes and occlusions, it woke up. *Don Alejandro told me things will be or will not be. I weigh the world; I judge.*

Don Alejandro had given him instructions with the skull, and he still remembered every word. *This is miraculous. I can fulfill my duty just before the end of the Calendar! I've waited so long for the sign—twenty. Those bastards! Just think how amazed people would be if they knew the whole truth!* David knew the world would be shocked to realize that global elite insiders had known all about the Calendar's end, shocked to realize the elite had anticipated the end for four hundred years! He had always thought it odd that people couldn't see something so obvious: When the conquistadors, Jesuits, and Dominicans plundered the villages and massacred the people, they gathered their books and calendars and brought them back to Europe. For many years secret cabals studied the records in their cloistered libraries to dissect the cycle to get the Maya galactic knowledge. The Maya timeline indicated when Earth would go back into phase with the Milky Way Galaxy. If people lost hope, the synchronization would fail. The priests and conquistadors cleverly described bloody Aztec sacrificial rituals to keep the people from noticing that Mass is the blood sacrifice. They tortured people over four hundred years, polluted the world, sexually abused anyone in sight, and killed unmercifully.

David put the skull on the table and went back to the cabinet for a leather notebook. *Now the test.* The notebook fell open on his knees. His eyes were drawn to beautiful scrolled red symbols and letters on skin-colored parchment. The skull in his right hand buzzed and vibrated. The notebook contained the specific list of all the things the elite planned to accomplish by December 21. If they made it, Earth's multidimensional fields would collapse and lose form. If these things didn't happen on time, reality could reweave itself into the golden threads of Earth's dream.

- *Pole shift caused by a discontinuity in the core*
- *Nuclear meltdown that destroys the oceans*
- *Complete melt at the North and South poles*
- *Total war between Judeo-Christianity and Islam*
- *Death of love in the human heart*
- *Human physical form is distorted and gender confusion rampant*
- *Elite weather control blocks sound waves from the universe*
- *Humans forget how to co-create life with the divine*
- *Electronic pollution blocks high energy from the Galactic Center*

David had forgotten how scientific the list was. It had seemed outlandish when he reviewed it thirty-six years ago when he couldn't even begin to imagine such things; he didn't even know what they were. Now he could see that great forces had been conspiring to make all this happen; millions knew the truth. Elements of this list had happened, but not enough to end the world by December 21. Fukushima was a warning bell, but not the death of the oceans.

He closed the notebook and vowed: *I'll be with this skull at dawn on the winter solstice.*

David still remembered what don Alejandro had said, which could never be written down: "David, you are among a few initiates given this knowledge. When you activate the skull at the end of the Calendar, do not think you carry the burden alone. Thirteen of you will judge whether the evil ones have taken over your planet, the heartless ones who seek only pleasure and riches.

"If the list is not fulfilled, an infusion of power from the higher dimensions into the lower ones will begin reweaving the dream of Earth. I warn you, however, this convergence will be so intense that many will not be able to bear it. Those who can will experience life in nine dimensions. This includes your children and grandchildren. I warn you, David, reality will be so chaotic and insane through 2016 that few will be able to stand it. But many will. You will. Your children will. You must because anything is better than the end of a world, anything."

The skull was buzzing. At first he thought he was crazy, but for sure it was. *Is it trying to speak to me?* His temporal bones vibrated with the skull, and a stream of thoughts came through a hologram, a diamond that emitted sound: *I am the Primum Mobile. Feel my tightly woven cord enter your body from deep in Earth and move through your energy centers, out through the top of your head, and into the spinning Galactic Center. David, listen to primordial sound. The game is over! The evolutionary push, nine phases of creation, completed November 28, 2011. The epiphany, a galactic superwave, approaches your solar system. When cosmic consciousness arrives, matter regenerates. In your zone, screaming metal parts vibrate within the iridescent hides of dying dinosaurs, the completion of the extinctions. Listen to them gnash their teeth! Tell them to surrender and leave their bodies to avoid the maelstrom.*

David took a deep breath and came back into focus, but he couldn't register what had deposited in his mind. He was disturbed by what he was feeling. It was as if a huge black machine made of metallic cords and whirring drives was reading him. *I wonder if this is the elite computer—the inter-dimensional brain that monitors everything and mind-controls people. Maybe it ran out of fuel?*

31

The Pierleoni Garden

On the evening of December 21, 2012, light suffused Claudia's elegant apartment. The marble floors glowed in the subtle light of recessed designer lights. When Sarah walked in, her eyes were drawn to reflected golden flames in dripping beeswax wall sconces. The sheen on the new glossy embossed satin fabric of Claudia's loveseat was sensual like excited skin. Sarah loved how going to Claudia's apartment felt like visiting the eighteenth century.

"Sarah, I'm so happy to see you, and I promise to never call you darling again. Do you love my new satin coverings? I found the fabric in Milan and waited nearly a year for it." Sarah admired everything and then they sat down as Claudia got right into it. "Here we are, the big moment; *has* anything really changed?"

"Well, of course, many things have changed. We are meeting to discuss the unspeakables, to unmask evil. I'm tired of the repression. I'm ready, Claudia. Tell me all about your love affair with Armando. I mean *all* of it."

The ash glowed when Claudia sucked her enameled cigarette holder. She looked at Sarah through lowered eyelashes, thinking about where to begin. *This is all or nothing but can I do it?* She watched Sarah's simple diamond pendant glitter in the candlelight and then raised her glance to Sarah's eyes, where she saw openness and compassion. *I will tell her,* Claudia decided. *I will tell my story because I may never have another chance. I can't carry the pain around anymore; I feel like a war refugee.*

She exhaled slowly and began. "All right, it happened when I was nineteen. We Romans have our customs for presenting eligible women to the right men. Our families give selective parties, and the men know they've been invited to view a daughter. The parents think they are in control of the girls because they select the men. Once a girl is ready, they start with the most eligible bachelors and go down the list until a few accept the invitation. Of course in a Catholic country, to get a rich husband a girl must be a virgin, so my parents watched me day and night. These parties are seduction opportunities, since avoiding marriage as long as possible is a game for wealthy Roman men. Well, why not? I first saw Armando at a party given by my great-aunt, Amanda Castiglione, a dear friend of the Pierleonis. I was excited because he is old Roman aristocracy. He took my breath away." She sighed. "Oh Sarah, you should have seen him when he was twenty!

"Of course, I wasn't playing by my dear aunt's rules; I just wanted to have sex with somebody. When Armando handed me a glass of champagne and searched my eyes as if he was seeking my soul, he knew. I sensed danger when his eyes flashed red like the eyes of a snake; I should have paid attention. Being a stupid young girl, I ignored my first impression because he was so handsome. He asked if he could pick me up in a few nights. Of course, I said yes."

Claudia's eyes were far away as she remembered. "He arrived at my parent's house with carnations for my mother and a gold embossed Pierleoni family crest card for my father. They were thrilled he was interested in me, since he is from an ancient lineage. After greetings were exchanged, they said goodnight to us as we went out the front door. It was my first time alone with a man; I was so excited! My mother told me nothing about sex so all I had to go on was French novels. And my father paid no attention to

Armando's notorious reputation because he was very rich. He asked me if I'd like to have a walk in the back garden of his ancestral house in Rome. Everybody knows about the Pierleoni walled garden, since they have owned it for a thousand years. I suppose you've been there, Sarah?" Sarah nodded but remained silent, encouraging Claudia to go on. "What harm could come from walking in the garden with a Pierleoni scion?" Claudia laughed bitterly.

"We passed through the old rounded stone gate as I wondered why he hadn't first shown me the house. Perhaps he thought I'd be nervous about going in if no one was at home? We strolled among beautiful exotic pruned trees, aromatic flowering plants, and lovely small ponds. I was especially taken with an ancient cedar as we sat on a white marble bench. When he put his arm around me, I thought being with him was the meaning of my life! We got up and walked around in circles; the entire garden is a labyrinth. I shared the ritual with him as if he were Pan or the Green Man. All the while he led me closer to a stone cottage with mottled leaded glass windows and a thick ancient mossy slate roof. I asked him if it was the cottage of the original vineyard? He laughed, putting his arm around my waist, and I smelled his body. I was so innocent and so attracted to him."

Claudia slowly exhaled a mouthful of smoke, her eyes filled with nostalgia for the young girl she had been. "I just wanted to have sex with somebody to see what it felt like. What I was doing felt right; it was my time. I am amazed still that my mother didn't teach me how to protect myself." Claudia looked over to Sarah to see deep sadness in her eyes, a faraway look of pain and concern. Sarah tried to break in, but Claudia protested, "No, no! Let me go on, I must."

Claudia began to speak more quickly. "He led me into a small front room with a little table and chairs by a window in a small kitchen. A heavy oak door with iron hinges that seemingly led into another room was closed. He pointed at the table; I sat down. He brought me a delicious red wine, a Pierleoni vintage, and a small

Pierleoni garden and cottage

plate of luscious Belgium chocolates. We talked about Rome and our families. He acted like he was impressed by the Tagliatti Company, as if I were something. He moved me relentlessly along by touching my thighs and pulling his hand higher to reach my hips with his thumb pressing into my sacrum close to my groin. His hands are big, so this was very sexy. All the while his eyes burned into mine while my body coursed with intense fire! I was taught by the nuns to never touch myself, so a latent nervous system was waking up! I drank in his eyes as he stood up and pulled me to him, grabbing my butt. I still remember desperately searching his eyes, wondering what he wanted yet I knew I would stay. He pressed his body against mine and I got hot. He was continually looking into my eyes, searching for something. 'What are you looking for, what are you asking for?' I said.

"He pushed away from me, laughing, which made me want to kiss his sensual mouth. He lowered his voice and spoke in this hoarse voice, sounding like the hero in a movie saying I was the only woman left in the world: 'I want to *know* what you want. Your eyes are beautiful, like deep pools at the bottom of a jungle waterfall. With your young, hungry body, you are a lioness. You are innocent and don't know how sensual you are. I want to know if you want *all* of it. Tell me!'"

Claudia lip's twisted in a half-smile. "Of course at that point, I thought he was wondering if I wanted all of his penis. Since I'd never seen one, I wasn't sure I did. I needed him to reassure me about what we were going to do to help me feel like it was right."

"Claudia," Sarah broke in, "Are you sure you want to tell me all of this? You don't have to, you know."

Claudia waved her hand at Sarah. "Oh, but I need to tell you; I need to tell you more than you know. If I don't share this story with at least one other person, I will die." *I sure can't share it with another Roman,* she thought. "You and I have talked a lot about what we're feeling during these crazy end times! Well, I am up against a wall. The things I've stuffed deep inside are eating my soul. I have to get them out because I am living a lie; nobody knows me. I have built an elaborate façade around myself with my apartment and business. Can you listen and accept me? Can you take it?'"

"Okay, Claudia, go ahead," Sarah replied in a warm and genuine voice, understanding that Claudia would never be able to tell her story to a Roman. *This gossipy city is a dangerous place where honesty is gauche, truth a joke.* "I think I can handle whatever you need to tell me." Sarah had offered her one more chance to back out. Maybe it would be just another intellectual rant, one topic to the next, but Claudia sounded dreadfully serious.

"I answered him very smartly by saying I wasn't stupid and knew exactly what he was after when he brought me here tonight. I was breathing heavily while I said it as he fingered my tailbone pressing his hand between my legs. One of his hands crept under my suede miniskirt as he removed my blouse with his other hand, tearing off the top button. I wanted it to go on forever. 'You are beautiful like a jaguar or an ocelot. Our bodies are perfectly matched as cat people from Sirius. You are the one I've been looking for, the one to take all of me as no one ever has before,' he said in a deep and masculine voice.

"'But surely you've had sex with a woman before,' I said, feeling disappointed because I wanted my first lover to be very experienced.

"'Sweet one, I've been having sex since I was twelve and plan to have it until I'm ninety. I am talking about something very special that I have never enjoyed before. Do I have your permission?' he said as he kneaded my ass intensely and breathed on my neck. I burned as if in a high fever. It sounds like a cliché, but my temperature must have been 106! I felt dizzy and drugged; I wonder whether he'd slipped something into my wine. Could anyone nearby hear me? I was afraid because my body was making me lose my mind. He pulled me against him, tightly pulling my pelvis to his and I felt his manhood. I was passing out like a robot running out of juice.

"'Come little sweet one,' he said, leading me over to the mysterious dark door. He got a scarf or something and tied it firmly over my eyes; it was soft like cashmere. We went into the room; I couldn't see anything. He took my brassiere off while kissing me with his tongue down my throat, making me wild and wet between my thighs. He reached down to touch me after he'd gotten my skirt and panties off, and he groaned. 'Maybe I will change my plans,' he said, massaging my pubis, stroking my clitoris, and penetrating my vagina with his fingers. I had no idea what he was talking about, no way to know. Oddly at that moment I remember wishing my mother would come for me. Subliminally I knew something.

"Then he got weird, very weird when my body quelled and I went rigid. He detected resistance and wariness, so he pushed me forcefully onto a bed on my stomach and grabbed my shoulders hard. I said I didn't understand what he was doing. Then his voice got mean. 'You said you wanted it. You can't tempt a man and go back on your word. You could make me angry, *very* angry. We don't make Armando angry.' I froze and stayed where he put me with my mind racing insanely. I could hear something, like the twisting of fabric or leather at the bed corners that made me nervous. He tied my wrists and pulled them to the corners while rasping in my ear, 'You will love this, little one; it is the best.' I had no idea what he was talking about. Can you believe that? He tied my ankles and pulled my legs tight, and I hurt with my crotch spread as wide as possible. I felt such awful vulnerability, hearing grunting sounds, animal sounds. There I was exposed and all splayed out like a cheap whore! *Still* I didn't know what was going on, so I asked him to tell me what he was doing! He said in a snarling voice, 'You will know in a moment, so don't worry. All that matters is you will love it.' I heard him unzip his pants and I heard them crumple on the floor. I heard something swishing on the floor." Claudia seemed unaware she had completely crushed the cigarette in her fingers. She looked at Sarah pleadingly. "Sarah, I was *terrified!*

"He rubbed me all over my back with an essential oil that smelled delicious, maybe ylang ylang. He rubbed my arms, my breasts, and then he rubbed oil all over my legs while his hands slowly moved over my thighs closer to my ass. The oil made me feel sensual, and suddenly fire shot through my body. There was nothing I could do to stop it, the bastard! He said, 'You want it now, don't you, beautiful one? It's your time tonight! The back of your body is incredible; you are a gazelle.' I thought of how long I'd waited to be taken, how I'd wanted to be forcefully seduced so that I couldn't resist like in French novels. So I felt myself weakening, a sickening feeling, and then I felt his greasy finger in my anus penetrating me."

Quickly, though Claudia was talking very fast, Sarah broke in again. "Claudia, you *don't* have to go on. I get the point. You don't have to give me all the details. I understand what happened. Let's stop so we can deal with how much this hurt you when you were so young and innocent. It was natural to respond. You have nothing to feel guilty about."

Claudia dropped her broken cigarette in the ashtray and fixed Sarah with a commanding stare. "Oh yes, I do have to go on, because you don't *know* what he did; somebody has to know or I can't bear it. I wish it were as simple as you think it is, but it is not." She paused for a moment, and then she started again like a train pushing to its destination. "He massaged me and prepared me with grease, and he penetrated me with his rock-hard, huge penis. The burning pain was incredible. I whimpered and objected, but the more I struggled the more he hurt me. He kept pushing, then pulling back, and then moving in deeper, thrusting into my stretched anus. He got in and took total control of me. Then while gripping my left hip hard, he rained blows on my back and buttocks with a leather strap. He lashed me like a horse!" She saw Sarah open her mouth and snapped, "Do not interrupt me, Sarah! I have to get this out." At this point tears were pouring down Claudia's face. Sarah was shaking and wondered if she could take it. *This is hideous, yet I feel such love for her. I have to listen to her ugly story.*

"He kept plunging in and whipping me harder and harder while whispering in my ear that he could do it till I came. He moved his hand to my throat, rasping and spitting, 'Come on, baby, come; you can do it. You are my lioness.'

"Then something started to happen in my body, and you have to understand that I had only read about orgasms; I had never felt that sensation or had anyone explain this to me. My back and hips burned from the blows, with blood rushing to the wounds. I synchronized my breath to his rhythmic thrusting because if I didn't breathe with him, I choked. He was strong like a monster! Finally, my anus didn't hurt anymore. A pleasurable thickening sensation started at the bottom of my spine as my vulva swelled because he was fingering me while thrusting in and out screeching, 'Yes, baby, Yes!' I arched when my vagina convulsed, hot energy filled my groin and thighs, and then fire moved out in a great wave into my arms and legs to my fingers and toes. I screamed! He lurched heavy on me, groaning in agony as he shot me with semen. Then he collapsed down beside me. It was over, but I couldn't move because I was tied. I was in shock and confusion. I didn't understand until later it was because he'd stolen my soul.

"He got out of bed and shuffled around doing something, maybe putting on clothes. I could hear water running. He untied my ankles and wrists, told me the bathroom was ready, and he left the room. I hurt all over but somehow I washed myself and got dressed. Sobbing as if I could never stop, I walked into the other room and said in an angry, blubbering voice, 'What was *that?!* How could you *do* that?!? Are you an animal, a dog in heat? What is wrong with you, Armando? I'm going to tell my father.'

"'Oh no, you won't, sweet one,' he said. I will never forget his sickening cynical voice. He said, 'If anybody ever finds out what we did—Claudia's orgasm—you will be nothing. I got you and if you tell them and they take you to the doctor, you are still a virgin. You won't get pregnant. You won't be able to tell them where I put it because you will be too embarrassed. I got you, you've been taken, Claudia, our delicious little secret. If you will be a good girl, next time I will do it the way you want it if you are on birth control, and maybe you'll like it even more. I got you, Claudia, and I can have you anytime I want.'"

Claudia's terrible story left Sarah feeling re-traumatized. *What is wrong with men? How could anybody do that to a young woman, like a Fallen Angel raping a woman? Do demons waiting to possess women lurk in male genes? How far would Armando go to turn himself on?* "Claudia, I am so sorry. I could say it so many ways. How did you ever get over it? Why are you still alive and sitting here tonight?" She looked at Claudia, who was staring pleadingly into her eyes.

"Sarah, can you come to me and hold me for a moment? It has been wonderful to get this *out* of my soul. You've helped me by being able to listen to me. Come hold me."

Sarah got up to sit beside Claudia, placing Claudia's head on her heart. "There now, this wasn't your fault, there was no way you could have known. Your mother didn't protect you when she should have. I'm here for you. I will always be your friend. I love you, Claudia, for your magnificent strength, the essence of feminine power. I want to learn more from you. It is a privilege to know you."

Delicious relief washed through Claudia. She felt her soul return; she felt good about herself again. "Sarah, I have to finish this so that I can let it all go. I think you are aware that we have two lower energy centers or chakras, the root chakra and the sexual chakra? The root chakra is in the anus, our physiological connection with the first dimension, the center of Earth. Our second chakra, the sexual chakra, connects us to the telluric realm, which is why sex can be like an earthquake or a volcano. The rape forced me to comprehend things most people can't fathom: I'm very sensitized to the first dimension, Earth's core. I think people ravage Earth because they feel guilty about this part of their bodies!"

The idea intrigued Sarah, so she broke in. "Surely there are other ways people can sensitize themselves to this part of their body and the Earth? Do you think people would stop destroying the planet if this chakra was not abused?"

Back to her normal mental mode, Claudia sat up straight, gently disengaging herself from Sarah's arms. "I think so, Sarah. I feel sure that things would at least be better. In light of what I had to endure while I was Armando's lover for ten years, I *had* to learn from it. I never liked it but it taught me things. But you're right, we don't have to learn through trauma—we can also sensitize ourselves by feeling the earth, being in nature. Observing the world through my somewhat tainted view, since my awakening began in this forceful way, I've noticed the worst destroyers are abusive and homophobic men, especially those who cannot come to terms with who they truly are—those who marry as a cover, those who are religious, righteous, and cruel because they feel guilty about what they do or want to do in private. Abusive and repressed men are amoral and vicious because they have not found a way to have sex without guilt. They cannot admit who they are. Men who repress their feminine aspects and over-emphasize their masculine aspects become men who hurt, force, and dominate. They get turned on when others suffer, like the profile of a priest who rapes children.

"I never wanted this form of sex. I don't care what anybody else is doing, but I know what I want. After ten years, I told Armando to go do it to a man if he wanted it that way, and then I dumped him. My last words to him were, 'If you like it so much then go out and find a guy who will do it to you. See if *you* like what you dish out before you fuck another man or woman in the ass.' He'd never let anybody do it to him, so he's stuck between worlds. He's just another man who doesn't know where the entrance to the sacred cave is. As you well know, he's been on the loose abusing women because he's too much of a coward to deal with his own distorted masculine aspect and his repressed feminine aspect. And I think repressed sexual guilt such as his is what causes humans to abuse our planet."

Sarah reached for Claudia's hand. "Claudia, I am deeply honored you shared your story with me. And I am in awe of the way you have survived and become who you are despite of what he did. Not only that, you have sought to understand and see what was at the heart of the disgusting way he treated you. Now I see why you are so functional and well-adjusted while Armando is a creep in rich man's clothes. That is the key, isn't it? No matter what happens to us, we must *learn* from what comes our way; it's the only way to evolve. Guilt isolates us from our surroundings and our world. It is a wonder this planet hasn't self-destructed. Thank you for choosing me to share this with. I will never reveal this to anyone, not even Simon. This is between us; we are now sisters, which means more to me than you realize. Will you be my sister?"

Claudia turned to Sarah, grasping both Sarah's hands with her own. "Yes. I'm so glad to have finally told someone. I just wish men would stop using women they don't really want. He didn't care about me; he was just trying to amuse himself. But he damaged me terribly, while he just chalked it up as some fun and stimulation. Someday I hope he will realize he is playing with very dangerous forces. Sex is dangerous when people aren't totally conscious of what's going on. He is so repressed he doesn't even seem to feel guilty about anything he does; I know that because our relationship continued."

Sarah's cell phone chimed. Sarah moved to turn it off, but Claudia said, "No, answer it. It could be Simon!"

Sarah smiled gratefully at Claudia as she answered the call.

"Sarah, it's me, Simon! I'm at the Rome airport. Can you come for me right away, or should I take a cab and meet you at home? I am home for the holidays!"

Sarah raised her eyes to Claudia's. They were sitting so close together she knew Claudia had heard Simon's words. Sarah didn't want to leave her newly sworn sister unless she was okay and wondered what she should tell Simon, but Claudia nodded. "You can go to him. Just telling my story has healed me."

32

Armando's Analysis

Lorenzo Gianinni, one of Rome's most celebrated Jungian analysts, sat on a comfortable leather chair in front of a large, dark, wooden desk with various ancient artifacts spread all over its surface. He tapped a pencil while running his eyes over them one by one. They were his tools, which held historic and symbolic information, the computer hard drives of ancient civilizations. He needed them because his clients were apt to dig up almost anything in the past, especially arcane symbols. He cast a glance at a small lapis lazuli statue of Sekhmet from the Eighteenth Dynasty in Egypt. Her broad prominent nose and fierce lion eyes seemed to be watching ferocious religious battles between the priests of Amun and the Amenhoteps. His gaze moved over to a Sumerian wall relief that depicted a strange chimera—lion body, chicken feet, and the head of a menacing man carrying a staff. *They made these so that people can remember something that happened long ago, but what?*

Putting down the pencil, Lorenzo reached for a soft limestone tablet with the twenty Maya day signs carved in raised relief; and he brushed his fingertips over the peculiar symbols. *Hmmm, my fingers go to Cauac, not Ahau. Funny, since Ahau is today's sign and Cauac means cataclysm, chaos.* He was thinking and thinking, as if somehow that would get him someplace; he of all people knew it never did.

Maybe if I free-associate it will tell me how to get Armando moving. Damn it! Ten years wasting time with this spoiled ass. He still goes around abusing young women, probably a repressed homosexual. Today he'll show up on the last day at the end of time. Ha! Maybe time will end for him, and I won't have to put up with him anymore! Most of Lorenzo's patients needed only two or three years of analysis, but he thought Armando could continue for the rest of his life, or at least the rest of Lorenzo's life. *I am so sick of the pompous creep!* As he thought of his life ending before Armando went away, Lorenzo's face flashed in the crackled glass of a Victorian mirror. It was a wily and smart face, like a happy little mouse stuffed with cheese. Even though he was almost sixty, his skin was tight, his hair black and gray, his mouth sensual.

I've had to listen to so many seductions and descriptions of his goddamned paintings that I'd like to gas the bastard. Lorenzo would have loved to end his work with him; Armando was the only patient he'd ever truly hated, but he was afraid to turn Armando loose. Over the past few months he'd grown more and more concerned that Armando was ready to kill somebody. *I can feel it coming; I have to confront him. Maybe if I threaten to end it with him, maybe that's what it will take to get him to see his dark side?* Startled, he looked up. Had the Sumerian lion just switched its long tail? His bright brown eyes sparkled in the mirror.

After parking and passing through the iron bolted gate off the Via del Portico d'Ottavia in the medieval Jewish ghetto, Armando ascended an ancient stone spiral staircase up to Lorenzo's office in a tower that was more than nine hundred years old. Once he got to a certain level, his awareness melted into another time and place. He was startled by something dark and hairy on the damp stonewall to his right. *Ugh! What a hideous spider! Looks dangerous too.* He took off a Ferragamo loafer, stood slightly back, and Whap! He squished it all over the wall. As it writhed and convulsed he thought, *There! Take it! You shitty thing!* Armando could hear its high-pitched death scream, a siren inaudible to most ears.

"Hello, Armando. How are you today?" Lorenzo said as Armando sat down, his head resting on the tufted dark green leather analyst's couch that could spin long tales going back to the mid-1980s. Lorenzo was invisible while he sat with clipboard and pen in a comfortable easy chair. He turned off the light on the table next to him and waited.

"The same, always the same," Armando said in a distinctly bored voice. "When am I going to change? We've been doing this for ten years! If only I could have Claudia just once more, I would change because she's the only woman I ever loved. And it would be even better because I know she is now Sarah's friend, the only woman I ever wanted to marry. Ironically, they are close these days. I have seen Sarah go into Claudia's apartment. I've waited around outside on the verandah for hours wondering what they talk about; Claudia should have a guard. I'm sure Sarah will go over there tonight, since it is the end of the Mayan Calendar. If only I could fuck Claudia just once more, maybe fuck both of them," he muttered as the heaviness came, the time to free associate.

"Armando, I want to make some changes today with your permission. We have been working together for ten years and making very little progress. You must be as tired of it as I am?"

"Of course I'm tired of it. I am sick of paying you, boring you, and never changing myself." That's what Armando verbalized, but it wasn't what he was thinking. *You worm, Lorenzo. I know you love me laying around here telling you about all my adventures. I'm sure I make you horny all the time.*

"Armando, I would like you to begin as usual by telling me the first thing that comes into your mind and then I'd like to regress you. We've never done that before, and I think it is time. I can lead you on a journey into the past, maybe to another place and time, possibly into another lifetime. We don't care what these experiences are, but they are usually valuable because regression accesses the deep subconscious where we find deeply repressed memories. I have been thinking of terminating our relationship because we aren't getting anywhere. This technique might help you; certainly it won't hurt you."

Armando gave his permission because his brain was thickening; something was flooding it, something was coming. He said, "I see a baseball bat."

"A baseball bat," Lorenzo noted. "Yes?"

"I'm swinging it hard over and over again, stretching out my shoulder muscles. I played baseball because I loved hitting the balls. Wham! Wham! Just like smashing that huge black spider in your filthy tower." His voice slurred; Lorenzo struggled to hear him. "I wonder if hitting a woman's skull with a bat could crack it open, thwack!"

Lorenzo shuddered.

"Armando, I want you to breathe deeply in sync with me for a few moments. Just allow yourself to relax . . . I am going to start at the number 100 and count slowly backward. Follow my voice coming through a tunnel . . . Here we go . . . 100. . . 99. . . 98. . . 97 . . . back. . . back. . . back. . . back in time to the place where you can see yourself with the baseball bat."

Armando's eyes closed. He felt like he was going to sleep, but suddenly he became hyper-alert. Rock was all around him, damp rock, creepy. He listened to Lorenzo's voice coming through a thick fog. "See your feet; what are you wearing? See your legs and torso; what do they look like? Look at your hands. *Tell* me what your hands look like."

Armando's eyelids fluttered as visions danced in his cornea. "This is very strange," he said in a sludgy voice. "This is very strange, I can't explain it."

"Just try!" Lorenzo encouraged in a soft voice. *He's gone somewhere.*

"Well, the backs of my hands are like snake skin, wormy, reptilian, scratchy snakeskin. I have claws with six fingers," he said in an awed voice.

Now Lorenzo was seeing what Armando was seeing. *I'm surprised Armando is so suggestible; I should've done this sooner.*

Armando's voice filled with wonder. "I am dying! I've come to the time when I am dying and my skin is horrible, dry, and cracked. I am dying because I've dried up and I'm ugly. Who am I? There are noises around me, other things around me that are like me. We are writhing together in a pit, writhing together because I squashed that spider. Oooh!"

"Armando, tell me about the creatures around you if you can. I would love to know all about them," Lorenzo said in a reassuring, curious, and seductive voice.

"They, we, WE are the fallen ones, the ones in the deep cave under the earth! Here we are in our prison; I am in the prison. Oh my God!" he said in a voice filled with amazement. "This is the part of me that exists simultaneously with Armando, like my double. I am a reptile, a snake, a being of great power. I am awesome, I am Armando Angelico Pierleoni."

Lorenzo looked around the room, detecting a potent, acrid stench in the room that seemed to be rising through the floorboards. *It's sulfur!* Nervously, he grabbed for a hematite crystal on the table and moved his awareness deep into the Earth, breathing in and out three times to balance his body. *I can always bring him out of it if I need to. What in God's name is this? What is he contacting?*

Armando's voice switched into its more familiar nasty, manipulative tone as he sneered at Lorenzo. "You're not so smart, doctor. You conjured me, Armando the Lizard, prince of the world. I can do anything to you if I want to; just wait."

"Now, Armando, let us not forget our agreements. You will not be doing anything here, only telling me what you see and feel. How does it *feel* to be a lizard? A reptile? Where is that part in your body?" At this point, Lorenzo was channeling questions because he was clearly seeing a vision of a huge cave filled with writhing monstrous reptiles, an underworld horror show. He remembered hearing an odd report twenty years earlier about Russian scientists doing deep drilling for oil five miles down. Out of curiosity they lowered a sensitive microphone down the hole and heard the sounds of voices screaming in agony. The scientists thought they were demons. *What if these are the souls of the reptiles that died in the cataclysm sixty-three million years ago?*

When Lorenzo asked him where the lizard was located in his body, Armando felt blood rushing loudly in his ears. "It, it's my blood, it is *in* my blood, my family blood. It is in all of us but we Pierleonis are born with more. My mother is so proud of our blue blood, but of course they are good aristocrats; I am an *evil* aristocrat."

"What is an evil aristocrat, Armando?"

Armando felt metallic power surging in his veins, the reptile in the deep cave. He barely heard what Lorenzo asked, but it registered somewhere in his brain. He replied vaguely, "I, I am there when I am here. When I have sex, my lizard grows. I was seven when I first felt him inside my body when I was playing baseball, and I was so proud of myself since I'd had my First Communion a few weeks before. When I whapped the ball, the lizard came into my body! He was licking me inside; it felt good. When I was twelve and saw a chambermaid's pubic hair when she leaned over the bed to pull the covers, again the lizard came into me! I swelled and got hard and pulled her into the stair closet and fucked her, my first fuck. She almost stopped breathing because the lizard was holding her mouth shut so she couldn't scream. My lizard does these things, the things that women don't like. I like to clutch their throats while I fuck them."

"Armando," Lorenzo said in a firm and commanding voice. "I want you to come back into the room with me when I count again. I want to talk to you about what we've discovered today."

In a few minutes, Armando was sitting across from Lorenzo in the dimly lit alcove again, feeling very odd.

Slouching over, Lorenzo was taking notes on a pad and considering things. *If he can integrate this and start to see it for what it is, he may be able to become aware of the pain he causes others. If he can't, I will warn the authorities about him.* He said, "Armando, now that you are fully here, what did you get in touch with today?"

"It can't be me, a *lizard*?" Armando said in an annoyed tone. "How could it be me? You think so because you regressed me into a lizard!" Even as he said that, he knew the lizard was a part of him, a part he knew very well. But talking about this with Lorenzo was too revealing. *I need help; I really need help.* "Even if that lizard is a part of me, then what will happen if I try to understand what it wants? What will happen to me? Will I turn into a snake or a reptile? *Am I a reptile?*"

"What do *you* think, Armando?" Lorenzo asked as he felt his skin crawl. *Better switch to mental right away.* "Maybe we all have a lizard inside? After all, we are descended from reptiles according to some evolutionary theories. Or maybe this is the serpent in the Bible that tempted Eve to bite the apple?"

As his mind grasped what Lorenzo was saying, Armando felt a rush of relief. Thinking about ideas always got him out of his snake body. "Lorenzo, have you heard of conspiracy theories that say the global elite are closet reptiles? People say during their secret rituals, they turn into reptiles to sacrifice and eat babies or have ritual sex. Since I come from an old elite family, maybe I was born that way? What do you think about that?"

"I think that is possible, even likely," Lorenzo said with a touch of amusement in his voice. "I don't mean possible that you eat babies, since I think you would have told me? But maybe the lizard is in your blood." In a commanding voice, he said, "Armando! You have been coming to see me for ten years, and I have been very patient. I have asked few things of you. I suggest you get to know this lizard because I think it is the part of you that hurts innocent women. Frankly, Armando, I've been appalled by what you do, horrified;

your cruelty is shocking. You must claim this part of yourself and change!"

"Everybody is appalled by me, especially women. But I've never cared, never cared a bit," he said as his voice slowed down becoming barely audible. Lorenzo leaned closer to him. "Doctor, I enjoy their pain; it makes me feel powerful. I am afraid I will kill one of them soon. I don't want to kill anybody," he said so softly Lorenzo could barely make out the words.

Armando felt a tiny sliver of hope come. "Do you think I *can* get to know that part of me? Can I learn to control it and not be ruled by it when I want sex? Lorenzo, now I will make the first honest statement of my life. I *hate* myself for what I do." He hunched over, hugging his lean torso and sobbing quietly. As the tears began to flow, his throat closed, and he felt as if hot liquid were flowing into his heart. He whispered, "I think I'm having a heart attack, Doctor. If I am, I deserve it."

"Breathe, Armando, breathe with me. I am your doctor. You are not having a heart attack; your heart is *opening*. You are forty-one, the time of mid-life crisis when many men have minor heart spasms during their heart opening. But, Armando, I am here with you and I know you will be fine if you let the energy flow. When we finish, I will order a complete array of tests just to be sure about your health. Do not worry. You are getting in touch with your feelings now, and I am very impressed with you. You *can* be a good man, Armando, and then you will be a good lover."

Simon sat at the kitchen table telling Sarah about his discoveries in Jerusalem and his experience in the Tomb of Mary, all the while marveling at the beauty of her face. She studied his eyes, looking for the sapphire blue flashes that revealed so much about what he was thinking. Instead of shyly turning away as he used to, he held her gaze and she shivered. "I see so much more in your eyes, Simon. Actually, I see profound spiritual beauty in your eyes."

"I am a different person, Sarah, a different person altogether. Something happened to me in the Tomb of Mary that awakened me. But it's hard to handle. When I went to the airport, everything was shining with extended light, and I was afraid the Israeli authorities would hassle me. They were about to give me a hard time because they could sense something about me, but when I told them I was going home to see my wife for Christmas, after running my passport again they let me through."

"Can you tell me anything more about feeling different?" Sarah asked. "I can feel it, but how would you describe it?"

He stroked her forearms while their foreheads touched. He found he could express himself if he looked down at the table. "I feel myself, you know, my solid body here in the room with you, as very small, much smaller than I have ever been, like a seed. Yet I am much bigger because I extend way out all around myself in a field that is shaped like an egg. When I was a young boy, my father taught me how to detect it, my extended cocoon, but I drew it back inside as soon as I went to school when I forgot about it. It is wavy and shimmery and has a greater intelligence than my mind has; it centers my heart. When I was walking through the airport, I could feel what everybody around me was thinking and feeling, and I was picking up accurate information. I can't wait to walk around the Vatican! 'Between the Sheets in Roma' is going to detect what is going on at the Holy See! Holy *See* indeed! But enough of me! You just saw Claudia this evening. How is she?"

Sarah smiled. "She's great. She shared some stories about her life that I'm not free to repeat. You'd have to hear it from her. But when she shared her truth, the glitzy, arrogant veneer stripped away. The woman within is a loving and brilliant goddess. I am so happy to have another friend in Rome."

"I sense what you mean," Simon said thoughtfully. "When I knew her and enjoyed her so much, sometimes the veneer cracked and I found the real Claudia. She is a proud, elegant, strong, and brilliant woman. I didn't want to drop our friendship when I found you, but I had to release the lover. I'd like to have her as my friend again now that you're fond of her. There is nothing greater in this world than friendship.

"My father is my friend, which seems like an odd thing to say. Because he knew I wouldn't always be his little boy, he befriended me by teaching me about the deeper aspects of life. He's the reason I was able to have that experience in the Tomb of Mary. He prepared me by initiating me. We can't be free in this sick world unless we are in touch with other dimensions. Now I realize my extended aura is multidimensional."

Sarah hung on to every word. She was joyful he was home, and she wanted to listen to him all night. She also felt there was something else, so she touched the ruby crystal while he told her more about Jerusalem. She said, "Something else prepared you for waking up; I feel there is something more. What is it?"

Simon followed her eyes to the ruby. "Maybe you know something, Sarah, since I see you touching the stone? Tell me if you know something. What do you know about my sense of being smaller yet extended? Anything? This is very disorienting and intense for me."

She replied, "Something is radically altered in your field, the field in this room, and the way I feel you. When you described the vibrating strings in the air above her tomb that extend out to cosmic zones, you woke up my cells. Something rearranged in my body." She dropped deeper into an altered state, with Simon holding her elbows to support her. "You made me feel less solid when you described yourself as a small seed and extended. I became filaments of dandelion seeds flying in the breeze. When I felt like that, I knew your seed would blossom soon within me, just like the filament carries the seed in the wind.

She swayed slightly, like the dandelion seeds in the breeze she had just described. "Right now the ruby crystal is downloading a file in my brain so complex and multidimensional that it will take me a lifetime to explore it. But there is one thing I must tell you: today was the end of the Calendar, and I am so happy you came home because something *did* happen today, something that will take many years to unravel. We are being lifted into a quantum realm; Claudia says it's the fourth dimension where everything functions in duality, non-locality, and by probable choice. Her definition is not the same as Einstein's, since she describes a series of higher dimensions above the fourth. I think this is detectable, like you being in Mary's tomb seeing the strings. When you told me about the icons of saints with golden auras, I could see the quantum fields in their halos."

She opened her eyes and continued. "We've had saints like Teresa of Avila, Hildegard of Bingen, and Jesus, who were in touch with these expanded fields. What's different now is many people won't be able to avoid seeing these multidimensional fields. Since most people are all locked up inside with unprocessed emotional trauma, this awakening will create massive waves of healing yet also chaos. More and more people expanding means we will see good and brave acts again, such as ending war and protecting children. If enough people expand, our world can heal. We will find peace when we open."

"Well," Simon said, laughing as he rose from the table, "If a cynical Jewish reporter can have a mystical experience in the Tomb of Mary, then anybody can. Let's go see what my new state of advanced consciousness creates in bed!"

Their lovemaking culminated in an ecstatic mutual orgasm that was so intense Sarah felt like she was passing out. Later as she drifted off to sleep, she felt something moving inside. She lay very quietly feeling new potent life, her egg in tension amid swimming sperms prodding it and pushing against its sheaf. Then one slipped inside. When Sarah awoke in the morning, she already knew she carried a new being in her womb, her secret for just a while.

33

Orvieto Cathedral

Armando swept down Lorenzo's tight spiral staircase and recoiled from the splattered blood and goo swarming with hungry little ants. *God, what a beast!* Emerging from the tower, he turned to his left to go out into the narrow alley and through an ancient round-topped iron-strapped gate to the garage where Lorenzo's clients parked. He climbed into his vintage Karmann Ghia, gunned the tightly wound engine, and backed out. He was ravenous as he snaked his way to the Lungotevere de Cenci to make his way out of Rome. Soon he was on the way north to Orvieto for an early supper.

Glancing up to his right as he drove along the Pozzo della Cava near Orvieto Cathedral, he noticed a placard that said the Cathedral would be open in the evening from now to Christmas. *Maybe I'll have the energy to go inside after dinner; now I need to think.* He left his car at the Hotel Palazzo Piccolomini and then walked over to I Sette Consoli, his favorite restaurant in Orvieto when he dined with Claudia. He sat down at the table they enjoyed when they were still lovers back in 2002 and asked for a Montepulciano bottled that same year. *Perhaps the taste of the grape will bring her back.* The wine was outstanding. Once he had ordered dinner, he fell into profound stillness. He remembered their final dinner here when she told him about the cathedral, that it was built on top of a volcanic plug that probably formed when this area of Umbria was a seismic hotbed 370,000 years ago when the nearby crater lake, Lago Bolsena, formed. They had both thought it was strange Urban IV built a cathedral on a magma plug to house the chapel for the "Corporal," an altar cloth said to be soaked in Christ's blood. *Why does the Church have to be so graphic?*

In 1263 a German priest on pilgrimage had offered Mass in a church in nearby Bolsena. The priest was in serious doubt about transubstantiation—the doctrine claiming that during Mass the wine is transformed into Christ's blood. When the priest raised the host and whispered the magical words in Latin, he felt blood dripping on his wrists from the chalice, so much blood that it stained the altar cloth! Alarmed, he stopped the Mass, something a priest must never do. Feeling confused he wrapped the altar cloth and took it to Pope Urban IV in Orvieto, who declared it a miracle and instituted The Feast of Corpus Christi: every year on that day the altar cloth in the reliquary was carried through Orvieto in procession and returned to the sacred chapel. The cathedral, which had been constructed in the thirteenth century, housed some of the finest works of medieval artists, such as Luca Signorelli and Fra Angelico.

When Armando made a pilgrimage to Orvieto, he always came here to view the magnificent frescoes, yet he had not returned since Claudia left him. He gazed out the window to a thick, rough stone ledge, wondering if he was going crazy while he shoveled pici all' Arrabiata into his mouth. *Never thought about it before: the name of this dish means "angry pasta." Maybe I like it because I'm angry all the time? Claudia insisted the chapel of the transubstantiation was built on a volcanic plug for some reason, yet I laughed at her. How could I? Considering what I found out with Lorenzo today, she knew a lot. She always knew things.*

His mind drifted back to that afternoon ten years ago when he had been in the Corporal Chapel staring at the exquisite gold and silver enameled reliquary wondering if Christ's blood was really inside. He had felt compelling energy coming from the reliquary that upset his stomach. Claudia had been very annoying that day and fomented a big crisis over the art. He thought she was losing it, so he told her in a loud voice to shut up, which upset the mumbling Christians gazing piously up at the reliquary. This made her so angry that she eventually broke with him. He could still see her proud ass from behind the very last time she went down his stairs; he felt panic in his heart. *Funny, here it is ten years later and I know I am supposed to be here tonight.* He finished his supper and thanked the waiter.

Armando climbed the magnificent stone stairs up to the golden façade and turned around to survey the wide piazza and the narrow streets below crammed with charming old houses divided into apartments and cafes. Everything was lit up to chase away the December gloom. It had been summer when he was here with Claudia ten years ago, when the flowerboxes on stairways and window ledges were filled with deep red geraniums and white daisies.

The cathedral in the Sienese Gothic style was like the Siena Cathedral by Giovanni Pisano, the great master who was discovered by Armando's ancestors. Lorenzo Maitani had added many Sienese features to Orvieto, maybe because they also patronized Maitani. *Claudia is right: the volcanic plug does make the cathedral feel like it's a mountaintop. Why would anybody go to all that trouble? It must have been almost impossible to build it! She said they did it because it collects deep earth forces that the Church broadcasts around the world. I laughed at her then; I wouldn't now. My father was privy to many arcane Catholic secrets. I wish he'd shared them with me, but he didn't want me to have more power. I wonder if my father thinks I am evil?*

He walked through the entrance into the dimly lit nave as things Claudia had said to him flooded back. *Do I still love her?* The alternating thick rows of alabaster and travertine on the high interior walls were like dramatic dark and light zebra stripes. The aisles on each side of the nave were sectioned off by round arches held up by thick round columns of alternating rows of travertine and basalt. He'd forgotten the beauty of the Gothic frescoes in the cavelike apse. Back then while he was admiring them, Claudia went on and on about the basic building materials. He got sick of her voice when she said the marble floors were resonating with the volcanic core. Like a witch she whispered in his ear that alabaster was the stone of the Egyptian goddess, Bast. If that wasn't enough, she insisted travertine resonated with sacred springs, since travertine formed when hot water mineral deposits harden the soil. She said these springs gushed with the fluids of the goddess hardened into crystal. Of course, then the basalt in the columns was cut out of the volcanic cone like columns in the Underworld! Right? All this was just *too* much. Right in the apse he had said in a loud and nasty voice, "No wonder my mother can't stand you! Don't you ever shut up? The only thing that shuts you up is a penis in your mouth!" Claudia was silenced while the pilgrims shuffled nervously away from her. *Why was I so mean to her?*

Be that as it may, the fight that ended their relationship had ignited over the art in the Chapel of the Madonna of San Brizio. Now he realized he had never understood what made her so mad; he knew his return to the chapel would be disturbing As he entered, he saw her angry face telling him she hated the way he hid from himself, the way he refused to see that this art expressed his spiritual journey. *What did she mean?* First he looked up to "Christ in Judgment" by Fra Angelico. *What was he thinking about when he was way up on the scaffold eight hundred years ago? He was a believer and I am not, yet I carry him in my blood. I wonder if he really believed in the themes he painted. Who did judge Christ? Was it Yahweh?*

He walked over to view the first painting in the Judgment Day series by Signorelli, the frescoes that always got Claudia's attention. "Deeds of the Antichrist" was very special because the lower left-hand corner had a very lifelike portrait of Fra Angelico standing with Luca Signorelli and viewing the scene with the Antichrist. When he was a little boy and his father brought him to see Fra Angelico and Signorelli, Armando was always captivated. He never looked much at the rest of the painting because seeing his ancestor standing with Signorelli was a thrill. *Maybe that's why I am a painter?* Fra Angelico was a grown-up version of himself, and by age thirty they were twins. *That's what made her mad: I wouldn't look at the rest of the painting even though she said it is about me. Well, what? The Antichrist looks like Christ while the devil whispers in his ear. I know all about that one!*

His gut hardened when he looked up at the sky above a crowd of contemporary historical figures—Raphael, Dante, Boccaccio, Christopher Columbus—all viewing the Antichrist. *I always looked at the famous people and never noticed they were staring at that yucky smoking black blob in the sky being chased out of the heavens by the Archangel Michael. Nearby, admirers of the Antichrist were dying in a rain of fire. Now I remember what she said to me: "Armando, Signorelli makes a point in this fresco: when devils whisper in your ear, evil forces are fighting a great battle with heaven for your soul." Her voice lowered to a raspy whisper to make sure nobody in the chapel could hear and she spit in my ear, "Now that I'm thirty, I realize the devil whispers in your ear when you use me sexually. The war in heaven rages and you transform into a Fallen Angel to ravage me. You will never touch me again."* She had strode haughtily away while he remained behind to admire the Pieta Ippolito Scalza, a disturbing painting of the grieving Madonna and the dying Christ. It was sad because Signorelli portrayed his son Antonio as the Christ, since Antonio died of the plague while Signorelli executed the painting.

I wonder if my father would care if I died?

His stomach was filling with acid and bile, and he wondered if he could go on. But he wanted answers. He went over to view "The Damned are taken to Hell and received by Demons," and this time he really looked at it. *My god, that is magnificent.* In an apocalypti-

Armando in tears in the Chapel of the Madonna of San Brizio

cal vision of entangled writhing bodies, Signorelli had evoked the agony of the damned. Decomposing demons staggering around with frayed wings picked at convoluted piles of naked bodies, a great collision of dimensional forces. *I am rotting inside and I'm only forty. My heart is made of stone; my cells weep while water flows through me as if I am the River Styx.*

Armando wasn't aware that he was standing in the middle of the chapel like a shrouded wraith with tears streaming down his gaunt cheeks and soaking his elegant linen shirt. People walked by him wondering, "Who is that wretch?" *I am one of them, the damned, and the whole rest of my life will be miserable. I can't go to Confession because the Antichrist lurks in the bowels of the Church like a tapeworm. I can't ravage women anymore to push hell out of my mind. How did I get this way?*

He walked over to "The End of the World." *Great thing to see on the day the world ends!* The painting was of cities being destroyed by great storms while people fled burning apocalyptic skies. The Sibyl sits on one side with her book of prophecies while King David raises his hand to predict the end of the world. *Funny, that's the Sibyl Claudia always talked about. Sarah too. I remember being disgusted with both of them and women in general. But now I am not sure. I must heed these warnings. What a terrible age I've grown up in, the age that abandoned belief. I studied these paintings when I was young to master Signorelli's fantastic technique, but I never thought about what he was trying to communicate. I need to be forgiven, but not by a priest. I need to be forgiven by the people I hurt. I need to remember how I became one of the damned.*

Later Armando climbed in between delicious linen sheets in an opulent suite in the Hotel Piccolomini, the same suite where he had spent his last night with Claudia before their final fight in the cathedral. They'd had too much red wine, and he pounded on her until she was nearly dead. Like a vampire he sucked the life out of her, not caring what she felt. Tonight before going to bed, he took a long luxurious bath in the white marble tub. Relief came with the warm water as the marble purified him, a cleansing baptism. He asked for one thing before he went to sleep. *Please give me a dream that will help me remember when I became one of the damned.* Drifting off, he felt very strange because he was getting younger. *I am getting smaller and smaller.*

Waves of white clouds in a pure blue sky passed through his mind as he felt his little hand clasped by the large hand of Father Cesare Vasari. "Now, come along with me, Armando. You are ready for your First Communion, so first you must confess to me. You cannot have Communion with Christ until first you tell me all of your sins." Deep green cedars passed by while dusty yellow soil crunched underfoot as they walked on the path through the woods to a tiny chapel. "This is our secret place, Armando, a special place where you can always come with me. Your mother loves this little chapel. But you must never tell her I brought you here because it is our secret. You will see what I mean."

"Forgive me, Father, for I have sinned," his little, high voice said expectantly. Armando was in a place in his mind that had closed long ago. A puppy floated by, the puppy he had crushed soon after he went to the chapel with Father Cesare. His mother Matilda's tear-filled blue eyes passed through the back of his mind. Back, back, as Lorenzo said . . . *My body is being stroked and massaged, I feel helpless.* "Now, Armando, this is our little secret, a secret you must never tell. Your time to *feel* Jesus has come; I am Jesus for your First Communion. When I become him, you will be in heaven." Father Cesare stroked him all over his small body. He felt jolts of hot energy when Father touched his little penis while rubbing his belly. "You've confessed, so you are pure and ready. You have told me you already touched it even though we told you not to. So you chose to have Jesus; you chose Jesus, Armando."

Darkness surrounded Armando with night sounds roaring in his ears—the wind, loud insects, and a barking dog. *I am a horse being ridden, a horse being pushed and pushed.* Around the chapel, the stars sparkled and a soft breeze came. He was in the starry heavens traveling to a planet. *Maybe I am going to the Moon?* Yet his body lay there in filth and pain, broken as if somebody had beaten him. A whisper came in his ear just when he thought he'd never get to go home, "Now you are ready for your First Communion next week. Do not tell your mother because this is our secret with Jesus. If you tell her, then it will be a sin and you will have to come for another Confession with me."

When Armando woke up the next morning, he didn't remember going to the chapel in his dream, but he sensed something. *I wonder if that priest my mother got rid of when I was small did something to me? Does my mother know something? Will she tell me?*

Armando searched his brain, struggling to remember something as he drove up the castle driveway. He'd phoned ahead to tell Matilda he needed to talk to her, so she was waiting for him in the breakfast room. The room was sunny and very private in the mornings when the staff took a break. He observed her from the hall while she sat drinking tea, staring out the window. Her blue eyes were as clear as the sky in his dream. Pietro had once told him that some people from Lucca have light blue eyes like hers because the invading Celts raped the women after the collapse of the Roman Empire.

She saw him and leaped up, the joy on her face replaced by concern as she took a closer look at him. "Armando, you look terrible! You'd think it was the end of the world, like all the silly fanatics have been screaming about!" She noted his rumpled clothes and haggard face. "What on earth is the matter? You look like you've just seen a ghost!"

"Well, maybe I have. Maybe I have seen my own ghost, the shroud Signorelli painted of me. We have been estranged for so long, Mother, as if I could not be your flesh and blood. As if I am a pariah. I had a chance to win you back when I was dating Sarah, but I could not keep it going." He paused to plead with her, "You are going to have to be honest with me because I'm trying to change myself. Can you believe that? I want to be different. Do not make too much fun of the end-of-time thing! I feel desperate. I will be condemned to be one of the damned if I don't find out what is wrong with me!"

Matilda's eyes filled with worry and fear. "What are you asking about, Armando? I want to tell you what you want to know, but I don't know what you are asking? Is it something in your past? When?"

She searched his agonized deep brown eyes. He looked like he was going to explode. Wondering what he'd done, she was almost afraid of him. It could be almost anything; that she knew. She had thought of meeting him in his studio for privacy. *Thank goodness I didn't go into his lair with him. God, what has he done?*

"Mother, something is wrong with me; I am really sick. Lorenzo almost terminated me because he can't stand me. I could get antipsychotic drugs, but I am afraid of them. I think they unleash demons in people, the forces I've spent my adult life trying to contain. The only thing that will help me is to get the truth." He lowered his eyes and demanded, "Did something happen to me around the time of my First Communion?"

Matilda slumped on the bench as air expelled from her lungs. *Oh, God, no. Do not ask me to remember this. I cannot stand the pain.* She raised an elbow to the table and looked off to the distant wintry fields, her eyebrows knit tightly together. Lines appeared above her upper lip and between her eyebrows; Armando thought she suddenly looked twenty years older. Her voice strained and breaking, she said, "Something did happen around that time. You were an absolutely cherubic little boy; everybody adored you. You used to sing all the time in the morning right in this room. Then you changed. It's hard to explain, but it was as if you had the evil eye."

She sighed deeply, her gaze still off in the fields. "People became afraid of you when you crushed the skull of your little butterscotch puppy with a rock. Pietro was very angry with you and hit you for the first time, but I had a bad feeling about that priest, Father Cesare. At your First Communion, I went out of my way to catch his eye, and he would not look at me. You have to understand that nobody in those days imagined priests harmed little children, but I put things together. One day I came into your room unexpectedly, and you were sitting on your bed crying. I tried to get you to talk to me but you wouldn't; I suppose you couldn't. One of the servant girls didn't like to be around you and I wondered about that. She told me I should watch you but she wouldn't tell me why, so I fired her. I don't know what it was, but I just sensed I could not trust Father Cesare. I asked the Archbishop to replace him and a new priest came. They sent Father Cesare to care for deaf children in a facility in Verona. You, you weren't a child any more; you acted like a knowing adult."

There was a hideous crawling feeling inside his intestines as if a lamprey eel had detached. He was feeling such dread and foreboding that he didn't know how to press Matilda. *But I have to know.* He said in a quiet and detached voice, "I think I wasn't a child anymore; I think that priest took my innocence from me. All I know is that once the world was white, and then it turned black. I felt like something awful was caged inside me, something he, he put inside me. But I was too small to comprehend it. Mother, I think that priest abused me. I think that priest raped me when I was only seven!"

"Oh my God, Armando. How could such a thing be?" she said in a barely audible, horrified voice. "How could such a terrible thing happen? How could a man do that to a little boy? I can't imagine that. I cannot understand that, but I know something happened to you. You trusted him; we trusted him." She paused, then continued, her voice now pleading. "Maybe it wasn't that bad? Maybe he did things to you that made you feel guilty, but he didn't do *that?*"

Armando met her eyes. "No, Mother, I think he raped me. I dimly remember terrible pain and I remember hiding in my room feeling sick. I can't remember it happening, but I was not myself after that. I had a foulness inside that made me want to crawl out of my own body! So I started hurting everybody. First I was just mean and bad-tempered, couldn't sleep at night, and it felt good to hurt others. My puppy annoyed me by licking me and wagging his tail, so I crushed him. I raped one of the young maids when I was twelve. I didn't care about the sex, but I enjoyed hurting her. I know this is horrible for you, Mother, but you have to hear it. Since that priest abused me, I have felt like I had to hurt women to escape my damnation. I like it when they are weak and helpless. Thank god I didn't kill anybody." Each confession seemed to hit his mother like a blow, but Armando had to keep going. His words now came out in a rush. "When I was eighteen I almost strangled Magdalena Pisano in the ravine below the lower vineyard after I tied her up and raped her. I will stab myself in my heart with a cross unless I can change. I can't go to a priest for Confession because I am afraid of all of them. The people I have hurt must forgive me. You are the first one, Mother. I have not made you happy, and I am sorry, deeply sorry."

Matilda tried to keep her composure as tears welled up. Her throat burned, her muscles ached, and her heart was expanding as if it would break. The numbness that had been her constant companion was leaving her, and it hurt. She had never thought she could ever feel anything for Armando, her only son, again. He'd hurt her so much by becoming a monster that a huge part of her happiness had just shut down. She squeaked out, "Oh, Armando, I don't know if I can take this. It's so overwhelming. I'm so sad this happened to you and to hear what you have done."

Armando sat with his mother for a long time with his arm around her thin shoulders while he quieted his body. Then he breathed with her as if they were again one body. A deep emotion emerged in his heart that he could not identify. As he stayed with her and allowed himself to feel her pain, his true masculinity came forth, his essence that had stopped growing when he was seven years old. *I am a man; I never knew it. She is my mother, the woman I lost. I love her and I regret all the time we will never get back.* "Mother, this is going to take time, I know it is going to take me a lot of time. I had to know; I have to face it. Suddenly yesterday I felt evil being unchained in the heavens. I can liberate myself by asking forgiveness from the ones I have harmed, all of them! Claudia will be the first because she is the one I have harmed the most."

"Oh, Armando, I know you always thought I didn't like her. But I did like her! I was afraid of what you were doing to her. You were so sophisticated at a young age that I hated to think about what you did to her behind closed doors. I was afraid for her and I was afraid for Sarah since you were so much older; I was very worried when she was alone with you. I never could get to know Claudia and now I've lost my friendship with Sarah, which makes me so unhappy."

Armando felt shame flood him again at the thought of how he

had hurt Claudia again and again, and how he had tried to hurt Sarah. "You were right to be afraid of what was going on behind closed doors. But that is over and it is never going to happen again. I actually think I can redeem myself! Forget about Confession and the so-called sacraments! I have to redeem myself! Nobody else is going to, not even Jesus."

Matilda shared the story with Pietro before dinner and when the three of them gathered in the library, Pietro was a different father. He put his arm around Armando and said, "My son, you never have to share any of this with me unless you want to. Your mother has told me about your conversation. I think that priest harmed you, but there is no going back on the past. Of course, I will report him immediately and demand an investigation if he's alive. All I care about is I love you. Your sharing with your mother has made her happy again because for her, you had died. If you ever have children, you will be amazed by how long you will wait until your child opens his or her heart to you. Welcome home, Armando."

34

Two Fathers

On December 21, 2012, for David and Rose "ordinary life" was gone. She retired early after a simple supper to go upstairs with *The Eustace Diamonds* by Anthony Trollope, hoping English high society trivia might help her forget about the children who died in Newtown.

The winds diminished enough for David to set a fire in his study. Sometimes the old chimney down-drafted, so he nursed the flames until they were burning brightly. He read an archaeology book for a few hours and then tiptoed upstairs to make sure Rose was asleep. It was almost midnight and her light was out, so he went back down to his study, shut the door, and contemplated the crackling fire. *It would be astonishing if the Maya actually knew the European invaders would begin their decline now. But then again, the Maya were the sacred high culture of this continent; maybe they did know.* The night deepened around him, and once he was sure the world wasn't going to end, he retrieved the crystal skull of Dzibichaltun. The mysterious skull intrigued him in a new way because the book he'd just read suggested the ancient Maya used crystal skulls for divination. *Maybe that's how they discovered the end time? Is this one of the skulls that can predict the future?*

He held the skull in his left hand, warming it with his body heat. He wished he still had the whale's ear. *Maybe the whale's ear could hear this skull speak?* He closed his eyes and felt a fluttering sensation in the lower cup of his ear canal. *I'll be damned. I do feel a vibration there.*

He knew what to do because he was adept at detecting the subtle energy of electromagnetic fields. He rubbed the skull's cerebellum with his fingers. The buzzing in his ears joined with a watery sensation in his temporal bones, and he felt the back of his skull expand relative to the size of the skull's large cerebellum. *With such a huge cerebellum, this skull must be Neanderthal. But how in hell would the Maya know anything about the Neanderthals?* Being of pure Near-Eastern Jewish lineage, David knew he carried many Neanderthal genes based on recent DNA studies. From just a light touch on the skull, his cerebellum filled with energy. *I wonder what Neanderthals were really like; maybe they were psychic?*

His sphenoid bone, the bird-shaped delicate bone over his eyebrows that balanced his body when he walked, clicked. He surrendered, knowing the click meant he could travel out of his body. *I am flying! I am flying way above the world over the jungle treetops to the land of the Maya. I see a very small pyramid glowing in a clearing, must be the Pyramid of Dzibichaltun. I fly home with the skull to deliver the records of time!*

David was sitting quietly by the firelight, deeply immersed in the most profound state of consciousness of his entire life. Outside the quarter moon in Aries rose in the night sky leaving a pathway of light on the surface of the calming sea. He cupped the skull's cerebellum to draw life out of it; his sphenoid bone began vibrating faster. He pressed the front face of the skull onto his thymus gland, and his chest and neck bones rattled slightly. The crystal skull spoke: *I am the Time Hologram, a superwave from the center of the galaxy. I travel through cosmic space to penetrate your solar system. The extinction of Neanderthal, the psychic human, holds you back. Their imprint is in everything, and you are lost unless you awaken their spirit.* **Remember us!** *The war in heaven of the past five thousand years ended tonight, and Neanderthal codes are* *to open again. Soon you will see people in power acting very differently; they will make new choices without knowing why. Many leaders will flounder. The ancient ones dream with you again. So open the doorway of your cerebellum, the world of archaic memory, your planet's ancient dream. You have brought me back to my temple so that I can awaken you. I am holographic. I can exist anywhere, anytime, to communicate with you; I am the essence of your thoughts. I am reborn in reality when you consider me. I have returned at the Calendar's end.*

While in the pyramid, David was simultaneously aware of himself in his study. Grounded by the magical night with his senses on high alert, this was a culminating moment. The idea popped into his mind that he could travel to the Pleiades from this pyramid. *Why the Pleiades? Why do I always find myself in that star cluster when I seek the time library? Maybe I can see them if I go to the window.* He went over to the moonlight-bathed window and could see the beautiful little jewel-like cluster shining way high above the moon. The bright twinkling beacon in the center was Alcyone, the central star. Still holding the skull in his left hand, he stood staring at Alcyone as his vision blurred and swirled into a cone.

Ah, excellent, David. Now you have the direct line. My crystalline matrix reduces to a line through Alcyone, which briefly draws me out of my spherical holographic presence in the universe, the ninth dimension. My dimensional reduction will enable you to see what I see. Now, what would you like to know?

As he continued holding the crystal skull, David's cerebellum was like an electrical circuit struck by lightning. Undaunted, he asked the skull, "You have a very large cerebellum, as if you are a Neanderthal. Is that important? Are you?"

David, notice your cerebellum connects with the whole universe, not just to your planet. But your culture denigrates universal wisdom. Now that we have made this connection, Neanderthal intelligence is going to reawaken in all human brains. This breakthrough will be intense and subliminal. People will start acting as if they are following a distant beacon. Watch current events carefully, and you will see this is true. When you see evil actions stifled and stomped on, evil men removed from power left and right, it will be quite a show!

David traveled around in his own cerebellum while the skull answered him. He saw incredible apocalyptical scenes—people drowning in rushing water; fire burning homes, forests, and cities; refugees moving along roads beyond the horizon; and everywhere frightened animals trying to escape. Once again, he asked the skull. "This is all well and good, but what I see in my cerebellum is terrible scenes of the maelstrom, the whirlwind, the complete unraveling of reality—Earth's nightmare. I can't see how that's going to do anybody any good. Why do I see this?"

This is where it gets complicated, because everything that you experience functions as particles and waves in the fourth dimension, the quantum world. So as you observe your reality from your perspective in third-dimensional space and time, when I add my greater view from the fifth dimension, my holographic sight lifts you out of your dimension. I pull you through particle-wave duality, the location of the nightmare you see. You are in particle land amid the disasters yet when you expand to traverse higher in the waves, you see good things happening. Let me put it this way to you: if you were caught in a flood, fire, or a mass murder, wouldn't you like to know a great elemental cleansing is going on that is dissipating evil? Answer me truthfully, David.

David thought carefully before answering. "I suppose having a higher perspective while in a world going to hell would make it easier to get along."

My last advice to you is to not miss the magic in your world at every turn. I will not abandon you while I move to the tenth dimension to become a rhapsodic sphere. By trusting your inner mind, you have given me this choice. When others on Earth trust their inner minds, I will link them to Alcyone. Whenever you see good things happening that you thought were impossible based on the previous events of your life, celebrate these breakthroughs! When you consciously acknowledge these new miracles, they pop into waves. You must herald each shift that penetrates the human heart because they come from very high worlds. Your world is transmuting to beauty and hope, love and compassion.

David felt a sudden withdrawal of energy from the skull, and he was left alone, feeling very tired. He wondered if the horrible scenes in his mind had caused his exhaustion. He walked over to the little cabinet in the corner, opened it, and put the skull back inside. *I wonder if the skull exists in the fifth dimension yet physically in my cabinet?* He closed the door and locked it, knowing he'd never see the skull again. He went over to the fire to spread the last of the coals and put the metal screen firmly in front of the fireplace. As he slowly climbed the stairs in the cooling house, the moon was setting below the horizon; a warm body awaited him in bed.

On the same night, William sat at his desk in his library drinking twelve-year-old Scotch while contemplating the apocalypse, which for him would be the fall of the Church. Wind and rain pummeled the old glass in his window seat. *What in hell is wrong with Benedict, or I should say Ratzinger? Why is he so stubborn while everything falls apart? "Between the Sheets in Roma" indeed! How could the pope invite my damned Jewish son-in-law to write gossipy trash about him? Does Sarah think this crap is funny?*

Simon's column had been translated into English and picked up by some online religious news services, and William's Opus Dei adviser, Mike O'Malley, had called him to rant about it. William didn't know what to say when O'Malley suggested he'd better get Simon to tone it down. He mumbled something about the tension these days in Rome and the Church after acquiescing that some people do go too far. Reading the column had thrown William into his spinning mental cage, which always caused a sleepless night. *I fear the wholesale abandonment of the Church by Catholics. My daughter did it, and even I think about leaving. The rumor is the Third Fatima Prophecy says the Church will fall, fall like a house of cards. Maybe Ratzinger is a mess and Cardinal Bertone went nuts because they know the game is up? What will happen to the world if the faith is gone?*

He poured another heavy slug of Scotch, thinking about the richness of the faith when he was young. *If only they'd just give us* an occasional benediction with chanting, the censer swaying back and forth, wafting the church with delicious aromas. Why did the Church let it all go—Latin mass, serious Confession, and pious priests and bishops? Why? Ratzinger tried to bring back the old ways and look what a mess everything is now. He tried living in a cave while the modern world rolled along; I did too. Come on, William, 'fess up, he said to himself. You know what they did to you, did to a lot of kids. Get your head out of the sand!

And what in hell is all this end-of-the world shit? he thought while staring at a "Doonesbury" cartoon strip that made fun of the Mayan Calendar. *Yeah, Trudeau is making a joke but why pay any attention at all? Here I sit here in my old and decrepit library filled with boring theological books. What could be worse than reading Aquinas, Chenu, and Lonergan? Maybe my world is ending? What the hell!* He slugged down a big gulp of Scotch, almost choking. *What if people stop growing and changing? Ratzinger has stayed completely the same, and look what a disaster that's been. What was the butler squealing about, anyway?*

William leaned forward in his seat and slammed down his Scotch glass rather loudly for three in the morning. He said in a loud voice, "No more Mayan Calendar!" and then sat there staring out into space. *Damn, maybe smart-assed Simon is on to something. Maybe the only way out at this juncture is to laugh! I mean, really, it is funny! Garry Trudeau, another sassy smartass, is right! It is a joke! The damned pope dresses up like a pole dancer in a gay bar while his butler vomits insider politics in the curia. Why does the pope have a pretty boy who ties his shoes after spoon-feeding him the daily news? Even I was embarrassed when* Vanity Fair *satirized Georg Gänswein calling him "Gorgeous Georg." Maybe there is something going on between the sheets? But Simon forgets that popes are infallible. What if this pope isn't infallible? What if the pope is just as much of an asshole as I am?*

He was about to get all bummed out, but there was still some holy Scotch in the decanter. So he poured it out and took out Simon's article again. *So Innocent X was tired of Olimpia and he incarcerated her. Simon hints that this is what happened to the leaky butler. Simon also hints at a gay underworld, which for me is an issue because gay priests have to hide, which makes them more prone to blackmail. Huh! What if the pope is getting blackmailed because he's gay? Well, if that's true then he might've covered up for all the abusers!* His thoughts were beginning to blur from all the Scotch. *Rule number one: we're in it together and nobody gets caught no matter what they do, same thing as any Boston contractor. That's the attitude that got me gored.*

"You know what," he said aloud as he raised his glass up to Jesus on the cross. "You know what, Jesus? You gotta come down before it's too late. As long as they keep you up there, none of *them* get crucified, but they're the ones that oughtta get nailed up, not me, not Jesus!" William stumbled up the stairs and fell onto bed in the guest bedroom, his favorite place to sleep when he stayed up too late.

PART THREE

The End of
the Mayan Calendar

35

The Pope Resigns!

For Simon and Sarah, January 2013 in Rome shot by like a grouse flushed out of its nest, never to return. February was nearly half gone when Sarah curled up by the fire one night, reflecting. Simon was out on Vatican watch; he sensed something big was brewing. The 2012 Christmas season had been like a game of musical chairs when the music stops: who would be the one who can't get a seat? *I wonder whether the obsession with the end of the Mayan Calendar has made us all crazy, especially me?* Sarah wondered. She'd come down with a nasty flu right after Christmas, suffering horrific backaches and a fever. *Maybe being sick is what made everything seem so peculiar?* She tried to recall that strange visit from Claudia, who had come to bring soup and good cheer just after Christmas while Sarah had lain aching and feverish in bed. She tried to listen to Simon and Claudia talking in the kitchen, but she couldn't register what they were saying. Later Simon had told her Claudia believed Armando had changed in some way, that Claudia thought he was getting honest with himself. Of course Simon had also said, "So what? As far as I'm concerned, he can sling his Italian ass up a tree."

Outside, the winter light was translucent and silvery as she thought about Armando. *I can imagine him changing, but I wonder what ever got him to do it?* Sarah wanted to know how evil got into the world, and knowing him was the closest she'd ever come to an encounter with a demon. She wondered if she'd even gotten the flu from listening to Claudia's ugly story. Regardless of what Simon thought, she wanted to know if Armando had really changed. She wasn't sure if a person could change that drastically so quickly. Yet at the same time she felt everything was in limbo and on the verge of great change.

Simon had been extremely excited during the last few weeks. It looked as if some truth might be breaking through, since accusations by victims of priestly abuse were creating a tidal wave of expensive lawsuits. Wild rumors about the Vatican flooded the Roman media. The pope's butler, Paolo Gabriele, had finally been tried for "Vatileaks," for leaking information to Gianluigi Nizzi for his book *Your Holiness: The Secret Papers of XVI.* The Tribunal convicted him, since he admitted he leaked information to Nuzzi. His lawyer said the butler had done it because he wanted to help the pope "root out evil in the heart of the Church," which fanned the flames even higher. The Vatican hoped a swift trial would quell the ferocious media pressure, but instead it whipped up a bigger frenzy with everybody wanting to know what was going on behind closed doors. *Something has definitely shifted,* Sarah thought. *Even though Georg Ganswein is always with the pope, Gabriele and Nuzzi got some truth out; now everybody wants more, more. The pressure on Benedict must be incredible!*

The unfolding of this historic crisis in Rome made Sarah's work on her thesis about Marcion feel urgent. People were now refusing to tolerate corruption and evil in the hierarchy. It was one thing for a politician like Silvio Berlusconi to rob the public and be sexually profligate and get caught, but such behavior was unforgivable in the clergy. Sitting down with Simon for dinner after a long day of writing, Sarah said, "I think something is going to break that will change everything; I can feel it in the air."

"Yeah, me too," Simon responded. "This city is about to explode!

The pope's mask has been torn away. His ridiculous liturgical pomposity draws too much attention. People wonder whether a paranoid, self-obsessed demon is leading the flock. Did you know this pope is totally obsessed with his liturgical apparel? He is a fop pruned to perfection every day by pretty boy Monsignor Ganswein, who pours wine in his glass to please him. You know, Sarah, his demonic shadow taunts the public!" His bizarre self-deification is going to crash the hierarchy; the rumor is nobody knows how to stop him! They are stuck with the tradition—he must continue until he dies."

Simon's comment was prophetic. He left right after breakfast the next morning, February 11, to go to the Vatican courtroom at Santa Marta Square in the center of the Vatican to write a good description of its paneled rooms. That was his excuse, but actually something drew him irresistibly to the Vatican. As he sat in the courtroom tapping away on his laptop, he noticed some extra commotion in the hallway. He rushed to the door and saw a group of cardinals moving in a tight huddle. He could tell right away that something was very wrong. The men's faces were pale, their lips compressed. No one spoke at all. *Did the pope die?*

As the morning passed, he noticed increased activity around him, guards and messengers rushing around with nervous eyes. He laid low, afraid someone would kick him out, not even leaving for lunch in the fear that he wouldn't be let back in. Finally, late that afternoon, he saw one messenger he knew hurrying past, a young priest named Giancarlo who'd often served as an anonymous source in the past. Simon caught Giancarlo's eye and motioned him to a secluded corner.

Giancarlo looked around to make sure no one was watching and followed him.

"What's going on?" Simon asked in Italian. "I can tell something has happened."

Despite his olive skin, Giancarlo looked pale and thoroughly shaken. "I do not know for sure, Simon," he murmured in heavily accented English. "And it is nothing I can talk about. It is bad, very bad."

Simon had to know now.

"Not for a story, then. Just for me," he pleaded. "I won't write about it yet. Just tell me. You know you can trust me."

Giancarlo hesitated, but the truth was he wanted to tell someone the shocking news. "I do not know for sure, but I heard that in the morning meeting with the cardinals, the pope announced that he was going to resign."

Simon's mouth dropped open. Whatever he'd expected, that wasn't it. He wasn't aware of any pope ever resigning. You were pope until the day you died.

"Because of the scandals?" he asked.

"No, for health. His heart is not so good," said Giancarlo. He cast another look around. "I have to go, Simon. Remember your promise!"

Simon walked out of the building in a fog. *What in the world?* As he was walking across St. Peter's Square trying to process this information, people started shouting and pointing their fingers and cameras. He looked back at the Basilica's dome, and right at that moment a huge bolt of lightning came down from high and struck it. *My god, what is going on?*

Simon hurried home and told Sarah what he had just found out. She shared his shock and they speculated on the reasons for Benedict's decision. He kept his promise to Giancarlo not to write about it beforehand, but he was at the paper first thing in the morning as soon as the official statement came out with a draft he'd written the night before. The official story in *L'Osservatore Romano* was that Benedict was stepping down on February 28 due to poor health. Simon didn't buy the health excuse for a second. He'd been following rumors that European powers had been considering taking criminal action against the pope for crimes against humanity and criminal conspiracy. He hadn't taken it seriously before, but just last week he'd heard Cardinal Tarcisio Bertone was informed about a coming arrest warrant, and even that the pope had gotten a warrant and ignored it. Suddenly these stories had a lot more credibility.

Simon had researched it the night before: Benedict was only the second pope to resign in two thousand years, the last one being Pope Celestine V eight hundred years ago. Celestine had been an odd duck, a hermit who was in office for only five months. Benedict's sudden resignation was much more significant, since he was the grand inquisitor for so many years before he became pope. He was a very powerful and sinister figure.

"I wonder what my father will think about this?" Sarah broke in as she combed through the paper. Even more interesting to Simon was that Benedict planned to return to the Vatican after a new pope was elected to live in a refurbished nunnery at the end of the Vatican gardens. That meant two popes would be in the Vatican at the same time. How could two popes both be infallible? Simon announced, "This will end up being the death of papal infallibility and the descent of power through the Petrine line no matter what kind of spin the Vatican puts on it. Would Ratzinger hang around to protect some kind of power thread that must be kept secret? Or if it was true that he was subpoenaed by a global legal entity, perhaps nobody could touch him as long as he stayed in the Vatican? Simon suspected that Benedict would go right back to his old role of being the bad guy in seclusion while the good guy—the next pope—played Mr. Nice Guy to mind-control the faithful. A new pope polished up like Eve's apple, yet it would be the same old game. He predicted next the cardinals would choose a friendly cover-up pope who will give the people permission to keep sucking on the mother tit, but with the same old rot going on in the rectory.

Since he'd had all night to think about it, Simon filed his story in record time and headed home to Sarah. He found her paging through the official story in *L'Osservatore Romano* and joined her at the little table.

"I still can't believe this!" she said. "Two popes?"

"I know," he said. "I still can't get the image of the lightning bolt striking the Basilica out of my head. You know, when you had the flu, Claudia and I talked for hours. She mostly wanted to tell how she believes Armando has changed. I couldn't care less about that; however, she brought up a subject with me for the second time that I shot down last year—the idea of a midline going through Rome that the Vatican uses to control the world. Now I'm reconsidering what she told me. I tell you, Sarah, that lightning bolt was the kind of huge bolt that strikes ungrounded power stations. Also, there must have been another bolt that preceded the one I saw because the crowd in the piazza was pointing at the dome just before I turned to look. There must be some kind of fantastic power under the Vatican that discharged that day. Otherwise, I don't see how a thick bolt like that could occur. Claudia explained again the recent scientific discoveries about her midline theory, about the midline creating some kind of telluric force, possibly plasma discharges from discontinuities between the spin of the Earth's core and the middle tectonic region."

Sarah got up to pour Simon a cup of coffee as he continued. "I have been watching the Church for many years and as we've talked about, I think they generate evil energy. The clerics who get possessed by it aren't even aware of what they're doing because this force is just below the threshold of their conscious minds, like a weird atavistic shadow. Now I'm more open to Claudia's idea that human sexual energy charges deep earth forces that also link us to higher dimensions. What else explains an institution located in Rome that drives incessant global rituals and the systemic culling of sexual energy?"

Sarah put the cup in front of Simon and sat back down. "Claudia and I have discussed this midline idea, and it always rang true for me although I don't understand it scientifically. In my own research I seek that boundary where evil penetrates the world and grabs people, the forces that obsessed the Gnostics. I think the greatest thing any one of us could do is to help redeem a person like Armando or abuser priests. If Armando has actually changed, he may know more about that boundary than any of us do. I bet he knows *why* he crossed that edge and how he found his way back. I think reaching out to a person who needs to draw away from evil is more important than my thesis or any article you could write."

Simon shook his head. "I don't want to talk about Armando after what he did to you. I'm not ready to hear about him; I probably will never be able to deal with him. But what I strongly disagree with is your statement that the redemption of one person is more important that the collective corruption you and I are exposing. Redemption can't happen unless people understand *why* they do evil things."

Sarah started to break in, but Simon held up his hand.

"Let me finish," he said, his voice annoyed. "Nobody can change anything—themselves or corrupt institutions—without mentally comprehending *why* they are the way they are. Screw Armando; I think you don't realize how important your own thesis is! You have found a central wrong turn nineteen hundred years ago when the great redeemer—Jesus Christ—was derailed. Marcion was right, and nothing is going to make sense until people understand how and why they lost the great teacher they awaited for thousands of years. You were right, Sarah," he said, gazing at her proudly.

"Yahweh triumphed," Simon continued. "And now he's seated on the Bernini throne in the Vatican. It is all about layers: Jewish wisdom and social justice were corrupted and defiled by the Christian overlay; the pure love teaching of Jesus was adulterated by attaching him to the old god; and Islam fractured into opposing sides because it was influenced by Judeo-Christian dualism. Each religion has beautiful wisdom and truth. But they haven't been able to share their

knowledge non-violently because their essential elements are polluted by alien ideas. That's why your work matters so much! These
days mystic Jews offer their wisdom by reviving the Kabbalah, Sufis
invoke pure light, so now Christianity must reclaim Christ's love
and compassion. The world's people can't stand the inner tension,
emotional pain, mental confusion, and spiritual angst in the major
religions; they will abandon faith unless it liberates them.

"Claudia says she thinks the midline influence may have changed
in some way on December 21. After seeing that lightning bolt, I
wonder if she is right. She thinks the Maya knew this would happen. When a pope resigns and plans to reside under the wing of the
next one, Catholic global control is over, just plain over. Nothing is
going to be the same ever again." He took a deep breath. "Okay, I'm
finished."

Sarah took his hand. "I'm not, Simon. Everything has changed
for us! We're going to have a child, the next generation to come
and enjoy Earth's beauty. This child will grow up in a world that's
throwing off the control of evil forces. Our child will begin in freedom and be a liberator. Your trust in my work enables me to go on,
and soon we will be three seeking transcendence and joy!"

Simon's mouth dropped open, and as awareness dawned, pure
joy transformed his features. "You're pregnant, Sarah? Why didn't
you tell me?"

"I got the doctor's confirmation yesterday when you were at the
Vatican, and I've been waiting for just the right moment to tell you.
I knew I was the moment I conceived, and I just wanted to nest
with it until I saw the doctor." Tears of joy dampened her eyes. "And
thank you for your belief in my work," she said softly. "I'm going to
need it."

36

Claudia and Armando

Claudia and Armando walked briskly past the obelisk in the Piazza del Popolo and aimed for the Via del Corso. Noting a directional sign to Florence, she said breathlessly, "Maybe someday we will go back to Florence. Do you remember what a weird time we had the last time we were there?" Without waiting for a response, she switched subjects in midstream. "You say you have some painful things to talk about?" She looked at him expectantly, her camel hair cape flapping in the biting February wind off the Tiber.

Armando tightened his scarf and tucked the ends into his flannel-lined trench coat. "Can we go to your apartment to talk?" he asked.

They got a cab, and soon she opened the door of her apartment. "I can't believe you are here with me. I never thought that would ever happen again." She turned in the foyer and stared into his eyes. Her expression was haughty and commanding; Armando's was nervous and evasive. Regardless, he was determined. He looked around the hallway opening into the main rooms. "Claudia, this is beautiful! You have really transformed this lovely old flat. It's so warm and welcoming, something I appreciate now." Armando and Claudia had been in touch over the phone, but Armando hadn't been in her apartment for ten years. "My mother would love what you have done. But please, pick a comfortable corner for us, hopefully with a fire, and let's sit down together. I have to get this over with."

She took him into her small library filled with floor-to-ceiling bookcases and grabbed the remote to light the gas fireplace set in a French eighteenth-century white marble mantle. Wall space not covered by bookcases was papered in rich burgundy with lacy golden vines that glowed in the firelight. They sat down on two elegant tapestry chairs by a low oak table littered with magazines and small objects. "Huh," he said, "these objects on the table remind me of Lorenzo's collection. Will you be my shrink tonight?"

"I don't think so, Armando," she said, lighting a cigarette and inhaling deeply. "I'm amazed to hear you still go to him after so long. What's it been, more than ten years?" She relaxed back in her chair, wishing she could pour some brandy, but she sensed they should have nothing until he was finished.

"Yes, over ten years. He's patient and it paid off," he said, looking her over intently. *She is still as beautiful as when I first met her. How does she do it?* Claudia was observing Armando just as closely because he seemed to be a different person. His nervous intensity always focused on "getting something" was gone, and he seemed tired. *I wonder what motivates him these days?*

"Are you still painting, Armando? I hope so because you are very good."

He relaxed as the fire warmed his face and hands. He took note of Claudia's tension, control, and guardedness. She looked as if she were ready to pounce. He flashed back momentarily to his first date with her, and he felt a painful stab. He hadn't thought of that night until now, and he dreaded what he had to say. "Yes, I am painting, seems to be the only thing I've ever done well, and, for the past two months I've been painting seven days a week, intense mythological dramas of the dark and light. Lorenzo is thrilled with my work now. He always thought there was more in me than Tuscan landscapes, and the only break I take is for quick meals or to eat with my mother.

Claudia's face tightened at the mention of his mother; Armando noticed. "Claudia, may I begin by saying that Matilda sends you her heartfelt regards? When I shared some unpleasant things about myself, she told me she always liked you and was impressed by you. But she was afraid of what I would do to you." He stopped to look at her face. It was so tight it looked like it was about to crack; however, the only movement in its marblelike surface was a fluttering right upper lip.

It's amazing how his beautiful face captivated me when I was young, Claudia thought while drawing on her cigarette and gazing evasively into the fire. She said ruefully, "Matilda had every reason to fear what you would do to me." She noted his lost and confused eyes. *That's the expression of a four-year-old; never saw that years ago.* "Anyway," she said rather matter-of-factly, "what do you have to say to me? You wouldn't be here unless it's important." She stared at him, noticing that his fine upper lip, still perfect and sensual as ever, was trembling. *How could I have been so addicted to him?*

"I begin by apologizing for every hurtful thing I ever did to you," he said, clasping and twisting his long perfect fingers. "It does not seem like enough and my apologies will not mean much to you unless you hear *why* I acted the way I did when I knew you. But I must begin with a sincere apology before going deeply into things so that you will not think I am just making excuses for my actions. Will you accept my apology provisionally? If you will, I can share my ugly story."

Claudia waited a long moment, then nodded coolly. "All right, Armando, I accept your apologies as long as you realize I feel nothing for you, nothing, but it would be good to understand why you treated me the way you did. Then, perhaps, I could feel something again and accept you. I don't hate you; however, I feel such contempt for you that I feel nothing." Her solar plexus ached from the deep wound in her heart, but her mind dominated her heart. She had him completely shut out.

Her arched coldness was oppressive and made him feel small; this made him angry. He felt twinges in his shoulders where his skin was tender. *Oh my god, I didn't think about that. My lizard might come back!* He looked over at her again and felt a rush as his eyes slithered over her exquisite long legs. She looked over at him, cold-eyed, like last night's unwarmed coals. She barely heard him whisper, *No you don't, slimy one, be gone!*

"What? Armando, what did you say?" She glared across at him, thinking about her small loaded pistol in the drawer, the reason she'd brought him into this particular room.

"Claudia, please, just listen as best you can," he requested in a measured and sincere voice. When she nodded in assent, he began. "I did see Lorenzo twice a week for ten years, and then in December he threatened to terminate me because we were getting nowhere. Yet he said he wanted to try one more thing—to regress me. Do you know what that is?" She said yes and he continued. "I won't go into the details because they are not what's important. We had a very long and intense session because I stopped resisting under hypnosis. I wish he'd regressed me years ago, but he says I might have been overwhelmed by my shadow. Maybe I wasn't ready before; perhaps knowing Sarah shifted me. Anyway, I got in touch with the repressed shadow stuff that made me unable to feel the pain of others, especially yours. During those ten years in analysis, *you* were the person I talked about because you were the only woman I loved. But that isn't the point of tonight.

"I got in touch with a vile, manipulative, and cruel part of myself, an evil reptilian being, the demon that took me over and gave me potency when I wanted sex. I don't know if I have any sexual desire anymore and I don't care. That part of me was killing me and would've killed one of my victims eventually." He stopped for a moment to breathe because his throat was closing. He was afraid he might not be able to finish, but he had to. "That part of me is the beast, a monster within. Yet once I got in touch with it, something changed in me, profoundly changed."

Claudia was perched on her chair like a raptor coolly assessing the distance to its prey. She felt cold-hearted and cruel and was very uncomfortable with that feeling. So she turned on her psychic eye and was stunned by what she saw on the fuzzy screen behind his head—a panoramic movie of writhing reptiles on craggy rocks surrounded by flying winged demons! Armando was twitching as if beaks were pecking his face, which made her nervous. She said, "Armando, please relax. I'm listening to you; I am not going to bite."

Armando's posture softened a tiny bit. "I left Lorenzo's office knowing the only thing I could do was go to Orvieto, my sacred place. If you can believe it, that day was that crazy end-of-the-world day! I went to our favorite old hotel and restaurant, ate dinner, and thought only about you. Even though I went to Orvieto every year as a child, I have not gone back since that terrible day when we had our last fight. I knew I had to go there to figure out why you acted the way you did; I had to face it. It was bizarre because I didn't yet understand what had happened with Lorenzo. All I knew was I had to get back to the place where you and I split.

"The moment I walked into the nave, I was terrified because I knew I was going to get the truth, every ugly shred. I went into the Chapel of the Madonna of San Brizio and studied Signorelli's paintings. Because of my analytic breakthrough, I saw what you meant about the battle for souls. I realized I was damned to hell unless I changed, but not in the way the Church says we can avoid hell. I stood in the center of the chapel and fully realized the rest of my life was going to be a living hell unless I changed; I really got that. But I knew it wasn't enough. I sensed I had to know how I got to be the way I was, what happened to me."

Claudia was totally absorbed in him and losing her boundaries. For a split second, it was as if their relationship was an ongoing continuum, and he'd scaled the wall between them. Then she jostled herself into the present, remembering she'd never let him hurt her again. She said in a distant and blasé voice as she sucked on her cigarette, "So, you finally got the point?"

Armando wouldn't let her deter him even though the bile in her voice churned his gut. *I wish she'd lash me with straps, beat me the way I used to beat her.* But he took a deep breath when he felt the lizard stir, which terrified him—he never wanted it out again. "Claudia, please just be patient for a little bit more. I'm seeking a way to tell you something that will free you, not to ask for your pity. You have to hear me! I don't want anything from you; I just want you to hear my honesty. I think if you can, others can, and then maybe that is what I will be—an honest person."

I'll believe that when I see it, she thought to herself. But she sat back in her chair and said, "Okay, Armando, *try* being honest."

"Back at the hotel, I stayed in our old room. The white marble sunken tub that you loved is still there, so I had a purification bath. Then I crawled under the sheets feeling like a child because I did something I have not done since I was very small: I asked God for a dream that would help me remember when and how I became one of the damned." He looked across to her and almost stopped when he saw her eyes. The depth of the pain they held made him shudder. She did not pull away her fixed gaze. "Go on, Armando; you are safe here."

"I had a dream of being seven and walking to the chapel in our woods with the parish priest holding my hand. My First Communion was coming up, so he took me there for my first Confession. When I woke up, I couldn't remember anything about the rest of the dream as hard as I tried. But I thought my mother might know something, so I went home to ask her what she knew about that time in my life and that priest. I could see this question upset her, but I had to know. She told me of the time I crushed my puppy, which saddened her. As we sat there together, I could see that she knew something had happened to me with that priest because I changed utterly after that day. She couldn't comprehend what he did to me, but while I was talking with her, I saw hideous flashes like in a movie in a black room. That priest raped me, Claudia, raped me when I was only seven." He stopped, exhausted, and turned his eyes to the gas flames.

A force ripped through Claudia's chest. She started to shake inside, almost dropping her cigarette, then leaned forward to put it out in the ashtray, struggling for composure. Emotionally she was being pulled back into the horrific chain of sexual abuse, the priest raping her through Armando. She did not feel any compassion because she was swooning in the sick vacancy of her dying cells. Abruptly she got up to get brandy and glasses. "How awful for Matilda, how awful for you. I hate the Church even more than I hate myself."

Armando froze, feeling as small and helpless as if he were seven again. "Why would you hate yourself?" he asked as she slammed down the brandy decanter. "*You,* Armando! Whether it was your fault or not, you dumped this goddamned bile in me! *You* shredded me to bits. You flayed me with your lust and beat me with your pain; you robbed me of my innocence only because yours was taken from you. That is *not* a good enough reason for what you did to me."

"Claudia," he said in a voice so quiet she strained to hear. "I am not here to ask you to help me. I am here because I hope that if you can see the path that led me to be the way I was, maybe you can find yourself again. What I did to you gives me greater pain, a thousand times greater, than what that sick priest did to me. If you can forgive me for what I did to you, then I will know I didn't kill you. We may be able to break the cycle. But I think this is too much, I think you need some time to think about this, and I am drained. I'm going now. I hope what I've shared will take some of your pain away. Please forgive me someday."

He's getting up to go! My god, I never thought I'd ever see Armando care more for someone else than himself. That is incredible! She grabbed his forearm as he was getting up and made him fall back into the chair. "Wait, stay and have brandy. The armor I've built to protect myself from you makes it hard for me to comprehend what happened to you. Do not go, Armando. I do not want to be a woman who cannot forgive. Without feeling compassion, I cannot live."

She poured the brandy and brought over some almond cookies with sugar on top. She looked at Armando as she set things down. *There is something really different about him, what is it?* He was gazing at the fire and seemed unaware of her presence. *I see sweetness in his hands and in the aura around his body. My god, I see Armando Pierleoni's innocence, of all people. Better be careful; he may be fooling me.* "Here, have a cookie with your brandy to take you back before you were seven."

"Claudia, *please* don't be sarcastic. This isn't something to joke about. A priest doing that to a little boy is as ugly as what I did to you. I can't forgive myself; you are the only one who can free me from my living hell. I am not expecting it of you, but *please* don't insult me with such a callous innuendo."

Few people ever successfully upbraided Claudia Tagliatti. If someone did, such as a rich bitch in her boutique, she always got him or her back; she was the master of acid cruelty. But Armando was right, absolutely right. "Armando, please give me your hand. I can't take all this in without touching you again."

He gave her his hand, and as she held it and put her other hand inside his, he felt cool fire in his spine, a shivering long wave all the way up and through his head. He raised his eyes to look into her eyes, and her bronze catlike eyes reached into his mind. *I will never again be able to lie to her, hurt her, or know her. I ruined the most beautiful thing I ever had, but all I care about now is forgiveness. If she can forgive me, she will be able to reclaim herself.* "I never thought you'd hold my hand again. You are like pure water, a light song, a deep canyon. It is an honor to feel your touch."

Unbridled warmth passed through her whole body and released a flood of stifled pain from her acidic cells. She sat there in suspended animation, holding his hand and occasionally looking into his eyes seeking the universe, and she found it. She could not deny it: there he was now—steady, respectful, and simple, a man who needed nothing more from her than compassion. Tears began to flow as she finally relaxed her facial muscles. He wanted to speak, but she said in a low voice, "No, let me do it; let me see and feel what happened to you." She stopped looking into his eyes, closed hers, and she saw the horror movie—*Armando's Confession.* Even though he himself couldn't remember what happened, she could see everything by holding his hand. She allowed herself to see it, and it was vile and unspeakable. Claudia allowed herself to behold man's inhumanity to man to find the source of her own inhumane treatment.

Armando just sat there with her until she opened her eyes and looked at him with love and respect. Then he knew she was going to be all right. She was going to be able to reclaim the young woman she had lost when she was nineteen. Warmth flowed back in, her mind cleared, her body relaxed, and then her spirit spoke. "Armando, I have seen it all and I will not talk to you about it. I forgive you for anything you have ever done or said to me. We will never be lovers again after all that has passed, but we will be friends, very, very dear friends. I survived because I figured out how to find deeper knowledge from the way you treated me, and when you became so bitter ten years ago that we could no longer learn from each other, I ended it. You also must ask Sarah for her forgiveness."

He settled back into the chair and closed his eyes in deep relief.

"Thank you, Claudia," he whispered. "I had no right to expect your forgiveness; you will never understand what it means to me. Of course I will also ask Sarah for her forgiveness, but I had to see you first. The Church teaches us that we have to go to a priest for Confession, but if I'd done that it would have circumvented the bonds and love that we've shared tonight. Confession encourages people to go on and on doing terrible things to each other and the world. It isolates people."

"Well, if anybody has the right to say that, you do!" Claudia said. "Can you take that comment without thinking it's a joke?"

"I know what you're probing for, since I still know you well. You wonder if I'm over it? I am, I think. I don't really remember the incident, and I think it is better if I do not. If I have to do that, I'll dump it on Lorenzo. Finally I might use him for what he's great at. I suppose he was right to take so much time with me. What matters to me now is the harm I've caused others, especially you. Do you think you can move past what I did to you, Claudia?"

"You know what, Armando?" she said, lighting another cigarette instead of eating a cookie. "I'm a tough broad. I either always was or my experiences with you made me into one. Either way, life is what teaches me. Yes, I wish things had been different, but we can't change that. Every day brings new surprises, today especially."

37

Via Lombardia

When Claudia called Simon and Sarah to say she urgently needed to meet with them, Simon's first reaction was annoyance. He was busy interviewing people about the pope's resignation and the upcoming conclave when the cardinals would gather to select a new pope. Romans gossiped without restraint about Vatican insiders, and the world was rife with rumors about who would be chosen. *Oh well, maybe Claudia will be a good distraction.* Sarah knew Claudia wouldn't ask right then unless it was important, so she offered to make Simon's favorite dish if she could invite Claudia for dinner. He came home early that night, poured a bourbon on the rocks, and said in a mildly irritated voice, "I suppose it's about that damned Armando?"

"I don't know, but she is our friend. If she needs to talk about him, I don't think we can refuse."

"Of course not," he grumbled as he kissed her. *I'm tired tonight; might as well be entertained by two gorgeous women,* he thought as Claudia rang from below. Simon pushed the code to buzz her in. In came Claudia looking very serious and flushed by the chilly wind. She sat down on the couch and Sarah gave her a glass of Chianti and brought out a tray of cheese and crackers.

"Hi, Claudia," Sarah said. "Nothing fancy tonight, just homemade lasagna and salad." *What is so urgent? Could one of her parents have died or something?*

Claudia smiled sweetly at Sarah. "That sounds delicious and also very grounding in light of what I have to tell you. I have forgiven Armando, and my bitterness has faded; I can hardly believe it!"

Simon planted both feet on the floor, staring at Claudia. Shifting her gaze to Claudia, Sarah said, "You know that I haven't told Simon anything about things you've said about Armando?"

"Well, I wasn't sure about that, Sarah; however, we don't need to go there because it doesn't matter. Simon, let me put it to you this way for the sake of conversation: Armando was very sexually abusive with me when I was young, which isn't hard to imagine considering what he tried to do to Sarah."

"That's for sure," he grumbled. "So you've forgiven him for that? Why?"

"He has been in analysis with Lorenzo Gianinni for over ten years, and he finally had a breakthrough a few months ago. I began seeing him as a friend after that." Simon interrupted her with a wry expression as he clicked his glass on his lower teeth. "I don't suppose this occurred at the end of the Mayan Calendar?"

"Well, yes, it did. But your skepticism will not divert me." Claudia explained what Armando had told her about being regressed by Gianinni and asking God for a dream to show him why he was one of the damned, and his eventual realization that he had been abused.

"He told me that Matilda says in those days nobody knew these things happened. No one could imagine a priest doing something like that to a little child, so things were suppressed. Armando thinks an evil possession was implanted in his body when he was only seven. I believe him because now he is sensitive and kind; he is a completely different person, the one I used to see below the surface and always hoped would come forth."

She stopped, only now noticing the tears filling Sarah's pained eyes and Sarah's hands clasped so tightly that her knuckles had turned white. "Oh, how utterly devastating," Sarah said. Simon looked at the floor with a furious and panicked expression on his face. He got up and went to Sarah, putting his hands on her shoulders. "Another one. How are we going to make the world better when so many children are broken so young?"

Sarah couldn't speak, so Claudia continued, "I look at this differently. Armando went on living for more than thirty years with that corrosive pain eating him alive. He projected his venom on others, especially on me. Yet now that we know about the pervasiveness of priestly sexual abuse, he realizes it was not entirely his fault because he was so young. Most importantly, now that he knows what happened, he feels he can transform the demonic force. Actually, he's getting his feelings back by exploring the dark side in his art."

Claudia could tell Simon was still skeptical, so she kept talking. "The abuse has been rampant since the fourth century when the Church became possessed by power, yet back in 1980 nobody would have believed him. He suffered terribly because nobody realized what was wrong with him; even Matilda was paralyzed. They couldn't find words for what was wrong because it was unspeakable. They could not access their trauma! This is changing because the truth is out, and you have made a real difference, Simon. Things *are* getting better. When you hear what happened to Armando, how does it make you feel? Now that you know about this, can you forgive him as I have? Can you forgive him for what he did to Sarah?"

There was a long pause while Simon and Sarah absorbed the enormity of Armando's story. Claudia stared at the gas flames. Sarah wanted Simon to speak first because she'd forgiven Armando long ago. She had always sensed that despite his actions, Armando needed her compassion and even her friendship. Friendship was her highest aspiration. Simon worked so hard that he had few friends, only colleagues. Actually she worried that he would miss out on the thing she most greatly valued, true friends. Ten silent minutes passed. Then Simon cleared his throat and spoke in a grave voice. "This is terrible, just terrible. I wonder if any Catholic is unscathed by this plague. I've never met Armando, so I can't judge the depth of his character; I can only form my opinions based on what I've heard about him, which isn't good. Since you've come into my life, Sarah, I find myself reflecting on how lucky I was to have the childhood I had. Nobody did anything like that to me, so I didn't get angry and take pain out on others. Nobody did anything like that to Sarah, so we are both very fortunate. Apparently something happened to Sarah's father with a priest when he was young, which is confidential, Claudia." He pointed his finger at her with a warning expression. Claudia felt slightly insulted. *Who did he think she would tell?* "This has created its own set of difficulties in his personality and life; yet he did not take it out on others."

"I'm still unsure that someone can change as quickly as you say Armando has. And his own hurt does not excuse how he hurt both of you. If he is willing and able to truly change his life and to try to liberate the women he hurt by sharing the realization of the source of his own pain, I can respect that. But I think trust needs to be built, and that you should be careful, Claudia."

Sarah was watching Simon with a distinct look of pride. "Simon," she said slowly and thoughtfully, "you do not fail me. Your willingness to extend kindness does not surprise me. I loved Armando, but not in the way I love you. I think I was often able to experience the man hidden beneath the monster, which is why I can more easily believe he could transform. His parents are special people, and I believe he is special too. Your response gives me hope. The world is so dire that we must forgive each other and extend a hand to the lost ones. That kid who murdered all the children in Newtown was isolated, lonely, obsessive, and probably possessed. I think he struck out against children to appease his inner torture. Something must have happened to him when he was in the first grade that slaughtered his inner child. Maybe if just one person had reached out to befriend him, maybe then the children would still be alive."

Ready to move on from that subject, Sarah caught Claudia's eyes and smiled. "Claudia, I'm pregnant! I'm due this fall, although sometimes I think we are completely crazy to bring a child into this world. But I am hopeful, and what would the world be like without our child?"

Claudia leaped up to hug her. "Oh, I am so happy for you! You two will have the most beautiful baby! I will be Aunt Claudia!"

Sarah held her at arm's length and looked into her eyes. "I know what Armando did to you, and I don't want anybody else to ever have to experience that. The minute you told us you forgave Armando, I could see the horror was gone for you, simply gone; you are really different, lighter and less sarcastic. Something entirely new is happening now. People are pushed to the wall, which makes many troubled and violent. Yet, the opposite pole—truth and healing—is expanding. I've never heard of an evil man like Armando finding his way back. But each person does have a choice as long as they are alive. Our will is the thread that can save us."

"I agree with you." Claudia said. "We seem to be mired in radical darkness amid extraordinary breakthroughs. I've carried this horrible pain for twenty years and suddenly it is beginning to fade. Who would imagine Armando would free me? I thought I'd take this angst to the grave with me. I've never stopped loving Armando. But as he got worse and worse, I couldn't bear his pain anymore." She turned to Simon to reassure him. "I do not intend to go back with him because I'm happy the way I am. Unlike the two of you, I like being alone. I think Armando is happy just painting for now. Besides with his genes, he should find a woman to love and have a family. Now that he's gotten through this, I think he could be a great father."

Casting a glance at the front door of the Hotel Hassler as he hurried by, Simon saw a sleek wealthy woman in a lynx coat walk in wearing gold spiked heels. *The greed scale sure is going up.* The wind was bitter on the Via Sistina, so he rushed along until he reached the Via di Porta Pinciana, and then he went on to the corner of the Via Lombardia, the corner with high walls surrounding the Pierleoni house. After Claudia had told Armando of their conversation, Armando had asked if Simon would meet with him. After some thought, Simon had agreed. He had to admit; he was curious about the man and also his famous home.

Noting the large garden behind the red wall, he assumed it must be part of a convent. Nobody had space like that in Rome. On the entrance on Via Lombardia, however, he noticed a worn family crest with a standing leopard mounted on a blue-and-red checked background above the garden gate. *That's a Sienese contrade crest, and the Pierleonis live near Siena. Maybe that's their garden, wow!* The high garden walls merged into the corner edge of a very dour red sandstone two-story house. The windows on the first floor were laced with iron bars on the diagonal that tricked the eye. *Are those medieval leaded windows? Nah, they're barred, have to be on the first floor in Rome.* The upper windows were shuttered with louvers latched from inside. The entrance was menacing with thick-cut stone columns that supported a carved lintel that ended in two snarling griffins with bulging eyes. An elaborately tiled stone family crest was displayed between the two griffins glowering down at Simon as he pulled the iron door loop. The door was thick, worm-eaten, and encrusted. *This certainly is an imposing house, almost threatening. It looks like it's more than five hundred years old!* His reporter persona was on high alert.

The door to the Pierleoni mansion creaked open, and the antiquated manservant led him through a fantastic great room. The two-storied stone walls were draped with exquisite Belgium tapestries; the Italian authenticity of the house enveloped him sensually. *This should be a museum; everybody should see this house.* The shriveled old man with paper-thin skin led him into a large library where a great fire roared at the end. Multicolored leather and gold-embossed books glowed in the firelight. The room was one of the most grandiose yet welcoming that Simon had ever seen. It was clearly the heart of the house.

A handsome and very elegant dark-haired man in an emerald green blazer stood by the fireplace. He stepped forward to take Simon's hand. "How kind of you to come, Simon; I am honored and deeply touched." Simon took his hand, feeling its delicacy, the hand of a serious painter. *His teeth are as perfect as a string of real pearls; I've never met anybody like this. I can see why Sarah was drawn in by him. If he hadn't attacked her, it would have been hard to resist his offer of marriage. The life this picture-perfect guy offers is every woman's fantasy. She could have become royalty!*

Armando had looked forward to meeting Simon, yet he was also very apprehensive. He certainly could see why Sarah had chosen Simon, a very good-looking and obviously fascinating man. He'd expected a tweedy and rather dull New York intellectual, not the intriguing, sophisticated man in front of him. He looked deeply into Simon's eyes and detected potent magnetic focus. He hoped this would not be too difficult.

"Thank you, Armando," Simon said tentatively. He felt disarmed by Armando's palpable femininity shrouded within potent sensual masculinity, a quality he'd noticed in a few other seasoned European men. "I didn't think we'd ever meet, but now the occasion has come. Your home is wonderful, spectacular, as I've always heard. Amazing to be able to live in a house like this in Rome these days!"

"Yes," Armando replied, wondering where to begin. He decided to just reveal himself, his usual way with women but a technique he rarely employed with another man. "The most wonderful thing about this ancient house is walking down hallways and being in rooms where twenty or thirty or more generations of my ancestors have lived. It is very comforting, an experience very few have. It is my great joy, yet also it isolates me from most of humanity. Of course, you can imagine all the things that have happened in this house over so much time in Rome! It has been a garrison, a brothel for cardinals, and the center for my family."

Armando brought his hands together. "Well, we both know what the real subject for this visit is, so without further ado, shall we talk about things? Lunch is ready for us any time, and would you like tea or coffee now?"

"Yes, coffee please."

"And congratulations on your marriage, you are most fortunate."

"Thank you; I am indeed fortunate. Ironically, even with all this family protection," Simon said accepting a cup of coffee that the butler produced almost instantaneously, "still you were not safe?"

Armando nodded. "Yes, that is true, especially since the clerics have always preferred picking off the children of the rich. Parents sent their beautiful adolescent daughters for spiritual counseling to bishops who seduced them. Little boys who got too close to the altar were ravaged. You have written about it, so you know. I have read your articles, and I very much admire you. Also you have given me more than a few laughs with 'Between the Sheets in Roma.' You are all the rage in Rome. Did you know?"

Simon smiled in acknowledgment of the praise. "That's good to hear because it will keep me employed, but may we stick to the subject? Now that Claudia has told us about your breakthrough in analysis and your recall of being abused when you were a small child, I am trying not to be angry about what you apparently did to her and tried to do to Sarah. As you can imagine, I've had nothing but contempt for you until now; in my mind you were a monster." While he said this, he was using his journalist's eye to look Armando over.

"Well, yes, Simon, I was a monster. If I ever told you about some of the things I've done, you would leave the room. You would never be able to get over your anger over what I did to Sarah. I assume you know that I hurt other women too, and I plan to apologize to every one of them if I can speak to them. It will not be easy to arrange that, but maybe I could see them if I brought my mother or someone they trusted. Today, I ask *your* permission to meet with Sarah to apologize to her. We had deep feelings for each other, and I need this last chance to be alone with her." Armando was watching Simon's darting eyes very closely, noting little wrinkles appearing on his forehead.

"That's not really up to me, but before I answer that," Simon said in a measured tone, taking a sip of coffee to get some space. "May I ask you some questions about what happened to you? As you know, I've covered the files on priestly abuse thoroughly and interviewed countless victims. You don't have to worry about confidentiality, and I would not be interviewing you for the press, only for my own understanding. Sarah is fond of your family and she is willing to forgive, I want to understand what happened to you and how it has affected you."

"Simon, you can ask me anything, and I will answer as best I can. However, I have little comprehension of what happened to me." He rang a little high-toned bell and paused as sandwiches and cold vegetables appeared and were put on the table between them.

"All right, good," Simon said as he bit into a chicken salad sandwich wedge. "What do you know about the priest who abused you when you were seven? Were there rumors about him in the parish? Did you notice any other children he might have molested?" This made Armando think for a moment, absently tapping a celery stick against his plate.

"Well, come to think of it, and I've never thought about it until now, there was one thing I noticed. I went to the rectory one day before anything had happened to me to deliver some cookies. When I walked into the back hall, a door slammed hard. I heard furniture scraping and a frightened cry; I didn't know what to make of it. It made me feel bad, so I left the rectory. Maybe he was doing something in there. My mother sensed something was going on so she had him sent away. She could do that because of our family. I suppose he got sent somewhere else and kept doing it."

"It is incredible, isn't it?" Simon remarked. "They were like weapons aimed at little children because the hierarchy protected them." While he spoke, Armando looked into Simon's eyes, noticing the deep blue flashes in dark brown, a captivating animation. "Now that you know what happened, does it still hurt? When you remember the scene, does it retraumatize you? Many of the victims I've spoken to have problems with flashbacks."

"Truthfully, I don't remember much about it, and I'm not sure it would do me much good if I did. I have a good analyst, Lorenzo Gianinni. He encourages me to be in the present, saying I must deal with the damage I've done to others and I think he is right. Now that I realize what I have done, I am getting better every time I can tell the truth. My relationship with my mother is blossoming, a joy for both of us. My father is now tender with me, and Claudia is so compassionate that I've found myself more in love with her than I ever was before because it is real love, not just lust."

For Simon the afternoon with Armando revealed the truth of something he had thought all along—that remembering buried trauma could generate change and sometimes free its victims. To be with an individual who had been terribly abusive for so long, but who was now so humbled and vulnerable gave him hope. By the end of their meeting, he was ready to give Armando a chance. "As long as she is comfortable with it, I am all right with you seeing Sarah. She amazes me; she really cares about you in spite of what you've done. Once she heard what had happened to you when you were so young, she was very anxious to see you. She will be happy if the two of you can just let it go by sharing your feelings; it would be good for her. If I were her, I don't think I'd want to see you alone but she may want to come here? I know she loves this house, and I can see why. I assume your parents are here in the winter? Under the circumstances, I'd be happier if they were around. She'd like to see your mother anyway, and you've told me she knows all about what's going on."

Armando set down his sandwich, his eyes riveted to Simon's avid, kind face. "I can't believe it! I can't believe I've come far enough to be offered your generosity. You know I would have married Sarah, but don't worry. I don't feel that way anymore. Thankfully, she kept me from doing the worst, or I'm sure you wouldn't be here with me today. To be honest, Sarah is the only one I didn't get. You don't know what a monster I was. I almost killed one young girl in a Tuscan ravine, and I abused Claudia until she was mindless."

Simon winced. But Armando seemed like a completely different person, and he could see that little boy before he was raped. Although Armando was an amazingly strong man, a very determined man, there was sweetness in him, a little child who wanted to be loved. "Will you be able to meet with this Tuscan woman?"

"I am hoping my mother can arrange that, since she still has family nearby. I may have to meet with her with my mother so she feels comfortable and feels safe. Yes, I think I will be able to do that and I dread it."

"Based on Claudia's experience, it seems to me each one of these meetings has the potential to heal you and release the women," Simon said, "but I can see why it's a hard thing to do."

Armando said in a deep voice, "Being accepted again by Claudia and knowing she is getting over the pain means everything to me; she is slowly unwinding her bitterness. We all have healing powers we do not use. The most awful thing I think about is what I would have done next. I was getting very close to murdering the next woman, and Lorenzo knew it." Simon shuddered, thinking how close Sarah came to being dreadfully hurt.

Armando went on. "As you can imagine, Simon, I have thought much about the monster I became—like Dr. Jekyll and Mr. Hyde! Claudia says the end of the Mayan Calendar was the completion of nine levels of evolution, and now many elements of each cycle will pass away. She says I reverted back to a primal phase, and she could actually see me reverting back by observing my body language. She thinks potent lust causes a lot of people to revert back to the time when humans evolved from primates, and they go out of control. What do you think about that idea?"

Simon glanced at his watch to see a few hours had passed. As much as the afternoon had made him think he could give Armando a second chance, he wasn't yet ready to discuss such matters with the man who had attempted to rape his wife.

"I'm sorry, Armando, but I have to leave. Maybe we will continue this discussion another time."

"Thank you, Simon, and thank you so much for meeting with me this afternoon."

As Simon made his way home, he thought about some of the things they had discussed. He did agree with Armando that lust could cause people to revert to their primal levels. He could feel the power involved in sex, especially sex with Sarah. It gave him power; in a way, he felt he became power. That was why marriage was very good for him because it allowed him to contain and safely express that part of himself. As he hurried down the Spanish Steps, he knew Sarah would be happy to hear he was willing to give Armando a second chance.

38

The First Quartet

The last days of February and the first few weeks of March 2013 were a very strange time. World attention was focused on Rome when Pope Benedict XVI stepped down February 28, yet would remain in Vatican City as Pope Emeritus. After a brief renovation, Benedict would reside in the Mater Ecclesiae, a convent on the edge of the Vatican gardens formerly used by nuns to pray for the pope and the Church. Simon grumbled to himself while pouring his morning coffee, "The nuns get dumped so their residence can be turned into a nursing home for an ailing pope. Ratzinger always gets what he wants. I suppose he'll spend a fortune to have Gorgeous Georg decorate it. Oh well, it's a very exciting day in Rome—the conclave."

Sarah sat on the couch next to him with a cup of green tea— these days coffee gave her morning sickness. She hoped Simon was in a good mood today. With Vatican events shifting so radically, he had withdrawn his next installment of "Between the Sheets in Roma." The papal interregnum was unprecedented, since nothing like it had occurred in eight hundred years, and the conclave's integrity was seriously tainted by the abuse scandal. A significant number of attending cardinals were implicated in the scandals but had not been defrocked. They still had the right to vote for the next pope!

The allegations against cardinals Godfried Danneels of Belgium, Sean Brady of Ireland, Roger Mahoney of Los Angeles, and Justin Rigall of Philadelphia were extensive and serious. Regardless, the perpetrators arrived for the conclave in long limousines like Hollywood stars attending the Oscars.

A new pope would be chosen to win back the laity's loyalty and adoration. In Simon's opinion, the conclave was not authentic and he said so in print. He resented having to let his next "Between the Sheets" article go, since it satirized the broad-based homosexual clergy easily blackmailed by higher-ups in the hierarchy. He felt that setting the present cast of characters back in the days of Olimpia Maidalchini and Innocent X perfectly captured the flavor of the uproar going on behind closed doors. *Oh well, at least I can pass it by Claudia for a good laugh, and I've had my chuckles.* Sarah snuggled next to him, her freshly washed hair smelling like peach blossoms. He treasured his newfound domestic joy. She was so patient and sweet! He put his arm around her shoulder not knowing she felt frustrated. She was experiencing bizarre reality distortions, and she was anxious to have a serious talk with Claudia and Armando about them.

She had met Armando for lunch just the week before, since Matilda and Pietro were still at the castle. Simon still didn't trust Armando enough to feel comfortable about Sarah meeting him alone at the Pierleoni house, so they'd agreed to lunch at a Chinese restaurant near her apartment. Her pregnancy was making her feel so sick, and the only thing she could eat was rice. Armando thought it was funny, saying what she really liked was the sweet and sour sauce, which was basically true. First he apologized to her again and she accepted it. Then he described his analysis with Lorenzo Gianinni and the landscape of his inner world. Mysterious archetypes and symbols were pouring out on his canvases; he'd become a fountain of creativity. She could easily see the change in him and promised she'd come with Simon to see his work as soon as possible.

Simon was waiting for her to speak, since he could see her wheels turning as she sipped her tea. "Simon, do you think we can have Claudia and Armando over as soon as the conclave concludes?"

Simon knew Sarah was delighted to see the change in Armando and wanted to have him as a friend. He wanted her to be happy, especially as she hadn't been feeling well. "Yes, I definitely want to find out more about Armando's transformation. I guess that means you still feel like it went well with him the other day."

Sarah smiled and snuggled in closer. "It did. I could see the change in him, just like Claudia said. He'd already apologized to me before for his behavior, but this time it was more sincere, perhaps because he understands more why he did what he did."

Simon nodded. "I'm glad you are happy." He gave her a brief hug and then stood and swung his laptop bag over his shoulder. "I'll be out on the streets this afternoon talking to people to describe the mood in Rome for the *Times*. Americans are always curious about conclaves, a throwback to the Middle Ages. But remember sometimes it's weeks before we see the smoke."

This time it didn't take weeks. Simon was gathered with some colleagues at their favorite café when everyone's phones started ringing at once. It was only the second day of the conclave, and Jorge Mario Bergoglio from Argentina had already been selected! He would be called Francis, and he was the first pope from the Americas as well as the first Jesuit. Simon was completely amazed, as were all the other reporters.

"Well," he began, "I think the world is having a psychosis! Any of you feel that way?"

Bergoglio had been so far off the radar that only a few of them even knew who he was. A reporter he'd always liked from the *Herald Tribune* said, "Can anybody tell me why a rotting pack of sexual predators in red hats and skirts picked a guy who actually may be a good person? I thought they were going to pull out another slimeball, didn't you?"

"I did," Simon said. "His Jesuit background intrigues me. The Jesuit order protects the pope, so how can one of them *be* pope? Anyway, it's done and we'll see what it means. Francis seems to be a fine choice. Do you suppose something good happened for a change? I'm going home to my wife." He got up to go as a reporter from the *San Francisco Chronicle* grabbed his arm. "Simon, I think maybe something good did happen for a change. I can just feel it."

About a week after the conclave, Simon, Sarah, Claudia, and Armando met together for the first time to look deeper into the truth they were all so interested in uncovering. Sarah had sprouted daffodil bulbs for the spring equinox, and the subtle aroma permeated the kitchen. The gas fire was on, taking off the chill as they gathered in the living room. Claudia opened the discussion. "I propose we become a quartet playing our minds as instruments to ascertain the nature of reality, since some kind of shift is happening that may jeopardize or accelerate our existence."

As the others nodded, Claudia began. "A bizarre acceleration of events occurred during 2011 and 2012—the Arab Spring, the Syrian war, Fukushima, Wikileaks, Vatileaks, and the pope's bizarre resignation. The failure of people in power is widely touted on the Internet, and everywhere tiny cell phone cameras expose previously hidden abuses. Widespread chaos is spreading even further because information technology achieved global connection in 2011, the unification of the collective mind. We don't need to discuss the details of these accelerating events, since we can barely track it. Rapid change is ubiquitous, and I can't remember what happened two days ago!

Claudia wished she could smoke; it helped her think, but Sarah had forbidden it in her house. "I am interested in the *forces* driving these collective events. Sarah and I are both certain something entirely new is going on. Armando, you are an artist and open to unusual ideas. Simon, you are the skeptic, the critical analyst. Sarah, you are the seer. My contribution is Mayan Calendar research. So with everyone's permission, I begin with the ending of the calendars, since millions have wondered what it means: if anything *did* happen within this time frame, would we actually be able to detect a shift? One major calendar tracks 5,125 years of history through 2012, and another main one tracks 16.4 billion years of evolution through 2011. I also think there were many more calendars that explore these cycles, things the elite have studied in secret."

"Well if there are so many versions of the calendar, how do we know which one to abide by, which one to believe?" the skeptic chimed in.

"For me," Claudia said, "the most meaningful interpretation is the 16.4 billion-year-long evolutionary analysis, as the 5,125-year calendar is only one of the nine phases of this greater calendar. However, the great value of the 5,125-year calendar is it calls attention to the domination of the patriarchy, the addictive control system that is destroying nature and the feminine. One thing we can be sure of is the old world is collapsing to create space for something new." She looked at Simon, thinking he would push the idea.

Simon leaned forward. "Well, I think these calendars *did* nail the shift, but how could the Maya have known that a few thousand years ago? Since being able to predict what will happen makes money, do you think the global elite know all about this? Is that the reason for the peculiar debunking of 2012 in the media? Also, does the Church know?" Simon stood up and began to pace as his train of thought ramped up. Claudia and Sarah settled in, knowing this could go on for a while. But Simon's enthusiasm was new to Armando, so he gave Simon his undivided attention. "After all, the European elite raided the Maya heritage and claimed they burned thousands of calendars, but who says they burned them all? Of course, a few of them survived that inform us of the end point, such as the remarkable Coba Stele, which is the source of the 16.4 billion-year calendar interpretation. Maybe the records that describe the *meaning* of 2012 were stolen and hidden for elite eyes only? Even though I'm the designated skeptic, I begin with the assumption the Maya *did* nail something that would happen now. If we start there, then we can use our time to figure out *what* they thought would happen now and how it might affect us. Armando, you had that life-changing regression the very day the Calendar ended. Do you think this was possible for you because some kind of new potential was suddenly available to you and your analyst?"

Claudia and Sarah both noticed Simon said "new potential." Both of them wondered if the great change would be in male behavior, something they both hoped for. The patriarchy was still holding on like a crab gripping rock in heavy surf. The resistance to male control, however, was playing out behind closed doors in personal relationships. Some men were genuinely supporting women in their careers and caring for infants and small children, blurring the lines of the defined gender roles that contributed so much to the patriarchy's dominance.

Armando cleared his throat. "I have been painting the scenes I see in strange parallel worlds where puppet masters pull the strings that make us dance. What if great change first starts in other worlds? Going back to that strange day, I was desperate; so was Lorenzo, so he regressed me. It was risky because he knew demons possessed me. When these forces are unleashed, sometimes an exorcism is needed. That day, something mysterious was leading both of us to the edge of reality. I don't even remember the drive to Orvieto because I was on autopilot. Since my personal hell terrorized you and Claudia, Sarah, combining this experience with your studies, I wonder what you have to say about how this all relates to our understanding of evil in the world. Do you think the Church unbinds demons in the faithful by means of sexual abuse? That's what they did to me, and I lived with a monster inside for over thirty years." He sighed. "I didn't have to let it out, I know. Yet, I liked the way it felt to be the lizard, the power over other people, especially women. I made that choice, and I have to live with the consequences. Regardless, it all began with a priest, with an act I believe was fully supported by the hierarchy. The most shocking thing is that he used my first Confession as an opportunity to get me. What are their ultimate plans? You've been to my family home. The Church has always wanted to get their hands on it, so maybe that's why they went after me."

Always able to answer questions through high sources when asked directly, Sarah answered clearly, "Sexual abuse, and that includes sexual repression, is used to beat the laity into slavery. This has been going on for at least sixteen hundred years with the Vatican as the control center. The hierarchy knows sexual abuse rips people open to black forces that implant demons, so my issue is, *why?* There seems to be only one answer: any god that would ask for the sacrifice of a child, like Yahweh asked of Abraham, is a demon! These bloodthirsty Canaanite practices are re-imprinted during Masses celebrated continuously all over the globe—the son sacrificing himself to the father. Notice this ritual was invented during the 5,125-year patriarchal phase, so the ending of this phase may signal the arrival of truth. It's even worse when sexual abuse is combined with the sacraments. So, Claudia, you say you learned things from Armando. *What* did you learn?"

Claudia was on the couch leaning way back in an effort to cut the tension, still longing for a cigarette. Nobody was drinking either. *It will be hard to answer this question without smoking or drinking.* She took the measure of Sarah's intent green eyes, and said, "You've heard about yin and yang, the balance between the dark and light? Well, that is not an idea for me; I *experience* it. You were in distress and I loved you, Armando. I had to endure sexual practices I despised, which made me strong against your demons. You were very dark, so you shoved me into the light where a magical world opened! All of us have light and darkness within; sometimes it is our interactions with others that bring out one side or the other. I have experienced realms beyond space and time where high beings live that are magnetically drawn into our lives. Most people don't know that, but I do. These beings live in me and inform me about astonishing things that almost no one believes could be true. This is a huge subject, one I've barely touched on even with Sarah. She travels in these worlds all the time, whether she knows it or not. To avoid getting too complicated for now, I'll allude to the second dimension just below this one, where Armando was trapped, the Underworld. I went there with him many times; I know the landscape of the lower world."

Indicating layers with her hands, she went on, "Demons inhabit the second dimension in semi-physical forms that express Earth's power. Demonic thoughts and feelings inhabit the fourth dimension, the source of sexual/power complexes that manipulate humans using symbols and rituals. We are designed to freely inhabit the third dimension, yet power mongers have learned how to entrap us in the fourth dimension. They also tap Earth's power at sacred sites like the Vatican to trap us in the second dimension. People who seem to be asleep throughout their whole lives are trapped in the second dimension. This energy manipulation is the basis of patriarchal power. You, Armando, lived in a wonderful family and were located solidly in the third dimension in a beautiful life. Then the priest wrenched you out of it by using sexual energy to throw you into the dark. When you expressed yourself sexually upon maturation, you trapped more people.

Disgust transformed Claudia's features. "Hot desire feeds the Church with power and sticky luxury. The Church uses hypnotic, lurid pomp and splendor to keep people's minds in the dark zone instead of freely living in the solid world, in a balance of light and dark. Your knowledge of this archetypal zone is what makes you a great painter, Armando, but you couldn't control these forces in yourself until now. Also, you are very reptilian because you are a blueblood, the perfect codes for possession. You've expressed yourself sexually like a reptile, and now you are dormant. Does creativity satisfy you?"

"Like all men, I have a penis that can be used as a weapon," Armando said gravely. "I am serious about this," he said because he knew Claudia thought women had some of the same problems. "The Church uses the male biology to perpetuate their agenda! There are penises under the cassocks and robes of the 'celibates.' Men who find their penis to be a problem are attracted to priestly roles because ordination announces publicly they don't use it. However instead many end up misusing it. Thank God I didn't become a priest!" He lowered his head for a moment. The others imagined he must be thinking about how this misuse had affected his own life. "Because of the yin and the yang, when sexuality is repressed, dark energy expands, but it also expands when perverted into violence and force. The hierarchy sends abuser priests from parish to parish because the agreement is based on protection. Ordination is used as a penis-control program! But back to your question, Claudia, creativity can help with these problems, but it is not the complete solution. Creative expression is the opposite of sexual repression and violence, so it can balance extreme urges and help people live in moderate ranges. Simon, how do you control urges?"

"Hmmm," Simon said, "I was just wondering the same thing myself. Off the top of my head, I think I use curiosity—*lust* for answers drives me. When I get a real answer, it is almost as good as great sex, pardon me, Sarah." With a smile, Sarah pretended to kick him under the table. "For me, the world is a gigantic creative soup filled with ideas I hold in constant consideration. I'm sure you all do this in your own way; however, for me this mental process is sensual. I weave an oriental rug out of the ideas being considered by humanity. Claudia, have you ever thought about what could break the chain of abuse, end the constant rituals and sacraments, to collapse the hierarchical power structures that threaten nature, or at the least humanity's survival? I know you learned from your abuse, but there must be another way to learn these things. Will things ever be different?"

Claudia tapped her long fingernails on the table. "That is a huge question, and as I've said already, things may change as the patriarchy collapses. Addictive rituals like the Mass, war, and sporting obsessions will go away when people are bored with them, a sign the feminine is coming back into balance. But that's a question for another day."

She looked across the table at Sarah, who was as deeply engrossed in the conversation as the rest of them. "Sarah, you haven't said a lot tonight," Claudia continued, "but in some ways you know more than all of us. You travel around in these higher realms; I've been with you when you do it. I sense you are more certain than any of us that something has changed very fundamentally in another dimension. Do you think processes in the higher realms have shifted in some way? Has something happened elsewhere that is changing or will change things on Earth?"

Simon saw Sarah put her fingers over the ruby crystal. She took a deep breath and said in a soft, mellifluous voice: *"The great cry from Earth is being heard on high. Beings in higher dimension—call them light angels if you like—can hear you now when you ask for them. You must ask for happy children, loving, strong, and brave women and men, good friends, and the cessation of war, poverty, and abuse. It is time to use your desires for good things; ask from your heart. Your reality is now a quantum field of creative change. If you ask for good things, leaders will use their power to make them happen, but you must ask. In the higher realms, countless beings wait to hear from you."*

39

The Conclave

Simon stood in the Piazza San Pietro with the rest of the huge crowd magnetically drawn to be near Pope Francis. Women gushed and cried with happiness, men grinned with otherworldly beatific expressions on their faces, and babies and dogs couldn't imagine what the fuss was about.

Despite the objective demeanor he liked to project as a journalist, Simon was just as excited as the rest of the crowd about the new pope. The more he discovered about the new pope, the more he thought of him as a symbol of the shift, a sign of real hope for the future.

Before the cardinals locked themselves up in the Sistine Chapel for the conclave, they had had a forum in the Synod Hall, the transcripts of which were publicly available. After a few days of speeches, Bergoglio from Argentina had spoken for only *four minutes,* yet in that time span he had turned the cardinals around! The others were sick of hearing about how to reform the Vatican's dysfunctional bureaucracy and the sex-abuse scandal. Instead, Bergoglio called for the Church to create a new story of evangelization to awaken Christ-centered consciousness. He said the Church must be the mother who cares for her children, the poor and marginalized people in pain. His vision was of a Church of justice and human dignity instead of one that drew attention to its own inner processes all the time. He said it was time to break down the Vatican walls, and miraculously the other cardinals selected *him!*

As soon as the choice had been made public, Simon had called a reporter friend at the *Buenos Aires Herald* to ask him whether Francis was all he seemed to be. His friend, Marcelo, said Francis was consistently good-hearted, honest, disciplined, and brilliant. The story was that he learned how to be a good leader by making a lot of mistakes after being appointed a provincial superior in the Society of Jesus when he was only thirty-six. He created a lot of problems by being too authoritarian. He had learned from that experience, and now he favored consultation. Unlike most popes who relished the chance to be the sole authority, Francis had already appointed a group of eight cardinals to make decisions *with* him.

Simon could feel his heart swell with the shared hope and excitement of the crowd. On this unusually warm April morning, the aroma of flowers, food, and the nearby Tiber was intoxicating. Next to Simon a hunky young Italian guy was passionately kissing a luscious girl in a beige miniskirt and mid-calf leather boots. Simon's cell rang, and he was surprised to see it was Sarah. She rarely called him while he was working, so it must be important. He put the phone to his ear, eyeing the couple with amusement. The guy was gripping the girl's firm buttocks with hungry hands while his tongue was down her throat.

"Simon, I have great news and a question. Your sister Jennifer just called, and she wants to come to Rome in a few weeks to do our photos here. Is it okay if she comes soon? If so, where will we put her?"

"That's fabulous, Sarah, and it's so nice to hear your sweet voice right now." He turned and walked away with his phone because the young guy had caught him looking and was now shooting him annoyed glances. "I'd love to have her visit! Ask her to let us know exactly when. Don't worry about putting her up because she never bunks with people. She needs lots of time alone. Suggest the Hotel

Gregoriana up past the Hassler. It's really charming, reasonable, and a short walk to our apartment. She'll love staying there. Tell her to ask for a balcony on the inner courtyard.'"

"Okay. Don't forget to come home on time because we're meeting at Armando's house tonight. Have a wonderful rest of the day!"

Armando tore up the spiral staircase to Lorenzo's office because he was late. He knocked, waited, and the door opened. "Sorry, Lorenzo. The traffic was hell. I hope I have not inconvenienced you?"

"No, not at all, Armando, I was reading. This office is the most contemplative place I have. My wife talks too much. Today I am taking the whole afternoon here, and you are my only appointment. Come, lie down on the couch, and let's see what's going on in your inner mind."

"No, please, Lorenzo. If you don't mind, I want to talk with you as a counselor. I'm happy to recline after that, but I would like to just talk for a while."

Lorenzo led Armando to an old studded leather chair and opened the leaded casement windows to bring in some air. "Lovely spring, isn't it? I don't remember one as warm as this for many years." Yiddish mixed with Italian and English wafted up and echoed in the room in the old tower, reminding them both of the many other worlds just below. Lorenzo sat down across from Armando. "Well, how are you? You've been doing so well, but after such an intense breakthrough, sometimes there is a backlash?" Armando looked troubled, though his manner was calm. Lorenzo had met Matilda once and had been impressed by her deep serenity. Since Armando's regression, a similar quality was emerging in Armando's eyes.

"Yes, of course, a backlash," Armando replied. "I have felt the lizard on occasion, and when he appears, I stuff him. Now that we've discovered him, I seem to have the upper hand so far. He comes out when I am attracted to women, so I have been painting all the time. Meanwhile, I'm very horny, Lorenzo."

"Well, of course you are. What do you want to do about it? I assume women are available if you want them?" Lorenzo had been waiting for this to come up.

"Of course, women are available. But I am terrified the lizard will get out again if I just go fuck somebody. Actually the lizard seems to be pushing me to do exactly that, so I jack off but that's not satisfying. When I am with my mother, I am reminded of how much I love the company of women, especially intelligent ones. If I order a Club Doria Pamphili slut, I think I'd be taking a big chance and reverting to my old ways, don't you?"

Funny what a little child he is. He was so seriously arrested emotionally at such a young age. Maybe I should try to get him to the couch, but he doesn't seem to want that. Perhaps he is right—by sitting here his conscious mind dominates. "Ahem, Armando, I am wondering what you liked in little girls and even older girls before that terrible day?"

Armando, who felt like he was being tested, studied Lorenzo's face intently. Then what came out of Armando's mouth was so innocent that Lorenzo wondered whether Armando was going to be able to take the next step—serious commitment to another person.

"When I was seven, before it happened, I thought a lot about the kind of woman I wanted to marry. I saw images of her when I daydreamed as well as in my dreams at night. Lately I am seeing her again as if she is about to arrive. My sense of her is palpable. She is tall and strong, very intense, and her intelligence is daunting. Now that I'm horny but also wanting something more, I dream about her constantly. I see her walk into our Tuscan library, piercing my soul with dark incisive eyes. Then I embarrass myself as she watches my eyes crawl all over her body; she is offended by my lack of restraint." He felt sensual just talking about her, yet he shivered and fell back in his chair, feeling like a little boy who was acting improperly.

Lorenzo knew Armando was describing his own latent inner feminine. He wondered if it would help to tell Armando that. No, he decided. I think he'd feel trivialized. "Have you ever seen or met any-one like the woman you dream about?" He watched Armando closely; he was perspiring because he was forcing himself not to cry.

"Yes, I have and I ruined her," he said very slowly, his voice strained. "Claudia was very much this woman, but by abusing her I destroyed her image within myself. I kept on trying to reach her again, but whenever I got close I ruined her more. I can't do this again; I can't. I think I could have Claudia again if I asked her to marry me. But I don't want to marry her and I don't know why I don't. Why don't I, Lorenzo?"

"Armando, I assume you know about the virgin and whore com-plex? Some men feel they must have a virgin when they marry, espe-cially wealthy men. Meanwhile, they go around deflowering every woman in sight, still expecting to find a virgin to marry when they feel ready. Perhaps that is why you proposed to Sarah?"

Armando felt truth in what Lorenzo was saying, but it seemed too trivial right now. He was more interested in this woman he had been sensing.

"We don't need to talk about stuff like that, Lorenzo, because it seems obvious to me now. So you think I should use my family background and money to pick off a sheltered Italian twenty-year-old? They bore me."

"What do you think, Armando?"

"I think now that I'm not a monster, I have to stop being an ass. The world has had quite enough of me. My mother thinks I should marry, and I listen to her. You know what? If I can quell the damned lizard, then I could handle a relationship with a real woman. That's what I think. But I still don't know what to do."

Lorenzo Gianinni listened to Armando descending the stairs. Oh god, how many more years?

Evening came. The air was warm and aromatic when Armando opened the French doors out to the walled garden while he waited in anticipation of Simon and Sarah's arrival. Claudia had come early and asked to go to the garden cottage alone. More than an hour had passed, yet he knew he must not bother her. Soon after he opened the doors, she came to the threshold and stared at him while he sat quietly in a leather chair, his eyes closed. *He looks so lonely, but he seems to be serene, resigned almost. What does he think about?* She activated her psychic eye. *Hmmm . . . There is a beautiful exotic garden all around him and a tiger walks up to him. He puts his hand on the tiger's head, and they look at each other as if they are in love.* Armando's eyes flew open. "Oh, hello, Claudia," Armando said as he lowered his right hand, which was oddly suspended in mid-air. "I was beginning to worry about you," he said wanly.

She walked over to him and put her left hand on his left shoulder; hot shocks coursed through his body. *I wonder if she wants me? Anything that happens will have to come from her; I am incapable of making a move.* "I'm all right, Armando, all right now. Thank you for letting me finally shut that door." He felt a tense lock in his chest that he didn't know how to release. Feeling it, she put her right hand on his right shoulder, which released the energy. She continued, "You and I shall always be friends, always." He detected the aroma of her perfume.

Just then Sarah walked into the library with Simon lagging behind, fascinated by the elaborate family crests between the bookshelves. The four of them gathered in comfortable chairs around an ancient cedar shipper's trunk that served as a coffee table.

After greetings and small talk Simon initiated the real conversation. "We all agree some kind of field shift has occurred, but I want to know how something like that might work. Anybody want to take a stab?" he asked, looking at Claudia. *I wonder if Armando is taking an interest in her again.* Nobody did, so Simon went on. "For me, the selection of Pope Francis is the most perfect example of the shift. Bergoglio, now known as Francis, is said to be a brilliant man with a huge heart, who refers to himself as a sinner that God looks upon. A true Jesuit, he embraces community, discipline, and an open mind. He values discernment—making choices from God's perspective by intending to follow the spirit in all ways and in all times—a focus that comes from the Jesuit founder, Saint Ignatius. Francis appears to be a deeply spiritual man who refers to the Jesuits he admired as mystics—Ignatius, for example. On Church governance, he cites Pope John XXIII, who once said, 'See everything; turn a blind eye to much; correct a little.' I can only imagine what that advice would do the Church's ban on contraception or gay marriage! Francis seems to be a smart and dedicated pope. So, Claudia, what forces do you think could have created such a reversal in the Vatican?"

"Claudia shifted in her chair, crossing her legs. "Well, change comes first from the collective mind—in the fourth dimension—the dark and light range of all human thoughts and feelings. When Pope John Paul I was assassinated after only thirty-three days as pope in 1978, the mind of the Church turned very dark under John Paul II and Benedict XVI, who both attempted to nullify the Vatican II reforms that had defined the Church as the holy people of God. According to Vatican II, infallibility was in the body of the faithful—laity, clerics, the hierarchy, and the pope—and the hierarchy was merely a guide. The faithful felt hopeful for a brief period of time, but dark forces took over the inner structure when John Paul I died, and his body was immediately cremated and his apartments stripped. Next John Paul II used Ratzinger as his hit man while he went all over the globe speaking to adoring crowds in his bulletproof popemobile.

"The darkness expanded ominously when Ratzinger became Pope Benedict XVI, who covered up the sexual-abuse scandals and eliminated many of the Vatican II reforms. "The hierarchy thought the faithful would just forget the reforms, enslave themselves to pomp and ceremony, and hand over their children to the priests. But they were wrong. A tremendous entropic force was building in the minds of the faithful, a huge resistance to inauthentic authority; eventually the bishops and cardinals began to fear it. I could feel frustration all over Rome at that time, yet still they conspired among themselves to keep the same old Church. Thus an apostasy—the faithful abandoning the Church in droves—began, which meant the money would go away! Judging by the outcome of this conclave, the hierarchy has lost confidence in what they've been doing; they have lost their vision of the Church's future. Bergoglio offered a new Christ-centered vision; the light side seems to be emerging. However, let us remember the Italian Curia knows very well that Francis will appeal to Americans, their main revenue source. Even if Pope Francis is a deceiver, and some people say he is Petrus Romanus—the last pope according to Saint Malachy—people respond to hope en masse, which connects everyone in the dimension just above ours."

"Regardless," Claudia continued, "now that Francis is pope, resistance will build up against him from conservative elements in the Church. For example, a Catholic fundamentalist movement became very strong during the dark days of John Paul II and Benedict XVI. These elements are entrenched and they will attempt to undermine Pope Francis. Considering how easily previous gains in the Church were reversed during the past forty years, we shall see how far the Church can progress. People are desperate; they look for hope where they find it, and Francis seems to be such a warm and heartfelt man. Maybe something different is going on, although I doubt it, as the conclave was full of corrupt men and Francis is a Jesuit, an order known for secrecy and political manipulation.

She leaned back in her seat and shrugged. "If real positive change is coming, it would be because the world is exhausted by five thousand years of male dominance. I hope Francis represents the rise of the feminine to balance the masculine. He has even suggested he believes the feminine must rejuvenate the Church. But, you'd know he is serious about that if he advocates strong roles for women in the Church. Sarah and I went to the Sibyl's Oracle near Naples to tune in to the lower dimensions to see if we felt earth forces regenerating nature, the basis of life. I've noticed Francis says important decisions require feminine intelligence, earth wisdom. Yet, there sits the Vatican on the midline with only men running the show while the true feminine dries up in the collective mind because men and women lack creativity in a techie world. Sarah, what does the Sibyl say now?"

Sarah was concentrating deeply while listening to Claudia, so the question flipped her mind to a higher dimension. She replied in a clear and sure voice from another world: *"Pope Francis alluded to the feminine in men as well as women. The true feminine is severely under-represented in the collective mind. Feminine power is magnetic, which means it draws everything to it. It holds everything together like gravity; it may be gravity. Without it, things fall apart. When Sarah walked in the oracular tunnels, she felt the energy lines of the inner Earth. Realities shifted, signs the inner Earth is shifting. The lower world is a fast track propelled by those who flow with it, for example, the way Francis ignited the conclave. That is, our thoughts activate the telluric realm that affects us in our world. Francis may be reading positive forces in the collective mind accurately and moving with the lower energy pathways here in Rome; maybe that is why he knows when to act. There will be little resistance to Pope Francis in Rome, at least at first."*

Armando was feeling lost in so much intellectuality, so he hadn't heard much of what was said. Yet what Sarah had said about the inner Earth had jarred him, so he spoke up. "When I did the regression, I found a part of myself that was trapped in the lower world, which really is hell. The world we inhabit is purgatory. The hierarchy doesn't realize it is trapped in hell, even though Dante made it clear eight hundred years ago. Perhaps Francis can nudge them into purgatory where they would have to change. Certainly the Church is not in heaven! My new paintings are layered to depict these three levels simultaneously very much like some Renaissance painters. The archetypal level populated with images and beings that exist within us is where I find the puppet masters. When I depict them, I feel them; they hover above us all. We can't shift reality out of hell-bent destruction unless we detect what's influencing us by seeing our parts in the drama. I think the Church will just dissolve in hell eventually because the hierarchy got too inflated and pulled the dark and light down into our world by means of liturgy, rituals, symbolic clothing, and abuse. It will implode no matter who is in charge or how many white doves are sent to fly. I hope Pope Francis has a sense of humor! At least he seems to be very kind. I'm amazed anybody takes a leadership role during times like these."

Eventually they all said goodnight to Armando, and Claudia went home to bed exhausted. She kept thinking about her return to the garden cottage, which had brought the ugly feelings back. She'd picked a dozen multicolored tulips and put them in a mason jar on the kitchen table. Then her last act was to scatter them on the tapestry coverlet covering the infamous bed. Drifting off to sleep, she wondered, *Why did I go back there?*

She fell into a deep sleep and found herself rocking in a wedding bower—a great basket lined in gleaming white satin that was swaying in a tall tree over a winding pathway in the forest. The rattan basket leaned with her body weight as Umbrian folk music and birdsong filled the air. Her long ivory silk dress with blue scarves was spread out on the basket's puffy satin multicolored pillows. It was 1912. When her lover walked down the pathway, she tipped out of the bower . . . *I am sexy and beautiful, here to entice him as he comes!*

A beautiful man wearing a black satin tuxedo walks under the bower looking up. There on a nest he sees a golden goose with bright blue eyes and a floppy wide-brimmed hat tied with a red ribbon. The goose ties a blue silk scarf into a big bow while singing a love song. He grows feathers and webbed feet as his mouth and nose transform into a beak; his neck lengthens into the perfect curve. He is ready for her. Together they fly over a magical lake to a fish awaiting them for the wedding feast. For the female goose, slices of cantaloupe surround the large white fish. Orange cake bordered by cherries will be their dessert.

40

The Painter
and the Photographer

Jennifer Appel arrived in early May on a late evening flight from Paris to Rome, took a cab to the Hotel Gregoriana, and went straight to bed. Early the next morning, she strode briskly down the Spanish Steps on the way to her brother's apartment. Flower vendors were already opening their carts, so she bought tulips and daffodils. She noticed she was being watched. A few men sidled by her when she turned to go further down the stairs, but her haughty and determined look easily put them off. She was wearing loose beige linen pants and a skimpy black T-shirt stretched tight across her chest by a large leather backpack. She wore a hammered gold choker that gleamed in the morning sun as if she was in Rome to conquer. Leering local men wondered what she carried in her backpack.

She arrived at the apartment and rushed in to see Sarah's smiling face. Simon clenched her in a bear hug and then held her back to see her face. "You look happy, Jen. Are you in love?"

She handed him the flowers. "Oh, no, not at all. I just love walking around Rome, especially in the spring. Your apartment is wonderful! We'll have such a marvelous time. You are glowing, Sarah!" she said, admiring Sarah's rounded belly under a loose white blouse.

"Those pearls are fabulous. You look Edwardian, just perfect for being photographed in Rome. Simon, go put on a linen jacket, something romantic! Sarah, also bring a pretty shawl, maybe a hat, a few accoutrements to flatter you. I've got my cameras, so I'm all ready!"

They rushed around grabbing what they needed, but as they were heading out the door Sarah's phone rang. "Oh, hello, Sarah! I'm so happy I've reached you!" said a lilting, excited Italian voice. "This is Matilda Pierleoni! Armando will be here in a little while to prepare for a big show in Rome. Now that we have our country house fully open, will you please come visit this weekend and bring Simon with you? I am so anxious to meet him; Armando speaks so highly of him. Armando's newest work is here now and he wants you both to see it. Do come!" Sarah glanced at Jennifer and Simon, wondering what to say. "Matilda, how lovely of you to call, and of course I'd love to bring Simon to your villa. However, Simon's sister, Jennifer, just arrived from Paris to visit and photograph us."

"Oh, Sarah, excuse me for asking so much, but bring her too! We'd love to meet her. And she could take some photos of you and Simon in Tuscany! You could give one to William for his birthday in August. We'd love to have Jennifer come! You could even stop by Orvieto for lunch and a few photos."

Sarah needed to discuss it with Simon and Jennifer, so she said she'd call back in a few minutes. Simon and Jennifer couldn't resist the prospect of staying in an ancient castle in Tuscany, so the visit was arranged and they went out the door. They had a wonderful day walking around taking photos in piazzas, on the Spanish Steps, in the Borghese Gardens, in front of fountains, and in outdoor cafes. Jennifer took hundreds of photos and impressed Sarah with her focus and endurance, which nearly exhausted Sarah.

On the following morning, Guido picked them up, and in a few hours more photos were taken in front of Orvieto Cathedral's golden façade. Eventually the car made its way up the curving driveway up to Castel Vetulonia. The beautiful views of the countryside entranced Jennifer and Simon. Guido said, "Sarah, I assume you remember the room you stayed in and possibly the one your father stayed in? If you like, you and Simon can stay in your room, and you can show Jennifer to the other room across the hall? I will bring up your bags."

Sarah led them through the back gate where Matilda and Pietro waited. She took Matilda's hand and kissed her on the cheek, and then she kissed Pietro's glowing cheek. They both exclaimed over Sarah and her growing baby belly. Sarah smiled and accepted their gracious compliments, but she couldn't help but notice the sadness hidden deep in Matilda's eyes. Sarah turned to introduce Simon and Jennifer. Matilda took Jennifer's hand to welcome her, as did Pietro, and then Matilda turned to Simon with a warm smile. She looked into his dark, intense eyes, taking note of his sweet and handsome features. "Oh, what a pair you make, Simon, and your beautiful sister is just as charming."

Both Simon and Jennifer smiled to acknowledge the compliment, and then they went up the back stairs to the front entry hall. Jennifer looked up to the vaulted ceilings and then cast her eyes down to the ancient worn stone floors in front of a magnificent wide stairway. "This is just exquisite! It is so lived in and warm and I think early Renaissance? What a magnificent great hall! Sarah, you did not prepare me! *This* is a castle!"

Simon was taken aback by seeing what Sarah could have so easily chosen. He could hardly believe she'd resisted such romance and beauty. He was very impressed yet slightly stunned, so he took Sarah's hand and blurted out, "Now, *this* is a staircase for a bride's descent!"

There was a pause while Sarah blushed, causing Jennifer to shoot them both a quizzical look. Always the perfect hostess, Matilda said, "Oh, yes, Simon. I came down these stairs as a bride, as did Armando's older sister! When I was married here more than forty years ago, this hall was not restored, so our wedding was rustic and romantic. I will show you some photos while you are here. Now, go to your rooms to freshen, and we will all meet in the library for drinks at six when Armando will join us."

Sarah and Simon settled Jennifer in her room, which featured a heavily carved, dark oak medieval bed with a lavishly embroidered canopy. A sunny balcony with an intriguing view of a tower by a back courtyard beckoned. Jennifer looked out and exclaimed, "I will just sit *there* all afternoon! See you for dinner. But wait. Who is Armando?"

Simon and Sarah exchanged quick glances. He said, "He is their oldest son, a painter. We have recently become acquainted and I'm sure he will enjoy meeting *you!*" Jennifer rolled her eyes and showed them to the door.

Sarah opened the double doors to her room and led Simon in. A profound silence gripped them both as they stood gazing at golden Tuscan fields bathed in late afternoon sunlight. They were enthralled by the distant views of amber patchwork hay fields and grapevines in many shades of green and red interspersed with old walls and winding roads. Double rows of cypress trees marked neighboring ancient villas and roads. Simon said in a wistful, quiet voice, "If Armando had not attacked you it would have been hard to resist this. This is every woman's secret dream! His parents are delightful, this villa is magical; you might not have been able to turn him down."

"Simon," she replied thoughtfully, "it did all appeal to my vanity and my fantasies but being with Armando never felt quite right. Once he did what he did it made the decision pretty easy. Besides, he was not meant to be my husband, only my friend. You are my love." He embraced her, running his fingers through her hair and enjoying the feel of her rounded belly against his. " I think you might be able to feel little flutters," she said happily placing his hand on her belly.

At six the three of them went down to the library. Sarah had warned Jennifer to dress for dinner, so she walked in wearing a high fashion teal and gray geometric-print silk dress that resembled an abstract expressionist painting. It accentuated her long slender waist and slightly hugged her broad and strong hips. The neckline plunged in a deep V, offering subtle views of her small yet very shapely breasts, and a gold necklace with dramatic tourmaline teardrops accentuated her neck. Her entrance startled Armando; it was as if a tropical bird had flown into the library.

Jennifer was so distracted by the library that she had to remind herself to focus on her manners. She noticed a tall, catlike man in a beige linen jacket standing by an alcove with a tall window watching her. He seemed to pull through the room toward her! She felt awkward yet curiously dominated as she approached Matilda to greet her. "Hello, Matilda. What a stunning and warm library! The vaulting looks medieval, yet most of what I've seen of your villa is Renaissance. Is this room medieval?" She waited for an answer while Pietro gazed at her, and Armando appraised every inch of her body.

Matilda replied, "Yes, Jennifer. This room, my favorite, was the original great hall in the 1300s. This end of the castle is from the earlier period, as is the dining room. The kitchen area is the oldest part, possibly tenth century. I am so happy you like our library."

Simon joined them, saying with enthusiasm, "This is such a wonderful library! I could just stay right here forever."

Sarah noticed Armando standing slightly apart. "May I introduce you to Jennifer?" She crossed the room and took Jennifer's arm to lead her away from Pietro. Jennifer took a deep breath and forced herself to look directly into Armando's eyes, although she was exceedingly nervous. *I have never seen a man as beautiful as this one. I could cast him in my lenses for a hundred years; he is luminous.*

Armando's knees weakened when she came closer. This woman was the woman from his dreams! She seemed to fly into his chest and then fly out, distorting his vision. Cool waves flushed through his body edging out to rushes of hot fire when he extended his hand. *Oh my god, I'm going to touch her.* He took her hand and noticed it felt warm, so he held it for a moment lacing his long tapered fingers through her palm onto her pulse. His hand was locked into hers like a magnet. "Welcome, Jennifer. I do hope you like your room and your visit so far? It is my pleasure to meet you. If you enjoyed the afternoon sun out on your balcony, you may have noticed the square medieval tower just beyond the courtyard, my painting studio?"

The electric silkiness in his fingers thrilled her as he continued to hold her hand. *What do I do? Is this Italian? French guys do this when they want to go upstairs.* She smiled gloriously, revealing perfect teeth. "Yes, I am happy to be here, so honored to be graciously invited by your mother. I cannot imagine anything more marvelous than this castle." Then she boldly penetrated his sensual, distant eyes, which reflected her own enigmatic presence.

"How excellent! I am sure we will have a wonderful time together." He looked around acknowledging the others once again. "I am anxious to show all of you my work." Armando knew the others realized something big was going on. Simon could tell Jennifer was extremely attracted to Armando. This made him a little nervous. But he knew his sister was a strong woman who could hold her own, certainly more experienced than Sarah had been. Matilda and Pietro beheld the stunning woman standing by the window with their son as if she'd always been there. Watching them, Sarah recalled the first time she had seen Armando in that room. *She's older than I was and he is a different man; she can handle him.*

The party of six lingered with wine and sparkling water for Sarah. Once the conversation began, it flowed like a perfect dance. Jennifer relaxed in a large Windsor chair feasting her eyes on the books, rich fabric, and art. Armando came over to sit on the edge of a heavy oak bench next to her and said, "Everything is in this library, so please feel free to come down for books. Don't miss climbing the spiral staircase to the upper balcony where there are more." He knew this lovely woman was very taken with him. Her classic angular features and large dark eyes were exotic, and her body was strong yet delicate like Simon's. She was confident, bold, and didn't hide her attraction to him. He felt playful, so he said, "I feel like I've seen you before. Have you appeared in Parisian magazines, or did we know each other in another lifetime? I know that sounds like a naive come on, but I don't mean it that way. I am sincere."

What do I say to that? Making sure nobody else was listening she said, "Maybe there is something in me that reminds you of yourself?"

"Well, if so," Armando said, laughing, "then I must be beautiful inside, which I never thought was the case. Forgive me, Jennifer, I am an artist and I must say, you look exquisite in this room. It's as if it has been waiting for you."

Jennifer replied very discreetly in a low voice, "Since you are also an artist, I will not think of you as merely a flirtatious Italian. I accept the compliment. Now, may I return the favor?" He showed his assent by smiling enigmatically. "You are very elegant and serene; you would make a fabulous subject."

Armando tilted his head and smiled more warmly, accentuating his sensual lips and alluring dark eyes; he liked her boldness. He said outrageous things to her, and she handed them right back. He felt free and playful, the way he had been long ago before life got so complex. *She liberates me.*

Jennifer studied his beautiful features while he spoke. She, too, could sense that the others knew what was unfolding. She liked his flirtatiousness and sense of humor. He made her feel like an open box of Godiva chocolates.

"Come on, Jennifer and Armando, time for dinner. The cook won't wait any longer," Matilda said when they realized everybody else had already gotten up. As they filed into the dining room, Matilda said, "Armando, I always place the most eligible young lady next to your father, but tonight I'd like to switch you so that you can enjoy Jennifer's company. That is, if *you* don't mind, Pietro?"

"Oh, of course not. Tonight I will enjoy sitting with Sarah with pleasure. We will discuss Marcion, since I have looked into the sources myself. I found some very interesting Gnostic tractates in the upper section of the library for you to look at, Sarah. Tonight, Simon, she is mine." Thus Armando and Jennifer were free to probe into the events of their lives that led up to the present moment. Armando knew she was the one, and Matilda sensed that Armando might have finally found a woman he could care for in a real way.

After everyone went to bed, Sarah took Simon into the ancient chapel to meditate and then they snuggled into the cozy bed. Simon wasn't sure how he felt about Jennifer's interactions with Armando. He was becoming more comfortable with Armando and it seemed he truly had transformed, but he still worried about his only sister. On the other hand, now that she was thirty-two she wanted children, so he hoped she'd find someone to love soon. Her great success as a photographer challenged most men, and many of her colleagues were gay. Armando matched her in intelligence and personality, and it seemed his new view of life could support her strong spirit.

Sarah read a novel for a while. Just before turning out the light, she studied the embroidered tendrils and small flowers gracing the inside of the canopy, the same ones that had soothed her after Armando's attack. When she fell asleep, a big dream came. *I see Jesus in a woven white robe approaching the well where I wait for him in a hooded sapphire blue robe. I hold the alabaster jar. He comes close to me and I kneel in adoration. He says, "Rise, Mary, you are not beneath me." I rise. He kneels in front of me, and I anoint his forehead, temples, and lips. Light waves flowing out of his body lift him way above the well. He beckons me with his arms; his eyes draw me up to him.*

The guests enjoyed fresh orange juice, omelets, and homemade bread with jam, then Armando took Simon, Jennifer, and Sarah up to his studio. Sarah was very anxious to see Armando's work; however, as they reached the bottom of the stairs she hesitated, realizing she hadn't been back to his studio since the day he attacked her. Armando smiled reassuringly at her and led the way up the stairs. He pushed the door open and led them in. Holding Simon's hand, Sarah walked in and then gasped. More than twenty large canvases of powerful and compelling medieval-style paintings interspersed with modern touches were scattered around the floor and hanging at upper levels. Writhing bloody animals, grotesque suffering humans, and flying angels oozed through modern scenarios of freeways, tall buildings, nuclear power plants, digital screens, and storms. The medieval elements emerged in the modern scenes like the unconscious mind becoming conscious.

Nobody said anything; they just stared. After twenty minutes, Sarah realized she was viewing a hellish underworld, a suffering middle world, and a transcendent upper world of light and uplifted angelic beings. This activated the Underworld flow in her lower body and simultaneously lifted her soul into transcendence. Finally she said, "These are magnificent, magnificent. You depict the struggle we all have—the agony of life and the higher elements that give us hope. These paintings will awaken people's consciousness by forcing them to consider evil influences."

Jennifer had no idea what to say. Finally she said, "These are fantastic, but is this what comes out of you as a Catholic, I assume since you are Italian?"

"Yes, of course I am Catholic," Armando replied, smiling. "But these ideas are not inspired by the Church. These are the universal elements in our consciousness. I paint them to exorcise deep fear, to free us from possession so that we can take the next evolutionary step. We are all *in* the apocalypse now exposing hell, transforming our world, and transmuting to higher realms."

"Armando," Simon broke in, "these are truly great, so honest. But for them to create change, many people must see them. Are you selling them? Are you doing any big shows?" While he said that, he was thinking the paintings helped him understand Armando better. *What a tortured soul he is.*

"Thank you, Simon," he said. "I just had a major show in Florence, and two-thirds of these were sold, two of them to museums. I have a show coming up at a new gallery for modern art in Rome. I was very nervous about how the dealers would respond to such a radical shift, but I've simply lost interest in painting landscapes. Fortunately, I had previously sold enough to persuade the dealers to give my new work a try. So far these paintings have been received more enthusiastically than my landscapes ever were. The show in Florence ended and I've gathered them here for the show in Rome. I think people will come to see them, since they are hungry for real art, art that expresses the complexity of life. Not all the reviewers like them, but the reviews were mostly positive."

Jennifer contemplated his work. With the ability to express such artistic majesty, what is this guy like inside? He must be really sexual and deeply emotional. Armando is obviously not boring. I bet he's a real handful but my brother seems to like him. She looked over to Simon and noticed he was watching her. I bet he wonders what I think. She said to Armando, "How do you feel after you paint one of these? I think I would get all stirred up, maybe feel crazy. Your work is intense, apocalyptic, and very multidimensional. After a morning in this studio, how do you eat a tuna fish sandwich for lunch?" She spoke very earnestly because she really wanted to know. Sarah suppressed a snorting giggle, and Armando roared with laughter at the thought of eating a tuna fish sandwich after painting the apocalypse all morning.

"Forgive us, but the juxtaposition of this art with a tuna fish sandwich is very funny," Armando replied. Jennifer joined in and they all doubled over with mirth, releasing the high tension from studying such disturbing art. Armando put his arm around her shoulder and hugged her firmly, which she really liked. He said, "You know what? That's the most effective comic relief I've ever had, even though Italians rarely eat tuna sandwiches! To answer your real question, it is often very difficult to transition back into the mundane world after I've painted one of these. That's why I spend so much time up here when I'm painting. "

41

The Fonte Gaia

"Can we steal away together tonight?" Armando asked as he and Jennifer walked by the grape fields after lunch. "Tomorrow I will be our guide in Siena, but may I take you out to dinner tonight? Rosia is nearby, a little town with a nice bar with a good chef who wanted to escape Rome. I haven't been there for a while, and I'd love to take you." He stopped walking and took her hand, engaging her eyes. Jennifer felt like she was walking by the side of a swan.

"I'd love to, but are you sure the others won't mind?"

"Well," he replied, "we run our house so that people can go their own way. Our chef prepares the meals and all we do is tell her how many people will come. Our tour of Siena tomorrow will be very ambitious, and I am sure you will be constantly taking pictures. So we deserve a night out! I'm sure my parents would love some extra time with Sarah and Simon. My mother is very intrigued with Simon, and Pietro is determined to tell Sarah all about his Gnostic research, since he found some translations paid for by Lorenzo di Medici hidden away by our ancestors in the upper library. They probably were sequestered there in the 1550s before the Jesuits led a campaign against Sienese heretics that caused the horrific book burning in the Piazza di San Francesco. My parents have read Simon's articles, so they have more than enough to talk about."

Jennifer was more than happy to agree.

When Simon learned of their plans, he wanted to tell Jennifer everything he knew about Armando, just to prepare her, but Sarah convinced him not to. "Your sister is not me, and he is a different man now," she said. "Let them have an evening together without the shadow of his past. If he doesn't tell her himself, then you can." Simon reluctantly agreed.

Oltre Il Giardino was in a charming restored stone house with a terrace oriented to the setting sun. They sat on a bench at a simple wooden table with the western view. The low sun bathed the landscape in magical golden light while breezes rustled cypress and olive trees. Armando left her for a moment to get two glasses of red table wine, and then he sat behind her on the bench with his legs to either side. They were alone. He moved very close to her back while she gazed at the sunset; his soft breath tickled her bare shoulder.

He said, "I have some things to say because you will be here for only a few more days. Then you will go back to Paris and I might never see you again." He moved even closer. His taut thighs cradled hers. She turned her head to face him, saying nothing. Her face bronzed by golden light was exotic, Persian. "Perhaps I should kiss you on your neck instead of talking to you?" he murmured, intoxicated by the nearness of her wine-reddened lips and breathing in the scent of her hair.

"You said there is something you want to say?" She bored into his eyes as if she knew everything about him.

"Of course, yes, we must talk. I must be honest about myself. I don't know what Simon has told you about me?" He paused, wondering if she would make things easier.

She replied circumspectly, "We are a family of few words, and we rarely discuss a person we've just met. I have been here a few days, and I didn't know you existed until I arrived. I've noticed Simon and Sarah feel connected to you. You must be easy to connect with, since Simon is very ambitious and does not usually take the time to cultivate friends. I don't really know Sarah that well yet, but I think she's kind-hearted and rarely speaks negatively. So Armando, what's eating you? I see it in your eyes now, and I saw it in your paintings." She turned all the way around to face him, keeping some distance between them. "I perused a book on the history of Siena in your library. Do you have the Sienese madness, everybody's excuse for the annual Palio?"

Now what do I say? "Well, we will discuss our famous madness tomorrow, since it always comes up. You say they have not told you about me, so I am free to say what I think is important." Her eyes were dark brown with yellow flecks around large pupils, raptor eyes. He glanced at the chiseled indentations below her cheekbones that accentuated her strong jaw. He'd never dated a Jewish woman before or even thought he would want to, but times had changed and he found he didn't care at all. *After all, some of my early ancestors, who were forced to convert to Christianity to save their lives, were Jewish.* He grazed her cheek delicately with his fingers while holding her gaze. Shivers ran through her torso up to her neck.

He said, "I am forty-one and never married. I proposed only once, to Sarah. She turned me down, and now we are good friends." *I see that knowing spark in her eyes. She already sensed it, so I had to tell her.* "I have been a rake most of my life, and I am not exaggerating. But I recently finally had a breakthrough after more than ten years in analysis when I accessed a very dark part of myself. By becoming conscious of it, I loosened its grip. Maybe I did have Sienese madness? There are many things I have done that I am not proud of, but that is finished and I am trying to make amends." Sweetness came into his eyes and mellowed his face.

Jennifer said, "Thank you for telling me you proposed to Sarah; what man wouldn't? What a natural beauty she is and she seems to be angelic. Do you and Simon have the same taste in women? Just a moment ago when you spoke of your past, your facial expression was like your mother's beautiful face. I wish I could capture her whimsical charm on film, her childlike feminine nuances. I like your father and mother a lot; your heritage intrigues me. I don't care much about what you've been doing before now, unless there is a pack of illegitimate children? I hope you don't care what I've done; I'm thirty-two years old and an adventurous woman. We will both know more about this as we get to know each other. Is there anything else you want to say?"

Her forthrightness surprised him yet again. He was resisting her because he was still integrating his recently attained insights, yet she penetrated his fog. *I am disarmed because I don't know how to seduce her! Oh, what the hell, why not just say it?* "Jennifer, I have been dreaming about you for weeks." Even longer, if he were completely honest, but he didn't want to scare her away.

Jennifer's eyes widened slightly. She paused a few moments before responding. "Are you sure you were dreaming of me? Do you think you might recognize your feminine nature in me?"

Armando considered. "Maybe so, but why would I be dreaming about you and then you show up? This encounter is fated and will change our lives."

She knew there was nothing more to say. She reached for his taut neck, turned her face up to his, and they kissed long and passionately, savoring the taste of one another. When they pulled back to search each other's eyes, they were both surprised by the potent sexual force they felt. He stood her up and pressed her to himself to explore the shape and curves of her strong, slender body. They breathed together. He exhaled slowly, shaking his head slightly to free himself from the spell their kiss had cast on both of them. "Let's go into the dining room for dinner; I hear the bell."

They were served various courses of la cucina Toscana— bruschetta a pomadoro, risotto con zucchini e ricotta, and bistecca Florentina. She ate with abandon, obviously enjoying her food, and watching her made him wonder what she'd be like in bed. For her part, she detected his sexual hunger in the way he bit things. Though her own desire was volcanic, she wanted to savor this phase before basking in sensual delight. Armando was enjoying the smooth skin of her arms and hands and her perfect long neck. Her short skirt revealed her strong upper thighs, and he smelled her aroma. Despite his strong attraction to her, the lizard remained dormant while his heart beat with true joy. For once the attraction was more than physical for him. It was something deeper, something he had glimpsed with Claudia and Sarah but that had been smothered at the time by his unresolved past. After tiramisu was served, he captured her eyes and moved his hand onto her thigh, pushing it slowly up her leg. She put her fork and knife down on the plate, reached for his hand, and held it in hers. "Armando, I want to know you much better before, much better."

"Ah, then I will come to Paris in a few weeks! May I come to see you there?"

"Of course you can," she said, smiling at him enigmatically. "Anytime you want to, and there is a very special boutique hotel near my apartment."

Armando, Simon, Sarah, and Jennifer were up with the rising sun in the morning for a guided tour of Siena. Armando's family background meant he could take them to places that most tourists never see. Because ancient families such as the Pierleonis had preserved many elements of the Italian medieval synthesis, Siena contained the living remains of one of the most esoteric and complex alchemical cultures in the world.

They all piled into the car and Guido dropped them off on the edge of the old city, as cars were not allowed in the center. They wandered along narrow medieval streets looking into the shop windows and studying features of the ancient buildings, and then they came through a narrow alley that opened into the Piazza del Campo, the heart of the city. Armando and Jennifer had been traipsing along hand-in-hand like happy four-year-olds, a situation that had not escaped Simon's attention. But now Armando released Jennifer's hand because it was time to guide.

He began, "This piazza, Il Campo, was an open marketplace before the twelfth century, before that probably an Etruscan settlement, and the area has evidence of the ancient people since there are cyclopean walls in nearby Vetulonia, the inspiration for Castel Vetulonia to honor the Etruscans of this region. This piazza is one of the best-preserved original town centers in Europe, very protected since 1928. As you may know, there are seventeen ancient districts, or contrade, within Siena. Each group is represented by its own animal symbol. Here a bareback horse race among the contrade, the Palio di Siena, has been held twice a year for hundreds of years. It is wild, dangerous, sometimes bloody, and very medieval. Some say our people are all a bit mad, yet the Palio discharges our madness, the famous Sienese madness every year. Each contrade has a horse stall and a chapel in Siena, and I will take you to my family's meeting place in a few moments. Of course, we also have clubs and apartments up there in the upper floors of the buildings, and if any of you visit during the Palio, we will be up there for the view. First we go to the Fonte Gaia at the midpoint of nine divisions in the pavement, where there is very strong magnetism."

They strolled together to one edge of the piazza to a square fountain fed by aqueducts, while he continued. "The piazza is shell-shaped with ten sectors of red brick divided by nine long white travertine lines that fan out from the fountain. Being in the piazza is like being in a great shell." Near the fountain, Sarah felt nauseated and wondered if the morning sickness was coming back. She said, "Armando, I feel so much strong earth energy around this fountain, but the fountain can't be what's causing it. It looks so, well, very Catholic."

Armando smiled. "Ah, yes, Sarah, exactly. You expected to find a mermaid in the shell? The original fifteenth-century nude statues by Jacopo della Quercia were replaced because they were too pagan.

This is unfortunate because the original ones may have balanced the strong energy here that gets whipped into frenzy during the race. Quercia carved the Madonna and Child, protector of Siena, surrounded by two female nude statues of Rhea Silvia and Acca Laurentia, the mother and wet nurse of Romulus and Remus, the founders of Rome. The original ones are now in the Ospedale di St. Maria della Scala in the Piazza Duomo, and I hope they will be brought back here someday. The feeling here is very emotionally intense, and if we use Claudia's model of the nine dimensions, right here we are in the fifth dimension. Oh well, at least the original shape of the piazza has been retained and the fountain is in the fifth section. Claudia says this ancient piazza has very pure access to the nine dimensions that she first decoded here, so exchanging the statues interfered with access to higher levels."

"Claudia?" Jennifer whispered to Sarah.

Sarah had forgotten that Jennifer had not yet met Claudia. "Oh yes, she is our friend in Rome. She and Armando used to date a long time ago. You will meet her soon."

Sarah felt very drawn to an odd shell-shaped drain that was opposite the Fonte Gaia, a lower area where the long white lines pulled together like the bottom of a fan, the lowest point in the piazza. She stared at it and had a vision of the drain expanding into a huge shell, and then a tall nude goddess appearing in the shell. Then she heard Armando say, "Now we go to my family's meeting place for the Palio."

They left the piazza to walk down another narrow alley to a heavy and large rounded wooden door. Armando continued. "Now we come to our contrade, the Cantata of the Caochinio, the snail." He opened the heavy door with a huge iron key and inside was a small museum and a simple chapel. Heraldry was displayed in cases by the side of a complete suit of medieval armor and a helmet. "Other contrade are, for example, owl, caterpillar, panther, wolf, unicorn, and so on, real and mythological animals. On the surface, this is ancient tournament symbolism; however, to us it is deeply esoteric."

"What exactly do you mean, Armando?" Sarah broke in. "Please tell us the secrets!" Jennifer studied Armando's intense black eyes.

"Well, just a few months ago, I would not have been able to answer you because my father has only recently shared the secrets with me," said Armando. "He says the time for telling the truth has come, that all the secrets must be revealed, so I will do the best I can. We believe this ancient piazza is a great shell based on perfect stellar geometry that protects all species, all of nature. For example, my family is the keeper of snails. There are seventeen contrade, which is a very complex number that relates the species to the stars, and the shell connects us with the Pleiades. People go crazy here because this place pulls conduits of stellar light down into the inner Earth. My father says the people used to see balls of blue light come down from the sky before they removed the original statues. My father also says life will go on no matter what happens, which is deeply reassuring to me." Jennifer watched his catlike body language while he spoke, thinking, *I feel I will marry him.*

"Ah, there is so much to say," Armando continued. "I suppose what matters to me is that Pietro finally shared the knowledge with me. The secrets are not given to anyone who is destructive, since here we protect life." Simon, who had been observing his sister as she watched Armando, felt reassured by the fact that Armando's father had now chosen to trust him with these family secrets. Clearly his father was convinced that his transformation was indeed genuine.

"The door there in the back goes into our chapel, yet we cannot go in there today because it is only opened when we bring out our candle on the Feast of the Assumption of Mary. In 1348 the plague killed half our population, and we believe the power of nature saved us. Claudia has been teaching us about the meaning of the end of the Mayan Calendar, things we can tell you all about sometime if you want," Armando said as he turned toward Jennifer, remembering that she didn't even know who Claudia was. "Briefly, all of us think something has actually changed in our world, some kind of restart button. My father says the Etruscans had a complex stellar religion going way back into the Paleolithic, a religion that related the landscape to patterns in the sky. This knowledge is lost, but my father says these forces are in play whether anybody knows about them or not. And he says his father told him the ancient knowledge comes from the swan, and he hopes I will figure out what that means someday. He said that our symbols are encoded with stellar information, and he hopes I will be able to decode things he has never been able to understand. I hope I will be able to do that, but meanwhile the shell shape still connects the stars to Earth forces that protect the species. Siena is a nature temple.

"And despite the removal of the stabilizing statues in the Fonte Gaia, the forces under the piazza correctly emanate energy to the higher dimensions guarding our planet no matter what anybody changes. Siena is the place where people can trust evolution's unfolding, the reason I will always live here." Then he deliberately looked into Jennifer's eyes. Sarah felt a strong quiver in her abdomen and felt her child move. "Now we go to Siena Cathedral—Cattedrale Metropolitana di Santa Maria Assunta—the high point of our day because more esoteric wisdom is still visible there than in any other Catholic Church in the world; it is alchemical."

Coming out of a narrow street, close ahead they saw the looming west façade of Siena Cathedral. The complex mixture of French Gothic and Romanesque architecture took Jennifer's breath away as she aimed her camera at the tall black-and-white striped bell tower on the right side. The exterior walls made of large alternating black-and-white marble stripes and the front façade by Giovanni di Agostino were exquisite. Jennifer took photos of Simon and Sarah with the cathedral in the background while they were immersed in the beauty around them. Sarah was beatific and Simon was enthralled. Jennifer was thrilled to capture their radiance.

Armando led them to an unfinished back section of the cathedral. "The 1348 plague halted the construction of this section, which has been protected to be a reminder of how fragile life is. Now come with me because we are going to climb the bell tower to eat our sandwiches on top." As he unlocked the door at the bottom of the black-and-white striped tower with a large iron key, Jennifer photographed him for the first time because his face was reverential. *That is a photo I will cherish.* A tightly curving stone circular staircase carried them up inside the tower. Since the tower was much taller than the cathedral, they wondered how high they'd have to climb. Armando took up the rear behind Simon and noticed a big and menacing spider on the rough wall. *This time it lives. What are they? Wolf spiders?*

They made it to a top terrace. Sandwiches were unwrapped and lemonade poured, while they sat on stone benches to enjoy the view of the city's sloping terracotta roofs way below. The sun felt marvelous on Jennifer's face, giving her a feeling of peaceful serenity; everyone was smiling.

Armando stood up. "Now that we have eaten and have energy, let's go down to visit the cathedral."

They strolled into the nave where the effect of the black-and-white stripes intensified, dramatizing the haunting great Moorish-looking space, which was charged with palpable energy. "Here we see black and white emphasized, the colors of the Siena coat of arms inspired by the black-and-white horses of our legendary founders, Senius and Aschius, the sons of Remus. This connection to legendary horses draws the thread way back to the Paleolithic era because the contrasting layers stimulate our inner knowledge of the phases of time. These elements contain ancient secrets; for example, my father thinks the alternating layers remind us subliminally of the cycles of creation and extinction. Four twisted marble columns with writhing horses being killed by huge lions at the bases support the pulpit, a symbol that fascinates me. When you learn how to read them, a complex story of evolution emerges. Our city literally balances the dark and the light, especially in this cathedral, which accesses high spiritual realms.

"Now let us study the marble floor. When we entered, we walked over a curious marble mosaic that portrays Hermes Trismegistus. Yet why is the famous Greek/Egyptian magus here? On both sides we see marble mosaics that portray all the sibyls of the ancient world." Sarah walked closer to the mosaics, examining them with great interest. "Yet why are they here?" Armando asked. "Notice the huge statue of Artemis up high by the left side of the front entrance. These are all pagan magical symbols! The church was built mostly between 1215 and 1263, when medieval art successfully brought spirit down into our world, an alchemical synthesis that is returning now. Notice the capitals at the top of the columns where we see allegorical animals emphasizing the protection of all species." They were all looking up to the beauty of the high dome as they walked out of the nave, Sarah only reluctantly leaving behind the mosaics portraying the sibyls.

He led them closer to the pulpit to an intriguing red circular mosaic in the floor. "This is one of the most beautiful early mosaics showing the She-Wolf of Siena nursing Romulus and Remus in front of the tree of life. Siena is the mother teat of Rome! All around this center are the totemic emblems of the major cities, which links nurturance with our politics. Claudia says the She Wolf is Sirius, a stepping-stone into the Milky Way Galaxy. My father says the Pleiades were the stepping-stones out of the galaxy in the Paleolithic times. Consider the paintings, the panels, and I know you, Sarah, were especially intrigued by the mosaics we just looked at that depict the various sibyls from pagan cultures all over the world—the Delphic, Cumaean, Hellespontine, and Persian Sibyls. They are here to remind us that Gnostic wisdom was global for thousands of years before Christianity. This is a remnant of ancient knowledge because still in medieval times we had a wonderful balance between our pagan background and the Church. This great synthesis was

Mosaic of the She-Wolf of Siena

destroyed by the Inquisitions, yet fortunately this incredible pagan art was not tampered with here. Everything you see in Siena is very pagan and earthy. Now we go to the Piccolomini Library, my most favorite place in the world."

They filed into the library, looked up, and were stunned by the frescoes, detailed portrayals of late medieval and early Renaissance scenes. "These are by Pinturicchio based on Raphael's designs, and they tell the story of my ancestor, Siena's favorite son, Cardinal Enea Silvio Piccolomini, who became Pope Pius II. We see Enea at the various stages of his career, here launching a crusade, there visiting the court of James II of Scotland, and over there canonizing Catherine of Siena in 1461. These are wonderful portraits of an important life that are filled with realistic details of fifteenth-century living." Everybody was leaning way back to view the ceiling. "Ah," Armando said, "this incredibly beautiful ceiling of complex mythological symbolism is a great example of the pervasiveness·of arcane knowledge."

"Armando," Simon said, "how far back does your history reach?"

"Thank you for asking that, Simon. Of course, there is a lot we don't know. We have always thought we may go back to the Etruscans, and we probably actually do in our blood. Or possibly we were among the Franks who came down to establish power bases here called *contado*. The furthest I can go back for sure is to the twelfth century in our chapel records of our family offering wax candles to the Madonna on August 15, and later records of when we furnished the Palio with the silk banner for the winner. We go back to the beginning of everything here."

"It must be reassuring to be so consciously aware of your past," noted Simon.

"This is very true, yet we are all part of the stream. It is just easier to find the threads in Siena." He paused and said dramatically, "Maybe someday Jennifer will decide to share these threads with me."

Despite Armando's exaggerated boldness, everyone knew his words carried an undertone of the truth.

The library was airless as they stopped breathing and turned to Jennifer, who was staring at Armando with a thunderstruck expression that illuminated the room. Grandly as if she were in a procession, she walked over to Armando and put her hand in his, saying, "Only the Sibyl of Cumae knows, don't you agree, Sarah?"

"Yes, I agree. It really is that simple. Everything else is as complex as these exquisite portrayals of the past. Thank you, Armando, for showing us all of this."

Simon's cell phone rang while he stood in the bedroom looking out at the early evening view. Sarah was down in the library with Pietro before dinner. A large star brightened as the light waned, and he wondered if it was Jupiter or Venus or a bright star like Sirius. "Simon, it's Dad. How are you all doing? I had strange dreams about Jennifer last night. She is visiting you, right? Is there something I should know?"

David's psychic attunement always amazed Simon. *How does he know?* "Well, yes, something remarkable is going on with her. We are all here visiting the Pierleoni villa in Tuscany, and Jennifer is falling in love with Armando!" He heard his father catch his breath, since he hadn't told him about the great change that had come over his new friend.

"What? You are *all* there at Armando's house? Are you insane?"

Simon explained about the change in Armando and how their friendship was slowly growing as he was beginning to trust that Armando truly had changed. David said, "Are you sure about this, Simon? In my life I have never seen such a radical change in any man. Things like that don't happen. I dreamed a dark shadow of a huge bird came over Jennifer and she was lost in mist."

"I don't really think you should be that worried about her," Simon replied. "She seems to be very taken with him, and he is clearly falling deeply in love with her and doesn't mind showing it. But, Jen can hold her own, you know that. Sarah was right that his parents are lovely and Jen seems to like them. Who knows, maybe the new Armando will end up being the right man for her. Never thought I'd say that, but I suppose stranger things have happened."

"Simon," David said. "I am coming to Rome immediately to meet him. Is Jennifer staying long enough for that? I can be there in two days. Your mother doesn't have to come because she's very busy right now, but I must meet Armando."

Simon said, "Jennifer will be here four more days, so come! We'd all love to see you!"

42

La Sagrada Familia

Claudia called Armando at the castle. She wanted the four of them to discuss Pope Francis some more because she'd never seen someone walk such a razor's edge between the dark and light. Armando asked if they could include Jennifer, but as they talked about it, they realized they'd have to explain too many things. Armando used the meeting as an excuse to accompany Jennifer back to Rome because he didn't want to let her out of his sight. After they were all back for a day, they gathered at Simon and Sarah's apartment while Jennifer enjoyed a quiet evening alone at her hotel.

Claudia spread her arms wide at the table. "Every time I do anything, I either get blocked or I manifest something in an instant, like the way the conclave picked Francis. The patriarchy is definitely collapsing when all cardinals can do is bet on a dark horse! This *has* to happen, but it is so intense! I wonder if we can survive it? I take one step forward and then three back."

She paused to catch her breath, then continued, "I used to think I understood how things work, but the proverbial rug has been pulled out from under me! Sarah," she said, turning her pensive gaze toward Sarah, "we must discuss the amazing visions you had of the timeline under the Vatican. What do these visions mean to you considering the shocking changes in the papacy?"

Sarah put her fingers over the ruby, closed her eyes, and went very deep into her mind. Simon watched her aura pull inside her body, like watching the halo around an angel suck in. *She does that every time she's asked a direct question. Where does she go for those answers?*

After a few moments, Sarah said in a strained and scratchy voice, *"I am here fifty thousand years ago, a Neanderthal woman. A spirit penetrating my brain makes me watchful. What is it? Who is this? It is silvery and light and makes me feel cool. It whispers to me, 'I am your future self. You will not exist forever. But I exist! I draw you forward to me; you must trust the flow of time, which is all you have.' My Neanderthal self does not comprehend this message, but I understand what it means in my time, so I will explain,"* she said, screwing up her face a bit as if she were attempting to become more herself. Simon watched her intently as her eyelids fluttered.

"Comprehend this!" she ordered, addressing the other three in a loud voice. *"Forgive my time complexities! The being I was then as Neanderthal did not continue, but she is in my past. Armando's bloodline is similar: some have died out, yet he still knows about them because of his heritage. My Neanderthal self does not exist because her cultural pattern was obliterated, her cerebellum atrophied, and nobody remembered her until very recently. Possibly soon her heritage can be recovered, since she is being remembered; she is in our DNA, especially in Jewish DNA."*

Sarah turned to Claudia still speaking from her place of meditation. *"Regarding how you feel these days, intelligence from the deep past is waking up in your cells that does not resonate with what is around you; this will soon alter radically. Pope Francis knows he doesn't know what is going to happen. For him, the crafty Jesuitical side of him is waking up along with the kindly saint! You can see this in his wise eyes. We live in a hall of mirrors composed of a sphere of twenty triangular facets that reflect all the evolutionary stages. We know we can't live as we have before, yet none of us knows what the next stage will be. The old ways are fading away, yet we don't know what our new habitat will be. Deep inside, we are all scanning the time lines seeking images in the misty facets that could conceivably save us, give us a sense of direction. All paths led* to December 21, 2012, which the Jesuits anticipated from the information they found in Mesoamerica. That is why this pope is a Jesuit."

"Excuse me, Sarah," Claudia broke in. Sarah's trance-like state remained unchanged as Claudia spoke. "In the visions we observed simultaneously, we watched a timeline of human events under the Bernini altar. Even though the cultures—Neanderthal, Magdalenian, Etruscan, then early Christian—were different, each scene was a ritual, such as a burial or an act of sexual abuse. I want you to tell me now whether the papacy uses these rituals to influence, shape, and control the world. This includes the Masses on the four directions going on down there twenty-four hours seven days a week—24/7. The priest who told me about it was *also* a Jesuit."

Sarah jolted as if she'd received an electrical shock. Simon jumped up to go to her, but since she seemed to be okay, he sank back into his seat. She reached into her purse with her eyes shut and retrieved a leather pouch. From it she pulled out a smoky five-inch-long quartz point that looked ancient. She held it for a moment and then said in a clear incisive voice, *"I, Neanderthal, do not comprehend the higher angel that pushed me to evolve because I don't know how to change. "Yet as Sarah, I respond to the push. Armando, Sarah always saw the light around you. Abuse cut the tender angelic threads in your brain, but you are reconnecting them because the dimensions are opening."*

There was a pause as the words sunk in for the group, then she continued, *"Claudia, you saw these lineages playing out through time beneath the Vatican. In some way, these scenes are recorded in our minds like old photos. You and Sarah live in women's bodies scarred by the memory fields of mass rapes and child abuse going all the way back to the earliest rituals, such as the sacred burial of divine children. You could see these scenes because Earth is releasing the abuse. When someone like Armando recalls when his thread to spirit was cut, depression lifts and freedom can come! This opens space for stellar-connected ceremonies. The Church has enjoyed a long phase of patriarchal power; they nearly severed the ties to our lineages. This abusive ritual cap on the earlier sacred burials and visionary journeys began when the sibyls were suppressed.*

But, now we are awake and fully present." Sarah paused, an other-worldly aura still surrounding her.

"Sarah," Simon interjected, "can you tell us *when* you were the Sibyl of Cumae?"

"Yes, of course," Sarah replied immediately. *"I was the primary sibyl in the sixth century BCE, when I was brought from Delphi to Baia. Claudia was the Samian Sibyl then, and there were other sibyls living now. The high point of esoteric awakening was in the middle of the sixth century BCE, when the planet was flooded with knowledge from great spiritual teachers, such as the Buddha, Zoroaster, and the sibyls. Peter's Church systematically eliminated women's knowledge from that time, with, for example, the murder of Hypatia, the keeper of the Alexandrian Library, and the sibyls were silenced and reduced to mosaics in the floor. My ruby crystal is the keeper of the sibyls. It was cut and polished more than twelve thousand years ago and set in the third eye of a Buddha in a cave in Nepal a few thousand years ago to protect it. This sacred stone is from before the great cataclysm; it emanates a pure field that resonates within me. All over the world, these talismans are awakening as our inner minds awaken. The light has switched on and freedom is coming. The elite think they have all the talismans, but all they have are moldy old Sumerian artifacts and Masonic temples, implants of the patriarchy."*

Simon was fascinated by the answers Sarah was offering. "What does Marcion have to do with all of this, Sarah?"

Sarah felt a rush flow in from way below her body that feathered up her spine, widened her vertebrae, and went out the top of her head. She grounded it by touching the quartz tip. Her voice keened, *"I will tell you Marcion's secret. At the ancient Temple of Arataxta, Marcion fought the dragon, the great dragon of the apocalypse. He won the battle and guards the doorway to the Underworld. That is why he has been removed from history. Long ago, the sibyls held the keys that were used to open doors into the minds of those ready to go beyond fear.*

"Christ came to announce anyone can be healed and redeemed from hell, and Catholic dogma retained a trace of this by claiming Christ went down into hell and freed the damned. But they fail to say each one of us can win the battle with

the dragon! Marcion saved the whole story, which I will tell you now: the goddess, Mary Magdalene, welcomed Christ into herself to balance the error Sophia made when she created the species without Lucifer; Mary anointed Christ to create a sacred marriage with him. Now our challenge is to heal and purify the old dark ways with fathers mothering their children along with mothers. Sharing childrearing frees the woman, Sophia, to create, and brings the man, Lucifer, totally into Earth. It balances the error that occurred when the species were first created."

"Sarah," Claudia jumped in because she knew the whole Gnostic story, "were we transforming darkness and sexual abuse while we observed those scenes?"

Sarah's eyes brightened. *"Exactly! That is the meaning of the end of the Calendar. That is what the Maya saw in their visions—the transmutation of a pile of religious manure that nobody believes in anymore. We are to shovel the pile away and laugh. You are the best example, Armando. You have apologized to the ones you abused rather than go to Confession to turn on a priest."*

"Sarah," Armando broke in quietly, "do the sibyls hold the marriage keys, not the Church?"

"Yes, but for those who want to be sexual. Many of the sibyls choose sacred virginity. Listen to me carefully as I tell you the truth. There is only one morality: no human should dominate any person sexually, mentally, physically, or religiously because it destroys their will, their voice of God within. When this happens, the dragon is unleashed and creates pestilence. The greatest sin is domination of Earth, the great test in the near future. Claudia, the midline is loosening and reducing East/West duality, yet aligning with nature is the main agenda. Unity is forcing each person to face inner demons and cease blaming things on others. That is all I have to say."

Sarah's face suddenly relaxed and she began blinking. When she came fully out of the very deep trance, she didn't remember anything and was fascinated by what the others told her she'd said.

Simon and Sarah sat out on the balcony enjoying the last vestiges of a balmy late May evening. David had arrived and was on his way to the Hotel Gregoriana to see Jennifer, who agreed to stay a few more weeks to attend Armando's big Rome show. Simon said, "You know what? My sister and father are running up bills at the Gregoriana, your thesis is in for the first review, and I have a break. We should go on our honeymoon and let my father and Jennifer stay here! Would you like to go to England to see Hildegard? If you could go anywhere in the world, where would you like to go with me?"

Her eyes glistened with happiness; the morning sickness was long gone and her thesis was in. Soon their child would tie them down, so she'd been longing for time alone with Simon. She knew where she wanted to go. "Barcelona! I want to go to Barcelona! You've told me so much about it, and I've always wanted to see Antoni Gaudí's outrageous buildings. Let's go have fun, relax, and see his famous cathedral, La Sagrada Familia Basilica."

"That's a great idea, Sarah. We talked about it once, but it seemed to just slip away in all the busyness. I love it there. It may be my favorite European city, so yes, let's do it, take our first trip together! I'll get plane tickets right away and then check with a few of my favorite hotels. We should be able to stay down in the barrio, it's centrally located so we can walk everywhere from there. It is a walker's dream, which will be very good for you right now. Yes, Barcelona!"

Back at the Hotel Gregoriana, another scene was unfolding. David checked into his room and then joined Jennifer at the Sala Vietri Bar in the Hassler. After they embraced, she asked him if he was jet-lagged.

"No, not bad. To get a ticket on such short notice, I had to fly first class. So I slept half the way, which was ideal."

"You can't imagine how happy I am to see you!" she said.

He sat down facing her and asked, "So, who is this guy, Armando? Can I meet him? Are you serious about him?"

Jennifer smiled as her gaze landed in some faraway place. "I have dated a lot of men, but I have never dated anyone like him. I need your opinion because I'm not objective. I'm outrageously attracted to him. I haven't slept with him or anything; I'm just enjoying his company."

"Well, Jen, that's the best way if you are serious about him. I'm relieved because you must be very careful. Simon told me a few things about him and his family; certainly they are very aristocratic, but I hear he has his demons. Has he told you about what happened with Sarah?"

"Yes, he has told me what he thought I needed to know. No details though," Jennifer said. "You are right that he has had a big struggle, but I think he has overcome some of his problems. I don't think it will be easy to be with a man like him, but I also respect him for what he has overcome. Dad, I would like you to meet him. I want to see what you think." She smiled mischievously. "Wait until you see his house. The old saying is Americans have all the money and Europeans have the class. There may not be much difference in the money; but their home here in Rome and the one in Tuscany definitely have the class. The great spans of time in their family are quite daunting; you will see."

"Well, yes, it is often like that with Europeans," David said. "It is exciting to think of families that have been on home turf for centuries."

"More than a thousand years," Jennifer added. "Well, what matters to me is what you think of him. He has asked to meet you and invited you to have lunch with him tomorrow."

David walked slowly down the Via di Porta Pinciana to the Via Lombardia. His enjoyment of Rome's charm was dimmed by his worry for his daughter. Approaching number 33, he took note of a high-walled garden. *That can't possibly be their garden, not in Rome.* He walked up the steps to the grand entrance, vaguely noticing a panther on a family crest, and soon he was led through the hallway to the library. *Quite a house! I wish Rose was here right now; the tapestries are exquisite.* As he approached the entrance to the library, a dark, slender man stood and walked toward him.

"Hello, Mr. Appel. I am Armando, and it is so kind of you to come." He led David inside. He liked the look of Jennifer's father.

"Armando, Pierleoni, I believe?" David said precisely as he was led to a round club table with two leather chairs. A beautiful arrangement of multicolored cut flowers rose majestically out of a tall, narrow blue glass vase. "This library is spectacular. How old is your house? This room must be at least five hundred years old!"

"Yes, the most wonderful thing about our life is this home, which has been passed down to each new generation for at least eight hundred years. I will be very frank," he said deepening his voice once David tentatively settled in. "I am forty-one, and I don't want to break our lineage. As you can see, that would be rather sad. However, I didn't give things like that a thought until five months ago. I have led a life that I am not proud of, but I have learned from my mistakes, and I am ready to marry. I think I will want to marry Jennifer, but I doubt I will propose to her right away because we've known each other less than a week! We locked on to each other with no control over it. We plan to spend more time together to get to know each other, yet both of us realize we feel very serious, we just do. I can offer your only daughter a very happy and rich life, a life in which she can do anything she wants. Is there anything you would like to know about me?"

While Armando spoke earnestly and respectfully, David applied all the character wisdom he possessed to find some way to read him. *If he was a bad guy before, which I know from Simon and he is admitting, how can anybody be sure this current "good" guy is going to last?* David said, "Well, you are an artist? Would you give her enough time? I am aware money is not the point, but would you really give her your full attention?" Armando paused and became thoughtful, which gave David a moment to look him over. He wondered what Sarah thought about this sudden change in the guy who had tried to rape her. *The thing that is keeping me open to this guy is Simon's friendship with him.*

Armando continued, "Mr. Appel, your question gives me considerable pause because I never thought about giving her time. I have always lived alone and gone to my studio whenever I wanted to. I don't know how to answer except to say that our whole family is very warm and intimate. It is not just about me; it is about my parents who are very close. You see, we all live in the same houses even when children come in our family. My parents took to your daughter immediately. Jennifer is also an artist and would need her own time to be alone and creative, which is not a problem because we have more rooms than we ever use." He stopped.

"Well, that is an honest answer, I must say." David was impressed that Armando had not automatically said what he assumed David would want to hear. In fact, his answer had been so honest that it shifted the dynamic between them. "I suppose I was trying to decoy you somewhat, just to see what you'd say, and please call me David. Truthfully, there is nothing Jennifer loves more than having her own time."

David held out his hand. "Armando, I do not know you but you make a good first impression, and I am happy to hear you plan to take good time with Jennifer before possibly proposing. I would like to meet your parents. Can that be arranged?"

"Of course! They are returning to Rome today, and they have invited Jennifer for dinner here tonight. So, if you come with her that would be perfect. You will meet all of us, and I am certain we will enjoy each other very much."

Ocean breezes on the Barcelona quay soothed Sarah, who was staring out to sea as the sun rose. Simon stood behind her, enveloping her in his arms and losing himself in the fresh aroma of her hair. They had been in Barcelona for five days in a hotel that had once been a bishop's home. They shared leisurely breakfasts in the grand dining room, rode the subway all over the city, and took long walks in search of buildings by Gaudí. In the late afternoons, they had long and languid sex while twilight crept along the ancient alleyway outside their balcony. They'd longed for this purely romantic time together.

Today they'd gotten up early because it was the day of their spiritual quest—a tour of Gaudí's unfinished La Sagrada Familia Basilica, which he had begun constructing in 1883. Simon and Sarah approached La Sagrada Familia from the west, striding rapidly along the Avinguda Diagonal to the Carrer La Marina. Even though they'd both seen pictures of the famous church, they were astonished when they saw the bizarre honeycombed towers with colorful tiles at the top gleaming in the bright sun. The first thing Sarah noticed as they walked up the stairs was the Passion Façade, scenes of Christ's crucifixion. The scenes were the usual ones; however, Gaudí's use of rigid and angular sculptural forms created dark and deep shadows within sharp angles. Gaudí seemed to want the onlooker to feel fear. Sarah winced. "There we go again! As usual we're supposed to be drawn into the brutality of Christ's sacrifice!"

Once inside, they could see the Latin cross in the vault of the nave as they moved through the crowd to find a place to stand. Sarah was enveloped by an intense altered state when she looked up through a complex crossing of mind-boggling geometric forms. The columns colored in exquisite pastels rose up a few hundred feet from square bases that transformed into octagons, then into sixteen sides, and then into circles at the top, a three-dimensional intersection of helicoidal columns, some turned clockwise, some counterclockwise. As the columns rose higher, sometimes they split as trees do and some had mosaic medallions and lacy skirts. Multicolored light beamed from above and from the side through the columns, like sunlight filtering through ancient trees.

Sarah thought Gaudí revealed the plasticity of the spiritual

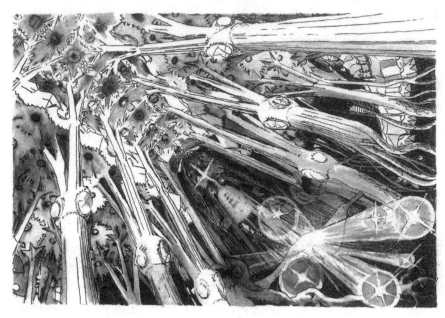

La Sagrada Familia

world. She remembered he had once said, "Hearing is the sense of Faith and seeing is the sense of Glory, because Glory is the vision of God. Seeing is the sense of light, of space, of plasticity, vision is the immensity of space; it sees what there is and what there is not."

Gaudí's ability to show what was usually invisible slammed Sarah into the battlefield of her own emotions because she was standing in the most perfect space between heaven and Earth she'd ever found. *Gaudí has transcended the greatest medieval cathedrals, even Chartres. This is ecstatic alchemy!* Simon watched her as she became so translucent that she looked like she would soar like Saint Theresa up into the columns. She was only able to remain standing because actually she was moving down into the inner Earth below the basilica where she was swimming in a cave. Looking up to the cave ceiling, she saw tree-root tendrils. She realized Gaudí had just cast her down under the root system of a great oak tree with twisting and turning roots. She could actually feel the roots delivering force to the trunk as it soared above and split out into great branches.

"Simon, this basilica is a vision of trees growing from within the root systems, to the trunks, and out through the sky! It is so intense to be here because all of humanity's possessions and obsessions are encoded here in stone. His rendition of the divine as a forest in our dimension contains all the elements of the lower and higher worlds in our solid world. Patrick is here," she whispered.

"Patrick?" he said quietly. "The brother you lost?"

"*Yes, he is here!* All the souls we've ever lost are here in this space. Someday my soul will come here, maybe yours. Here we are together beginning our lives while I carry our child. Like Gaudí, we are dedicated to finding the truth and expressing it as writers. Being here strengthens my faith that what we do with our lives matters, matters a lot. This is the holiest place on Earth, and we will always come back here. Gaudí has brought heaven to Earth in Barcelona. Simon, this basilica is the *future* of Christianity! *This* is the Christianity we are supposed to have. This could be the future Marcion envisioned! Sometimes I've felt that calling attention to Marcion's thoughts about Christianity two thousand years ago is a lost cause, but now I see the magnificence of Gaudí, a man with great personal pain. This makes me hopeful that Christianity can still transform into a religion of love and compassion, the pure intention of Jesus."

"Sarah, you warm my heart," Simon replied. "When we first met and talked about Marcion, I knew that what you were delving into was very important. Now that I am here in La Sagrada Familia, the Holy Family, I can see the masses need to have faith, a concept I have always been very skeptical about. People need to have something to believe in that transports them to higher dimensions."

BOOKS OF RELATED INTEREST

The Pleiadian Agenda
A New Cosmology for the Age of Light
by Barbara Hand Clow

Astrology and the Rising of Kundalini
The Transformative Power of Saturn, Chiron, and Uranus
by Barbara Hand Clow

Awakening the Planetary Mind
Beyond the Trauma of the Past to a New Era of Creativity
by Barbara Hand Clow

The Mayan Code
Time Acceleration and Awakening the World Mind
by Barbara Hand Clow
Foreword by Carl Johan Calleman, Ph.D.

The Mind Chronicles
A Visionary Guide into Past Lives
by Barbara Hand Clow

The Pleiadian House of Initiation
A Journey through the Rooms of the Wisdomkeepers
by Mary T. Beben
Foreword by Barbara Hand Clow

Return of the Golden Age
Ancient History and the Key to Our Collective Future
by Edward F. Malkowski
Foreword by Barbara Hand Clow

Visionary Shamanism
Activating the Imaginal Cells of the Human Energy Field
by Linda Star Wolf and Anne Dillon
Foreword by Barbara Hand Clow

INNER TRADITIONS • BEAR & COMPANY
P.O. Box 388
Rochester, VT 05767
1-800-246-8648
www.InnerTraditions.com

Or contact your local bookseller